P9-CEI-831

THE CAT IS OUT OF THE BAG

He was sitting on a fallen tree limb. A rather large limb with one end resting on the riverbank, the other end submerged. The cat was taunting me for some reason, and I was crazy to be out here in the middle of the night following the animal around.

"If you want to be friends, come and visit me tomorrow," I told the cat, then turned to retrace my steps.

I swear he meowed again, though I couldn't be sure over the sound of the river. I turned the light back toward him and stopped when I spotted a brown ostrich-skin boot propped on top of the fallen limb near the cat.

What the heck?

I walked as close as I safely could to the riverbank's edge, three feet or so above the water. The boot was actually lodged in the fork of a branch attached to the limb.

My heart raced. Was there still a foot in that boot?

I changed my position and saw the leg bent at an unnatural angle. A leg clad in khaki pants. A wave of nausea washed over me as I moved the light and discovered the rest of the body submerged in the water.

Earlier today I had wanted Bobby Joe Flowers to go away and leave us alone.

But not this way.

BLACK CAT CROSSING

KAY FINCH

BERKLEY PRIME CRIME, NEW YORK

BERKLEY PRIME CRIME

An imprint of Penguin Random House LLC
375 Hudson Street, New York, New York 10014

BLACK CAT CROSSING

A Berkley Prime Crime Book / published by arrangement with the author

Copyright © 2015 by Kay Finch.
Penguin supports copyright. Copyright fuels creativity, encourages diverse voices,
promotes free speech, and creates a vibrant culture. Thank you for buying an authorized
edition of this book and for complying with copyright laws by not reproducing, scanning, or
distributing any part of it in any form without permission. You are supporting writers and
allowing Penguin to continue to publish books for every reader.

BERKLEY® PRIME CRIME and the PRIME CRIME design are trademarks of
Penguin Random House LLC.
For more information, visit penguin.com.

ISBN: 978-0-425-27524-5

PUBLISHING HISTORY
Berkley Prime Crime mass-market edition / September 2015

PRINTED IN THE UNITED STATES OF AMERICA

10 9 8 7 6 5 4 3 2 1

Cover illustration by Brandon Dorman (Lott Reps).
Cover design by George Long.

This is a work of fiction. Names, characters, places, and incidents either are the product of
the author's imagination or are used fictitiously, and any resemblance to actual persons,
living or dead, business establishments, events, or locales is entirely coincidental.

PUBLISHER'S NOTE: The recipes contained in this book are to be followed
exactly as written. The publisher is not responsible for your specific health or
allergy needs that may require medical supervision. The publisher is not
responsible for any adverse reactions to the recipes contained in this book.

If you purchased this book without a cover, you should be aware that this book is stolen
property. It was reported as "unsold and destroyed" to the publisher, and neither the author
nor the publisher has received any payment for this "stripped book."

Penguin
Random
House

For London, our own cat whisperer

ACKNOWLEDGMENTS

My first heartfelt thanks go to Leann Sweeney and Jennifer Stanley. Without an extraordinary set of circumstances initiated by them, I would not be writing this series today. Thanks to my agent, Jessica Faust, for reaching out to me and for her enthusiastic encouragement. I'm so grateful for Michelle Vega, my editor, and the entire Berkley Prime Crime family, who have given me such a warm welcome. Getting to know you all has been a dream come true. Thanks to my husband, Benton, for willingly eating leftovers while I spend long hours at the computer. My critique group is top-notch in the advice and support department—thanks to Bob, Dean, Julie, Kay 2, Laura, Susie, and Millie. Thanks also to Amy, critiquer extraordinare, and to my coworkers Bobby, Cheryl, Lisa, and Susan, for listening patiently when I discuss the best way to kill my next victim. Last but not least, I appreciate my personal good luck cat, Alice, who sat with me and meowed her two cents during the writing of this book. Thank you, one and all, for everything.

LACED MY FINGERS, cracked my knuckles, and stared at the few words on my laptop screen. Behind me, the hum of early morning conversation in Hot Stuff Coffee Shop went on as usual. Back when I was a kid visiting my aunt Rowena, the shop was called Das Kaffeehaus, in keeping with the German heritage here in Lavender, heart of the Texas Hill Country. Then a transplant from San Antonio bought the place and changed the name to Hot Stuff. He traded the old *oom-pah-pah* background music for seventies disco tunes. I'd choose listening to Donna Summer over any polka band in history, but I had to wonder why he didn't go with a country music theme. After all, this was Texas.

Boot Scootin' Coffee, perhaps.

Or, if he had his heart set on Hot Stuff, he could stream songs by today's up-and-coming hunky performers. More good-looking guys than I can keep up with, but dang it, thinking about country singers wasn't supposed to be on my agenda this morning.

I yanked off one of the ponytail holders I wear on my wrist like extra bracelets and gathered my mop of hair at the nape of my neck. After fastening the hair with the pink elastic band, I tried to concentrate on my story. In the real world, I listened to the peaceful clinking of spoons against heavy crockery mugs and the Bee Gees crooning "How Deep Is Your Love," but on the pages of my novel in progress, all hell had broken loose. Scarlett Olson and her toddler Melody were on the run from a killer, having barely escaped plunging into an icy river in Calgary, which would have meant their sudden death.

I sat back and nibbled my lower lip. Would this plot line fly? Should Scarlett have had more sense than to leave the safety of their hideout? She'd seen the weather forecast for torrential rain on TV that morning. She knew the killer was nearby. Would the reader rag on my character for not calling the authorities, even though she couldn't risk turning on her cell phone for fear the villain would track her signal?

I blew out a breath and stared at the poster of John Travolta in *Saturday Night Fever* on the wall near me. I supposed he was considered "hot stuff" back in the day—around the time I'd been born. I rubbed my neck, feeling Scarlett's predicament in every tendon, but did it come across on the page? For the millionth time I wondered whether I'd ever finish this book or if I was destined to the status of wannabe mystery author forever. I lifted my cup and took a whiff of the heavenly vanilla-and-almond-scented coffee—a house blend called Lavender's Sunrise.

Try to relax, Sabrina. For God's sake, focus.

Before I could get back into the story, the shop's bell tinkled and the door thwacked open into the table behind it. I turned and saw Thomas Cortez marching straight for me. He wore a wide-brimmed straw hat, jeans over work boots, and a short-sleeved plaid shirt. I'd seen him—the handyman for Aunt Rowe's rental cottages and her most loyal friend—tackling an overgrown hedge when I'd left this morning. His grim expression told me he wasn't here for a great cup of coffee.

My heart leapt to my throat and I stood, fearing the worst. "Is Aunt Rowe okay?"

"She's fine, Miss Sabrina." Thomas pulled out a chair and plunked himself down.

"Thank goodness." I eased back into my seat.

Thomas took his hat off and placed it on the chair across from me. "Your aunt's having a good day so far. Glenda got her settled on the patio chaise so she can enjoy some sun before the day gets too hot. The physical therapist should be there shortly."

My aunt, Rowena Flowers, took a nasty fall in early spring and was recovering from a concussion and a broken leg. Which was my impetus for finally quitting my Houston paralegal job and accepting her offer to come live with her for a while. In addition to keeping my aunt company, I was helping Thomas and Glenda, the housekeeper, manage the cottages during Aunt Rowe's recuperation.

Thomas lifted his arm to check his watch, and I spotted a bloody cut on his forearm. Looked to me like he might need stitches.

"What happened to you?" I pulled a fresh napkin from the dispenser and handed it to him.

He accepted the napkin and dabbed at the wound. "El Gato Diablo is what. Gosh-darned cat crossed my path, next thing my toe caught on the curb, and I fell flat out. Arm caught the edge of one of them fancy metal planters in front of the wine shop. Better'n smacking my head, I guess."

"A devil cat?" My forehead creased. "What are you talking about?"

"The black cat," he said. "Big fella. Been around these parts since I was a kid."

Since he was a kid?

"You're what?" I said. "Thirtysomething?"

"Close enough."

The coffee shop's owner, Max Dieter, came up with a mug for Thomas in one hand and a steaming coffeepot in the other. The big man had a fringe of strawberry blond hair surrounding a bald crown and always offered a jolly smile. Without asking what Thomas wanted, he filled the fresh mug with a flourish.

"Heard you talking about the bad luck cat," he said. "Legend around town. I thought we'd seen the last of him when Wes Krane loaded him up and carted him off to Nolan County."

I'd met the crotchety Mr. Krane, owner of the local hardware store, and wasn't surprised that he'd drive across the state just because a cat annoyed him.

Thomas lifted his arm to show Max his injury. "The cat's here in Lavender. Did this to me."

Max shook his head. "The animal better steer clear of my place. I remodeled to bring in more business. Don't need bad luck scaring people away."

I stifled a giggle. If you asked me, Max's baby-blue leisure-suit-like pants and polyester print shirt were enough to drive customers away.

"Y'all be serious," I said. "Cats don't bring bad luck. And there's no black cat that's like thirty years old."

Thomas said, "Remember, cats have nine lives."

"Uh-huh." I rolled my eyes. "You took a fall this morning, that's all. It was an accident."

"You'll run into that cat one of these days," Max said. "Most folks do sooner or later. You've been warned."

"Right." Thomas nodded. "El Gato Diablo."

"We'll see," I said. "But you didn't come to talk about a cat."

Max took the hint and walked back to the counter, but that didn't mean he'd quit listening in on our conversation.

Thomas leaned forward and lowered his voice. "Weekend guests start arriving tonight."

I picked up my mug and sipped my coffee. "We discussed that earlier. Is there a problem?"

Thomas nodded. "Heard through a friend of my sister-in-law's neighbor that Bobby Joe Flowers is on his way here, too."

I frowned. "He was my dad's cousin."

"I know," Thomas said. "And Rowena's. She won't be glad to see him."

"Okay." My shoulders tightened, and this time my tension had nothing to do with fiction. "Dad had plenty of stories about cousin Bobby Joe, none of them good. He was the rowdy one in the family, the risk taker, the womanizer, the drinker. I never met the man. Maybe he's settled down by now."

"He hasn't." Thomas drained his mug in one long swallow and put it back on the table. "We can try to keep him away from Rowena, but she likes to face problems head-on, and he usually makes a beeline to her door."

I cocked my head. "Why is that?"

"Always lookin' for a handout," Thomas said. "Never has a dime to his name to hear him tell it. Rowena's done good for herself. But last time Bobby Joe didn't ask. Stole a couple thousand in cash from her safe."

My jaw dropped. "That's despicable. Did Aunt Rowe report him to the police?"

"Nope." Thomas placed his elbows on the table and folded his hands as if in prayer. "You know how she is about family."

"Did she get the money back?"

"What he hadn't already spent," Thomas said. "I mean to see nothing like that ever happens again. Expect he'll be here by dinnertime. We need to be ready."

The thought of anyone, family or not, treating Aunt Rowe so badly made the coffee in my gut churn. "What can I do to help?"

"Glad you asked." Thomas pulled a list from his pocket and handed it to me. "I'm runnin' over to Emerald Springs to pick up rosebushes Rowena special ordered. She wants 'em planted by tomorrow. You could get these lock kits at Krane's Hardware on your way back. Put them on the company account. I'll install them later in the main house. I'm betting ol' Bobby Joe hung on to a key."

I wasn't looking forward to meeting this relative whom, for some reason, I'd never laid eyes on—not even at Dad's funeral.

"Where does Bobby Joe stay when he's in town?" I said. "Not with Aunt Rowe, I hope."

"Too close for comfort," he said. "She usually gives him the Monte Carlo cottage, but now you're in there. Ought to send him off to the nearest La Quinta, but she won't. Since we're not fully booked, she'll probably put him up in one of the other cottages." Thomas stood abruptly and picked up his hat. "We need to be ready," he said again, then left me with the list.

I watched him go and wondered what his being "ready"

entailed and whether it involved firearms. His acting like we were the Texans hunkering down inside the Alamo as Santa Anna's army approached made me plenty nervous.

Good Lord, there was no way I could come up with a creative thought now. The writing would have to wait for another day. I shut down my computer and slid it into my carrying case, then felt around under the table with my feet until I found my flip-flops.

I waved bye to Max, wondering how much of our conversation he'd heard. I hadn't been around long enough to know whether he'd keep private information to himself. Assuming that everyone in town didn't already know our family's business.

Outside, the sky was brilliant blue, the air thick with humidity that was nothing compared to what we'd have in another couple of weeks. I hurried to my Accord, which was parked under the shade of a live oak, and stopped short when I spotted a huge, coal-black cat sitting on the car, still as a hood ornament. The feline sat tall, with its vivid green eyes focused on me.

This had to be the cat Thomas and Max referred to as the bad luck cat, but I didn't buy that for a second. I smiled at the animal and held out a nonthreatening hand as I took baby steps toward the car.

"Aren't you gorgeous?" I said, and that's when the cat took off through the flowering white oleander bushes that separated Hot Stuff's parking lot from the wine shop's lot next door.

I shrugged and climbed into the car. Technically, the cat had not crossed my path, so I should be good to go.

2

K̲RANE'S HARDWARE SAT on the outskirts of Lavender town proper and, as evidenced by the row of vehicles parked out front, the store did a bang-up business. I pulled my small car into a space between a couple of 4x4 pickups and climbed out, feeling like I'd arrived in the land of the giants.

Hardware made up only a portion of Krane's inventory. With departments devoted to household goods, hunting and fishing, plants, and pets, the place drew customers who didn't feel the need to drive an hour to the nearest Walmart. I pulled Thomas's list from my shorts pocket and headed inside, hoping they had the locks he wanted.

I was looking at the piece of paper in my hand while stepping up to the entrance and nearly got clobbered by a humongous bag of dog food perched on a cowboy's shoulder as he headed out. I ducked in the nick of time, and he went on to his truck without ever seeing me. I pushed through the swinging glass door and walked into the store.

A heavyset young woman in a green bib apron with "Krane's" embroidered on the breast pocket stood at the front window, staring into the parking lot. She glanced at me and said, "Isn't he dreamy?"

What? Who?

I walked over to her and followed her gaze. The cowboy who'd almost taken me down hefted the dog food from his shoulder into the bed of his white pickup. When he turned toward the driver's door, I got a good look at him.

"Pretty cute," I agreed, though that was an understatement. The man looked to be a little over six feet, late thirties or so, with dark hair and a five-o'clock shadow several days old. The rugged, outdoorsy type. Definitely dreamy. He wore a belt with the requisite Texas-sized belt buckle and jeans that fit him ever so well. The yellow Lab riding shotgun in his passenger seat was super cute, too.

"Who is he?" I asked the clerk.

"Luke Griffin," she said. "Lives on the Kauffman ranch."

I didn't know where that was, and I might have asked except that my attention was drawn to a fiftyish man getting out of a cherry red SUV. He approached Griffin, who sure didn't look happy to see him. In fact, he seemed downright perturbed. The two erupted into what looked like a verbal battle with a lot of waving arms and finger-pointing.

The store clerk and I exchanged glances.

"Who's *that* guy?" I said.

She shrugged. Behind us a loud voice snapped. "Hallie, where the devil are you? You have customers to take care of."

We turned away from the window in unison. At the U-shaped checkout counter, one cashier was efficiently ringing up an order while five people waited in line to check out. The second cash register stood unused.

"Sorry, Dad." Hallie hurried over to her register and said, "I'll take the next customer over here."

Until now, I hadn't known the clerk was related to the store's owner, though I had seen her a couple of times before. I approached Krane, who looked like he'd had a rough morning. The sleeves of his off-white shirt were soiled with dark, wet stains. His face and neck dripped sweat, and his sparse salt-and-pepper hair needed combing.

"Sorry," I said. "My fault. I distracted your daughter."

"Did she help you find what you came for?" He looked pointedly at my empty hands.

"No, not yet." I handed him Thomas's list. "I need to get these."

"She wasn't gonna find any deadbolt locks by staring into space," he said. "What to do with that girl, daydreaming one minute, listening to that noise she calls music the next? This way." He turned and strode down an aisle.

The man was so grumpy I wouldn't blame customers for driving to Walmart to avoid him. I needed the locks sooner rather than later, though, so I followed Krane. He stopped midway down an aisle, near another woman wearing a Krane's apron. She was unpacking a box of fire ant poison and stocking the shelf in front of her.

The woman gave Krane a once-over and said, "You go Dumpster diving?"

He scowled at her. "Stupid cat got in the garbage again. Dragged stuff all over the place."

"El Gato Diablo?" she said.

"Who else?" Krane said.

The woman looked at me. "Did he get you, too?"

"Gosh, do I look like I've been in a fight with a cat?"

She grinned. "No, I meant has the cat caused you bad luck?"

"Not yet," I said, playing along rather than pointing out that cats do not affect luck.

"Good for you," she said. "Just this morning the mailman came by and said he'd spotted the black cat. Next thing he knew a gust of wind ripped the mail he was about to deliver right out of his hand. Blew it into the street, and he nearly got plastered by a truck hauling a load of hay when he chased after the envelopes that got away."

The cat controlled the wind. Right.

"Lucky he wasn't hurt," I said.

"A miracle," she said with a touch of sarcasm.

Krane was focused on finding my locks and obviously didn't want to talk about the cat. He ran a finger down a row of packages and pulled one off the rack to check against the list. "These deadbolts for Rowena's place?"

"Yes," I said, "Thomas sent me for them."

"Having trouble out there?" He turned to me, and his brows drew together.

"No trouble." I wasn't about to give either of these people something else to blame on an innocent cat.

"Huh." He picked up four identical packages. "I'll take these to the checkout for you. Need anything else?"

"Not today."

I followed him to the front of the store, where he recorded the purchase on Aunt Rowe's account. He bagged the locks and handed them to me.

"Thanks, Mr. Krane. Have a good day."

"Yeah," he muttered. "You, too."

I left the store and found myself disappointed that Luke Griffin and the angry stranger were gone. The brief conflict I'd seen between the two men was interesting and mysterious. Maybe I could use a confrontation like theirs somewhere in my book. I tucked the thought into the overstuffed "ideas" section of my brain, the section that could stand to have its files better organized.

I climbed in my car, backtracked into town, and hung a left on Gazebo Street. The short drive from there to Aunt Rowe's property took me over rolling hills and past sparkling spring-fed creeks. My shoulders relaxed, and I sank back into my seat as I enjoyed the scenic drive. Two miles out of town, I turned again on Traveler's Lane, the driveway to Aunt Rowe's house and her Around-the-World cottages. I headed for my place first, the Monte Carlo cottage.

Guests who valued beauty over practicality chose to stay here rather than rent a typical Hill Country wood-sided, tin-roofed cabin. Aunt Rowe had designed each cottage in a style reminiscent of her trip to a particular city. In Monte Carlo, she had avoided overpriced lodging along the coastline and opted to rent a charming Tudor cottage.

I walked up the stone walkway, entered the cottage, and set my laptop on the small table in the combination kitchen/dining/living room. I opened the blinds on the window next to the stone fireplace to give myself a view of the steps leading down the steep incline to the river. Maybe creativity would flow better here today than it had at the coffee shop. I'd give the writing another try after checking in with my aunt. Thomas hadn't said whether she knew about Bobby Joe Flowers's impending visit, and I decided I wouldn't bring him up unless she did.

I grabbed a bottle of water from the mini-fridge in the kitchenette and took a long swig as I walked into the living area. Even though I'd never met Flowers, I wondered why he usually stayed in this cottage with its decidedly feminine decor, all pastels and lace. Aunt Rowe had decorated the Monte Carlo with posters and photographs of the French Riviera, casinos, and palaces. A framed photograph of her on a sailboat with one of the James Bond actors who had lived there when she visited stood on the mantel. A picture book from the Princess Grace Gardens sat on the coffee table next to a photo album of Aunt Rowe's shots from her trip, alongside a journal she kept there for all guests in the Monte Carlo cottage to record thoughts about their stay if they so desired.

I pulled off my ponytail holder and ran my fingers through my hair, then retrieved the new locks from my car and walked the short distance up a gravel lane to Aunt Rowe's house. I went in through the back door of her rambling one-story and left the locks in the utility room for Thomas.

Salsa music was playing, way too loud. I followed the music to the screened porch and found my aunt sitting on an oversized wicker chair surrounded by blue-striped pillows, her leg cast propped on a matching pillow atop a wicker ottoman. She wore a bright red off-one-shoulder top and a big yellow flower clipped in her dyed auburn hair.

"Wow," I shouted for her to hear me over the music. "What's the occasion?"

She looked up and gave me a big smile, then grabbed a remote and lowered the volume on her Bose sound system. "Sabrina, you're back early. How do you like my Zumba workout music?"

"Zumba?" The woman was closing in on seventy and had a cast on her leg.

I sat in a chair across from Aunt Rowe and watched with amusement as she started moving her arms and snapping her fingers in time with the music.

"Zumba's a workout without the work. More like dancing. And this—" She paused to run a hand across the fabric of her red top. "I bought in Paris and wore one night that I spent dancing with a special gentleman. It brings back good memories."

She was in a happy mood, a rarity in the six weeks since I'd moved here. "That's nice, but you might have to put the Zumba on the back burner for a few more months."

"It won't be months," she said. "I'm on a new quick-healing program."

"Oh? You saw your doctor today?"

"No. Claire Dubois came to visit and told me all about foods that promote bone healing. Glenda is off to the market as we speak, to make sure I'm stocked up on green leafy vegetables, calcium-fortified orange juice, sweet potatoes, yada yada yada."

"Claire from the wine shop?"

Aunt Rowe smiled. "The very one."

Odd that Claire would come here. She never seemed especially friendly, and Aunt Rowe had never mentioned her before. But now I was beginning to suspect the real reason for my aunt's better mood.

"I didn't know you and Claire were close," I said. "Did she tell you about the Zumba workouts, too?"

"No, the Zumba was my idea. I'm sick to death of crosswords and daytime TV."

"Did Claire happen to bring something with her to help you heal?"

Her smile disappeared. "For Pete's sake, Sabrina, so she brought me some wine. I knew you'd start nagging when you found out, but I didn't take any pain meds today, at least not after I started drinking."

"But, Aunt Rowe—"

"Don't 'but' me," she said. "If you'd rather have me grousing about my circulatory problems, the fact that I can't sleep worth a darn, or those flippin' crutches, I will. At least the wine made me forget about that crap for a little bit."

"Okay, okay." The wine had messed with whatever meds were still in her system. Aunt Rowe didn't normally fly off the handle so easily.

"I want to be up and about, ready to greet my new weekend guests," she said. "I live for that, you know."

"I know you do." Feeling sorry for getting on her about the wine, I moved from my chair and perched carefully on the edge of the ottoman supporting her cast. "I ran through the Barcelona, Florence, and Madrid cottages this morning and left your welcome baskets. Maybe you should try to take a nap this afternoon before the new guests arrive."

She nodded. "A nap might be the thing. The wine made me a bit drowsy."

We both started at the sound of a car on the gravel outside. I looked over Aunt Rowe's shoulder to the driveway and the vehicle that pulled up to the closed garage doors.

The red SUV looked awfully familiar.

"Is Glenda back?" She was trying to turn and look, but her rigid leg kept her from finding the right position.

"No, it's not her." The man who climbed out of the SUV was the guy from Krane's parking lot.

"Then who is it?" Aunt Rowe said.

"I'll go see." I walked over to the screen door, which was where the man immediately headed.

Was he one of the weekend guests? But why wouldn't he go to the front door of the house?

I opened the door before he reached it. Definitely the guy who'd argued with the cowboy. He wore khakis with a crease, a green golf shirt, and brown ostrich-skin boots that looked brand new. His longish hair was gray and thinning on top, and he sported a sparse beard.

"Hello," I said. "May I help you?"

He looked me up and down with a leer that would have made J. R. Ewing proud. "I'll sure bet you could, darlin'. I'm Bobby Joe Flowers."

3

ALL I COULD think of was Thomas warning me we needed to be ready when Bobby Joe Flowers arrived. I didn't feel ready.

The man standing in front of me was my father's first cousin. My first cousin, once removed. The ne'er-do-well prodigal cousin I'd heard about my whole life but had never met.

"Is Rojo here?" he said.

A lump the size of an apricot formed in my throat. Rojo. My dad's nickname for his sister, Rowena Josephine. I didn't like the sound of her pet name coming from this man's lips.

I cleared my throat. "She's recovering from a serious injury," I said, intending to send him on his way, but my aunt was too close and had heard every word.

"Bobby Joe, don't even think about hitting on this young lady," Aunt Rowe said.

I turned, surprised to see she had managed to get up and now stood a few feet behind me on her crutches.

"Give me some credit," he said. "Would I hit on Saint Richard's daughter?"

He gave me a smarmy smile that made me cringe inwardly. How did he know who I was? Even if he'd received childhood pictures of me in annual Christmas cards, which I doubted, it didn't make sense that he would recognize me at thirty-eight. And what was up with him referring to Dad in that snide tone of voice?

Bobby Joe entered the house as if he lived here and went up to his cousin. "Place looks nice." He leaned in and gave Aunt Rowe a kiss on the cheek. "Sorry to hear about your leg. What happened?"

Aunt Rowe and I exchanged glances. This was normally where she'd offer refreshments to someone who came calling, but her stiff posture and the lack of warmth in her expression told me how she felt about this unexpected visit. By her silence, I guessed she didn't even want to tell him how she'd tumbled down the stone steps leading to the river. I checked my watch. This would be a great time for Thomas to get back.

Using the most formal tone I could muster, I said, "What brings you to Lavender, Mr. Flowers?"

His lips curled up, and he laughed. "Well ain't you a chip off the old aunt? Call me Bobby. We'll be gettin' to know each other right quick seein' how I'll be living in these parts from now on."

"Living here?" Aunt Rowe said. "In Lavender?"

"That's right. I'm stayin' with a friend, so you don't have to worry about puttin' me up for now. But you might want to have a seat before I fill you in on the rest of my news. Wouldn't want you to take another fall."

So he already knew she'd fallen? How? Not everyone with their leg in a cast had injured themselves by falling. My stomach twisted into a tighter knot with every word the man said.

He wasn't the type to care if Aunt Rowe asked him to leave. Unless we could bodily throw him out—an impossible task—we were stuck with the guy.

I went over to Aunt Rowe and put a hand on her arm. "Let me help you."

She went willingly to her seat on the wicker chair, but she didn't relax against the pillows. Bobby Joe took one of the chairs facing her, and I sat in the other.

"Spit it out, Bobby Joe," Aunt Rowe said. "I don't have all day."

He grinned, drawing out the telling of whatever he'd come to say. He propped one of his spanking-new boots on the opposite knee. "I had a medical procedure recently, too. Not so serious as yours, Rojo, but it led to finding out a damn interesting fact about my blood."

"And you came to share your medical history with me," Aunt Rowe said, regaining some of her composure. "How special."

He ignored her sarcasm. "See, my blood don't have much in common with my brother's or sister's. Imagine my surprise. I'm here to tell you I think my blood's a lot more similar to what you got runnin' through your veins, Rojo."

"What?" I blurted. "That's a ridiculous thing to say."

He chuckled. "Let me finish, little lady."

"Explain yourself," Aunt Rowe said. "Before I throw you out of here on your ear."

Bobby Joe leaned forward and fixed his gaze on her face. "Ran into some people over in Austin. The Staffords. Remember them? They knew our folks real well back when we were kids."

"I remember." Aunt Rowe spoke slowly, as if she wished she didn't know who he was talking about.

"Miz Stafford's near ninety, still sharp as ever. She was

surprised to hear my folks stayed together till their dying day."

I remembered seeing Henry and Eliza Flowers and their other children, Becky and J. T., from time to time at family reunions. Bobby Joe was never with them.

"Your folks had issues," Aunt Rowe admitted. "Lots of folks did."

He shook his head. "But not yours. They were perfect, just like Saint Richard. And you. Always better than the rest of us."

"Cut the crap." Aunt Rowe raised her voice. "No one's perfect."

"Not your daddy, that's for sure." He gave us the smarmy grin again. "See, Miz Stafford tells me your daddy and my mama were especially close, right before the time I came along. Put two and two together, Rojo. I think I'm your baby brother."

Aunt Rowe gaped at him. I gasped. He was saying PawPaw cheated on Granny. I wanted to call Bobby Joe a big fat liar. My grandparents were the happiest couple I'd ever known.

"Given this new information," he went on, "I'd say the land we're sittin' on, including those profitable little cottages you rent out, is rightly half mine."

Aunt Rowe moved quick as a snake. She jumped up from her seat and took a couple of steps toward him on her cast. She gripped a crutch in her right hand and swung it toward his head like a batter itching to hit a home run.

The crutch connected with his temple, and the impact sent his chair flying over backward.

Aunt Rowe's face was beet red. "How dare you come into my house and slander my father's good name," she yelled. "You can take your lies somewhere else, 'cause you will *never* get your slimy hands on one square inch of this property. No. Way. In. Hell."

Bobby Joe was down on the floor, flailing on top of the wicker chair, protecting his face with his arms. Blood spurted from the place where her weapon had connected with his head. She stood over him with a crutch poised in the air like she planned to clobber him again.

I jumped up. "No, Aunt Rowe. Stop."

She was zoned out, livid, and didn't seem to hear me. "You're a lying sack of—"

A loud voice interrupted the melee. "Excuse me."

I glanced up to see a man standing at the screen door. He had two children with him—a boy and a girl—and their mouths were hanging open.

"I'm Tim Hartman," the man said. "And we have reservations for the Barcelona cottage. We're, um, kind of early."

T wo hours later, I was at my friend Tyanne Clark's bookstore. The store had closed at five, and we sat in a cozy reading nook in the back enjoying glasses of sweet tea with lemon. Ty had kicked off her Crocs—I swear she had every new style they made and a pair in every color—and sat with her legs curled under her. She was as petite and blond as I was gangly and dark, and the easy chair seemed to swallow her.

Ty and I had met when we were eight, during one of my summer visits to Aunt Rowe's. Since then, I'd married, divorced after four difficult years, and given up on finding a man I was willing to live with. Instead, I spent all my passion at the computer, trying in fits and starts to write a book I could sell. So far all I had to show for my trouble was a pile of rejection letters.

Tyanne had married, given birth to three children, and opened Lavender's only bookstore, Knead to Read, a name inspired by her bookstore cats, Zelda and Willis. With Internet sales, e-book rentals, and a booth at every Hill Country bazaar and festival in three counties, Ty kept her business hopping.

At the moment, the store mascots were winding down their day. Zelda, an orange female, was asleep on Ty's lap. Willis, a big tabby tomcat with striking markings, sat nearby kneading the braided rug under her chair.

After I spilled the whole sordid story about what had happened at Aunt Rowe's, Ty said, "You're lucky Thomas showed up when he did, before Rowe killed the man."

"I know. Thomas even managed to convince Mr. Hartman to keep his reservation and checked the family into the Barcelona cottage. I'm not sure how, given what the poor guy and his children witnessed." I took a sip of tea and put my glass down on a side table. "Aunt Rowe went ballistic, but if she hadn't hit Bobby Joe, I might have done it for her."

"Do you believe his story that he's her brother?" Ty asked.

I shrugged. "I'd rather believe this is another ploy to get money. If it's true his mother and my grandfather had an affair, then why didn't anyone hear rumors before now?"

"People were more discreet about their private lives when your grandparents were young," she said. "These days people don't mind showing up on reality TV and announcing to the whole world: 'I was seduced by my brother-in-law and I'm having his baby.'"

"Stop," I said. "My grandfather didn't seduce anyone."

"Maybe you're right." Ty ran a hand through her short blond curls and gave me a conciliatory smile. "You think Flowers will turn your aunt in for assault?"

I shook my head. "He was laughing about the whole incident when he left. Stayed only long enough for Thomas to patch up the cut on his forehead with a butterfly bandage from the first aid kit. His head bled like crazy."

"With all that blood, you should have collected a sample. Had it tested against your aunt's and gotten an answer. Wouldn't have to make yourself sick wondering."

I shook my head. "I don't think collecting a blood sample would do the trick. Years ago, I did some DNA research for a book. Don't you need the father's blood to get conclusive test results?"

"They have more-advanced tests these days," Ty said.

I didn't want to hear that. "Bobby Joe has to know Aunt Rowe's not handing over her inheritance on his say-so. Probably won't give him a dime even if science can prove he really is her brother. The law might protect her, too, depending on what exactly PawPaw's will said. I'm sure Bobby Joe has a plan. He said Aunt Rowe would hear from him again soon."

Ty raised her eyebrows. "Or his lawyer. Or the cops. Or both."

"He can bring it on," I said. "I'm angry that he tarnished the memory of my grandfather. And I sure hope he can't lay claim to Aunt Rowe's property."

Willis walked over and rubbed against my leg as if he knew I needed comforting. I reached down to scratch behind his ears.

"Don't let this change your feelings about family," Ty said. "I mean the family you've known and loved, not this Flowers character."

"Easier said than done."

She grinned. "I know exactly what you need to do."

"Find an attorney to represent my aunt against criminal charges?" I said dejectedly.

"No. Use this somehow in your book. Conflict on every page, remember?"

Tyanne was always harping about conflict. She was the

only person I allowed to read my manuscript pages, and though she was a harsh critic her insights were usually spot on. I sat back and thought about how I might weave details of what had happened today into my book. Maybe a twist on real events. I could have Scarlett Olson run to an uncle she hopes will keep her and her daughter safe, only to learn he isn't her uncle at all.

"You gave me an idea," I said. "I'm going home to write."

B ACK at the house, I learned from Thomas that Aunt Rowe had taken a sedative and was sleeping like the dead. Bobby Joe Flowers hadn't been seen or heard from again. Thank goodness.

In my cottage, I booted up my laptop and read over the last few pages of my novel. I mapped out possible plot changes but wasn't happy with any of the ideas I came up with. Sometimes writing was nothing but a big time suck. Around eleven I called it a night and went to bed.

I tried to sleep, but apparently I was too wound up after what had happened today to write or to sleep. By two, I gave up on the bed and decided to bake. I had a craving for pecan tarts. I changed my nightgown for shorts and a T-shirt, added socks and tennies, then grabbed a flashlight and keys and headed to Aunt Rowe's. Not my first middle-of-the-night foray into her large country kitchen. I had baked things there as a cure for insomnia two or three times a week since coming to live in Lavender. Though Aunt Rowe claimed she had trouble sleeping, she had yet to interrupt me during a baking frenzy.

The night was humid and still. From the path, I could barely hear the gurgle of the Glidden River—a narrow section of which ran through Aunt Rowe's property. Clouds drifted across the half-moon, and I flipped on the flashlight to guide me. At her back door, I stubbornly tried my key three times and then smacked my forehead with the heel of my hand.

Of course. Thomas had changed the locks.

I stood there for a few seconds, grieving for the pecan tarts I would not be eating. I'd have to settle for the banana bread I had leftover from my last middle-of-the-night bake-fest. I hurried back along the path toward my cottage. The clouds slid away from the moon, and I switched the flashlight off to conserve the batteries.

Something darted across the path in front of me.

I stopped and scanned the area. Up ahead, eyes glowed in the dark. My heart raced. I turned the flashlight back on and found a large black cat sitting about twenty yards ahead of me. The same cat I'd seen sitting on my car the day before.

This time it had crossed my path.

If that had happened before Bobby Joe Flowers's visit, I'd say *he* was the bad luck. Or if the cat had shown itself on the way to Aunt Rowe's house, I'd say the bad luck was that I didn't have the right house key.

Black cats don't cause bad luck, Sabrina, remember?

I resumed walking, and the cat stayed right where it was until I got closer. Then it jumped up and ran ahead.

When I reached my cottage, I saw the cat sitting on the top stone of the steps leading to the river. I stooped down and talked to the animal.

"You've made quite a trip coming all the way out here from town," I said. "You might want to steer clear of Thomas, though. He probably won't be happy to see you."

The cat meowed.

"Glad to meet you, too," I said. "You remind me of a cat I used to have. Smoky went all the way through college with me, but then I married Elliott and he was allergic. Should

have made *him* move out instead of the cat. But Dad kept
Smoky for me until he passed. Smoky, I mean, not Dad, but
Dad's gone now, too." My eyes teared.

Get a grip. You're talking to a cat as if it's your therapist.

The cat stood and looked at me, then turned and darted
down the steps.

"Wait." I ran to the top of the steps and shone my light in
the direction the cat had run.

There, another flash of black.

Where was the danged cat going? I thought cats didn't like
water.

I took the steps a little too quickly and had to stop for a
moment to catch my balance on one flat stone that rocked
when I put my weight on it. I slowed down, taking care so I
wouldn't slip and fall. When I reached the bottom, the cat's
green eyes appeared in a place that made it seem like the
animal was suspended over the water.

No, he was sitting on a fallen tree limb. A rather large limb
with one end resting on the riverbank, the other end submerged. The cat was taunting me for some reason, and I was
crazy to be out here in the middle of the night following the
animal around.

"If you want to be friends, come and visit me tomorrow,"
I told the cat, then turned to retrace my steps.

I swear he meowed again, though I couldn't be sure over
the sound of the river. I turned the light back toward him and
stopped when I spotted a brown ostrich-skin boot propped
on top of the fallen limb near the cat.

What the heck?

I walked as close as I safely could to the riverbank's edge,
three feet or so above the water. The boot was actually lodged
in the fork of a branch attached to the limb.

My heart raced. Was there still a foot in that boot?

I changed my position and saw the leg bent at an unnatural angle. A leg clad in khaki pants. A wave of nausea washed over me as I moved the light and discovered the rest of the body submerged in the water.

Earlier today I had wanted Bobby Joe Flowers to go away and leave us alone.

But not this way.

4

FOR A FEW seconds I considered jumping in to rescue Bobby Joe. I had years of experience leaping into the water from this bank. The river pooled here and was about eight feet in the deepest section. There were some large rocks I'd have to avoid, a tricky maneuver to pull in the dark. I slipped off my tennis shoes, but then logic kicked in. Bobby Joe was facedown in the water and looked like he'd been there for a while. I was too late.

With shaking hands, I patted my pockets for my cell phone. No luck. I'd left it on my nightstand. Not very far away, but now that I'd found the body, I felt weird about leaving Bobby Joe. Like I was abandoning a long-lost cousin. What if the river's current dislodged him and carried him downstream? I told myself he couldn't be swept off into some large body of water and lost forever, at least I didn't think so. Still—

Move, Sabrina. Make the call.

I turned and took the steps with care so I wouldn't fall and

meet the same fate as Bobby Joe. I shone the flashlight around
the sparsely wooded area surrounding me, looking for the
black cat. He was nowhere in sight. He had led me to the body,
then disappeared as though his work was done.

After reaching the top of the steps, I hurried inside and
retrieved my phone. I dialed 911 and told the dispatcher about
Bobby Joe. The woman took my information and told me the
authorities would be on their way and I should stay on the
line.

This whole scene seemed surreal, like something out of a
book. In the kind of books I read, though, there would typi-
cally be a killer on the loose. Thank goodness that wasn't the
case here.

Or was it?

I dropped onto the cedar bench outside my cottage door.
My whole life I'd heard nothing but bad things about Bobby
Joe Flowers, and now he was dead. In less than twenty-four
hours, I'd learned that the man was a thief, witnessed him
having an argument, and formed a decidedly bad impression
of the guy after finally meeting him for the first time. He
seemed like a good murder victim to me, but maybe it was
simply my mystery-writer brain conjuring up unlikely possibilities. I had subconsciously been thinking of interesting
plot points involving the man ever since Aunt Rowe hit him
upside the head.

I stood quickly. Aunt Rowe. She needed to know what
happened before sirens woke her. Calling the house at this
hour might scare her silly. Without asking permission, I put
the dispatcher on hold and dialed the housekeeper's cell
phone. Since Aunt Rowe's accident, Glenda had been spending the night, though she actually lived a few miles away with
her husband, Lloyd, and two teenagers.

She answered on the first ring and said, "Heard the news about Bobby Joe."

"How? I just found him."

"Laurelle, the dispatcher, and I are Bingo pals. She called me."

So the dispatcher had put me on hold, too. I sure hoped she'd notified emergency personnel before calling Glenda.

"Be there in a jiffy," Glenda said.

"No, you should stay with Aunt Rowe."

"I'm not with her. Just left my house, and I have the pedal to the metal, so I'll get there before anyone else."

"I thought you stayed with my aunt every night." If she didn't, I would move into the house myself.

"I usually do," Glenda said, "but last night, Rowe was worked up after what happened with her cousin. We watched *North by Northwest*, but I could tell she wasn't paying attention to the movie. Afterward, she told me in no uncertain terms to go home for a change and hug my kids, so I did. She was out like a light before dark, and I made sure she had her cell phone charged and within reach before I left."

After a few seconds of my silence, Glenda said, "You okay, honey?"

"I'm fine."

"Guess I should say I'm sorry to hear what happened to that man, but I can't lie. I've seen him in action a couple times."

"I totally understand."

"Be there in two minutes," Glenda said. "I'll break the news to Rowe. EMS has a pretty fast response time around here. Stay by your cottage to flag them down."

"Will do." I disconnected from Glenda and went back to the dispatcher call, then flipped on all the cottage lights to make it easier for the first responders to find me.

About ten minutes later, the EMS van crawled down the narrow winding lane toward my cottage. Thankfully they weren't running the siren. I hoped the guests in the other cottages were sound sleepers and didn't notice the flashing lights. Maybe no one would realize what was going on outside. I couldn't see the spot where Glenda usually parked from where I stood, but she had sent me a text to let me know she'd arrived at the house and that I shouldn't worry about Aunt Rowe.

When the van reached me, the dispatcher disconnected our call. Two men jumped out and took a backboard from the van. They put on hats with spotlights mounted over the brims and grabbed a duffel along with some other supplies. I pointed them in the right direction, and they double-timed down the steps to the river.

My mouth felt as dry as peanut shells, and I wished I'd thought to bring a bottle of water with me. Before I could go inside to grab one, another set of headlights coming down the lane claimed my attention. A sheriff's department car pulled up behind the van, and a woman climbed out. Deputy Patricia Rosales. I would have rather seen the kindly, older Sheriff Jeb Crawford, a longtime friend of my aunt, but I wasn't surprised that one of his deputies had night duty.

I'd met Rosales a couple of times at Sheriff Crawford's office when I visited to ask him about crime scene details to use in my book. She always seemed annoyed with me for taking up her boss's time, and she didn't look any happier to see me tonight.

Rosales was slim, but the legs of her heavily starched uniform pants swished together and practically crackled when she walked. Her sleek black hair was drawn into a bun so tight it had to hurt. The woman was tall, a good five foot ten, and I looked up slightly as she got closer.

"So, Miss Mystery Writer," she said, "you got a real body this time. You find that pretty exciting?"

"I—no—what an odd thing to say."

She smirked, then turned and looked toward the river. "I'm going to speak with the EMS folks." She signaled me with her palm out. "You stay."

I didn't appreciate her talking to me like I was a dog. *Stay, Sabrina. Be a good girl.*

No matter how much I wanted to talk back to Rosales, the woman's manner intimidated me enough that I didn't dare move. When she was out of sight, though, I edged closer to the river to see if I could overhear her conversation with the EMTs. The noise of the rushing water plus the chirping of night creatures drowned out any words, but I saw a spotlight moving across the area. I sighed and moved back to the place where she'd left me. A long ten minutes later, she returned clutching a notebook and pen.

I swallowed and asked an obvious question. "He's dead, isn't he?"

"Yes." She poised her pen over the notebook and asked me to spell my name for her, which I did even though she should already know the answer. She made me sign the visitor's log every time I showed up at her office, and how hard is it to remember Sabrina Tate? I wondered if she was purposely trying to annoy me.

"Do you know the identity of the man you saw in the river?"

"Yes. It's Bobby Joe Flowers. I—"

She silenced me with a look. "Was he drinking this evening?"

I frowned. "I have no idea."

"Did the two of you have an argument?"

"No, we barely spoke earlier—"

She cut me off with, "How long have you two been here?"

"*We* haven't been here. I mean, I moved here six weeks ago. He arrived yesterday afternoon."

"Where do y'all live?"

"*We* don't live together." My voice grew unintentionally louder, and I took a few seconds to compose myself before going on to explain about Bobby Joe's arrival at Aunt Rowe's house. I stressed the fact that I had never met him before and left out the part about Aunt Rowe hitting the man.

When I finished, Rosales said, "Do you have any idea why Flowers was at the river tonight?"

I shook my head. "No."

"Perhaps he and your aunt were visiting."

"Out here? No way. For one thing, Aunt Rowe's an early-to-bed person."

"Maybe they met earlier in the evening," Rosales said.

I hesitated. Was she trying to say Aunt Rowe had something to do with his death? I felt heat rise up to my cheeks and took a deep breath before continuing.

"Deputy Rosales, my aunt has a broken leg and is on crutches. She's barely able to leave the house, and she certainly can't traipse around the place or navigate on such uneven ground."

Rosales stared at me for a few seconds, then said, "One thing especially puzzles me. What brought you outside in the dead of night to find this body?"

As I launched into my explanation about my insomnia and love of baking, I noticed a group of people congregating near a stand of live oaks between my cottage and the next one. Aunt Rowe's guests had awakened after all. The EMS van's headlights illuminated the area enough for me to identify one onlooker who towered above the others. Tim Hartman, the man who'd witnessed the scene with Aunt Rowe and Bobby

Joe. I sure hoped Rosales wouldn't talk to him. I quickly looked away, not wanting to draw her attention to Hartman.

Rosales watched me closely through narrowed eyes, and my stomach clenched.

"So you headed off to bake pecan tarts," she said, "but then you went down to the river. Why?"

I didn't want to discuss the black cat leading me to the body. First of all, I realized that sounded crazy—though maybe no more crazy than walking through the woods to bake at two in the morning—and I didn't want to give anyone fodder for more stories about the cat bringing bad luck. I could already hear the superstitious townspeople accusing the cat of crossing Bobby Joe's path and causing his death.

I forced myself to smile at the deputy. "The river is soothing. Some people buy those little machines that play sounds to help them sleep. There's a phone app, too. But I have the real thing within walking distance."

She looked skeptical but flipped her notebook closed.

A relieved sigh escaped my lips. Fortunately for me, Rosales's attention was drawn to voices coming from the riverside.

"Excuse me," she said and headed that way.

While she was out of sight, another set of headlights came down the drive. When the vehicle veered across the grass to where the guests had congregated, I realized it was Aunt Rowe's golf cart. Next thing I knew, Aunt Rowe climbed off the cart with the aid of her crutches to approach the guests.

What a bad idea. I had told the deputy that Aunt Rowe would never come out here in her present condition. And where the heck was Glenda?

I started in my aunt's direction, but then noticed Rosales coming up from the river, followed by the EMTs who carted the backboard holding Bobby Joe's sheet-draped body. At the top of the steps, the men placed the backboard on the ground. One of them folded the sheet back. The other illuminated the body with his flashlight while Deputy Rosales stooped down and took a couple of close-up pictures with her phone. Then she turned away from them and made a call.

From what I could tell, Aunt Rowe and the others had stopped talking among themselves to watch the action. I looked at the ground, feeling sick to my stomach, and wished once again that Sheriff Crawford had responded to the emergency himself. There was something about his presence that comforted me, not that anything would seem comforting at the moment.

The deputy's voice carried in the slight breeze. She had ended her call and was talking with the medical personnel. I heard the words "head injury" as the three of them leaned over the body. After a minute, Rosales turned away from the EMTs and headed toward the group where Aunt Rowe stood. Tim Hartman separated himself from the others and walked in her direction.

Uh-oh. No doubt he would share with the deputy the argument he'd witnessed when he arrived. Aunt Rowe was going to need all the support she could get after Rosales grilled her about what she did to Bobby Joe.

No one was looking at me, so I ducked around the side of my cottage and pulled out my phone. I scrolled through some old e-mails until I found the one I'd saved from Sheriff Crawford that listed his cell number in case I had more questions for him while writing my book. I paused for a moment and checked the time. Nearly dawn. The sheriff would be up soon if he wasn't already, so I quickly punched in the number to call him.

"Hear you have some trouble over there, Sabrina," he said after we'd exchanged greetings. "You okay?"

"I'm fine." I kept my voice low. "But I'm getting a bad feeling about what's going on. Have you talked to Deputy Rosales lately?"

"Ten seconds ago," he said. "You must have ESP."

I didn't feel like joking. "Have you ever met Aunt Rowe's cousin Bobby Joe?"

"Not that I recall," he said. "Why do you ask?"

"It's a long story," I said. "I want to be sure that if there's anything suspicious about his death, your department will investigate thoroughly. Bobby Joe Flowers was not a likable person."

"I would say not," the sheriff said. "The man has two distinct head injuries. Now don't tell Deputy Pat I mentioned that little detail."

"Two injuries?" My mind raced. "He must have hit his head on a rock or maybe on one of the stone steps when he fell."

"We'll know more after the autopsy," the sheriff said, "but I get the feeling there's something you're not telling me."

I took a deep breath, then filled him in on what had happened upon Bobby Joe's arrival at Aunt Rowe's house.

"That's unfortunate," he said in a somber tone when I'd finished.

I paced alongside the cottage in an effort to tamp down my rising panic. "Bobby Joe laughed after it was all said and done, and he walked out of there on his own two feet."

"That may be true, but head injuries can affect people in various ways," the sheriff said. "We have to—"

"You have to figure out what happened," I blurted, "and it will *not* be that Aunt Rowe caused him to die."

"Calm down, Sabrina. I didn't say she caused his death."

"There's no telling how many enemies a man like Bobby Joe had or how many of them would be happy to be rid of him." I paused to collect my thoughts. "For example, I saw him having a heated argument with this cowboy in the hardware store parking lot yesterday."

"Aha," the sheriff said, "and you're suggesting the cowboy had a hand in what happened to Flowers?"

I didn't appreciate the mocking tone of his voice. "I don't *know* anything. I'm only mentioning this as an example, in case the autopsy shows there was foul play."

"Spoken like a true mystery writer," he said. "You know this cowboy's name?"

"I never met him," I explained, "but Hallie Krane told me his name is Luke Griffin."

The sheriff chuckled.

"Why are you laughing?"

The sky was beginning to brighten as dawn approached. Across the property, I could see Rosales writing in her notebook as Hartman talked.

"Do yourself a favor," Sheriff Crawford said. "No matter what, do *not* mention the name Luke Griffin to my deputy."

"But he should be a person of interest," I said. "If anyone hurt Bobby Joe Flowers, this Griffin character—"

"Listen to me. I repeat, do *not* mention Griffin to Deputy Rosales."

"But why not?" I said. "He might have been here tonight for all I know."

"'Cause Griffin is the game warden in these parts," Crawford said, "and Deputy Pat has a crush the size of Texas on the man."

5

B Y EIGHT THAT morning the scene was cleared and Deputy Rosales had left. Except for the chaos in my head, things were pretty much back to normal. I leaned against the island in Aunt Rowe's kitchen, sluggish from lack of sleep, and waited for the oven timer to go off. The stress of finding a body had sent me inside to bake those pecan tarts I'd had on my mind the night before.

Baking didn't have its usual calming effect on me today. I couldn't seem to get my heart rate back to a natural rhythm. I'd have to remember this freaked-out feeling the next time I wrote about a character finding a body.

I couldn't believe that Aunt Rowe was down the hall in her office checking on website reservations—business as usual. After the scene I'd witnessed, I knew there was no love lost between her and Bobby Joe, but didn't she feel distracted? Was she simply better at compartmentalizing issues than I was?

Glenda, in a knee-length denim skirt, white short-sleeved shirt, and flats, stood at the counter near the sink, adding fresh strawberries to a colorful fruit salad. She wore her straight, dark hair in a carefree pixie cut and had a pair of reading glasses perched on top of her head. Even though I had told her about the scene she missed while she was at the grocery store the day before, she didn't seem concerned.

"Just because the deputy left doesn't mean Aunt Rowe is off the hook," I said.

"Just because Mr. Hartman talked to the deputy doesn't mean she has a reason to come back," Glenda countered. "Do you know what he told her?"

"No, but I have an excellent guess, since the whole fight took place right before my eyes. It wasn't pretty."

Glenda turned to me and put a hand on one hip. "No need to be snarky."

I frowned at her. "I'm not snarky."

"I have teenagers. I know snarky when I hear it."

I sighed. "Point taken."

"The deputy's not going to haul Rowe in for hitting her cousin," Glenda said. "If she took in everyone involved in a family dispute, there wouldn't be enough room at the jail. Besides, it's not like Bobby Joe can file a complaint."

"You didn't see the look in Rosales's eyes when she noticed Aunt Rowe gallivanting outside right after I said she couldn't get around."

Glenda left her fruit salad and walked over to me. "You can stop blaming me for that right now. You told me to come and break the news to Rowe, not that I should tie her to the bed to keep her in the house. She wanted out, so she sent me to the kitchen for a cup of tea and skedaddled the second I turned my back."

"Doesn't raising teenagers prepare a person for that sort

of trickery?" I immediately regretted my snide tone. "Sorry, I'm just worried."

I grabbed my potholders and went to the oven to check on the tarts. I didn't even know what I was going to do with eight dozen of the things. As usual, once I got to baking I had a hard time stopping.

"I know this is eating at you, honey," Glenda said, "but you have to trust the sheriff's department will figure out what happened to the man. Does anyone know why he came back here last night?"

"No idea." I opened the oven, pulled out a cookie sheet, and breathed in the sweet, buttery scent. "He said he was staying with a friend. If that wasn't true, he may have come in search of a bed for the night."

"Where was his car?"

"Parked in a blind spot behind the Paris cottage." I touched the edges of a crust with my fingertip and decided the tarts were ready, then took the last tray out and turned off the oven. "Seems like he didn't want anyone to know he was here."

"I don't like the sound of that," Glenda said.

"Me neither." I got out the basket I routinely used to hold pastries and lined it with a red-and-white gingham napkin. "I also don't like that Aunt Rowe's acting like nothing happened."

"She's in denial." Glenda finished adding the strawberries, covered the bowl with plastic wrap, and put it in the refrigerator. "She'll be okay."

"I know she disliked the guy," I said, "but he was family. At some point, she's going to feel the effects."

Glenda patted my shoulder. "Don't worry. We'll help her get through whatever comes. Listen, I'm on my way to refill the coffee supplies in Zurich and Venice. It's time you get to writing if you want to make your daily word count."

Like I could focus on a day like this.

Glenda left without waiting for a response. When the back door closed behind her, I took a glass from the cupboard and filled it with milk. I promptly ate five tarts that were still a little too warm and washed them down with the cold drink. Maybe the sugar in the filling would give me a much-needed energy rush.

I put half of the remaining tarts in a container for Aunt Rowe and filled my basket with the others. Tyanne was always happy to offer treats to her bookstore customers. My friend had probably already learned of Bobby Joe's death through the town grapevine, and I wondered what she'd heard.

Aunt Rowe was on the phone spouting facts about local wineries, probably talking with a prospective guest, so I left a plate with some tarts on the corner of her desk and gave her a little wave before leaving the house.

I headed out with the basket over my arm and my mind on Bobby Joe. How did a guy so familiar with the place, who had run around this property as a kid, miss his step and fall into the river? Had he been drinking, careless, rushing to some unknown destination? Why had he come back in the first place? To antagonize Aunt Rowe some more? To see me? If so, he hadn't knocked on my door.

I walked down Aunt Rowe's driveway and cut across the grass, taking the shortcut to my cottage to change clothes before I left for the bookstore. The morning was on the dreary side with a lot of cloud cover, but the sun usually burned through by ten and the forecast called for temps in the high eighties.

As I skirted the property surrounding the Barcelona cottage, I noticed movement in a thick patch of flowering lantana bushes. A girl's blond head poked out between the shrubs. Tim Hartman's daughter. She crawled out of the bushes and stood to brush yellow blooms off her pink polka-dotted shirt and denim shorts. She wore silver sparkly sandals, and her toenails were painted baby blue. I guessed her age at about eight.

She looked at the basket over my arm. "Is that breakfast?"

Surprised, I said, "No, at least that wasn't the plan. I guess it could be breakfast if your dad says it's okay."

"He's sleeping," she said.

I didn't want to feed the girl anything without a parent's permission, so I changed the subject. "My name's Sabrina, what's yours?"

"Molly." The girl regarded me thoughtfully for a few seconds, then said, "Do you work for the lady who hit that man?"

The question surprised me. "No, well, sort of. She's my aunt Rowe, and she doesn't usually hit people." The girl probably didn't know about Bobby Joe's death, and it wasn't my place to tell her.

"What got you up and out so early, Molly?" I said. "Don't you like to sleep late?"

"I'm too excited," she said. "We're gonna float on the river today. Dad said, 'Don't you dare wake me earlier than nine.' Is it nine yet?"

I checked my watch. "Not quite. What were you doing in the bushes?"

"Looking for the cat."

"You brought your cat on vacation with you?"

Molly giggled. "No, our cat's at home with my mom. I'm talking about the cat that lives here. He let me pet him."

"Really?"

"He likes me to rub under his chin."

I couldn't imagine the skittish cat I'd seen sitting still for that. "What color was this cat?"

"All black," she said. "He's a real cutie."

I grinned. There could be several black cats in the vicinity, but since I'd never seen one around here until the day before, what were the odds?

"I guess you don't think black cats bring bad luck," I said.

"No way." Molly shook her head. "That's silly. He's a good cat. He likes me so much."

"I'm sure he does," I said.

"All cats like me," she went on. "Mom calls me the cat whisperer. Do you like cats?"

"I sure do," I said in a whoever-doesn't-love-cats-is-crazy tone.

"Does your mom call *you* the cat whisperer?"

I hesitated, trying to remember how long it had been since Mom called me at all. It seemed her travels with her new husband took precedence over everything and everyone else.

Quit feeling sorry for yourself and answer the girl.

"Cat whisperers are only girls with a special talent like yours."

That brought a smile from Molly and made me feel better.

"I'm glad you and your family are staying here. I thought your dad might be upset when he saw my aunt arguing with that man. I'm glad you didn't leave."

"We can't leave," Molly said with an eye roll. "My dad has this new girlfriend—Sophia—and she's coming here after she's finished working today."

"That should be fun," I said.

"Maybe. At least Dad will think so." The girl had a very matter-of-fact personality, which I liked.

"Where did you see the black cat last night?" I said.

"He was on the porch of that cabin with the Paris sign. At first he ran away from me and sat under the red Jeep."

Bobby Joe's vehicle.

"Did you see a man in the Jeep?" I said.

Molly shook her head. "My flashlight wasn't very bright. I could hardly see the cat except for his shiny green eyes."

"It was already dark?"

Molly nodded. "Pitch black."

I didn't like the thought of this girl wandering around outside after dark. "Where were your brother and your father?"

"Nate's always playing video games. I don't know what Dad was doing. But don't tell him I was outside," she said hurriedly.

"I won't, but, Molly, you really need to be careful about going outside by yourself at night."

She looked down and kicked a sandal at the grass. "I know."

I didn't want to harp on danger too much, but I did want to know where Bobby Joe had been while Molly was outside chasing the cat around. "Are you sure you didn't see any other people outside?"

"I did, but not a man."

"Then who?" I said.

"That lady—your aunt. She was riding around on her little cart. I thought maybe she was looking for the cat, too."

"That couldn't have been my aunt you saw," I said. "She went to bed early last night."

"It was definitely her," Molly said. "I could tell because of the cast on her leg."

6

I QUIZZED MOLLY ABOUT what Aunt Rowe had been doing when she saw her the night before, but the girl didn't have an answer. She was focused on the cat, then and now, and as soon as I told her it was nearly nine o'clock, she was off like a shot to go wake her dad and brother.

Aunt Rowe might have been responding to a tenant's call, I told myself. Maybe she woke up and remembered she'd left the thermostat turned too low in one of the cottages. Maybe she heard a strange noise and went to investigate. Maybe I should charge back into the house and ask her point-blank what the heck she was doing outside on the night her cousin, or should I say alleged brother, ended up dead in the river.

Nah, that wouldn't go over too well.

I speculated this way when I was trying to figure out where a plot was headed, and I was the type of person who could "maybe" and "what if" myself to death. There could be a dozen legitimate reasons for Aunt Rowe to be out on the grounds at night. She was a grown woman, and she had done a fine job of handling her own business before I got here. She didn't need me asking a bunch of crazy questions. I had to trust that there was nothing nefarious about her nighttime trek in the golf cart. Now if only I could block the image of her belting Bobby Joe Flowers with her crutch, I'd be fine. For this morning, I'd stick with my original plan to visit the bookstore.

NEAR eleven, I walked into Knead to Read and found Ethan Brady, Tyanne's sixteen-year-old employee, standing on top of the sales counter. The boy wore a purple crushed-velvet cape with metallic gold trim over his jeans and T-shirt. He was thumbtacking lengths of purple ribbon fastened to gold stars and cover copies of the latest Wetherby Wizard fantasy novel to the ceiling tiles.

The cats usually loved to sit on the front windowsill and watch sidewalk traffic. They were on the sill now, but facing into the store, their attention riveted on Ethan's ribbons. A stuffed brown dog, representing Wetherby Wizard's sidekick Wendell, sat next to the cash register, wearing a small pointed hat decorated with gold stars and a cape similar to Ethan's.

"Morning," I said. "Hope you go all out for *me* if my book is published."

Ethan stooped to pick up another ribbon, and his overly long blond bangs fell into his face. He stood and stretched to tack the ribbon to the ceiling. "Write a fantasy, and I'm all over it."

"Never mind." Fantasy wasn't my thing. "Is Tyanne in?"

Before he responded I heard the murmur of voices coming from the stacks.

"She's with a customer in mysteries." Ethan homed in on the basket I had over my arm. "Again with the baking?"

He was the only teenage boy I'd ever known who didn't like sweets. If I had a basket full of hamburgers, he'd inhale them in one sitting. "Don't give me grief today," I said. "I'll get back to writing. Promise."

"Swear?"

"I swear."

"Hey, I was thinking, you could give that kid in your book some special powers. Like, she can do stuff her mom doesn't realize. Make things appear, disappear, you know?"

I laughed. "Yeah, and I can change her name from Melody to Tabitha."

He shrugged. "Tabitha's cool."

I smiled. Obviously, the kid had never seen *Bewitched*. I left my basket on the counter near the stuffed dog, gave Zelda and Willis each a little scratch behind the ears, then headed toward the mystery shelves. I heard Tyanne naming some of her favorite cozy authors. I didn't want to barge in on her conversation, so I stopped out of sight and grabbed a couple of new thrillers to check out the cover copy. Reading bits from other books sometimes jogs my brain and helps me solve plot problems.

"She'd pick the flower shop book," a man on the other side of the shelf said, "and maybe the one with the librarian."

"Those are good choices," Ty said. "I'll get you the first in each series."

"So long as the stories are light," the man responded. "Something relaxing. Take her mind off things."

"They're fun books," Ty said. "I think your mother will enjoy them."

Sweet. A man shopping for his mama. Sexy voice, too.

I edged forward to get a glimpse of the nice son. Before I got that far, he rounded the corner and slammed his muscled body straight into me. I lost my grip on the books I was hold-

ing and they fell. One of the hardcovers hit my toes, bare in
flip-flops.

Ye-oww.

My face burned as I stooped to pick up the books, but the
man went down to do the same and we ended up face-to-face
and both reaching for them. Which is when I realized I was
staring into Luke Griffin's chocolate brown eyes. He smelled
of citrusy cologne and peppermint.

"Sorry about that." He scooped up the hardbacks in one
hand.

"My fault, I, I mean, I'm Sabrina."

We stood in unison, and he handed the books to me. He
was in uniform today, and his khaki shirt stretched across
a broad chest. "Luke Griffin." He tipped his head in greeting
but didn't linger, taking off toward the checkout. I watched
his retreat and decided he looked as good in the uniform as
he had in those jeans the day before.

Tyanne stopped at my side and whispered, "Enjoying the
view, huh? Don't go anywhere. There's something I have to
tell you."

I nodded and replaced the thrillers on the shelf, then wandered casually toward the front of the store. Ethan had finished his decorating project and was carrying an armload of
new books to a table near the door. Griffin had already paid
for his purchases. He tipped his head to Ty, then walked by
the windowsill and patted each of the cats on the head before
leaving.

Two middle-aged women in Sunday-go-to-meeting outfits
passed him, coming in as he left. Most women would glance
at a man as good-looking as Luke Griffin, especially one in
uniform, but not these two. I looked out to the parking lot and
watched Griffin climb into his pickup. His yellow Lab occupied the passenger seat again. I liked a guy who appreciated

animals, unlike my ex, who acted like he was in mortal danger every time an animal came into view.

Belatedly, I remembered the argument between Griffin
and Bobby Joe Flowers, and my implying to the sheriff that
Griffin might have played a part in Bobby Joe's demise. Still
a possibility, but I hoped that wasn't the case.

I turned my attention back to Tyanne, but the customers
had gotten to her first. I pegged them as out-of-towners, but
then again I didn't yet know everyone who lived in Lavender.
The woman in front, stocky and in a floral print dress, said,
"Good day. We're interested in discussing new releases in
inspirational fiction."

Tyanne welcomed them to Knead to Read and after a short
conversation offered to print out a list of the newest titles. The
woman said she'd like that, and she followed Tyanne to her
office at the rear of the store. The other woman, this one
pencil-thin with a pinched face and dressed in drab gray,
stayed behind and watched Ethan.

"Young man," she said, looking down her nose at the fantasy novel display Ethan had set up, "such books are the work
of Satan, and it would behoove you to abstain from every
appearance of evil."

"Yes, ma'am," Ethan responded politely. "I'll be real
careful."

The thin woman, who reminded me of *The Wizard of Oz*'s
Miss Gulch, had her back to the front window where Willis
stood and stretched. The tabby cat silently jumped to the floor,
then took a flying leap, barely clearing the dour woman's
shoulder, to land on the sales counter with a thump.

The woman jumped back, and her hand flew to her throat.
"Keep that thing away from me."

Ethan hid a smile with his hand, but her statement annoyed

me. "His name is Willis," I said, "and if you don't like cats just say so, and I can move him to another room."

"Cats are pawns of the devil," she said.

Definitely from out of town. Otherwise, I would have already heard about this wacko woman.

"That's a preposterous statement," I said. "Cats are lovable pets."

This customer wasn't backing down. "They are evil."

Ethan retreated in the direction of Tyanne's office. I went to the counter and picked Willis up. Cuddling him against my chest, I stood before the misguided woman. "He's a sweet kitty, and if you knew him, you definitely wouldn't associate him with the devil."

Zelda, not interested in the conflict, got down from the sill and without the woman noticing her slinked off behind a shelf.

The woman sniffed. "In my opinion, this cat is no better than that black cat we saw on our way in here. I wanted to leave town right then and avoid the bad luck, misery, disease, even death that might befall us."

"What a crock!" The words slipped out before I could stop them.

"Noreen," the thin woman yelled. "We need to leave. Now."

Tyanne hurried toward us, clutching a sheaf of papers. "Ma'am? I'm sorry if my cats are upsetting you. Ethan will take them to the back. Noreen and I are in the midst of placing an order for the church's study group." She gave me the eye, and I felt only slightly guilty for aggravating the prospective customer.

"We'll talk later," I told Ty as I handed the cat to her.

"Yes, we will." With a stern expression, she turned her back on me.

Walking out into the humid morning, I shook my head at the weird opinions of some people. I wasn't worried about Tyanne. She wouldn't hold it against me that the woman had gotten under my skin, but now I'd have to wait before I could find out what she had to tell me. Dang it all.

I scanned the street, hoping to catch a glimpse of the black cat whom I felt needed protection from people like the woman inside the bookstore. He wasn't in sight, so there was nothing I could do for him now. He was probably pretty good at taking care of himself; at least I hoped so.

Exhaustion from my early morning was beginning to overtake me. A protein-filled lunch might perk me up, so I headed for McKetta's Barbeque. It seemed that every town in Texas had a handful of establishments where you could buy barbeque, if not from a random barbeque pit hooked up to a pickup and parked alongside the road. I'd decided that the small mom-and-pop places had the best sauce, which was about as important when eating barbeque as the meat itself. Daisy and Mitch McKetta ran the café where I was headed, and I voted theirs the best barbeque in and around Lavender.

The building housing my favorite lunch spot sat in a strip between Hill Country Gifts and Sweet Stop, the local candy store. With weathered planks and a rusty tin roof, McKetta's appeared at least a hundred years old. The front porch posts were a tad crooked, and the air surrounding the building was heavy with the scent of smoked meat.

Inside, a half dozen people waited in line to place their orders, and I was glad I'd arrived before the lunch rush. I went to the end of the line, and the woman ahead of me turned to smile at me briefly.

After my eyes had adjusted better to the indoor lighting, I realized the woman wore a Krane's Hardware apron. She was about five seven and a bit overweight, with blond-highlighted hair—the woman who'd teased Mr. Krane about Dumpster diving the day before.

"Popular place, huh?" I said.

"Best barbeque in town," she said, mirroring my opinion. "We're having a customer appreciation day today at Krane's, noon to two. If you don't mind waiting a bit longer for your lunch, you could come by the store."

"Now that I've smelled this food I don't want to wait," I said, "but thanks for the invite. I saw you at the store yesterday. Don't believe we've met."

"Judith Krane." The woman offered a hand and we shook. "Wesley's wife."

"Oh." I smiled and introduced myself. "And Hallie's your daughter?"

"She is."

A bell sounded, and we looked toward the counter. "Mrs. Krane," Mitch McKetta said. "Your order's up."

A box lid filled with quart containers sat on the counter in front of him next to a stack of crowd-sized trays covered in heavy foil. I offered to give her a hand, and she accepted my help carrying the food out to her pickup.

"I owe you one," she said before driving away, and I wondered if she would consider making a free delivery next time Thomas asked me to pick up something from the hardware store.

Back inside, Daisy waved me over to a dining table. She sported a new super-short haircut, and she had opted to dye her hair a soft reddish color this time instead of her usual ash brown. Daisy was a small woman, and the new hairstyle suited her.

"Appreciate your helping Mrs. Krane," she said. "I took the liberty of serving your usual. Hope that's okay."

The plate on the table held a sliced-beef barbeque sandwich on a homemade bun with a container of sauce on the side for dipping and a small dish of mustard potato salad.

I grinned. "Perfect."

"Heard about the man in the river," she said. "Bad business. Mind if I join you for a minute?"

"Pull up a chair." We often visited over a meal.

"Give me a sec to grab us some Cokes."

"Takin' five, Mitch," she hollered to her husband, who wouldn't complain if she took five hours off from working in the kitchen. Mitch, the polar opposite of his wife size-wise, was always saying she worked too hard. They were good together, and I envied their cheerful, easygoing relationship.

I dipped the edge of my sandwich in the sauce and took a big bite, savoring the tangy flavor. Daisy returned with two extra-large drinks.

"Is Rowe doing all right?" She slid into a chair across from me. "I understand the man who died was her cousin."

At least the grapevine didn't know about Bobby Joe's claim of being Aunt Rowe's brother. Yet. "She's okay, I guess. She's not saying much."

"Probably better that way. Last thing she needs is for the press to blow this whole thing out of proportion."

The press? Here in Lavender? The town newspaper was printed once a month and consisted mostly of advertisements.

"I wasn't even thinking about news coverage," I said. "If this makes the paper, it'd be one of those teensy articles." I indicated a little square with my fingers.

"The paper? Girl, we're in the Internet age. They connect stories from decades ago to current events all the time. I'll bet this is one of those times."

"Decades ago?" I said around a mouthful of creamy potato salad.

Daisy nodded. "It'll be one of those history-repeats-itself pieces. Except the first time it was a girl; now it's a man."

I put my fork down. "What in the world are you talking about?"

Daisy sat back in her chair. "Well, I thought surely Rowe would have mentioned this to you now even if you never heard about it way back when 'cause you were a kid. I was in middle school at the time."

I held out my hands, palms up. "Mentioned what?"

"That girl who was murdered 'bout thirty years ago. Vicki Palmer."

"I never heard of Vicki Palmer. Who was she?"

"A teenager living here in Lavender. They found her body in the Glidden River right about the spot where you found Bobby Joe Flowers. Dollars to donuts this is right up the alley of whoever writes those news stories I see on Yahoo.com."

7

"**W**HO SAYS BOBBY Joe Flowers was murdered?" I asked Daisy even though I'd been pretty much assuming that someone actually *had* murdered the man.

"Clete Lester's brother was one of the EMS techs at the scene," she said. "Told Clete somebody took a chunk out of Flowers's head, wound was shaped like the edge of a shovel." She cupped her right hand slightly and ran the index finger of her left along the curved pinkie-finger side. "Like this."

I winced and pushed my plate away from me. There went my last hope that Bobby Joe accidentally clunked his head on a rock and died.

"You know how head injuries bleed," Daisy said. "He probably didn't last long after he got hit."

I tried to block the image she was painting, but I could feel the color drain from my face. My skin felt clammy.

"Doggone," Daisy said. "Here I am running my mouth

about a murder while you're trying to eat." She touched my hand. "You okay?"

"Sure. Fine." I didn't want Daisy to realize how bothered I was by what she'd told me. I imagined a shadowy figure creeping outside my cottage and carrying a shovel. Premeditated murder for sure. I mean, no one carries a shovel around in the middle of the night. I took heart in the fact that my imaginary figure was walking normally and not hobbling on crutches. Aunt Rowe was absolutely *not* involved. Even so, I didn't want to discuss Bobby Joe with Daisy and have my comments come up in her conversations with customers.

I picked up my cup and took a long swallow. "So who killed Vicki Palmer?"

Daisy shrugged. "From what I recall, they never solved the case."

"Really? I'd expect the sheriff, whoever it was at the time, would have worked day and night on that one, local girl and all. Did they have any suspects?"

"I'm not sure. Deputies came out to the school. Talked to Vicki's friends. That's all I remember. I was thirteen or so at the time." She glanced toward the kitchen and said, "Better get back to work."

"Let me ask you one more thing real quick. Have you ever heard some crazy legend about a black cat in town that brings bad luck?"

"One cat?" Daisy laughed. "There's more like two dozen cats hanging around our back door every night lookin' for handouts."

"Two dozen, seriously?" I said.

She nodded. "Come back after dark if you don't believe me. There must be a kitty billboard somewhere, says 'C'mon over to McKetta's for leftover meat.' Why are you askin' about a black cat?"

"A couple people have mentioned this town legend to me lately." I pushed my chair back.

"I don't have time to fool with that kind of nonsense," Daisy said.

But plenty of time to gossip about murders.

I didn't say what I was thinking, though, and told Daisy good-bye after turning down a to-go box for the rest of my sandwich. The thought of food no longer appealed, and I wasn't going straight home where I could refrigerate the leftovers.

As I made my way back to the bookstore, I hoped Daisy was wrong about Bobby Joe's death making the Internet news. Aunt Rowe's rental cottage business would probably suffer if it did—either that or business would pick up because of the types who like to visit tragic scenes.

With all traces of cloud cover gone, the early afternoon sun beat down on me. I was looking forward to stepping into the bookstore's cool interior when I spotted Tyanne across the oleander hedge from her place. She disappeared into the Taste of Texas Wines shop.

I was glad to see she wasn't still tied up with the church ladies and decided to follow her. Perhaps the shop would be a better place for us to chat for a minute, with no bookstore customers waiting in the wings.

The bell over the door sounded like crystal wind chimes. I stepped inside to a cool and serene atmosphere with classical piano music playing at low volume. Shelves lined with wine bottles took up the left side of the space. A corner cabinet held a selection of gifts—fancy napkins, corkscrews, liqueur-centered chocolates, wine-bottle stoppers. Tyanne stood by a bar, nearly shoulder high to her, made of burled walnut. No one else was in sight.

"Hey," I said.

She turned and smiled. "Great, you're back. Boy, do I have big news for you."

A crashing that sounded like breaking glassware came from the back, followed by a woman's voice. "Oh, dear, now look what you made me do."

"Go ahead, blame me," a man responded. "I'm used to it."

Tyanne looked at me and whispered, "I haven't seen a man in here before, and that doesn't sound like Claire."

I shrugged and said, "What's your big news?"

Tyanne held up an index finger, her head cocked as she listened to the people in the other room.

The woman said, "Leo, please, I know you're upset, but why don't you go on back? I can handle the store by myself."

"For how long?" The man spoke in a loud voice like a person who's hard of hearing and doesn't realize he's shouting. "Did she ever give that a thought? Did she ever for once in her life think about anyone other than herself?"

Tyanne and I exchanged a glance. She knocked on the bar and said, "Hello?"

"You have a customer," the man said.

"Be right there," the woman called. Then, "If you would get out of my way, Leo, I could tend to business. And clean up that glass."

An elderly woman with wavy white hair emerged through swinging saloon-style louvered doors. She carried a wooden tray that held empty wineglasses, and her wide smile gave away nothing of the bickering we'd overheard.

"Good day, ladies." She placed her tray on the bar. "What can I help you with on this lovely afternoon? Would you care to sample our new cabernet?"

She was an attractive woman, closer to eighty than seventy

I'd say, and her face was expertly made up. She wore an elegant burgundy sheath dress with layered beaded necklaces that drew my attention.

"Not today, but thanks." Tyanne introduced us and mentioned that she owned the bookstore next door. "Is Claire in?"

The woman's smile dimmed a watt. "Not at the moment. I can leave her a message if you like."

Tyanne shook her head. "That's okay. I believe I know which wines she would recommend. I'm having a gathering this weekend, and I need to place an order."

"I can help you with that." The woman walked over to the sales counter and pulled out a pad and pen.

The louvered doors swung open a second time, and a portly man approached us. He wore olive slacks that had seen better days and a green plaid shirt. His bald head contrasted with bushy gray eyebrows that drew together as he looked from me to Tyanne. "Which one of you is from next door?"

Tyanne raised her hand. "I am."

Before the man could say more, the woman turned to him and put a hand on one hip. "Leo, please, I'm in the middle of taking an order."

He ignored her and addressed Tyanne. "Claire is our daughter," he said, "and I'm sure my wife is about to kick me in the shins to shut me up, but I'm not gonna listen to her with our girl missing."

The woman looked up at the ceiling. "Heaven help me. I told you, Leo, she's not missing."

She turned to us and smiled. "I'm Felice Dubois, Claire's mother, and don't be alarmed. She's not missing."

"Then where is she?" Leo yelled, throwing his arms out. "She's not here, is she?"

Felice rolled her eyes. "Claire is an adult, and she asked me to take care of the store today. We don't need to know every little detail. I'm sure she'll be back to work soon. In the meantime . . ." She picked up the pen and smiled at Tyanne.

Leo looked like he wanted to shove his wife out of the way. He stared at us. "Are you two friends of our daughter or not?"

"I don't know Claire very well," Tyanne said.

He focused on me. "How about you?"

I felt uncomfortable under his scrutiny. "Um, I'm pretty new around here." I thought of Aunt Rowe's mention that Claire had come by to see her the day before, but I didn't intend to bring that up. "Claire and I have waved to each other a few times, that's about it."

"Is there cause for concern?" Tyanne said.

Felice shook her head.

Leo said, "A father's always concerned, especially when his daughter hangs out with a no-good—"

Felice cut off his words by grasping his forearm tightly. "Stop now, and let me proceed with this young lady's order."

If looks could kill, Leo might be on the floor and burnt to a crisp. Instead of continuing the discussion, he stomped out of the room.

"I apologize for my husband's behavior," Felice said. "Would either of you care to taste-test some wine while you're here?" She reached under the counter and came out with a bottle that had already been opened, a silver filigreed topper stuck where the cork would have been. "I could use some myself."

We declined, but that didn't stop Felice from pouring herself a glass and drinking half of it before she took down Tyanne's order.

After paying for her purchase, Tyanne said she'd pick up the wine on Sunday afternoon. We left before the bickering could start up again.

Outside the door we stopped, and I looked at my friend. "Now there's a happy couple."

"Giving them the benefit of the doubt," Tyanne said, "maybe they're not always this way. Sounds like Claire has done something unusual that's rocked their world."

"Claire's like fifty years old, isn't she?" I said. "Maybe she wanted to have time off from the parents. Are they the Dubois Vineyards owners?"

"I think so, though I imagine they've retired from running the operation themselves." Tyanne shrugged. "Claire's dad is really worried about her."

"I'll bet Mom knows something about why Claire's not at work and doesn't want to tell Dad."

"That was my take," Tyanne said. "And now I'd better get back to work myself. I only meant to leave for five minutes."

"What about the big news?" I asked again.

"Oh, right." Tyanne's eyes sparkled. "You won't believe this."

"Does it have anything to do with Bobby Joe Flowers's death?" I said.

"No, but I'm so sorry I forgot to mention that before now. Is everyone holding up okay?"

"Pretty well under the circumstances." Earlier, I had wanted to know what she'd heard, but I could catch up on that later. For now I was more interested in her news.

Tyanne grinned. "Brace yourself."

"Enough with the suspense," I said. "Out with it."

"Kree Vanderpool is in town this weekend." She paused and watched me expectantly.

"Kree Vanderpool, as in the literary agent Kree Vanderpool?"

"The very same."

"Doesn't she live in New York City?"

"Yes, but her sister in Austin had a baby. Kree came to visit the family."

Tyanne had met Kree at a conference a few years ago and sang her praises after listening to Kree's keynote speech. I was in awe of several mystery authors represented by the woman, and Tyanne had told me more than once that Kree would be the perfect agent for my work. If I ever got my work ready to send to an agent, that is.

"Austin is hours away," I said. "So what's the big deal?"

"She told me way back she'd look me up whenever she was in the area, but I didn't think it would ever happen." Tyanne waved a hand dismissively. "But then Kree called late yesterday and said she'd love to come over and see my store."

"Well you *can* be a pleasant person when you try," I teased. "So she liked you. It's awesome that she called."

"What's super awesome," Tyanne said, "is that she's interested in talking with *you* about *your* book."

My lower jaw dropped. "She what?"

"I told her about your book," she said, "then on the spur of the moment I decided to have a small dinner party Sunday afternoon after the store closes at five so the two of you can meet. Kree goes back to New York on Monday. Hope you're free on Sunday. You are, aren't you?"

Kree Vanderpool wanted to talk to me? Never in my wildest dreams did I imagine a personal audience with an agent the caliber of Kree Vanderpool. This was a writer's dream come true, so why did it seem like my heart had quit beating?

"Well?" Tyanne said. "What do you say?"

"I don't have plans for Sunday, but, but—"

"But what?"

"I can't pitch my book. I'm nowhere near ready."

"Then get ready, Sabrina, 'cause she invited you to bring your proposal along to dinner."

I gulped. "I could get the first three chapters fixed up," I said, "maybe. But I don't even have a synopsis written."

"Then write one," she said. "That shouldn't be a problem. You have two days."

Tyanne was super familiar with the book world, but even she didn't realize that to many authors, completing a coherent synopsis was the equivalent of a rodeo cowboy staying atop a bucking bull for thirty minutes.

8

DROVE FASTER THAN usual on the way home. As butterflies
swarmed my stomach, I couldn't decide if I was more excited or scared about the prospect of meeting with Kree
Vanderpool. This opportunity was more than I could ever
have hoped for, but a black cloud marred my elation. A synopsis by Sunday.

Holy moly.

Writing a synopsis might not be a huge hurdle for every
writer. For me, who changed my mind about the plot every
two paragraphs, it was a problem. If I wanted to succeed as
an author, I had to focus and make concrete decisions for once
in my life.

I yawned so hard that my eyes watered, reminding me how
little sleep I'd had the night before. Of all the times for my
big chance to arrive. I was the world's worst at blocking dis-
tractions. I had to set aside the questions running through my
brain—everything from who killed Bobby Joe and what had

happened to Vicki Palmer so many years ago to why Claire Dubois wasn't at work today—and concentrate on my novel. Could I do that? Good Lord, I hoped so.

I took a deep, calming breath as I turned onto Traveler's Lane, determined to head straight to my cottage and immerse myself in writing. For two days, I would put everything else out of my head. A mere two days.

Approaching the Venice cottage, I noticed a gray Tundra pickup in the parking slot. Venice had been marked as vacant when I scanned the schedule earlier, but we had walk-ins from time to time.

A blond man sat on the Adirondack chair out front, his long, denim-clad legs propped on the porch railing. I slowed the car to a crawl, succumbing to the distraction. I couldn't get as good a look at the man as I would have liked, but then he probably had a cute little wife or girlfriend inside.

Irrelevant information, Sabrina. You need to write.

I watched the man, surreptitiously I hoped, as I drove by. He tipped a bottle to his lips, then looked straight at me and toasted me with it. I gave him a little wave and nudged the gas, embarrassed that he'd caught me watching.

I rounded the next bend, surprised to see Thomas standing alongside the road. His Wrangler was parked at an angle near the pump house that kept water flowing through a decorative man-made waterfall. He motioned for me to stop, so I pulled in behind his vehicle and put the car in park. I lowered my side window as he approached.

"What's up?" I said. "You need help?"

He leaned down to look at me, his face shaded by his straw hat. "You seen a black cat around here?"

My heart skipped a beat as I remembered his attitude about the legendary black cat. "Uh, no. Why do you ask?"

"Heard the girl in Barcelona talking to Rowena about a

cat," he said. "If El Gato Diablo is here at the cottages, I need
to do something."

"Something like what?" My pulse kicked up. "It's a harmless cat who happens to be black."

"So you *have* seen it?"

"There's no cat around here." I shook my head, then felt
like a traitor for not taking a more aggressive stance. "And
so what if there *is* a cat, Thomas? This is a lovely place for a
cat to live. In fact, we could stand to adopt several cats. I'm
sure the guests would—"

"*Not* El Gato Diablo," he said. "People come here to relax
and unwind. We need to keep them safe."

Good grief.

I wanted to voice my frustration, but decided I'd be wasting my breath with him. Better to discuss the topic with Aunt
Rowe. She liked animals, and I was pretty sure the only reason she didn't have pets of her own was because she used to
travel a lot. She could convince Thomas to back off.

"What exactly do you plan to do?" I said.

"I'm gettin' me a big net," he said.

The thought of Thomas trying to catch a cat in a net made
me stifle a grin.

"And a couple traps," he added.

"You can't do that," I shrieked.

He motioned with his hand for me to keep it down. "I'm
not planning to hurt the cat, if that's what you're worried
about. I just want that thing far away from Lavender."

I didn't want to think about any kind of trap. I could only
hope the cat I'd met would lay low and never show himself
in Thomas's presence.

"Why not find the poor thing a good home instead?" I said.

"No one would want that critter."

I already felt a kinship with the black cat who seemed to

have the odds stacked against him. Thomas would never un-derstand how I felt, so I changed the subject.

"I see someone's in the Venice cottage."

"Yeah, fella checked in alone and spent hours doing nothin' but sitting on the porch." He shrugged. "Something strange about the dude."

"The fact that he's sitting there doing nothing doesn't mean he's strange," I said.

Thomas didn't argue the fact. He took a step back. "I'll keep looking for the gosh-darned cat. Let you know if I get him."

I cringed at the thought. "If you do, please tell me before you make any rash decisions."

He stared at me for a few seconds, maybe reminding him-self that I was the boss's niece, which would be silly given that Aunt Rowe helped raise him and he was practically as close to her as I was. Finally, he answered, "If you say so."

I drove the rest of the way to my cottage, praying that the black cat had found a nice and unobtrusive place to hang out in town—a place where superstitious people like Thomas would never be able to get their hands on him.

Inside my cottage, I did my best to put the issue out of my mind. My first instinct was to rush to Aunt Rowe and discuss the cat with her, but she'd be smack in the middle of her physical therapy session now. Besides, I'd promised myself that I would focus on work. I changed into my most comfy and probably least flattering knit shorts and T-shirt, then pulled my hair back and used the neon green band to secure it into a tight ponytail.

I started a pot of coffee, then opened the window overlook-ing the back porch a few inches to enjoy the river air before the stifling heat of summer set in. I booted up my laptop and pulled out my collection of flash drives. Everything from my first attempt at writing a short story to prior drafts of the current work in progress lurked somewhere on these gadgets. I flexed my fingers and stuck in the flash drive that I hoped held my early attempts at writing a synopsis for this book. The first file I opened was only two paragraphs long—a failed attempt.

For the next several minutes, I opened and rejected drafts that weren't worth using as a starting point. It didn't help that worry for the cat was foremost on my mind. Maybe I could wage some sort of campaign to support the love of black cats. According to Daisy, Lavender had a population of strays. Odds were plenty of those homeless cats were black, not only the one that I'd seen. Could I convince people to jump on my bandwagon? Maybe. I needed to write a mission statement and enlist volunteers who thought superstitions were ridiculous.

Save that thought. Write the synopsis.

I stared at the laptop screen and sighed. Went to the kitchen and poured myself a cup of coffee. Returned to the computer and plopped into my chair. I decided to wing it with the synopsis and started typing from scratch.

Hours later, I had three pages of an extremely sketchy first draft, nowhere near the length I'd need to tell the whole story. What I'd written seemed hopelessly out of order, similar to the thoughts running through my head. I also had a seriously numb butt from sitting far too long.

I stood, stretched, and checked the clock. I could take a short break, go talk with Aunt Rowe about the cat, among other things, and pray that some epiphany would come over me before I got back to writing.

Sounded like a great idea, but I knew leaving the cottage now would destroy my focus for the day. Better to grab a quick snack and plug away for a couple more hours. I scarfed down a banana and a scoop of peanut butter straight from the jar and was back at the computer a few minutes later.

I leaned back in my chair to review what I'd written and picked up my cup for a sip of coffee. That's when I noticed the black cat stretched out on the sill by the open window.

I set my cup down carefully so I wouldn't startle him and spoke in a low voice. "Hi there, you handsome boy."

The cat's ears wiggled. I doubted that he'd look so calm if Thomas was nearby—he'd sense it if a man was skulking around in search of him, wouldn't he?

"You doing okay out there? You'll take off if you see any bad guys, right?" I'd feel better if he'd come inside where I wouldn't have to worry about Thomas spotting him, but that wasn't likely to happen.

He bent his head and calmly began washing a paw. I smiled, pushed aside my worries for his safety, and continued working.

My snack had perked me up, and I was able to edit what I'd written, giving it a more logical flow. My fingers flew over the keyboard as I added details to tie my plot points together. Every few minutes, I checked the windowsill and saw my friend was still with me, overseeing my work. I came up with a more interesting twist for the ending, and when I'd written the final sentence of the draft I sat back with a sigh. Granted, this was rough, but at least I now had something to work with.

I looked at the cat, who watched me through slitted eyes, and felt an overwhelming urge to cuddle him. He probably wouldn't sit still for that, though. It occurred to me that my writing had improved after the cat showed up. Was it possible that this black cat—the one Thomas was so paranoid about— had brought me *good* luck? Or inspiration, to say the least.

"Make sure you stay out of sight whenever Thomas is

around," I told the cat. "I for one am glad you're here. You added some much-needed suspense to my writing."

The cat stood and stretched.

"Suspense," I mused. "And I know the perfect name for you. How'd you like the name Hitchcock?"

He blinked slowly and answered, "Mrreow."

I smiled. "Molly was right. You're a cutie."

He turned swiftly and jumped off the sill. I ran to the window, feeling panicky with him out of sight. A knock at the door startled me, and I realized that Hitchcock had heard someone approach.

My heart thudded as I walked over to the door. I called out. "Who is it?"

"Sheriff Crawford. I need to talk to you about the murder."

9

SHERIFF CRAWFORD. THE murder. So much for blocking out thoughts of everything except writing.

I opened the door. "Evening, Sheriff."

He stood on my porch, Stetson in hand, and I was reminded of the reason the sheriff was considered the most eligible bachelor among the senior women in Lawton County. Jebediah Crawford had a Tom Selleck build, tall and muscular for his age. He had the mustache, too, though Crawford's hair was solid gray. He'd lost his wife a few years ago, and I suspected that if his admirers knew he was out gathering facts for an investigation, they'd be lining up and claiming knowledge of Bobby Joe Flowers's killer.

"Come on in." I opened the door wider and stepped back, self-conscious about my worn hanging-around-the-house clothes and bare feet. "I'm surprised to see you here."

"Not sure why that is, Sabrina. Thought you'd be bustin' down my door today, hounding me for clues, tryin' your darndest to solve the mystery." He stepped inside, and his girth dwarfed the space.

"I've been hoping the whole thing would turn out to be a bad accident," I said. "That or a nightmare. No mystery to solve. Have a seat."

Crawford rounded my sofa. His knees creaked as he lowered himself onto the cushions. "Now, Sabrina, you knew right off the bat this was a suspicious death when you called me at two a.m. Don't backpedal on me."

"Can't pull one over on you." I smiled. "Can I get you something to drink? Coffee, Coke, water?"

He opted for water, and I brought him a fresh bottle, then sat in the armchair opposite him. "This works a little different from what I see on TV, huh? You aren't dragging people down to the station to take their statements."

He chuckled. "We do that sometimes, but it hardly has the desired effect on a suspect seeing as we're located in the back half of a church building."

"That's small-town Texas for you," I said.

"Doesn't make us take the work any less seriously."

My palms had started to sweat, probably around the moment the sheriff spoke the word "suspect."

Take it easy. This is normal procedure.

I forced myself to breathe naturally. "I'm surprised you didn't assign the mundane statement-taking to Deputy Rosales."

"She's doing her share." He looked away for a moment before turning back and meeting my eyes. "Matter of fact, she's talking with your aunt as we speak."

I popped up off the chair. "But *I'm* the one who found the body. Why's she talking to Aunt Rowe? Aunt Rowe wasn't there."

"Sit down, Sabrina," he said, his voice stern. "Your aunt owns the property, the deceased was related to her, she has the names of the guests so we can be sure we've talked to everyone who was checked in last night. Then there's the small matter of the deceased's claim to be Rowe's brother and her subsequent clubbing him on the head, as you yourself reported to me. Need I go on?"

I dropped back into the chair. "No, I get it, but I wish you wouldn't talk to the guests. I'd hate for the business to suffer because of this incident."

I wouldn't normally belittle a murder by referring to it as an incident, but I felt like I'd reverted to my argumentative teenage years, maybe because the sheriff reminded me of my dad. I was worried, too, about them talking to the girl who'd seen Aunt Rowe outside last night. Maybe we'd get lucky and they'd only question adults.

"Rowe's business will be fine," Crawford said.

"At least *you* could have talked to Aunt Rowe instead of sending Rosales. She's so, so . . . The right word is escaping me."

"Businesslike?" he suggested. "No nonsense?"

"Harsh," I said. "That's the word. She's way too harsh."

"Deputy Pat's personality has many facets." He unscrewed the cap on his water, took a long swallow, and replaced the cap. "In Rowe's case, I needed my deputy to do the professional interrogation."

"Oh my God, she's *interrogating* Aunt Rowe?" The coffee I'd been drinking all day sat like a gallon of acid in my stomach.

"She's taking a *statement*," Crawford said. "Because of my friendship with Rowe, it's better that I distance myself from discussing the case with her personally."

"But it's okay for you to talk to *me*," I said, "even though we're friends, too?"

"You're my good friend's niece. There's a difference."

Crawford put a hand up to his face and smoothed his mustache with a thumb and index finger. "Have you thought of any details that didn't occur to you when you spoke with Deputy Pat after finding the body?"

I shrugged. "Nothing comes to mind."

At least nothing I wanted to tell him.

"Any idea if Bobby Joe Flowers had enemies?"

"I'd be shocked if he didn't, but I don't know anything about his life or people who knew him. I don't even know where he lives, though he claimed he was staying with a friend in the area."

A small notebook protruded from the sheriff's shirt pocket, but he didn't take it out. "What do you know about his claim that he was Rowe's half brother?"

"Not a thing," I said. "The first I heard such crazy talk was when he walked in yesterday and blurted it out. That was clearly news to Aunt Rowe, too. She was as shocked as she could be. Her reaction was one of those heat-of-the-moment things. If she had stopped to think, there's no way she'd ever do—" I was talking way too much. "Anything so rash."

"Could your mother shed any light on Flowers's claim?"

"My mother?" I had to laugh. "I'm not sure if my mother ever spent two seconds thinking about Dad's relatives, especially not one who estranged himself from the whole family. Anyway, she's on a perpetual trip with the new husband. Couldn't even tell you where to find her. *If* you wanted to take her statement, that is. Probably a waste of your time."

Crawford watched me for a moment. "Guess I touched a sore spot. Sorry about that."

"No problem." My right eye began to twitch, an annoying reaction that often happens when I get worked up. I looked at the window, hoping to see Hitchcock had returned to watch over me, but the sill was empty.

I turned back to the sheriff. "You could talk to Bobby Joe's siblings, I suppose, though I don't know where you'd find *them* either."

"We've already made notification to next of kin," Crawford said. "They're in Dallas, by the way. Brother didn't seem to care one way or the other 'bout what happened. The sister, Becky, I believe, is more affected, ready to take charge of making arrangements for the burial. Which will have to wait until after the autopsy."

"Maybe the brother was an enemy to Bobby Joe," I said.

The sheriff nodded. "We'll check out their whereabouts at the time of death. Speaking of which, and you know I hate to ask you this, Sabrina, but where were you between the hours of nine last night and two this morning?"

My pulse raced. "Are you kidding me?"

He shook his head.

"I was right here, at home."

He raised his eyebrows. "Inside?"

"For the most part. I'm not a hermit, for goodness' sake. I'd been to the bookstore in town. Came back and spent some time writing. Went to bed, but I couldn't sleep so I was going to bake at Aunt Rowe's. Ended up finding the body instead. Are you asking everyone for an alibi, or am I just lucky?"

"We'll ask everyone," he said.

I wasn't sure I believed that, but they *would* ask Aunt Rowe. Dang it all. What had she been up to last night? I wish I'd had a chance to talk with her before Rosales showed up, but what difference would that have actually made? I wouldn't have encouraged her to lie. A cold sweat came over me at the thought of how their discussion might be going. The sheriff and his deputy needed a diversion—something to take their attention away from Aunt Rowe's anger with Bobby Joe. I thought about my talk with Daisy McKetta.

I looked at the sheriff, who seemed to be watching me carefully.

"Have you remembered something important?" he said.

"Maybe. I was thinking about a story I heard in town today. Did you know the body of a girl named Vicki Palmer was found in the same place as Bobby Joe Flowers? Seems like a huge coincidence, don't you think?"

"I knew the Palmer case," Crawford said slowly, with no change in his expression. "There's no connection."

"You can't be sure," I said, "with her case being unsolved all this time. Sure is a shame, poor thing dies and nobody knows what happened to her, even thirty years later?"

"Enough," Crawford said. "There's a lot you don't know about all the hours the sheriff back then poured into investigating the Palmer case. Sometimes answers can't be found no matter how—" He broke off and looked away.

"Were you on that case?" I said quietly.

He nodded. "We worked it for over a year. Hard. Nobody could say we didn't try our damnedest."

I'd caused a diversion all right, but now I felt sorry for bringing up the disturbing topic.

Crawford sat up straight and clapped his palms on his thighs. "That won't happen with the Flowers case. We're going to nail the killer this time." He stood to leave. "I'm hoping that Rowe has a good story—a solid alibi. 'Cause I mean to tell you, Sabrina, if the autopsy proves Bobby Joe Flowers was your aunt's brother and had any legal claim to this property, she has one doozy of a motive for killing the man."

10

AFTER SHERIFF CRAWFORD left my cottage, I was champing at the bit to see Aunt Rowe. I didn't want anyone to spot me racing over to her place, though. How would that look? Like there was something suspicious going on. Some big secret I had to pass on to my aunt before it was too late.

I sighed. I spent way too much time living in a fictional, mysterious world. Still, it didn't seem wise to let my frantic emotions show through to anyone who might be watching. Chances were the sheriff and his deputy would be in the area for a while, until they had crossed everyone they wanted to question off their list.

Aunt Rowe, Glenda, Thomas, the guests.

How many people did we expect this weekend? I ticked them off on my fingers. The Hartmans in Barcelona, the as-yet-unidentified man in Venice, and guests checking into Florence and Madrid sometime today. Of course, the people just arriving wouldn't have anything to tell about last night's events.

My growling stomach reminded me of my half-uneaten lunch umpteen hours ago. I looked at the clock hanging on the wall over the table that also served as my desk. Seven. Close enough to the usual dinnertime, a perfect reason for heading to the house. Glenda always cooked a nice meal for Aunt Rowe, and I was famished. There was absolutely nothing suspicious about me joining my aunt for dinner, right?

I slipped into my flip-flops and rushed out the door, making sure to lock up behind myself. I purposefully slowed to a natural pace and scanned the area. No one was in sight, not that the sheriff would conduct his interviews outdoors. He'd invite himself inside to conduct proper, authoritative interrogations. Worrying about what he might learn made me as jumpy as a cricket.

The evening was pleasant with a slight breeze and a hint of honeysuckle in the air. I headed diagonally across the common yard between the cottages, which were scattered around the property rather than lined up in rows. The sheriff had probably parked somewhere on the meandering lane that connected the cottages, and I'd be more likely to escape notice by taking this shortcut.

I passed the Paris cottage, then slipped around a stand of trees behind Venice to avoid the porch-sitting guy. I scanned the property to my right in hopes of spotting Hitchcock, but the cat was nowhere in sight. He might still be somewhere near my place, in hiding for the moment, and I hoped that was the case. He'd be safer if he stayed put instead of gallivanting around the grounds.

When my gaze tracked back across to the Venice cottage, I spotted the man I had hoped to avoid standing not ten feet in front of me. He was behind the cottage, facing away from me and holding a camera up to his face. As luck would have it, a twig snapped under my foot. The man jumped, startled, and turned around.

He recovered quickly and grinned. "Well, hello."

"Hi." I cringed inwardly, regretting that I'd left my place without giving one thought to my bedraggled appearance.

The man was on the tall side, thirtyish, with a couple days of blond beard growth that hadn't showed up from a distance. He wore a black Rolling Stones T-shirt with his jeans and Top-Siders. Now that he'd recovered from my taking him by surprise, he had a confident, easygoing look about him. His camera was the type my ex-husband had insisted on buying, a newfangled digital with a bunch of buttons and switches. Way too complicated, not to mention expensive, for my liking. I wondered what this guy was taking pictures of—all I saw was grass, trees, cottages, and Aunt Rowe's house in the distance.

"Find any interesting subjects?" I said.

He nodded. "This is a great place. Very peaceful."

"Peaceful doesn't exactly show up on a picture," I said.

He grinned again. "It does if I do a good job."

"You're a photographer?"

"Yeah. I specialize in wildlife, mostly birds." He smiled and offered his hand. "Adam Lee."

We shook and I introduced myself. "Sorry I interrupted. I need to run."

"Where you off to in such a hurry?"

"Dinner." I took a few steps, then stopped when he snapped his fingers.

"You must be the niece. Am I right?"

"That's me." I kept walking.

"You're the writer, moved here from Houston. I'm a Houstonian myself."

Good grief, had Aunt Rowe told this guy my life story?

And if she had, why didn't he keep the information to himself? Did he want me to ask for his personal details? I was in no mood, so I waved and kept going.

"Stop back and visit anytime," he said. "I could take your picture."

I'd had a better impression of him before the close encounter. I certainly didn't want him taking my picture. What an odd thing for him to even bring up.

Belatedly, I remembered Aunt Rowe's preaching about making all guests feel welcome. I looked over my shoulder and called, "Enjoy your stay."

The man had already turned away from me and was fiddling with the camera.

Fine.

I stalked toward Aunt Rowe's house, feeling unreasonably annoyed about my conversation with the stranger. Something about the guy bugged me. I couldn't quite put my finger on it.

I passed the Madrid cottage and noted a car, indicating the arrival of a new guest. Across the way, Florence still appeared empty. At the Barcelona cottage, a second car was parked next to Tim Hartman's. I hoped the girlfriend liked kids and that the family enjoyed their stay.

Diversions had made me forget my concerns for a few minutes. When I saw a sheriff's department car in Aunt Rowe's driveway, worries flooded back. I hesitated for a moment, then decided to go around back to the screened porch. The door was unlocked—not good, given that someone had been murdered nearby last night—and I let myself in.

The delicious scent of Glenda's enchilada casserole hit me the moment I stepped over the threshold. Normally, I'd head straight for that yummy dish, but eating wasn't at the top of my priority list tonight. I peeked into an empty kitchen. I tiptoed toward the living room and listened for voices. All quiet. The house was dim as the last vestiges of daylight slipped away, and it felt deserted. I caught the faint clack of a keyboard and followed the noise to Aunt Rowe's office.

I stopped before reaching the door and poked my head around the corner like a cop checking for an intruder before entering. Aunt Rowe was alone, seated behind her desk, her hand on the computer mouse. She had earbuds plugged in her ears. She looked tired and a bit pale, but her head bopped, presumably to the beat of music. Was she rocking out after the tension of Rosales's interrogation?

She noticed me and pulled the earbuds out. "How's my favorite writer?"

She sounded way too relaxed. "I'm good, but I'm more concerned about you. Where's Rosales? Her car's parked in the driveway. I thought she'd be in here."

Aunt Rowe held an index finger to her lips. "Shh. She's down the hall with Glenda."

"Oh, great." I turned to push the door against the jamb without latching it. "Sheriff Crawford just left my place. Seems to me they're concentrating on the wrong people."

"Ach." Aunt Rowe waved a hand. "They'll get on track eventually. Don't be a worrywart."

She turned her computer monitor so I could see the screen. "How do you feel about cruising to Bangkok? There's a great deal coming up this September. My cast should come off way before then."

I raised my eyebrows. "You're thinking about traveling?"

"It's been too long," she said. "Work, work, work, that's all I've been up to lately. I miss going places. I'd like you to come along this time."

"What?" Were her meds talking?

"You don't want to see the world?" she asked.

I shook my head and lowered my voice. "I have nothing

against travel, but how can you even be thinking about going anywhere at a time like this?"

"A time like what? The deputy talked to me, but she didn't give me any kind of warning like I shouldn't leave town. Is that what you're looking all panic-stricken about?"

I pulled out a chair parked across the desk from her and plopped into it. "Yeah, partly."

"They'll have this mess figured out way before the cruise date. The only thing that annoys me is Jeb not coming here to talk to me himself. And he claims he's my friend."

"The fact that the sheriff is your friend is exactly why he *didn't* come here," I said. "Aunt Rowe, this is dead serious. They're looking for a killer."

"I know that." She rolled her eyes. "I'm not a moron."

My shoulders sagged. "I didn't mean to insult you, but listen. I don't think they're getting anywhere with the investigation. We need to help them solve this. Do you have any idea who would have wanted Bobby Joe dead?"

Rowe grinned. "You mean besides me?"

I opened my eyes wide, trying to send a warning message, and spoke even lower. "Hush. I hope you didn't act so glib in front of Deputy Rosales. What did you tell her?"

Aunt Rowe gave me a palms-up gesture. "The truth. I'm sorry that this happened, but I'm not terribly sorry Bobby Joe is dead."

"Aunt Rowe!"

Footsteps tapped on the hallway's wood floor, but Aunt Rowe wasn't finished and apparently hadn't heard them.

"Sweetie, quit your worrying," she went on. "Bobby Joe Flowers isn't worth it. Trust me, if you'd known him all your life you'd have killed him in a book years ago."

Behind me, the door creaked open.

11

GLENDA PEERED AROUND the door at us.

"Y'all are darn lucky the deputy left," she said. "We don't need her hearing your fool talk about killing nobody."

I slumped in my chair and willed my heart rate to slow down. "Thank goodness it's only you."

"I'll ignore that jab," Glenda said. "Who wants enchilada casserole? It's way past ready."

"Count me in," Aunt Rowe said. With some effort and a grimace, she pushed herself up from the desk and grabbed her crutches, which were leaning against the file cabinet behind her. At least Rosales hadn't confiscated the crutches as evidence. Yet.

Aunt Rowe maneuvered herself out from behind the desk and followed Glenda down the hall. I hung back, wishing I could be as relaxed about the situation as my aunt was. Or was she? I shook my head to clear that line of thought and followed the others.

In the kitchen, Glenda had set the table for two.

"You're not joining us?" I asked.

She shook her head. "I ate leftovers earlier. Sandra's having issues with her youngest, and I promised I'd call her tonight. That'll take up the next couple hours."

Glenda's sister was notorious for her long-winded phone conversations.

Aunt Rowe settled herself at the table and didn't waste any time digging into what looked like a double helping of casserole. She'd piled tortilla chips on the edge of her plate. I doubted this meal fit into the bone-healing eating program she'd mentioned the day before, but decided not to bring that up. This was good comfort food, and at this point we could use an extra helping.

I went to the window and looked out at the driveway to be sure the deputy had left. She had, thank goodness.

I took the seat across from Aunt Rowe, and Glenda brought us each a glass of iced tea.

"How'd your talk with Deputy Rosales go?" I asked Glenda.

"Short and sweet. I didn't have much of anything to report. Hey, you meet the new guy? He's a writer."

"What new guy?" I said around a bite of casserole.

"The one in Venice," she said.

"Good-looking fella," Aunt Rowe said. "Came in from Austin. You might want to get to know him, Sabrina."

Since I'd come to live in Lavender, Aunt Rowe had refrained from trying to set me up, and I was fine with that. I finished chewing my food and swallowed. "Adam Lee? He's a photographer, and I thought he came from Houston."

Glenda wiped the flat cooktop surface with a damp cloth. "Photographer. Writer. Could be both. Told me he's working on something for a travel magazine. I thought he said Austin. He stopped in today, hoping we'd have a vacancy, and we did."

"Yesterday." Rowe crunched into a large chip.

"He checked in today," Glenda said.

Rowe nodded. "Right, but he was here yesterday asking whether we'd have a vacancy beginning tonight."

"Huh." Glenda shrugged. "You ladies need anything else before I make my call?"

We both declined, and she took off down the hall to the guest room.

"Let's not go on about Adam Lee," I said when Glenda was out of earshot. "We have more important things to discuss."

"Like what?" Aunt Rowe said.

Lord, give me strength.

"Did Deputy Rosales ask what you were doing outside last night after dark?" I said.

Aunt Rowe picked up her napkin, unfolded it, and placed it in her lap. "Outside?"

"You heard me. You might have thought no one saw you, but you were spotted out there."

She hesitated, and I wondered if she would continue on her path of denial.

Finally, she said, "Who saw me?"

"Does that really matter? What were you doing?"

My mental list of possibilities had grown. A guest might have called to ask for extra towels. She could have gone to open a door for someone who'd accidentally locked themselves out. Or maybe she'd decided to do some star gazing.

Aunt Rowe took her time drinking her tea, then put the glass down and twirled it in the ring of condensation left on her coaster before answering. "I was looking for Bobby Joe."

My heart sank. "Did you tell the deputy?"

Aunt Rowe sat up straighter. "She didn't ask, and I decided I was only answering exactly what she asked, nothing more, nothing less. That's what they tell people to do on those cop shows."

She'd held back information. Good grief.

"We're not in a cop show," I said. "Now tell me, why did you go looking for him? That wasn't the best idea you ever had, and keeping this little fact to yourself might backfire."

"How so?"

"If the deputy finds out later, she'll wonder why you didn't mention it. You'll look suspicious, and suspicious people end up on suspect lists."

"You're being melodramatic," Aunt Rowe said. "Guess that goes with being a fiction writer."

I sighed. "Believe me, I'm not planning to turn this into a script for a TV movie. *Why* did you go looking for Bobby Joe?"

Aunt Rowe puffed out a breath. "For one thing, I live here, and I can do what I want. Bobby Joe *said* he was staying with a friend, but I didn't believe that BS. I figured he'd break into a cottage when he thought I wasn't looking."

Okay, maybe that wasn't far-fetched, but in my opinion she should have told Rosales.

"Did you see him?" I said.

"No."

"Did you see his SUV parked behind the Paris cottage?"

"No."

"How long were you outside?"

"Thirty minutes? An hour? Heck, I don't know. I wasn't running a stopwatch."

"Don't get mad at me. I didn't create this problem."

"I didn't either."

We had a stare-down lasting all of five seconds. I gave in first and shoved a bite of casserole in my mouth. This stuff was impossible to resist. Ground beef layered between chunks of flour tortillas with a creamy sauce in between, enchilada sauce and melted cheese on top. Yum. Aunt Rowe must have felt the same, because she attacked her dinner with a vengeance. I cleared my plate, thought about seconds, then put down my fork and looked at Aunt Rowe.

"Why didn't you tell Deputy Rosales you were out there?" I said.

Aunt Rowe dabbed her napkin at melted cheese on her mouth. "Like I said, she didn't ask and there was nothing to tell. I didn't see Bobby Joe anywhere. I came back in. Period."

I sure hoped that was the truth, the whole truth, and nothing but the truth.

"We probably haven't seen the last of the deputy," I said. "It would be great if we had new information to report when that happens."

"I don't have any information." Aunt Rowe shoveled her last bite of food into her mouth. "Jeb and his people can do their own work."

She simply wasn't concerned about being a suspect. I was worried enough for both of us.

"Who else does Bobby Joe know in town?"

Rowe shrugged, still chewing.

"Any idea who his friend was? The one he claimed to be staying with?"

"Of course not. I'm the one who thought he was lying about the friend and squatting in one of my cottages."

"You think Becky or J. T. would know his friends?" I wondered how much information the sheriff had gotten from the brother and sister. Even if he'd learned something important, though, he wouldn't be sharing his knowledge with us.

Aunt Rowe sat back in her chair. "I can't see Bobby Joe keeping up with his siblings. Hard to imagine him having a friend at all, unless it's somebody he's trying to scam who hasn't caught on to his shenanigans."

I put my elbows on the table and propped my chin on my fists. Bobby Joe, the known scammer. How many people had he taken advantage of over the years?

"Bobby Joe grew up here in Lavender, didn't he?" I said.

"Stayed till high school graduation," Aunt Rowe said. "I was living in London about that time. Mom and Dad were running the cottage business."

I nodded, remembering that Aunt Rowe had lived abroad with her second husband for several years.

Or was it her third husband? Whichever.

I wiped my mouth and balled up my napkin. "I hope the sheriff plans to get Bobby Joe's phone records and check his credit card charges to see where he's been lately. Maybe then he'll have some clues to go by."

Aunt Rowe pushed her chair away from the table. "This has been one heck of a day, Sabrina, and I'm through talking about Bobby Joe. I vote for some mindless TV watching."

I considered asking her about the girl who had died in the river, but Vicki Palmer's death had most likely happened when Aunt Rowe lived in London, too. She might not know anything about it, and she obviously didn't want to talk. I could find a better time to bring that up.

I went with her to the den and helped her get comfortable in an easy chair with her cast propped on an ottoman. She turned the TV to one of those reality shows that don't even tempt me to watch. I told her I would clean up the kitchen before heading back to my cottage, and we said good night.

Back in the kitchen, I cleared the table and loaded our dishes into the dishwasher. I refrigerated the leftover casserole and spent a few minutes scanning other containers in hopes of finding something I could feed to Hitchcock. Leftover chicken strips looked promising, so I snatched two of them and found some foil to wrap them up. I checked the pantry for cans of tuna but came up empty.

I'd go to Krane's in the morning and pick up cat food and some treats. Stray cats were not all that predictable, but I had a feeling I'd be seeing a lot more of Hitchcock. The thought made me smile.

When I left the house, though, the vision of Bobby Joe's body in the river crowded into my head. The sheriff might be Aunt Rowe's friend, but that wouldn't affect Rosales's attitude about the investigation. I wondered if she'd been told about Aunt Rowe's nighttime escapade and what she made of that information, given that Aunt Rowe hadn't mentioned it herself.

If I wanted to keep Aunt Rowe off the top of the suspect list, I had a lot more to do in town tomorrow than pick up things for the cat. I needed to search for answers about Bobby Joe, his friends, and especially his enemies.

12

I SLEPT LIKE THE dead and woke when the first sliver of light fell across the crimson-and-cream silk duvet that Aunt Rowe had brought back from her Monaco trip. My thoughts instantly went to Hitchcock. I hurried to the back door and pushed it open to check the dishes I'd left out on the deck for him the night before. The chicken was gone, but that only meant some critter had come by—could have been a raccoon as easily as a cat.

I knew it was futile to search for Hitchcock. Even well-behaved cats do what they want to when they want to. I'd feel a lot better if I had him contained inside my cottage. For now, I could only hope he'd watch his back while he was out and about. Good advice for anyone, actually, human or feline.

Shortly after seven, I slid into a booth at Hot Stuff. "Knock on Wood" played on the jukebox, and Max did a solo line dance behind the bar, pausing to do quick mug fill-ups for the customers seated there. The coffee shop had a good crowd, many of them locals, which was why I'd come in so early. These were the folks who knew a neighbor from an out-of-towner. They noticed everything and gossiped like crazy. Bobby Joe Flowers had not been invisible in his red SUV, and I was betting a good number of people would know whom I was talking about when I began asking questions.

Or maybe I wouldn't even need to ask—information was headed my way in the form of Amos Whittle, a seventysomething man who'd lived in Lavender all his life. Amos didn't have a shy bone in his body, and he loved to talk. I'd met the man on my first visit to Hot Stuff when he'd introduced himself and promptly given me a summary of his life story. Then he proceeded to ask me everything from where I was born to why I wanted to write books since there were already so many books out there to be read.

Amos took the chair across from me and plunked his coffee mug on the table. He tipped his John Deere cap farther back on his head. "How's our local author doing this morning?"

"I'll let you know after I wake up."

Lacy Colter, a college student who worked part-time for Max, filled mugs at a nearby table and gave me a be-with-you-shortly signal. I smiled at her and nodded.

"No laptop?" Amos said.

"Not today." I'd stuck a copy of my synopsis in my tote, though, with the thought that I'd read over it at some point and mark up the draft. I was enjoying the afterglow of having written and preferred thinking my words were genius. Re-reading would tell me the truth, and I wasn't ready for that stage yet.

"Heard you had some excitement over at your place," Amos said.

"I could do without that sort of excitement. What have you heard?"

"Nothin' much, 'cept Rowe's in trouble for tryin' to kill her cousin."

I frowned at him. "She didn't try to kill anyone."

Lacy came up behind me with her coffeepot, and she'd obviously heard us. "You talking about that dude who's like older than my dad and acted like I should be interested in dating him?" She wrinkled her nose in distaste.

"I'm not sure," I said. "Am I?"

She gave a fairly accurate description of Bobby Joe, and when she got to the part about his red vehicle, I knew we had the same man. She ended with, "I heard he died."

"That's right," I said. "When he talked to you, did he tell you anything about himself?"

"Only that he was single, loads of fun, and looking for a good time."

I wasn't surprised that Bobby Joe would come on to the cute blonde with freckled cheeks and a nice tan. "Guess you turned him down?"

"For sure," Lacy said. "And next day I saw him with a woman more his age. Probably his wife."

I sat up straighter. "What did she look like?"

Lacy shrugged. "I wasn't all that interested, you know? Lady had dark hair, that's all I remember."

"Where did you see them?"

"Sitting in his SUV," she said. "They were parked on the street, couple blocks down."

The bell over the door jangled and more customers streamed in. Lacy glanced that way and said, "Here comes the Saturday rush. What can I get you?"

I ordered a vanilla latte and a cinnamon cruller, then turned back to Amos when Lacy walked away.

"Where were we?" I snapped my fingers. "I remember. You were accusing my aunt of trying to kill a man."

"Just tellin' what I heard," Amos said. "Not that I blame Rowe. Man threatens someone's property, there's gonna be trouble. Hard as we worked to pay off our mortgage, I could see my Edith taking out a man if he tried to stake a claim to our place."

"That sounds pretty drastic."

"Lucky for us we don't have relatives the likes of Bobby Joe Flowers."

"So you knew Bobby Joe?"

"Everybody who lived here back when Bobby Joe was in high school knew that rascal. He was impossible to miss."

"What do you mean?"

"Lights shot out at the courthouse, ask Bobby Joe," he said. "The 4-H steers let loose in the school gym, Bobby Joe was in on it. Principal gets up in the morning, finds his car on its roof. I could make you a list."

"Might be why Bobby Joe's been living elsewhere," I said. "You know anyone who's kept up with him all these years?"

Amos shook his head. "Most folks were glad to see him go."

"When's the last time you saw him?"

"Maybe a week ago."

Interesting. Bobby Joe was in town and hadn't told anyone. Or Aunt Rowe knew he was around and didn't mention it.

"Where did you see him?"

"Once on the street, near the bakery." Amos rubbed his gray whiskers. "Another time I passed him on the road. He was headed out of town."

"Anyone with him?"

He shook his head. "Nope. He was alone both times."

"He told us he was staying with a friend. Any idea who that might be?"

"Nah, all I heard is he'd been pretty free with the cash

lately. Heard he bought a round of drinks out at The Wild Pony Saloon a couple times."

The Wild Pony was a local beer joint that featured live country music on weekends. "Who told you that?"

"I think it was Twila, over at the antiques store." He checked his watch. "Edith is expecting me home. We're sitting for the four grandkids today. Wish us luck."

"Enjoy," I said and watched him go. I was processing the information I'd learned from Amos when I noticed Luke Griffin stride into the shop.

Lacy brought my order and apologized for the wait time. She glanced Griffin's way. He looked very official wearing his game warden uniform and a stern expression.

"Now there's an older man I wouldn't mind dating," she said and hurried over to the counter where Griffin was waiting for someone to take his order.

Guess Griffin appealed to all the young women in town. I remembered Hallie Krane's reaction to the man the other day. He *was* pretty dang attractive, but I reminded myself that Griffin had argued with Bobby Joe Flowers. He might have had a hand in Bobby Joe's death, and this was my chance to ask the man what they had fought about.

My mind raced as I tried to decide on the best way to broach the subject. Should I be straightforward with my questioning? "I saw you arguing with the murder victim" didn't seem like a good start if I wanted to get information. Chances were he was ordering a coffee to go. I grabbed my cruller and slung my tote over my shoulder, ready to follow him outside where I could casually waylay him with questions in relative privacy.

Lacy handed the warden his coffee. He turned, but didn't head for the door. Instead, he walked in my direction. I dropped my cruller on the table. Yanked the tote off my shoulder and reached into it. Grabbed the pages of my synopsis and slapped the paper down on the table. I bent over the pages and tried to look inconspicuous as I watched Griffin through the fringe of my lashes.

He passed the bar and approached a booth catty-corner from mine. He stopped with his back to me and addressed two men seated in the booth, though I couldn't quite make out his words. One of the men, a heavyset guy wearing dusty jeans with suspenders over a T-shirt, looked up at Griffin and said, "I didn't do nothin', Warden. You got the wrong man."

"No, Bart, I don't." Griffin spoke louder now. "You're the right man with the wrong gear in your truck."

What did he mean? I leaned to my left to get a better view of the guy with Bart. He was about half Bart's size with long, stringy hair, his attention trained on his coffee cup.

"C'mon, Warden," Bart responded. "I clean out my truck but once every couple a years. Got everything in there I need from now till three years from now."

"You're poaching deer," Griffin said in a low voice. "You don't want me to catch you red-handed 'cause I'll make sure you're justly punished and, trust me, you don't want to go there. If I were you, I'd store that deer hunting gear in your house till the fall and quit poaching while the quitting's good. You hear what I'm telling you, Bart?"

My attention had been riveted on the men from the moment Bart said he was the wrong man. He stared at Griffin like an alligator homing in on its next meal. His muscles tensed, and I felt sure Bart was about to haul off and punch Griffin in the face. I didn't want to witness a fistfight. Why didn't the game warden walk away? It seemed like he'd delivered the message he'd come to give.

Without much thought, I popped up from my booth and

crossed the aisle to stand next to Griffin. I put a hand on his sleeve and tried not to think about the feel of his forearm beneath my fingers.

"Excuse me, Warden?" I said. "Could I speak with you for a moment?"

I didn't look at Bart or his friend, though I could feel them staring. Griffin turned to me with a glimmer of humor in his eyes.

"Yes, ma'am. What can I do for you?"

"Could I have a word, please?" I turned and went back to my booth. Griffin followed and slid in across from me. I held my breath for a moment in hopes that Bart and his friend would go back to whatever they were doing before Griffin showed up, then breathed a sigh of relief when they stood and left the shop.

Luke Griffin smiled at me as if we met here for coffee on a regular basis, but his tone was anything but friendly. "So, you're the woman who sicced the sheriff on me."

"I, uh—" So much for plotting a casual way to begin the conversation. "That's not exactly what happened."

"Okay. Why don't you set me straight?" He wrapped his hands around the tall to-go cup and leaned forward. His brown eyes glinted as if he wasn't entirely serious, and his tone didn't sound nearly as severe as it had during his conversation with Bart. Was he making fun of me?

I sipped my coffee, then cleared my throat. "I saw you the other day. Thursday. At Krane's, in the parking lot. You were there with your dog."

He nodded. "Angie."

"Excuse me?"

"Her name's Angie. She's out in the truck now if you'd like to come out and meet her."

"What? You mean now?"

"Sure," he said.

"No. I mean, I'd love to meet her, but not right now. Angie? That's a cute name."

Not very manly, though. I wondered if a woman had named the warden's dog for him. I glanced at Griffin's left hand. No ring. No tan line.

What are you doing, Sabrina? Ask your questions.

"You saw us at Krane's," Griffin prompted.

"Right. And you were arguing with a man. The same man who ended up dead in the river, and I was wondering—"

"Whether I killed him?" Griffin said.

"No." I hesitated briefly. "Well, did you?"

He shook his head. "I'm not a fan of killing. I don't even hunt, and as you may have heard, I don't cut poachers any slack."

"But you didn't like Bobby Joe Flowers."

"Not especially."

"Why?"

Griffin sipped his coffee, then said, "I don't like people who break the rules or those who go outside the boundaries of what's good and decent."

I didn't either. I'd had a very short acquaintance with Bobby Joe Flowers, but I couldn't imagine the words "good" or "decent" ever applying to him. "Did Sheriff Crawford seriously question you about what I told him?"

"He did," Griffin said.

"Were you reprimanding Bobby Joe Flowers for breaking rules when I saw you?"

"In a manner of speaking."

"And would you say the sheriff is convinced you weren't involved in Flowers's death?"

"I would."

I stared at Griffin, thinking how I hadn't gotten straight answers out of him. I needed to ask more specific questions.

"So I'm free to go?" Griffin said. "Or did you want Deputy Rosales here to arrest me?"

Huh?

I followed Griffin's gaze to Deputy Rosales, who was approaching us at a fast clip. Of all the bad luck. I wasn't finished with Luke Griffin, and now I wouldn't be able to continue the conversation. Not in front of Rosales.

She was out of uniform and looking attractive with her silky black hair down around her shoulders. She wore white slacks with platform espadrilles and a red sleeveless top that showed off her well-toned arms. I wondered if she had expected to see Luke Griffin when she dressed for the day.

Rosales reached our table with a big smile for the game warden. Sheriff Crawford had mentioned her crush on Griffin, and I could see from the woman's face that was the truth.

"Luke," she said in greeting.

He nodded. "Morning, Patricia."

Then Rosales turned to me, and I feared her scathing expression would singe the eyebrows right off my face.

13

Luke Griffin didn't wait for the deputy to speak. He looked from Rosales to me to the papers on the table in front of me. He slid from the booth and stood. "I'll let you get back to your work, ma'am."

I nodded to Griffin and looked at Rosales. I knew better than to start something with the deputy, but sometimes my mouth doesn't listen to my better judgment. I pasted on a fake smile.

"You look lovely this morning, Deputy Rosales," I said. "You must be off duty. I sure hope that means you've solved the Flowers case."

"*This* is never off duty." Rosales tapped her temple with an index finger. "We're hot on the trail, so to speak, and I suspect you'll be seeing me again real soon."

With that, she took Griffin's arm. The game warden looked about as happy as a guilty man picked out of a lineup, but he allowed her to lead him across the room and out the door. I stared after them for a few seconds, then jammed the cruller into my mouth and gulped down the rest of my latte.

Dang it. What did she mean about seeing me again soon? Whatever she was getting at, I didn't look forward to that meeting. And what was with the possessive way she took hold of Griffin's arm? Was there more to the relationship than her one-way infatuation with the man? Griffin sure had been quick to disconnect from me when Rosales showed up, almost as if he was afraid of her seeing him with another woman.

Whatever. Rosales was his problem for now. What I needed to focus on was figuring out who had killed Bobby Joe before Rosales came to her own conclusion.

I got a latte refill and pulled a red pen from my tote. I flipped my synopsis pages over to write on the blank side of the paper. If I looked at the situation the way I went about plotting a book, things might start to make sense.

I wrote "WHAT IF" in capital letters at the top of the page, then continued writing out my stream of consciousness. What if an unlikable cousin came to visit and someone killed him at the river behind your house? The cops naturally look at you because you have a motive, namely to keep your inheritance and not have to share it with the cousin.

I stopped writing and looked at the page. I had to admit that if I read the actual events that had transpired in a mystery novel, Aunt Rowe would look like the guilty party. But everyone knows that the character who looks guilty at the beginning of a whodunit never turns out to be the villain, right? Well, maybe not *never*, but certainly not in this true-to-life case.

So who else had a motive to be rid of Bobby Joe? Love is a well-known motive for murder. Maybe a jealous husband or boyfriend killed him. If I could learn the identity of the dark-haired woman Lacy had seen with Bobby Joe, she might lead me to a suspect.

Money was also a popular motive. According to Thomas, Bobby Joe usually came to Aunt Rowe for money. Recently, he'd bought drinks for the crowd at The Wild Pony Saloon. At least that was the word around town. No one was going to murder a man for spending money on them. I wondered where the money had come from. Bobby Joe could have Las Vegas winnings for all I knew. Back to the elusive dark-haired woman. She might know more about the source of his funds.

I straightened against the bench seat and tapped my foot to "I Will Survive" coming over the sound system. My thoughts drifted to what Amos had said about Bobby Joe and the pranks he pulled as a teenager. Revenge was also a powerful motive. Was it possible someone from high school held a big-time grudge against Bobby Joe and had waited this long to act on that grudge? Nah, that was weak. I was going with the theory that Bobby Joe's recent actions led to his death.

But what if his recent actions had a connection to events from the past? I had already made one connection—Bobby Joe and Vicki Palmer had died in the same place. I drew a line across my page and beneath it wrote a new idea.

What if a man returns to his hometown and is killed in the same spot where his high-school sweetheart was killed thirty years ago? The sweetheart part being entirely fictional, of course, since no one had connected Bobby Joe to Vicki Palmer romantically. I could write a story using this plot, though, and the man should be the main character. That meant I couldn't kill him off, but perhaps someone attempts to kill him and misses. Then—

For God's sake, Sabrina, this is real life, not some book you're writing.

I threw my pen down and blew out a breath. I should trust
the sheriff's department to do a thorough investigation and
nail the killer. I should mind my own business and work on
my synopsis instead of running helter-skelter searching for
clues. Instead, I flagged down Max and asked him who would
know the most about events in Lavender thirty years ago.

He referred me to Twila Baxter at the antiques store. That
was the second time I'd heard her name today, and I took that
as a sign.

WAGON Wheel Antiques was located at the far end of
Saltgrass Road in a 1900s two-story building with a
wide front porch filled with collectibles from days gone by. I
had never visited the store, though I had driven by dozens of
times. I like antiques, but the ones I owned were in storage
along with everything else from my house in Houston. I had
no extra space in the Monte Carlo cottage for new, or should
I say antique, purchases.

I pulled into a parking slot directly in front of the entrance
and took a moment to survey the crowded porch. Old chairs,
a red Texaco gasoline pump, crocks, and a large black pot
that reminded me of the stereotypical witch's cauldron sat
near the front door. Vintage Americana signs were nailed to
the white clapboard exterior advertising Grape-Nuts, Dutch
Boy paints, Crisco, and Chesterfield cigarettes.

Looked like I was their first customer of the day, but the
Open sign in the front window was lit, so I climbed out of my
car and headed up the front steps.

The door opened with a screeching haunted-house-like
noise. I stepped inside, my senses assaulted by a combination
of mustiness and potpourri. A variety of chandeliers draped
with crystal teardrops lit the area, albeit dimly.

A trio of wooden pumpkins sat on top of a glass display case next to a stuffed black cat that looked a little too real for my liking. Next to the cat, a covered glass dish held candy corn, popular around Halloween. It was May. At this point I guessed the fall decor might as well stay out for next October.

Beyond the entrance, a dining table with six chairs was set with two dinner places. Pewter candlesticks topped with hurricane globes held orange taper candles, lit as if dinner would be announced any second.

As my eyes adjusted to my surroundings, I noticed thick spiderwebs in the window frames and hanging from lamps. They looked like the fake webs used as Halloween decorations rather than the fine webs spun by real spiders.

"Hello?" I called out, hoping that Twila was here today. No one answered. The place was huge and had a cavernous feeling not unusual for an antiques store. Twila could be in another section and not hear me.

I followed a path to my left and wove through collections of horsehair sofas, armchairs, and occasional tables. I was startled when I came upon a short church pew with a skeleton seated there. A skeleton dressed in a black suit. Unlike the fake spiderwebs, these bones looked like the real thing.

Surely not.

I couldn't seem to tear my gaze away from the pew and was thinking about leaving, when footsteps slipped up behind me.

"Hello, my dear." The voice sounded creaky and very old, like a lot of stuff in this place.

I spun around to face a small woman with blue-tinted curly hair, eighty if she was a day. She wore a stark black dress buttoned up to the neck with a stand-up collar. Her skirt brushed the floor, not surprising as she had to be under five feet tall.

"Uh, hi," I said. "Are you Twila?"

The woman smiled. "Of course, my dear. Welcome to our home."

Home? I glanced around and wondered about the woo-woo vibe that slithered up my spine. I reminded myself that I'd come for information. Now that I was here, I needed to go ahead and talk with the woman.

I smiled at her. "I'm Sabrina Tate. You have a nice place here."

"We do, don't we?" Twila said. "Cornelius and I snapped up the property when Oberlin's Drugstore went out of business. Shame, really. They'd been here since 1908, but my Connie always wanted an antique store, so here we are. This way, my dear. You've come to ask me questions. Let us find a nice place to sit." She turned and walked down an aisle.

How the heck did she know why I'd come? I could just as well have intended to shop for one of these smelly old armchairs.

Suck it up, Sabrina. She's simply an eccentric woman.

I followed Twila down the aisle that wound back around to the dining table with the lit candles. She sat in a chair at the opposite end from the place settings and indicated that I should join her.

The dining chair had a lumpy cushioned seat. I sat with one leg curled under me, trying to get comfortable, when I noticed a living room suite behind Twila. Ghosts occupied the sofa and chairs. Five of them. Merely sheets with black painted-on eyes draped over wire frames, I told myself, but that didn't stop goose bumps from racing up my arms.

Twila followed my gaze and said, "Do you like my guests, dear?"

"They're rather, uh, quiet," I said.

Twila made a rasping noise that may have been giggling.

"I forgot to turn on my music this morning. Excuse me for a moment."

She rose and shuffled toward the front counter. A few minutes later organ music began playing. Eerie music. I felt like I'd landed in an episode of the old vampire soap opera, *Dark Shadows*.

Twila returned to the table, carrying a tray that held a teapot and two china cups and saucers, with a matching sugar and creamer set.

"Tea, Sabrina?" she asked.

I nodded, though I wasn't too crazy about trying whatever she had in that pot. She filled each of our cups with the steaming drink and took her seat.

"Is your husband—" I didn't want to say *dead*, though I had a feeling Cornelius was long gone.

"In limbo," Twila said. "Over ten years now."

What exactly did she mean by that? I wasn't surprised when she went on to explain.

"You know, some souls are not given entry to heaven or hell. Poor Connie is in that state, and I need to figure out how to get him past this point before I die so that we can both go to heaven."

I nodded with what I hoped was an understanding expression, though I guessed the whites of my eyes were showing in a big way.

"The souls of the dead revisit their homes, you know." Twila poured cream into her cup and picked up a spoon.

She kept saying I knew things that I'd never even thought about and didn't believe for a second. I curled my hands around my teacup to warm them.

"That's very interesting."

"Dear Connie showed up on Halloween eight years ago. It was dinnertime, and I'd fixed his favorite pot roast."

Max may have been right when he'd named Twila as a person who knew the most about the goings-on in Lavender thirty years ago. But this woman was loony tunes, fixing dinner for a dead husband and believing that he had showed up years after his death. She might not know one thing about what happened in the real world over the past week.

No way was I going to ask if Connie ate some of the pot roast, so I said, "I'm sure you miss him very much."

"I do, but I trust he will return. He didn't come back the next Halloween or on any Halloween since then. Not yet. But he will, so I've decided to act like it's Halloween every day to be ready when he comes."

I stifled the urge to roll my eyes. "Good idea."

Twila leaned forward and fixed her cloudy blue eyes on me. "I'm hopeful that you'll be able to help us."

A shiver crawled up my spine. "Me? How?"

"Well, you're a witch, my dear, and now you've been re-united with your black cat. I believe it's in your power to restore Connie's soul."

14

SLID MY CHAIR back so fast it nearly toppled backward. "I am *not* a witch, and I don't know what on earth would make you suggest such a thing."

"Your name, for one," Twila said.

"Ha-ha. That's not a good reason."

When I was in high school, kids had teased me at times about my name, given that there was a TV witch named Sabrina. I hadn't expected the same joke from an eighty-year-old woman. I studied Twila's face—she wasn't kidding.

"Don't worry," she said. "I won't tell a soul."

One thing was for sure. I really should have reviewed the synopsis for my novel earlier, because whatever I wrote was liable to sound pretty boring after meeting this lady. I wasn't sure how best to handle her.

"I'm sorry, Twila," I said. "There's nothing I can do to help you and your late husband."

She smiled. "I understand this isn't the best time. You're

troubled. Perhaps after the murder is solved your powers will be stronger. Then we can readdress this issue."

Of course she knew about Bobby Joe. I was pretty sure everyone in Lavender knew. If only I could get her off this witch hang-up.

I leaned forward and was about to change the subject when a burst of male laughter startled me. I prayed the sound had nothing to do with the churchgoing skeleton I'd spotted when I came in. Thankfully, a live man, pudgy and fiftyish and wearing a denim short-sleeved shirt, walked out of the shadows toward us. He had a cell phone to his ear.

"We can have the settee you're looking for by the middle of the week," he said into the phone. "I located one up in Amarillo, and it's in pretty good shape."

After listening for a beat, he said, "Sounds like a plan. I'll get back to you."

He ended the call and turned to us with a smile.

"Mom, have you been sharing your tall tales about Dad with this young lady?" He looked at me. "Sorry if she bothered you. Some people are interested, most aren't."

He extended a hand. "I'm Ernie Baxter."

He looked like a relatively normal and sane person. I accepted the handshake and introduced myself.

"I don't mind listening to stories," I said, "except for the part where your mother called me a witch."

Ernie chuckled. "Your name's Sabrina?"

"That's right."

"I'm not surprised she'd make that connection. Mom's a big sitcom fan, always has been. Right, Mom?"

Twila played deaf and twirled her teacup on the saucer.

Ernie was probably accustomed to the silent treatment. He turned to me. "Now, Sabrina, are you looking for anything specific?"

"What?" It took me a second to catch his meaning. "Oh, I wasn't shopping. I came to talk to your mother."

Twila nodded. "About Bobby Joe Flowers and Vicki Palmer."

My heart rate kicked up. How could she know I wanted to talk about Vicki?

Ernie said, "I knew Flowers back in the day. He was a few years behind me in school."

I dragged my gaze away from Twila.

"Then you might be able to help," I said to Ernie. "I'm trying to find out where Bobby Joe was staying while he was in town."

The man shrugged. "I've been busy here at the store. I didn't even know Bobby Joe was around till I heard about his death."

I looked at Twila. "Amos Whittle said you told him a story about Bobby Joe being at The Wild Pony Saloon."

Twila said, "I only repeated to Amos what I heard from my son."

I ping-ponged back to Ernie.

He said, "That would have been my brother, Eddie."

"Ernest is my eldest son," Twila said, "by about six minutes."

My brows scrunched together, but Ernie quickly cleared up my confusion.

"I'm an identical twin," he explained. "The responsible one, the one who helps Mom run this place. Eddie's the care-free twin, the one who sleeps past noon every day and doesn't give a— You catch my drift."

I nodded. "Got it."

"We don't favor each other as much as we used to as kids," he said, "but you might recognize Eddie if you see him around town."

Now that he mentioned it, there *was* something slightly familiar about Ernie. Maybe I had run across the brother somewhere.

"Eddie shoots pool at The Wild Pony most every night," Ernie said. "If anyone knows what goes on at that bar, you can bet it's my brother."

"Where does he live?" I said.

"Here and there." Ernie shrugged again. "I'd say wherever he can find a bed. We don't see much of him. If I do, I can tell him to give you a shout."

"I'd appreciate that." I gave Ernie my cell number and he stored it in his phone's memory. "If your brother saw Bobby Joe with a woman, I'd be interested in knowing who she is."

"Sure thing," Ernie said, then excused himself to get back to work.

After he walked away, Twila said, "Bobby Joe Flowers thought himself quite the ladies' man as a teenager. Used to take girls out to his grandparents' cottages by the river during the off-season."

"Really?" The cottages had been quite a bit more rustic back then. Aunt Rowe had refurbished them about ten years ago. Teenagers probably didn't care about the decor, though, only that the cottages provided a place for them to be alone.

"One of his girls was our neighbor at the time," Twila said. "She'd climb out her bedroom window and take off with him."

"Was it Vicki Palmer?" I wondered if my fictional brainstorming earlier had been on point.

"No," Twila said. "Vicki was a sweet little thing, not the type to fall for Bobby Joe's antics, though she might have been better off. Poor girl dated a boy who roughed her up."

"Is that who killed her?" I had to ask, though if that were the case, the sheriff would have likely solved the crime.

"No, the boy moved away, but not till after he had terrorized Vicki on a regular basis. The sheriff finally ran him out of town."

Now there was something I thought only happened in the movies. In films, though, the villain always came back to finish what he'd started.

I said, "How did the sheriff know this guy didn't come back to hurt Vicki?"

"He was locked up when she died," Twila said, "for assaulting another girl in his new hometown."

I wondered about the odds of Vicki dating one bad boy, then being killed after he was out of the picture by a second bad boy. Maybe Vicki's relatives could shed more light on what had happened back then.

"Do you know Vicki's parents?" I said.

"Not well," Twila said. "They moved away after Vicki died. Opened a produce stand just this side of Riverview."

"Perhaps putting some distance between themselves and the tragedy has helped the family heal."

"Didn't help Vicki any," Twila said. "She and my dear husband are both restless, waiting on someone with the right powers to bring them peace."

Like these deceased people were comparing notes and reporting back to the living. Give me a break.

Twila looked at me, her eyebrows raised.

"Don't start," I warned her. "I am no witch, and I have no powers. I do have one more question for you, though, before I leave." I grabbed my tote and stood.

"What is it, my dear?"

"You said my name was one reason you thought I'm a witch. Do you have another reason?"

"Of course," Twila said. "You live very near the home place of Hildegard Vesta."

"Who's that?"

"Hildegard was a witch who came to Lavender in the sixties. I'm sure you've heard the legend. She and the bad luck cat lived on the banks of the Glidden River."

I should have left it alone, but I'd come this far, and her mention of a bad luck cat bugged the heck out of me.

"Why would anyone claim her cat was bad luck?"

Twila clucked her tongue. "He was, and he still is. Back then, shortly after Hildegard and the cat moved in, torrential rains came. Much of the town flooded."

"Everyone knows the hill country is prone to flash flooding when we have a downpour," I said. "People truly blamed the flood on a cat?"

"The flood and many other strokes of bad luck," she said, "even today."

I sighed. "If there was such a thing as a cat that causes bad luck, which there is *not*, that same cat is *not* here today."

"Of course he is, my dear."

"What on earth makes you think so?"

"He's sitting outside on your car as we speak, big as life."

I told Twila good-bye and hightailed it out to my car.

Sure enough, there was a black cat sitting on the roof, but not some cat Twila knew from the sixties. It was Hitchcock. He had a familiar way of cocking his head when he looked at me. His tail swished across the metal roof.

I approached the car slowly and glanced around me to make sure we had no witnesses, other than Twila, who would end up accusing me of harboring the town's legendary bad luck cat.

"Hitchcock, you have no idea what kind of rumors you're starting by sitting out here in broad daylight," I said.

The cat's eyes slitted, and he meowed at me.

"Oh, you think this is funny?"

I inched closer to the car. Hitchcock sat near the driver's

side door, and we were nearly eye level to each other. "I sure wish you'd stayed at my place. You can't trust everyone. Only me, you can trust me."

I held out my hand, palm up, over the edge of the car roof. Hitchcock stood and stretched. He tentatively walked closer to my hand and bent his head to sniff at my fingers.

My phone blared the Pink Panther theme, my ringtone for Tyanne.

Hitchcock dove off the car roof. I ran around the car to look for him, but he'd already disappeared.

I sighed and answered the phone. "Hey, Tyanne."

"Tomorrow's the big meeting," she said cheerfully. "Is your synopsis ready?"

I circled the car and stooped down to look underneath. No cat.

"Well?" Ty said. "Did you write the synopsis?"

"Kind of."

"That's not the answer I was hoping for," she said. "I was going to offer you a critique."

"I'm sure you and your red pen are raring to go," I said.

"Aren't we in a jolly mood this morning?"

"Sorry. I will welcome your critique. Honest."

"Then what's the problem?"

"There's this cat," I said. "Well, actually, there *was* a cat right here in front of me, a minute ago, right before you called. Now he's gone."

"A stray cat?" she said.

"Yes." I nibbled my lower lip. "Well, not exactly. Last night he was sitting on my windowsill and watching me write."

"How sweet. And he came back to your cottage this morning?"

"No, he's in town."

"Are you writing at Hot Stuff?" she said.

"I was there earlier. I've come from a meeting with Twila Baxter. Got sidetracked from thinking about my book when she started talking about me saving her late husband's soul."

"Oh, my. How did you get mixed up with her? I mean, she's a sweet lady, but as eccentric as the day is long."

"You think?" I laughed. "She accused me of being a witch. Maybe 'accused' is the wrong word. She didn't seem to think being a witch was a bad thing. By the way, have you ever heard of Hildegard Vesta?"

"No. Should I have?"

"She's someone Twila mentioned. Forget I asked."

"What's all this about, Sabrina? Sounds like you've lost focus in a major way. Talking with Twila about saving souls. Chasing a cat. I've seen you avoid writing before, but this isn't the time, not with the agent meeting tomorrow."

"I hear you." I walked to the edge of the antiques store and looked down the side yard for Hitchcock. He wasn't there.

"I know you hear me, but you need to take action," Ty said. "How soon can you have a copy of the synopsis to me?"

"Later today," I said.

"What time later?" She paused. "Hey, what color is this cat you're talking about?"

"Black. Why?"

"Thomas Cortez passed by the bookstore this morning. Early. As I was opening."

"He didn't come to buy books, did he?"

"Huh-uh. He said something about a bad luck cat sighting. Wanted to know if I'd seen a black cat this morning. I hadn't. Sounded like someone called him to report it."

"That's ridiculous," I said. "What's he going to do? It's one cat. Black, gray, white, purple. A cat is a cat."

"Hey, don't get riled up with me. I agree with you."

"It's so aggravating that some people believe a black cat will cause bad luck. I feel like I need to do something."

"If you figure out what can be done, let me know and I'll do whatever I can to help," Ty said. "You'd better hurry 'cause Thomas was on his way to Krane's Hardware. Seems he and Wes Krane have a grand plan to set up traps and capture the cat they claim causes bad luck for the entire town."

15

TYANNE AND I decided that two voices were better than one when it came to protesting the trapping of an innocent cat, so I swung by the bookstore and picked her up on my way to Krane's Hardware. She looked perky in a blue-and-white tie-dyed top with royal blue slacks and matching Crocs. Saturday was her busiest day at the bookstore, but she was okay leaving Ethan and Billie Spengler, her grandmotherly part-timer, alone for a little while.

She said, "I take it you believe the cat at your place is the same cat Mr. Krane and Thomas want to capture."

I nodded. "Right."

"How do you know that?"

"I just know."

"How?"

I cast a sideways glance at my friend and knew she wasn't going to back down. "Okay, I realize this sounds crazy, but Twila saw Hitchcock sitting on my car. She called him the bad luck cat, and I think she's right. Not that he's bad luck, only he's the black cat that superstitious people around here *think* is bad. I have to do something to stop them. I can't let them take him away."

Tyanne patted my shoulder. "It'll be okay. You sound like the kids when they begged us to keep the fawn they found in our backyard. They named him Spot, and you've named this cat, huh?"

I grinned. "Yeah. I'd love for Hitchcock to stick around. Not that I'm set up for a cat yet, but I planned to pick up some supplies today."

"I'm all for you getting a pet," Tyanne said, "though it might be better if you found a cat that likes to sit in your lap while you write instead of such a wanderer." She paused for a few seconds. "How many miles does this cat cover in a day anyway?"

"I've wondered the same thing," I said. "I've read that a stray cat can travel up to five miles a day, but why would he want to?"

Did Hitchcock have a goal, I wondered, in making these trips to town to sit on my car? Was he trying to tell me something? I decided not to share with Ty the fact that Hitchcock had led me to Bobby Joe's body in the river. Better if she believed he was a completely innocuous cat that I wanted to rescue.

We reached the hardware store in three minutes flat, and I scanned the lot.

"Thomas's truck isn't here." I pulled the Accord into a narrow spot in the front row. "What if he's already left with a truckload of traps?"

"Don't panic." Tyanne opened her door carefully and squeezed out. "Let's go inside and see what we can learn. Worse comes to worst I have a customer who has a rescue group nearby. I'll bet she could assemble a team right quick to disable any traps these jerks might have set."

"Great idea," I said, "and maybe they could keep an eye out for Hitchcock, too."

"You bet."

We pushed through the hardware store entrance. Wes Krane wasn't in sight. Judith and Hallie Krane were each working a checkout register. Judith's hair was fixed in a smooth bob and she wore a stylish print blouse under her green apron. Unlike her mother, Hallie looked like she'd crawled out of bed in a wrinkled gray T-shirt, her long hair fastened in a messy ponytail. Hallie chatted happily with her customer while her mother exhibited an all-business demeanor.

"Is Mr. Krane here?" I said when Judith glanced up from the customer she was waiting on.

"Not right now." Her fingers skimmed the register keys. "He's making an emergency delivery—customer had a water heater burst this morning."

"That sounds serious." I turned to Tyanne and lowered my voice. "At least he's not doing you-know-what."

"What's he done now?" Judith had finished with her customer, and she had obviously heard my comment.

"We hope nothing," Tyanne said. "Rumor has it he intends to trap a black cat."

In spite of the fact that Hallie had customers waiting in her checkout line, Judith left her register and walked over to us, shaking her head and tsk-tsking.

"Wes got his ridiculous superstitious streak from his mama," she said. "That man would drive five miles to avoid a black cat. I know of a few others in town like him."

"Thomas Cortez for one," I said. "Have you seen *him* today?"

"I have. He was here a little bit ago. Thomas and my husband are in cahoots, I'm ashamed to admit, but the traps they plan to use haven't come in yet. Wes tracked the shipment. Due to arrive Tuesday."

I looked at Tyanne and blew out a breath. Hitchcock might have a short reprieve. That is, unless the men rigged up some homemade traps.

"You have a pet cat you're worried about?" Judith said.

"I'm offended on behalf of all black cats," I said. "Something needs to change. Treating them differently from any other cat is plain wrong."

"I don't disagree," Judith said, "but you sure don't need any more on your plate right now. You must be worried sick about your aunt Rowena."

"I'm concerned, yes." I paused. "You mean about her broken leg?"

"The leg will heal," Judith said. "I'm talking about the law coming down on her for, you know, what happened to her cousin."

"She didn't do anything." I couldn't keep the sharpness out of my tone. "And to my knowledge the law isn't saying differently."

"Good to hear, it's just, well—" Judith paused and held a finger to her lips like she wanted to keep the wrong words from escaping. "You know how people talk. Sorry I mentioned anything." She turned and headed toward her register.

People gossiping about what happened to Bobby Joe and jumping to conclusions about Aunt Rowe's involvement aggravated the heck out of me. I attempted to tamp down my annoyance. The hardware store could well have been a place Bobby Joe frequented when he came to town, and I hadn't asked the Kranes about him yet. Rather than criticize Judith for listening to idle chatter, I needed to ask her a question. She must have felt me walk up behind her because she turned around before I spoke.

Her brows rose. "Yes?"

"Did you by chance know Bobby Joe Flowers, the man who died?"

She thought for a second before replying. "Very vaguely. I wasn't raised here in Lavender."

"Oh."

"I remember meeting your grandparents, though," she added, "after Wes and I married. As I recall, they were good customers. Good people."

"My aunt Rowe is good, too," I said.

"Oh, I know that's right," Judith said. "I'm not judging Rowena. I understand tensions can get mighty high between relatives and sometimes things, well, things happen."

Tension was about to get high between her and me if she actually believed my aunt was responsible for Bobby Joe's death. Or maybe she was only referring to the crutch incident.

Tyanne took my arm before I could pursue the issue and said, "Let's pick up those supplies we need so I can get back to work."

She practically dragged me over to the shopping carts and grabbed one while still holding on to my arm. I glanced over my shoulder. Judith had returned to her register and was busy with a customer as if she hadn't insinuated that my aunt had committed murder.

"Let's hit the cat supplies before you hit the store owner," Tyanne said under her breath. We headed to aisle seven, where anything and everything needed for a cat lined the shelves.

With our cart parked in front of the wide variety of cat foods, Tyanne chanced releasing my arm. She picked up a small bag of dry food and turned it over to read the back. "Any idea how old Hitchcock is?"

"No, and I can't think about that right now. I need to figure out what really happened to Bobby Joe before half the town convicts Aunt Rowe on hearsay."

"I thought you wanted to get supplies for the cat," Ty said.

"I do, but—"

"Let's concentrate on one thing at a time. You need to get back to your book, too. Don't forget that."

I wondered when she was going to bring that up.

"I don't know how to guess a cat's age," I said. "He's definitely full grown, twenty pounds at least, but very lean. He's a tall cat."

"This is a good choice," Tyanne decided and placed the dry food in the basket. "And you should alternate it with wet food. Start out with small meals so he can adjust slowly from whatever's been keeping him going till now."

"Okay." I scanned the variety of cat dishes on the shelf, and my thoughts strayed back to Vicki Palmer. "You know I haven't been running around town blindly wasting time. I've done some investigating and turned up some interesting facts."

Tyanne was holding a can of food and peering at the small print on the label. Her head turned in my direction. "What kind of facts?"

I told her what I'd learned about Vicki Palmer and about Bobby Joe giving teenagers access to the cottages when he was in high school. "That has me wondering about the rest of the Palmer family and whether they somehow blamed Bobby Joe for what happened to their daughter. His death could be a revenge killing."

"Lower your voice." Tyanne loaded cans of cat food into

the basket. "You don't want to start yet another line of gossip. Why would this family allegedly have waited three decades to take their revenge?"

"Not a clue." I picked up two midsized stainless steel bowls for water—one for my porch and another for inside in hopes that Hitchcock could be coaxed indoors. I chose a smaller ceramic dish with a decorative blue stripe for the cat's food.

Tyanne had moved down the aisle to the kitty litter section. "You need some of this?"

I hesitated.

She picked up a litter pan and put it in the cart. "If you decide no, you can return this later."

"I want to bring him inside where he'll be safe," I said. "That doesn't mean he'll cooperate."

"If things don't work out between you two, my friend can help you choose a rescue cat."

I didn't want a different cat, at least not now while my heart was set on Hitchcock.

"There's something to this Vicki Palmer connection," I said. "I can feel it. Did you know the Palmers?"

"No." Tyanne hoisted a container of litter and put it on the cart's bottom rack. "I think you're getting carried away. You should leave the investigating to the authorities and keep that imagination free for fiction writing."

"Maybe you're right."

Tyanne scanned the cart. "I think we have the essentials."

I grabbed a wand with multicolored feathers attached to the end. "Every cat needs one of these toys."

At the front of the store, a different woman had taken Judith's place at one register. We chose Hallie's line, which was shorter. When we reached the counter, I piled our selections on the conveyor belt.

"Aww," Hallie said. "Are you getting a new kitten?"

I shook my head. "No, I've found a grown cat that needs a good home."

Hallie smiled. "I love to hear about people rescuing pets. You're a real good-deed-doer."

I pulled my wallet out. "No one's ever called me that before. Thank you."

She rang up my purchases. After hearing the larger-than-expected total, I stuffed my cash back into my wallet and pulled out a credit card.

Hallie swiped the card, looked around surreptitiously, and leaned closer to me. "I heard you asking my mom about the dead guy."

I leaned in and said, "Did you know him?"

"Not really," she said, "but the woman from the wine store does."

I straightened. "You mean Claire Dubois?"

Hallie nodded. "Yeah, she and Bobby Joe Flowers seemed close. They came in here once, and I saw them together at McKetta's Barbeque, too."

Tyanne had been checking out a display of vegetable seeds near the exit, but she heard us and came over. "Did you mention Claire Dubois?" she asked Hallie.

"Uh-huh." The girl nodded.

Tyanne said, "Claire's father told me this morning she's still missing. He and his wife are running the store in her absence."

I looked at Hallie. "When's the last time you saw Claire?"

The girl began bagging my purchases. "Sorry, I don't know exactly. A couple days ago?"

She didn't sound at all sure of herself. I said, "That's okay. Thanks for telling me about her."

We headed for my car with the purchases, and I punched

the button on my key fob to open the trunk. Tyanne and I deposited the cat supplies inside, then slid into the front seat. Before turning the ignition, I looked at my friend.

"Say whatever you want about my imagination working overtime, but right this minute I'm wondering if Claire Dubois has left town for good and whether she committed a crime right before she disappeared."

16

I DROPPED TYANNE OFF at the bookstore. Since she wouldn't quit hounding me about the synopsis, I gave her the copy I'd been carrying around with me all day. The draft I hadn't read since the printer spit it out. Ty would tell me the truth about my work, be it good or bad. Until then, I would go home and talk to Aunt Rowe. Claire Dubois had come by on Thursday. Her visit had struck me as odd from the moment I heard about it. Now that Claire was allegedly missing, I wanted to know more about her conversation with my aunt.

As I drove along the winding two-lane road back to the cottages, the brilliant midafternoon sun glared off my hood. I put on my cheap drugstore sunglasses and scanned the countryside for any sign of Hitchcock. Of course, the cat didn't have to travel by road. If he cut diagonally across properties between here and town, the trek wouldn't be as long as I had imagined. Still, it seemed odd for a cat to exert so much effort.

Cats normally liked to sleep away the day in a patch of sun-light, right?

I saw no sign of Hitchcock, or any cat for that matter, and my thoughts jumped back to Claire and the odds of her involve-ment in Bobby Joe's death. Not hard to imagine a relationship with him leading a woman to murderous thoughts. Acting on the emotions was a different matter entirely. Claire might not be guilty, but she could know facts that would lead to the killer. She might have witnessed something that scared the bejeebers out of her like Scarlett, my character who was on the run after witnessing a murder. The possibility worried me.

I turned onto Traveler's Lane, hoping Aunt Rowe would remember something from Claire's visit that could help to locate the woman. I hoped my aunt hadn't heard the gossip around town that she had a part in her cousin's death. If she had, she'd likely be in too foul a mood to discuss Claire. Because of those ridiculous rumors, I was even more eager to find the missing woman. I'd go straight to Aunt Rowe's house before taking the cat purchases to my place, and find out what she knew.

I rounded the last curve, nearing my aunt's house, and stomped on the brake when I saw horses in the road ahead of me.

My heart beat double time. I'd never seen horses on Aunt Rowe's property before, though I knew several ranches in the area offered horseback riding to guests. There were five rid-ers. A couple of the animals stood on the lawn next to a decorative section of split-rail fence accented by bushes filled with bright pink knockout roses. Aunt Rowe wasn't going to like the horses tearing up her grass.

Wait a second. One of the riders *was* Aunt Rowe.

I threw my car into park and jumped out, leaving the door

open behind me. I jogged toward the animals, and as I drew closer I saw Adam Lee standing next to the bay mare that carried my aunt. Lee was in a pair of snug Wranglers, a Harley T-shirt, and boots. He held his camera in one hand and pointed across the road with the other to a spot where I saw he had a tripod set up.

Aunt Rowe wore her Stetson duster with the chin cord, a chambray shirt, and her calf-length split skirt over timeworn riding boots. From this angle, I saw her good leg. How in blazes had she gotten on the horse with her cast, and why?

Lee took the lead of Aunt Rowe's horse and directed the animal across the road to stand beneath a majestic oak.

"Y'all stay over there," he called to the other riders. Only then did I realize they were the Hartman family—Molly, her brother, her dad, and his lady friend.

I marched over to Lee. "What on earth is going on here?"

He gave me a what-does-it-look-like expression. "I'm taking pictures."

I walked around Aunt Rowe's horse to get a look at her cast leg, which stuck out at an awkward angle. I removed my sunglasses and propped them on top of my head. "I doubt the doctor cleared you for horseback riding. Why are you out here?"

"Publicity shots," she said. "Adam's idea, and I thought it was a darn good one."

Lee grinned up at her, then turned to me. "This nice family was heading out for a ride." He nodded at the Hartmans. "Rowe and I discussed taking some shots for her new brochure, and they agreed to be included."

"What new brochure?" One of my so-called duties since moving here was to help Aunt Rowe with advertising and publicity for the cottage business. I felt a twinge of guilt for not having spent much time on the job.

Aunt Rowe said, "The brochure that will demonstrate how

much fun we have at Around-the-World Cottages. Right, Adam?"

"Right," he said.

I cleared my throat. "Uh, Adam, would you mind if I had a word with my aunt? In private?"

"She's all yours." He took his camera and rejoined the Hartmans.

"I don't understand why you're in such a snit, Sabrina," Aunt Rowe said. "I'm not actually *riding*, I'm sitting here on a horse and having my picture taken."

"Well, this isn't the best time for pictures showing *anyone* having fun at the cottages. Remember, there was a murder on-site. *Two* days ago."

Aunt Rowe waved a hand. "Nobody will know the pictures were taken right after the murder."

"The Hartmans will know, along with anyone else Adam happens to tell. I'm sure he knows about the murder." I raised my eyebrows in question.

Aunt Rowe nodded slowly. "He may have brought it up."

"Yeah, and he brought up he's writing a magazine article. What magazine does he have in mind, and what's he planning to include in his article?"

"I don't know." Aunt Rowe lifted her chin. "He mentioned a travel magazine."

"Let's hope it's not some publication like the *National Enquirer*," I said, "and his headline isn't 'Landowner Cavorts on Horseback Near Site of Slain Brother,' uh, I mean *cousin*."

Aunt Rowe's eyes hardened. "There's no need for such sarcasm."

"I'm only looking out for you, the same as you would for me," I said in a low voice. "As you *have* done for me in the past."

Aunt Rowe nodded. "Understood, and of course I appreciate you having my best interests at heart."

I smiled. "Good. Now that we've cleared the air I *really* need to ask you some questions about Claire Dubois."

Aunt Rowe scowled. "Claire? What about her?"

I supported the back of my neck with a hand as I looked up to her. "I'd rather talk face-to-face instead of with you up on that horse, but for the life of me I don't know how you're going to get down from there with your cast."

"Adam will help me."

I didn't like the familiar way she talked about this guy. I glanced at him and saw him posing the Hartmans for a family shot. Probably planned to charge them a hefty price for the print. I turned back to Aunt Rowe.

"According to Claire's parents, she's been missing," I said. "You may have been one of the last people to see her. What did you two talk about when she visited?"

Aunt Rowe shifted in the saddle. She waved at a bee buzzing near her head. "Do we have to discuss this now?"

I wasn't budging. "Yes. It's important."

Aunt Rowe looked thoughtful for a few seconds, like she was having to dredge information up from the depths of her memory. Finally, she said, "First off, she wanted to know why I turned down Jeb's invitation to the chamber of commerce dance, the one right before I broke this leg."

"The sheriff invited you to a dance?" I said.

"The dance, dinners, the chili cook-off," she said. "He's a very persistent man."

This was news to me. "Sheriff Crawford wants to date you, and you're turning him down?"

"He's a friend," she said. "And I'd like to keep it that way. You sound like Claire."

"Did she ask because she's interested in the sheriff herself?" If that were the case, I wondered how Claire's relationship with Bobby Joe fit into the scenario.

"I don't think so," Aunt Rowe said. "Jeb's quite a bit older than Claire, and they're not at all suited for each other."

"Has she ever visited you before?" I said.

Aunt Rowe shook her head. "No."

"Did she say anything about leaving town?"

"Not to me."

"Unless her visit lasted a total of two minutes, she must have talked about something else." Or they spent the rest of the time drinking the wine Claire had brought. I wasn't about to bring that up again.

"She asked some questions about the history of the area," Aunt Rowe said. "Wanted to know when the cottages were built, if they were always owned by our family. Matter of fact, we chatted about family for some time."

"Your family or hers?" I said.

"Both. Why?"

"Did she mention she was dating Bobby Joe?"

"Good Lord, no." Aunt Rowe looked down at me. "I thought the girl was brighter than that."

"Did Bobby Joe come up in your conversation?"

"Not specifically," she said. "I may have mentioned that he was the shady limb on the family tree."

"If Claire already had an inkling about Bobby Joe's true character, that might have been enough to make her break things off and get out of Dodge for a while."

Or she had a confrontation with Bobby Joe and ended up killing him.

I ignored my wild imagination, though I wasn't the only one in town coming up with groundless speculations. Some people assumed Aunt Rowe had killed her cousin, for crying out loud. The sooner the truth came out, the better, and standing here wasn't accomplishing anything.

"I need to leave, Aunt Rowe, if you're sure you don't need

my help here. I hope Adam doesn't plan to keep you on that horse much longer."

"We're riding out to the entrance," she said. "Adam's going to pose us by the sign. He says that will make a great shot."

"I'm sure Adam knows best." I rolled my eyes as I turned toward my car.

Molly Hartman waved at me as I drove slowly past the group. I waved back to the girl and studiously ignored Adam Lee. What was up with him, coming to rent a cottage and now suddenly involving himself with Aunt Rowe's publicity? That didn't make sense. I found his cozying up to her down-right suspicious. What if he had an ulterior motive for getting close to her?

As I neared my cottage, a far more disturbing idea crossed my mind. What if Adam Lee had come to Lavender for some nefarious purpose and Bobby Joe Flowers got in his way? Was that a crazy idea, or what? I pulled to a stop next to the Monte Carlo cottage. Now, while Lee was otherwise occu-pied, might be a good time to see if I could learn more about the man.

I climbed out of the Accord and scanned the grounds around me to make sure there were no people or horses in sight. All clear. I set my cell phone on "Do Not Disturb" and stuffed it in my back pocket, then hurried toward Venice. Lee's four-door Tundra was parked next to the cottage. I glanced over my shoulder. Still no one.

Perfect.

I turned back to the pickup and caught a flash of black near the front tire.

Hitchcock.

I ran over to the truck and found the cat perched in the open driver's side window.

"Hey, boy," I said. "Good to see you."

He responded with a meow and then jumped into the truck.

I peered inside. Hitchcock leapt over the front seat and landed in back. A gray sweatshirt lay on the seat next to an *Austin American-Statesman* newspaper dated a week ago. The cat jumped from the seat to the floor and pawed at something. I opened the door slowly so as not to startle him and saw that a black duffel bag had attracted his attention. Hitchcock looked up at me, then moved as far as he could from me and the open door. He sat down and watched the duffel as if he expected a mouse to burst from the canvas.

"What is it? There something about this guy you don't like?"

I patted the bag, trying to determine what Lee carried in it, but I wasn't in a patient mood. What the heck, enough of the guessing. I unzipped the bag and looked inside.

Tennis shoes. T-shirts. An iPod. Large padded headphones.

"Nothing exciting here," I told the cat.

Hitchcock meowed again, never taking his eyes off the duffel. I took another look, then shoved a hand deeper into the bag. Sure enough, I'd missed something. I pulled out a black device with a grip on one end and a plastic dish on the other. I'd seen a similar listening device when touring a spy museum in Houston with a group of mystery writers.

What did this guy need a high-tech listening gadget for? I put it back and zipped up the duffel.

I backed out and closed the door, then went around and opened the passenger door. Clicked the glove box and held my breath before opening it.

Whew. No gun.

Now that I'd found the listening device, I was on edge. I hoped Lee wasn't carrying a firearm on his person. I pulled out a handful of paper along with the owner's manual. An insurance ID card identifying the policyholder as Alvin Ledwosinski, with an Austin address, sat on top.

I placed the ID card on the passenger seat, pulled out my phone, and took a picture. Alvin Ledwosinski. Adam Lee. Huh. I couldn't help wondering if Lee was actually Ledwosinski. I could see this obnoxious guy using a fake, more cool-sounding name.

"What are you doing in there?" The man's voice came from behind me.

I spun around. It wasn't Lee, thank my lucky stars. Thomas stood there, wearing work gloves and holding a shovel in one hand.

Maybe not so lucky.

I prayed his hearing wasn't as good as mine, because I could hear Hitchcock purring not two feet away from where Thomas stood.

17

THE BRIGHT SUN hit Thomas square in the eyes, and I hoped the glare prevented him from seeing into the truck. A quick glance assured me Hitchcock was calmly sitting on the backseat, out of Thomas's line of vision. So long as the cat didn't choose this moment to jump through the open window, we were good. Except I didn't want Thomas to see that I'd removed papers from the glove box either. He might report my actions to Aunt Rowe, and she wouldn't approve of my snooping in a guest's vehicle no matter what the circumstances.

"One second," I said and stuffed everything back where I'd found it. I closed the truck door and turned around.

Thomas tipped his head toward the Venice cottage. "I hope Lee isn't in there."

"Give me more credit," I said. "He's not here, but let's move away before he gets back."

We skirted the cottage and headed toward my place. I felt

better now that we'd put some distance between Thomas and the cat. I looked at his shovel and, since I hadn't yet decided how to explain my actions, changed the subject. "What are you working on?"

"Steps to the river," he said. "Where Rowena took her fall."

"I noticed those stones seemed dangerous."

He nodded. "Like they loosened up or somebody moved them."

"Why would anyone have done that?"

"I don't know," he said, "but we're not taking chances. Rowena asked me to put up a handrail."

"Good idea."

"What's with Lee's truck?" he said.

I stopped and looked at him. "Do you know about the picture taking?"

"I've seen the dude with a camera."

I gave him a quick rundown about the horseback riders and Lee's photo shoot.

"I don't like it," Thomas said when I'd finished. "If he's shooting scenery for some magazine, why's he parked in the same spot for days?"

"Exactly," I said. "He'd be all over Lavender and move on to neighboring towns. I'm afraid it's Aunt Rowe he's zeroed in on for some reason. That's why I looked in his truck. His insurance is under the name Alvin Ledwosinski, which could be Lee's real name. Or else Lee borrowed the truck from a friend. Whichever. I'm going to check him out."

"Good," Thomas said. "Rowena doesn't need more trouble. Bad enough the law is after her."

I stopped in my tracks. "What?"

Thomas propped his shovel on the ground and leaned on the handle. "My wife has a friend who works at the church building next to the sheriff's department. She hears things."

"What has she heard?" I tried to swallow, but my throat felt too parched.

"Deputy Rosales is making a case against Rowena," he said. "An eyewitness placed her outside the night Bobby Joe died. Rosales knows he claimed to be her brother and how Rowena smacked him in the head."

"She didn't kill him," I said.

"I know, but there's more." Thomas scuffed the toe of his boot in the dirt. "Rosales talked to relatives. One of them said Rowena threatened to kill Bobby Joe in the past."

I groaned. "If she did say those words, she didn't mean it. Lots of people say *I could kill him*. No one believes they intend to do anything."

"I'm saying what I heard, that's all."

"Have you told Aunt Rowe?" I said.

Thomas gave me an are-you-out-of-your-mind glare. "Not yet."

"Which relative gave Rosales that tidbit?"

Thomas shrugged. "Maybe Bobby Joe's brother or sister."

"I have to believe the sheriff will push Rosales to investigate other suspects," I said.

"Sheriff is sweet on your aunt," Thomas said. "You know that, right?"

I nodded, but I was miffed that this was news I had only heard today. Thomas obviously had known about the sheriff and Aunt Rowe for some time.

"Crawford is honest and fair," Thomas said, "but if Rosales has evidence—"

He let that sentence hang, and we were silent for a few seconds.

"Aunt Rowe needs to hire an attorney," I said. "The sooner, the better."

"Try convincing *her*." Thomas picked up his shovel. "I'm going back to work."

"Don't worry. I won't let Rosales get the best of us. I'm gathering facts on other suspects. I have a feeling there's no shortage of people who wanted Bobby Joe Flowers dead. Maybe even this Lee character."

"Don't forget the game warden," he said.

I turned to Thomas, my eyes wide. "Why him?"

"Griffin was out here late Thursday evening."

"How late?"

"Eight or nine. I saw him in the woods across the river."

"Does Rosales know?"

"I told her. She's paying it no mind, even though she knows Griffin had no use for Bobby Joe."

"Why do you say that?"

"Bad blood between those two." He shook his head. "I heard they had some knock-down-drag-outs."

"I'll add him to my list." Griffin *had* been on my list, but I'd mentally crossed him off after our discussion at Hot Stuff.

"Let me know if there's anything I can do to help." Thomas tucked his shovel under his arm and walked away.

I thought about Luke Griffin as I watched Thomas trudge toward the river. Griffin hadn't given me a specific reason for the argument I'd witnessed between him and Bobby Joe. Nor had he mentioned he was here on the night Bobby Joe died, but then why would he? He was a game warden. I imagined his work was largely done outside. He kept his eye on woods, rivers, animals. I hated to admit he belonged on the suspect list, along with Claire Dubois and Adam Lee, but knowing he was in the vicinity of Bobby Joe's murder made him a possibility. Which reminded me, I had some research to do when it came to Adam Lee and Alvin Ledwosinski.

As soon as Thomas was out of sight, I took the opportunity to carry the cat supplies in from my car. I didn't want him quizzing me about them when we already had enough on our minds. I could have read him the riot act about his plan to trap Hitchcock, but I feared broaching the subject would have the opposite effect and bring Thomas straight to my cottage. I'd have to tread carefully.

I left my door ajar and emptied a can of grilled tuna into one of the new dishes. If Hitchcock wandered in this direction again, I hoped the smell would bring him inside. The cat and I were becoming more familiar with each other. I had to believe he'd let me feed him. Whether he'd agree to live inside with me remained to be seen.

I sat down and turned on my laptop. As I waited for it to boot up, worry for Aunt Rowe flooded over me. Maybe I should search for criminal attorneys first, probably someone from the city. Somebody top-notch. The prospect turned my worry to anger. Aunt Rowe should *not* need an attorney. She was innocent. I had to find a way to convince Rosales to look for the real killer.

With that resolve, I did a computer search for Adam Lee that resulted in so many hits I'd have been sitting there for a month if I tried to read them all. I checked a dozen of the sites before deciding to start over with the less common name. I typed in Alvin Ledwosinski and clicked "Search."

No matches.

I took a break to glance at my e-mails and saw one from Tyanne with an "Urgent" icon next to the message. The subject line read, *Synopsis Critique—Call me ASAP*. I promised myself I'd call her soon, but I wasn't in the right frame of mind to deal with that yet.

I stared at the computer screen for a minute and thought about similar searches I'd conducted as a paralegal. The law firm where I'd worked subscribed to several services that provided access to databases full of information about people and companies. I didn't want to wait until Monday to call a former co-worker and ask for help, so I took a chance and opened one of my favorite sites. Feeling only slightly guilty, I tried the log-on ID and password I'd used dozens of times before and, luckily, they hadn't changed since I left my job.

The site opened. Before I was allowed to proceed, I had to check a box that claimed the search was related to a criminal proceeding. Well, it *was*, right?

I went to the "People Finder" page and typed in the name Alvin Ledwosinski, then drummed my fingers on the edge of the laptop while the computer generated a report. My pulse quickened as I scrolled through every address associated with the guy, all in Austin, though none matched the insurance card address. I zipped past credit records and paused to spot a Toyota Tundra, last year's model, on the list of vehicles owned by the man. This had to be my guy. I reached "Possible Business Affiliations" and stopped.

Ledwosinski Enterprises and ALE Associates.

I opened a new window and did a Google search for Ledwosinski Enterprises.

Nothing.

I tried ALE Associates, which led me to a company website. My heart raced when I read the site headings. *Surveillance— Family Investigations—Criminal Investigations—Corporate Investigations*. I read the blurb—*ALE Associates offers a wide range of investigative expertise*. The company address matched the address on the insurance card.

"Dang it," I said aloud. "Did someone hire a PI to check out Aunt Rowe?"

And his name is Alvin Ledwosinski, not Adam Lee.

"Who would do that and why?"

I pushed my chair back, startled to catch sight of Hitchcock out of the corner of my eye. He was chowing down on the food I'd left in the dish. The sight calmed me a bit.

"You're a smart boy, aren't you, Hitchcock?" I used a baby-talk voice, as people commonly did with their pets, but he didn't seem to mind. He looked up at me briefly, then went back to the food. I stood, found the other dish I'd bought, and filled it with water. I moved cautiously and placed the dish on the floor near the food dish. He kept eating. I wanted badly to stroke his sleek black fur, but I backed off and sat in my chair instead.

I watched the cat as he finished his meal. He went to the water bowl and lapped eagerly. That made me smile, but my happiness at being able to care for Hitchcock was overshadowed by concern about the PI spending time with my aunt.

Should I contact Sheriff Crawford? Before I could make up my mind, Glenda tapped on the cottage door.

"Knock, knock." She walked in without waiting for a response from me.

Hitchcock streaked past her, out the door.

"What was that?" Glenda scanned my kitchen counter and took in the cat food and other supplies. "You got a cat?"

"Sort of," I said.

"Glad to see you're working on your book," she said with a big smile. "Tyanne told me about the agent meeting. How exciting."

"When did you talk to Tyanne?"

"She called the house a few minutes ago, looking for you. I told her you were probably hunkered down over the computer, and I was right."

"Why didn't she call my cell?" I felt my empty pockets then spotted the phone on the kitchen counter. Belatedly, I remembered changing the settings.

Glenda went to the phone, picked it up, and brought it to me. "Your head's buried in that book, and that's a good thing. All your hard work is about to pay off when you meet with that woman tomorrow."

I glanced at my missed messages from Tyanne and turned the "Do Not Disturb" off. "I hope so."

I considered telling Glenda what I'd learned about Adam Lee, but then she'd go off on a tangent and I'd end up discussing my suspect list with her, and she'd go back and tell Aunt Rowe everything. I wasn't ready for that yet, not to mention the time it would take.

Glenda must have noticed the faraway expression on my face as these thoughts ran through my head. She said, "Sorry, I've obviously interrupted the creative flow. I took some fresh towels over to Paris. We have guests checking in there tonight. I'm glad news of the murder hasn't chased away business."

"Me, too." That might change if Aunt Rowe was arrested.

"Come over for dinner," Glenda said. "I'm making barbeque ribs, one of your favorites."

Despite my preoccupied thoughts, the mention of her ribs made my mouth water. "Okay."

"Tyanne's coming, too," she said. "Six o'clock straight up. Rowe and I won't mind if you two discuss fiction. In fact, we'd be glad to hear about your novel. You can practice your pitch. Got to run now."

She left before I could respond.

I checked the clock and saw that I had a couple of hours before dinner. I had no pitch prepared for the agent, and I sure as heck needed to read over the synopsis before I saw Tyanne. So much had happened since I finished the draft, I wasn't even sure I remembered the plot. Maybe it would be good to let this news about the PI sit before making a decision on whether to confront him, go to the authorities, or simply wait and watch what the guy was up to.

I sighed, logged off the Internet, and opened the synopsis document. I hadn't even decided on a book title. I pulled up a list of ideas I'd typed ages ago. Reading the list now, the ideas sounded corny, and I knew some of them were titles of published books. A new idea popped into my head, because it signified how I felt at the moment.

Grasping at Straws.

I reminded myself that my goal when I came to Lavender was to devote myself to becoming a successful author. I wasn't doing a very good job of staying on task. Bobby Joe Flowers's arrival and then his death had ruined my momentum. I'd do better after the killer was caught and behind bars. But my big opportunity with the agent was tomorrow. Tyanne was right to push me. This was important, though not as important as keeping Aunt Rowe out of jail. I decided to let my investigation simmer for at least the next hour while I read through my synopsis.

It didn't take long before I was moaning to myself about gaps in the logic of my plot. No doubt Tyanne had picked up on the same issues. I started editing, and by the time I'd reached page three, I noticed Hitchcock sitting outside on the windowsill.

Glenda had closed the door when she left. I got up and opened it before returning to my chair. Within minutes, the cat was back at the water bowl. He took a good long drink, then sat on the kitchen mat in front of the sink and began bathing himself. I took a chance in closing the door, and the cat didn't seem to notice. The fact that he wasn't skittish with me made me feel warm inside.

"I'm so glad you're back," I said, happy that he was protected from Thomas for the time being.

My cell phone rang just as I sat at the computer and started typing.

I'd never make progress at this rate.

Hitchcock darted from the kitchen and jumped up on the

fireplace hearth. I grabbed the phone and answered quickly so the ringing wouldn't disturb him further.

"Sabrina, sweetheart, so good to hear your voice."

I slouched in my chair. My mother, who hadn't bothered to contact me in the four months since she'd married Dave Harrison in Fiji. I pulled the phone away from my ear and looked at the screen. Brenda Harrison. She'd already changed the name on her account.

Of course. Mom was not one to procrastinate except when it came to keeping up with her children. Last I'd talked with my brother, Nick, he hadn't heard from Mom either. I considered tapping the phone against the desk and claiming a bad connection before losing the call.

"Are you there?" she said.

"Yes, Mom. What do you need?"

"I wanted to be sure you're all right. I heard about the murder, and I'm hoping you're back in Houston where it's safe."

Houston safer than Lavender? What a hoot.

"I'm at Aunt Rowe's, Mom, and I'm fine. Better than fine. I'm working on my book as we speak."

Her exaggerated sigh traveled over the line. "I was hoping you'd gone back to the firm by now. Dave said they'd take you back in a heartbeat. Good paralegals are so hard to find."

My new stepfather, Dave, was a senior partner at the firm where I'd worked. Mom insisted they met well after my father's death, but neither my brother nor I was convinced.

"I'm not going back," I said.

"We'll be home by the end of next week." She went on as if I hadn't spoken. "Dad and I would be thrilled to have you stay with us. I mean, Dave and I."

"No thanks," I said in what I hoped was a civil tone. Whenever I talked to her I had to keep reminding myself of my age, because I wanted to throw a childish tantrum.

Mom seemed to have blocked the fact that she was the reason I loved the Hill Country. She had sent me to Aunt Rowe's every summer to get me out of the way. Aunt Rowe was the one who had taken pictures at my college graduation, encouraged my writing, and held my hand when I cried about my divorce. I couldn't say Aunt Rowe was warm and fuzzy, but she was exactly what I needed her to be, unlike my mother.

"We can set up a writing desk at the window overlooking the gardens," she continued. "It's the perfect spot to be creative. You don't need to stay in the Hill Country to continue your little hobby."

I wanted to hang up on her so badly I could taste it.

"I'm not leaving Aunt Rowe," I said, not bothering to temper my angry tone this time.

"I don't think staying is wise, Sabrina," she said. "Sounds like Rowe finally did it this time."

"What do you mean?"

"She's wanted to kill Bobby Joe for years. I'm surprised it took her this long."

Realization hit me like a brick. "*You* talked to Deputy Rosales."

"Why yes, I did. She called me."

"In Fiji or wherever the heck you are?"

"We're in New Zealand now," she said. "Yes, the deputy called my cell."

"And you told her what?"

"The truth, of course. I would never lie to the authorities."

"You told her Aunt Rowe threatened to kill Bobby Joe Flowers?"

"That's what happened," she said, "and that's what I told her."

This time I did hang up.

18

COULD HAVE ASKED my mother a dozen more questions, but I didn't want to hear another word from her mouth. What on earth was she thinking when she offered Deputy Rosales damning evidence against her own sister-in-law? Or maybe she didn't consider Aunt Rowe a relative anymore now that Dad was gone.

Her crack about my decision to write fiction came as no surprise, but I could never seem to ignore her jabs. Hitchcock came over and rubbed against my leg as if he knew I needed consoling.

"That was my mother, in case you're wondering," I told the cat, "and boy-oh-boy is *she* ever a piece of work."

I reached for the cat tentatively, unsure whether he'd let me touch him. Apparently he knew how to take advantage of a good situation and allowed me to scratch behind his ears. The cat was a lot more relaxed than I was, judging by his

purring. *He* wasn't worried about how Aunt Rowe would react to questions about the alleged death threat she'd made.

After seeing her club Bobby Joe with her crutch the other
day, I had no problem imagining her making a threat to kill
him. I'd bet it had been another heat-of-the-moment reaction.
Aunt Rowe was human, and Bobby Joe was a jerk, so she
lashed out. Verbally. No crime in that. Lord knew I was angry
enough right now with my mother that I couldn't trust what
would have come out of my mouth next if I hadn't hung up
on her.

"I'm not taking Mom's word on anything," I told Hitchcock. "I'll get my facts straight from Aunt Rowe."

I stroked the cat from tip to tail, and I swear he smiled
at me.

"Be a good boy and stay inside while I'm gone, so I don't
have to worry about you, too." I found a spot in a corner of
the bathroom for the new cat box. Hitchcock watched from
his perch on my bed as I gave him a quick here's-how-you-
should-scratch-in-the-litter demonstration. The cat probably
would have rolled his eyes if he could. Rather than come over
to get a closer look for himself, he turned in a circle and
settled down on the comforter for a nap.

He seemed so at ease that for a moment I wondered if he
had a home elsewhere. I hated to think he might have a family searching for their beloved pet, but I couldn't very well
put up posters announcing I'd found a cat. That would be like
hanging a neon arrow above Hitchcock's head, leading
Thomas and his superstitious pal, Wes Krane, straight to their
supposed "bad luck cat."

Grilling Aunt Rowe about her past with Bobby Joe was
more pressing, and I had just enough time before dinner to
get that done. The sky was overcast and looked like rain, so

I threw on jeans and tennis shoes and grabbed a light jacket before leaving the cottage. Eager to put this discussion behind me, I opted to drive up the hill to the house. The appetizing scent of Glenda's pork ribs with her peppery yet sweet sauce hit me the second I climbed out of my car.

Talk first, food second.

I waved at Glenda as I dashed through the kitchen and headed to Aunt Rowe's study.

She wasn't there.

I checked the screened porch.

No luck.

I walked down the hall and saw a light coming from the master bedroom, its door ajar. I knocked lightly and stuck my head into the room.

"Hello?"

No response.

"Aunt Rowe?"

I stepped into the room and saw my aunt dozing in the chaise by the window overlooking her cherished rose garden. She had a Lone Star quilt pulled over her legs, but her cast stuck out on one side. The lamp on the nightstand cast its glow over her, and I couldn't help but think how much older she looked in sleep than when she was wide awake and talking a mile a minute. Poor thing was probably wiped out from the horseback riding.

"I'm not dead." Aunt Rowe opened one eye. "Say something."

She might not be so eager once she knew what I wanted to discuss. "Sorry to interrupt your nap."

"No biggie." Aunt Rowe threw off the quilt. "Is it dinner-time yet? A person can only smell those ribs for so long before it's considered torture." She struggled to swing her legs round so she could sit upright.

"A few more minutes," I said. "I have some questions be-fore dinner. Between us." I pulled the quilt out of her way and began folding it, taking my time with the task.

Aunt Rowe fidgeted on the chaise and looked at me. "Go on and ask. Cat got your tongue?"

I was momentarily startled at the saying she had used often when I was a child. No way she knew about the cat in my cottage. I meant to discuss Hitchcock with her, but later. No sense hemming and hawing, so I spit out what was on my mind.

"Deputy Rosales was told you threatened Bobby Joe's life in the past," I said. "What was that about?"

"Wondered how long that would take." Aunt Rowe frowned. "Who told her?"

"Does it really matter?" I said.

She hesitated as if she couldn't decide whether to answer yes or no, then said, "Yes, it does."

"I'll tell you later. Maybe. After you fess up."

"Have it your way." She cleared her throat before going on. "It was a holiday weekend—Thanksgiving. Bobby Joe was thirtysomething, rebellious and loudmouthed. He never did outgrow those traits."

She paused, and I said, "Was I there?"

Granny and PawPaw had lived in this very house. I re-membered large shoulder-to-shoulder family gatherings with enough food to feed the crowd for a week straight.

"I'm sure you came to town with your folks for the holi-day." She smiled briefly. "You youngsters loved to race around the property, hootin' and hollerin'."

"Yes, we did, but I don't remember ever seeing Bobby Joe."

Aunt Rowe waved a hand. "He wasn't interested in spend-ing time with family."

"Then how did this threat come about?"

"Happened at my house, the Friday night after Thanksgiving." Aunt Rowe clucked her tongue. "Earlier that fall, Bobby Joe came up with some brainstorm to start a business. Said he needed a cash infusion. My husband—you remember Uncle Trace, right?"

I nodded. The uncle with the easy smile, perhaps due to the ever-present glass of Scotch in his hand.

"Trace was doing well," Aunt Rowe continued, "and he was willing to help Bobby Joe out. I should have known better, but we went ahead and loaned him some money."

Aunt Rowe stretched her arms overhead, twisted one way, then the other before placing her hands in her lap. "We opened an account for Bobby Joe. Later, we learned he'd drained the account in two days. There was no business, and he never intended to pay back a dime."

I wasn't yet hearing any good reason to threaten death, but Aunt Rowe was building up her steam to tell the rest of the story, so I waited. She tipped her head toward one shoulder and used a hand to pull it into a deeper stretch. My neck ached, so I perched on the corner of the bed and did what she was doing.

"Fast-forward to Thanksgiving week." Aunt Rowe took a deep breath and stretched her neck to the other side. "Bobby Joe came over to the house trying to weasel more money, but Trace wasn't falling for his shenanigans a second time. Then my jewelry went missing. Every last piece."

"Uh-oh," I said.

"I accused Bobby Joe, and he denied having anything to do with the theft. He'd ticked me off by pissing away that money, so I kept after him. Your granny's wedding ring was stolen along with everything else."

"That's terrible." I straightened. "Did you ever get it back?"

Aunt Rowe shook her head. "Breaks my heart to this day.

Should have kept it in a safe-deposit box, but that's neither here nor there."

"What did you do?"

"Trace and I went around to pawnshops from here to Austin," she said. "Tracked down some of the pieces at a place over near Blackjack Creek."

"Did they tell you where they got the jewelry?"

She shook her head. "Didn't matter. I knew it was Bobby Joe."

"That's really low," I said.

She nodded. "Keep in mind, this was shortly after Thomas came to live with us."

"Poor little guy," I said. "He always looked so sad."

"That he was," Aunt Rowe said. "I know he hated to leave home, but fourteen is too young to live alone. His daddy was working out in the Gulf for weeks at a time, his mama battling that brain tumor, God rest her soul. I'm glad we were able to help him out."

Aunt Rowe grabbed the crutches that leaned against the dresser. "Got to wash off some of this grit from the horseback riding before we eat."

"Need any help?" I said.

"Nope."

I waited in suspense while Aunt Rowe hobbled into the bathroom. From where I sat I could see her bend over the sink to splash water on her face. She brushed her teeth and ran a comb through her hair before coming back into the bedroom and standing in front of me.

"Long story short," she said, "I caught Bobby Joe planting the pawnshop ticket in Thomas's bedroom. I knew right then he planned to sic the sheriff on Thomas and that he didn't give a rat's you-know-what about what happened to the boy."

I gasped. "What a horrible thing to do."

"Exactly," Aunt Rowe said. "*That's* when I said I would kill his ass if I *ever* found out he did something so despicable again."

"I can't say I blame you."

"And I'll bet it was your mama who told the deputy this little story."

I grimaced and nodded.

"I'm not surprised," Aunt Rowe said. "Brenda was always a nervous Nellie. The gunshot about scared the pants right off her."

After a few seconds, I closed my gaping mouth and said, "What gunshot?"

"When I saw Bobby Joe go into Thomas's bedroom, I pulled my pistol and followed. I knew he was up to no good. I shot a hole through the wall right next to Bobby Joe's head. He needed to be taught a lesson."

Good Lord, this was worse than I could have imagined.

"I was hoping it'd scare him straight," she said, "but that didn't happen."

"Does Thomas know what Bobby Joe did?"

Aunt Rowe shook her head. "Better if he didn't."

That may be true, but I had a feeling Thomas had heard the whole story at some point in his life. Probably from my mother.

I wondered if Rosales would get corroborating reports from other witnesses. "Who else knows about this?"

"Chester Mosley," she said without hesitation, "Unless he's drunk so much over the years that he's pickled his brain."

"Who is he?"

"Chester was Bobby Joe's best friend," she said. "He was in the house that day. In the kitchen, no doubt. Kid was always stuffing his face and had the weight to prove it."

"What happened when he heard the gunshot?"

"He was at my side in a split second, looking from the pistol to the hole in the wall. Then he backed away with his hands in the air as if he thought I meant to shoot him right then and there." Aunt Rowe chuckled. "Claimed he wasn't in on the jewelry theft, though, and I believed him."

When I'd asked her about Bobby Joe's friends the other day, she claimed no knowledge. Had she purposely avoided discussing this episode? My stomach churned.

"Did Bobby Joe and Chester keep up with each other all these years?" I said.

Aunt Rowe shrugged. "Don't know. Why's it matter?"

"Chester might talk to Deputy Rosales and repeat the story Mom already told her."

"So what?" Aunt Rowe said. "That's ancient history."

"We're talking about a murder. It doesn't matter how long ago you threatened him. Aunt Rowe, you know I hate telling you what to do, but you need to hire a criminal attorney, like right now."

"What I need to do now is eat dinner, and you can bet your britches I'm not hiring any lawyer." She lined up her crutches and headed for the door.

"Does this guy Chester still live around here?" I said.

"Sure does."

"Where can I find him?"

"The Wild Pony Saloon," she said. "He owns the place. But for Pete's sake, Sabrina, why bother with that old coot?"

"He may know something that would lead us to Bobby Joe's killer, which would keep you out of a boatload of trouble."

Aunt Rowe turned to look at me. "Relax and go back to your book writing. The sheriff will take care of everything. No way he's going to arrest me. He knows better." She left the room, her crutches thumping on hardwood as she walked toward the kitchen.

The sheriff might want to take care of Aunt Rowe, but he wouldn't overlook evidence. I wasn't so sure he could control his deputy. A smidgen of doubt crossed my mind. What if Aunt Rowe really *was* guilty and counting on her relationship with Jeb Crawford to get away with murder? I hadn't heard a denial from her. What if Bobby Joe had pulled some new scam that sent my aunt over the edge?

I wanted to leave right then and drive out to The Wild Pony Saloon to interview Chester. Two things stopped me.

I'd heard The Wild Pony didn't open until seven in the evening.

Plus, I didn't want to irritate Tyanne any more than I already had, and she was coming to dinner primarily to talk to me.

Those ribs sure smelled great.

Okay, three things.

I found Glenda in the kitchen, ladling steaming pinto beans from the Crock-Pot into a serving dish. I could hear Aunt Rowe scuffling around in the dining room, probably trying to get herself and the cast situated in her chair.

"Hope you brought your appetite," Glenda said.

"Some people can't eat when they're worried to death," I said. "Guess that doesn't apply to me 'cause I'm starving."

"Nervous about that agent meeting?" she said.

"For one thing." I wanted to share my concerns with Glenda, but not while Aunt Rowe was in earshot.

The doorbell rang.

Glenda said, "Could you get that? It's probably Tyanne."

I went to the front door, steeling myself. I could always pray for my brain to miraculously kick into creative gear when she asked me to give my book pitch, but that was a long shot.

I'd have to admit to Ty that my book proposal was far from finished.

I pasted on a big smile as I opened the door, but Tyanne wasn't the one standing there on the front stoop. Another woman, red faced and puffy eyed, held a wad of tissues in her hand, and before I could say a word she burst into tears.

19

THE SLIM, SIXTYISH woman standing on Aunt Rowe's porch wore designer jeans and a turquoise top, accessorized with tasteful gold jewelry, bronze flats, and a Coach handbag. She was the most well-put-together sobbing wreck I'd ever seen. Just our luck she'd show up now when we were about to sit down for dinner.

"Is there something I can do for you?" I said.

She looked me up and down, then drew a big breath. "I *knew* you'd be younger."

"Excuse me?"

"I've been wondering. And hoping. Praying some, too, for all the good that did." She sniffled and wiped the balled-up tissues across her mascara-streaked eyes. "So now I know. You're the one."

"The one what?"

"The one he left me for." She lifted her chin. "The other woman."

I took an involuntary step back. "I am no such thing." Kind of funny someone would call me that, seeing as I wasn't even dating.

She blinked rapidly and studied my face. "You *are* pretty, no denying that. And younger, *so* much younger."

"Ma'am," I said. "You're mistaken. I think you have the wrong address."

"Oh, no." The woman's blond-highlighted hair swirled as she shook her head emphatically. Her tone grew self-righteous as she continued. "He told me he lived here, right here, at the Around-the-World Cottages, so there's no use in denying the truth, little missy."

I stepped down from the front door stoop, bringing myself to the porch level to stand next to her. I was a good six inches taller than this woman, whoever the heck she was, so enough with the "little missy" talk.

"Look, lady, maybe you should tell me who you are and who you're looking for, 'cause it's not me. Perhaps I can point you in the right direction." I gazed down at her. "Whoever *he* is, I can tell you for a fact *he* does not live here, because there's only one person living in this house, and that's my aunt."

"Oh." The woman deflated with that one word, and she hung her head.

I'd shut her up, but now what?

"You'll have to excuse me," she said after a few seconds of silence. "I've got no control over my emotions right now."

"You're excused." Curiosity more than anything kept me from stepping back inside and shutting the door in her face. "If you could tell me what's going on, I'd appreciate it."

"I've had more than my share of loss." She sighed heavily. "Widowed twice, and I thought I could never hurt so much again."

I hoped she didn't intend to go through her whole life story. "I'm sorry to hear it. What happened?"

"He dumped me. Maybe I would have gotten over that eventually, but then he *died*." She paused. "I can live without him, but I didn't want him to *die*. Every man I've ever loved is dead." The tears started up again.

Finally, enough information to connect the dots. "You're talking about Bobby Joe Flowers."

"Uh-huh." She wiped her eyes again and sniffed loudly.

"And he told you he lived here?"

She nodded.

A new thought gave me a moment of dread.

"You and Bobby Joe weren't married, were you?"

She shook her head and sniffed some more. I wasn't sure whether to be relieved or upset. A bitter widow would make a great suspect to take the heat off of Aunt Rowe. On the other hand, she might have come here to take revenge on the woman she thought had killed her beloved, and her tale of getting dumped was a ploy to get inside. Nah. Her tears and body language came across as the genuine article.

This elegant woman didn't strike me as the type who would give Bobby Joe Flowers a second look. But she had, and I wanted to know what he'd done to hook her.

I put a hand on her arm. "Bobby Joe was my aunt's and my late father's cousin. I assure you there was nothing going on between him and me. I'm so sorry for your loss."

She gave me a tentative smile through the tears.

"What's your name?" I said.

"Marian Kauffman."

I'd heard the name Kauffman before, but couldn't place it this second.

"And, Marian, you came here today to—"

"I—" She paused. "I wanted to pay my respects and find

out what the arrangements are. You know, for the memorial service."

I nodded. Jeez, we hadn't even discussed a service. Did that make us terrible people?

Before I could decide how to handle the situation, I noticed Tyanne's Volkswagen coming up the drive. She parked quickly and hurried up the walk toward us.

"Marian," she said, "What are you doing here?" She peered at the other woman's red eyes and blotchy skin and didn't wait for a response. "My goodness, are you okay?"

She gave the older woman a hug.

"Sabrina, why didn't you invite Marian to come in?" she said. "I think she needs to sit down."

"I was about to do that. How do you two know each other?"

"She's a customer at the bookstore." Tyanne turned to the other woman. "Whatever is going on, Marian, it will be all right. You'll be fine. Come on in."

"Wait," I said.

Tyanne didn't realize my predicament. Bringing in Marian, who was so enamored of Bobby Joe, to meet Aunt Rowe without paving the way first was a disaster waiting to happen.

"Could you possibly stay here for a minute? I'll be right back, promise."

"Okay," Tyanne said, but I knew by her frown she thought I was being incredibly rude.

I rushed into the dining room as Glenda placed a large platter of ribs on the table. Clearly she had made more than enough food to add one guest for dinner, but that wasn't the issue.

"What took you so long?" Aunt Rowe said.

Glenda chimed in. "Where's Tyanne?"

"Out on the porch," I said, "and she's not alone. There's another woman here, and I'm going to invite her to join us."

"Is it the agent?" Glenda said.

I shook my head. "No."

"Tyanne brought a friend?" Aunt Rowe said.

"No, Tyanne showed up after the other woman arrived, and it turns out she's one of Ty's customers."

"Well, tell 'em to come on in." Aunt Rowe picked up a roll she'd already buttered. "I take it she's come to hear your book speech."

Aunt Rowe wasn't picking up my nervous vibe, but Glenda was a different story.

"What aren't you telling us?" she said.

"This lady, Marian, is a former girlfriend of Bobby Joe." I held up a hand like a stop sign. "And let me finish before you say anything. She's super upset, brokenhearted because Bobby Joe dumped her, and grief-stricken about his death. We need to play along as if we're grieving as much as she is."

"In your dreams." Aunt Rowe snorted.

I threw up my hands. "In that case, Ty and I will take her elsewhere for dinner."

"You can't go out to eat when I have this table full of food," Glenda said. "Explain. Why do you want us to playact?"

"Because I've been trying my darnedest to find someone who knew Bobby Joe well. Who might know where he was living, who he hung out with, where he got the money he's been throwing around. Most important, who might have wanted him dead." I lowered my voice and looked at my aunt. "Besides *you*, that is. I'm doing all of this to clear you, because you're looking mighty suspicious at the moment, and I don't want to see you arrested. This lady may have the answers I've been looking for."

"She's right, Rowe," Glenda said. "There's a lot of talk about you and Bobby Joe around town."

Aunt Rowe slumped against the back of her chair.

"So I'm inviting Marian in," I said. "And if she accepts and joins us, you'll behave?"

"She will," Glenda said. "I'll sit next to her and kick her if she speaks out of turn."

"You gonna kick my good leg or my cast?" Aunt Rowe said.

"Oh, you." Glenda waved a hand at Aunt Rowe. "This should be fun, kind of like one of those murder mystery dinners."

"Right." I rolled my eyes. "I'll be back in a sec."

"I feel a bout of indigestion coming on," Aunt Rowe said, "and I haven't even taken one bite."

"I'll set another place," Glenda said.

I went back to the porch and found Tyanne had Marian sitting on a wrought iron bench under the front window. Their heads were close together, and I could hear Tyanne murmuring. She was an expert at smoothing things over, and I was glad she'd shown up when she had.

"Aunt Rowe asked me to invite you ladies to join us for dinner," I said. "There's more than enough food."

"I don't want to intrude," Marian said.

Tyanne said, "You shouldn't be alone at a time like this. We won't take no for an answer."

They stood, and Tyanne urged Marian along with a hand on the other woman's back.

"It's just me, my aunt, and Glenda," I said. "Glenda works here at the cottages, but she's more of a friend than an employee."

"That's how I feel about the people who work on my late husband's ranch," Marian said as we headed for the dining room.

"Marian moved here from Fort Worth a few years ago when she married Farley Kauffman," Tyanne explained. "She and your Aunt Rowe may know each other."

Marian shook her head. "Farley and I were such homebodies, I only know a few people in Lavender."

We entered the dining room, and Tyanne made introductions all around as we settled into our seats.

"I appreciate your hospitality," Marian said with a catch in her voice, "though I don't have much of an appetite lately."

"None of us do," Aunt Rowe said in a melodramatic tone. "I can't tell you how many tears I've shed the past two days. Rest in peace, my dear, sweet cousin." She bowed her head and put a hand on her forehead. "Such a tragic loss. I can't believe he's gone."

Tyanne looked at me and raised her eyebrows. I suppressed a smile. Aunt Rowe was laying it on way too thick. The plate she'd piled with food belied her claim of no appetite, but Marian didn't seem to notice.

"Where did you and Bobby Joe meet?" Glenda asked as she passed the bread basket to Marian.

"He was looking to buy property abutting the ranch," Marian said. "I was out riding, and I saw him sitting on a rock and looking out over the hills. Enjoying the countryside." Marian smiled at the fond memory. "He asked me about the area, and he was so pleasant. Such a gentleman."

She was the only person I'd heard say anything nice about Bobby Joe.

"Our family raises 'em right," Aunt Rowe said.

As we passed the food around, Marian put one rib and a small scoop of beans on her plate.

"Odd that he didn't introduce us," she said, "being that we lived so close. He and I dated for several months."

Aunt Rowe said, "He probably didn't want to share you with anyone else. Bobby Joe was *such* a romantic, so loving."

I thought about pitching a roll at her head.

Marian sighed. "I would have come to pay my respects

sooner, but I didn't hear about his death until last night. Luke likes to keep me sheltered, but he couldn't keep news like this from me forever."

Tyanne elbowed me. "Her son is Luke Griffin, the game warden."

"Oh," I said. "I saw him in the bookstore the other day."

Marian nodded. "Yes, he bought me some books. He's a sweetheart."

She thought Bobby Joe was a great guy, too, so I wasn't holding much stock in her complimenting her own son.

"About the services," Marian said. "Have arrangements been made? Will the memorial be held here in Lavender?"

I looked at Aunt Rowe, who had picked up a rib. She placed the meat back on her plate and said, "We have to wait until the sheriff gives us the go-ahead. Bobby Joe's brother and sister will have the last word on what happens and when."

Marian nodded thoughtfully.

Aunt Rowe looked like a powder keg about to explode. I wanted more information before she went off on Marian.

I said, "The sheriff needs all the help he can get to figure this thing out. Do you know if Bobby Joe had any enemies? Had he argued with anyone? Gotten into a disagreement lately that you know of?"

Marian frowned as she shook her head. "I don't know of any such thing."

"Was he fond of spending time on the river? I'm wondering why he would have gone out to the river that night."

"I never saw him on the water," she said. "The river doesn't cross the ranch property. We spent most of our time together riding."

"You say he'd left you," I said. "How long has it been since you last saw Bobby Joe?"

Marian stirred her beans with the tip of her fork. "A couple weeks, I guess. I really needed to talk to him, too. Even though he broke it off with me, and I believe he already found another woman, we still have our partnership to deal with."

"What partnership?" Aunt Rowe said, her tone stern.

"We invested together in a car rental business," Marian said. "It's in Dallas, and Bobby Joe took the signed documents to have a copy made for me. Since he was living here with y'all, I'm thinking that the paperwork is here, too. We signed everything about a month ago."

Aunt Rowe slapped the table. "And I'll bet you gave him some money for the deal."

"Yes." Marian eyed Aunt Rowe. "We were partners. Fifty-fifty."

Aunt Rowe shook her head sadly. "Partners? Girl, were his lips moving when he told you that line of BS?"

Marian looked at me. "What's she talking about?"

"She doesn't know anything," I said. "I'm wondering if you have any idea where Bobby Joe was really living. As I told you, he wasn't living here. Have you heard him say anything—"

"She deserves to hear the truth," Aunt Rowe interrupted. "Bobby Joe was a scammer, I'm sorry to say, but that's what he was. He cozied up to you, Marian, got his grubby paws on your money, then took off. That's about how it happened, isn't it?"

"Rowe," Tyanne said. "Take it easy."

Marian pushed her chair back. "I've heard enough. Maybe Bobby Joe wasn't what he seemed to be, but I daresay you aren't either. You don't know anything about the funeral service because you don't care. You didn't care about Bobby Joe at all."

"You got that right, sister," Aunt Rowe said.

20

AN HOUR LATER, Tyanne and I slouched on my sofa with bowls of peach cobbler, the dessert we'd brought with us from the disastrous dinner gathering. Marian Kauffman had left without hers. Aunt Rowe stalked off to her room, as best she could on crutches. After eating our fill of the juicy ribs, Tyanne and I had helped Glenda clear the table before heading to my place.

The printed pages of my book and synopsis lay on the coffee table before us, but the chances of my focusing on them right now were slim to none. Hitchcock moved from his napping spot on the bed and crept to the doorway to peer out at us, then folded his legs under himself and assumed his meatloaf pose.

"There he is," I said quietly. "My new friend, Hitchcock. The cat Thomas calls El Gato Diablo. Isn't it crazy that anyone would call such a sweet kitty a bad luck cat?"

"He sure is handsome." Tyanne placed her bowl on the end

table and studied Hitchcock. "Where do you think he came from?"

"I don't know, and I'm worried that he has an owner who's searching for him."

"Let's find out," she said, and within seconds she had used her phone to log onto a website for missing and adoptable pets. "You know Magnolia Jensen, the vet?"

"I don't," I said and shrugged. "No reason till now."

"Doc Jensen runs the rescue group," Tyanne said, "and she keeps this list of every animal within a couple hundred miles reported missing or available for adoption. Complete with pictures."

"*If* they've been reported missing," I said.

"Well, yeah, but—" She scrolled down the screen. "No black cats on this missing list."

"You're assuming that every owner whose cat goes missing knows about that site."

"Regardless, I think Hitchcock needed a home, and now he has one. Think he'll let me pet him?"

"Give him a minute. He'll probably come over to check you out."

"About the luck thing." She looked over at me. "You know I'm not superstitious, but y'all haven't exactly had the best luck around here lately."

"That's not the cat's fault." I took a bite of cobbler and licked the spoon.

"I'm sure it's not," Tyanne agreed. "Your Aunt Rowe might be causing some of her own bad luck."

"She *was* a little too gruff with Marian. It's like she forgets her manners whenever it comes to discussing Bobby Joe."

"That's not good." Ty picked up her bowl. "If Deputy Rosales hears the talk around town—"

I put up a hand. "Don't say it. I already know Aunt Rowe's

in trouble, but Bobby Joe was not a nice guy. If I can find out whose bad side he got on this time, I might find the killer. Seems to me Marian Kauffman belongs on the suspect list."

"Get real," Ty said. "Marian is a gentle soul. Her only fault is she's way too naive."

"That's for sure," I said. "She believes there's a business she needs to take over now that her partner is dead."

"Maybe there *is* a business." Tyanne shrugged.

I started to laugh that off, but realized this was something to investigate further.

"You're right. I could do a web search, but I'll bet Bobby Joe wouldn't put his real name on anything. If he *was* telling the truth about a business, he could have still been lying about the fifty-fifty partnership. There may be another person out there, or maybe even a different business deal with a different partner, who realized Bobby Joe was screwing him over and decided to do him in."

"That's a lot of speculating," Tyanne said, "and the sheriff's department's in charge of investigating, not you, and not now. You have a book proposal to finish."

"I'll get to that." I stuffed another spoonful of cobbler in my mouth.

"Show, don't tell," Tyanne said. "You keep saying you'll do it, but I'm not seeing any progress. It won't be my fault if the meeting with Kree Vanderpool is a bust."

"But it *will* be my fault if Aunt Rowe ends up in jail because I didn't research all these suspicious people who might have killed Bobby Joe."

Tyanne sighed. "I hate to say it, but I understand how you feel. So who are *all these* suspects, and what kind of evidence have you collected?"

Now it was my turn to sigh. My list was sketchy at best, evidence sadly lacking. I launched into what I'd learned about

Alvin Ledwosinski, aka Adam Lee, the fake photographer, who was in reality a private eye investigating God knows what. "He was in town the night Bobby Joe died," I said, "even though he didn't check in here at the cottages until the next day."

"Huh." Tyanne stirred her cobbler absently. "Let's say he *is* an investigator. You don't know he's here on a job. He might actually be here to take pictures and watch birds like he says."

"And for that he needs to use a fake name?"

"I don't know," she said. "Maybe he's sick and tired of having to sign the name Ledwosinski on the guest register."

I rolled my eyes. "So how are you going to excuse Claire Dubois, dating Bobby Joe one day, then fleeing the scene the next?"

"I have no explanation for her," Tyanne said, "and you don't know that she fled."

"I *do* know she isn't around. She vanished for some reason, and that in itself is suspicious."

"What motive would Claire have for killing the guy?"

"Maybe the same as Marian," I said. "A woman scorned and all that."

Hitchcock had come closer to us while I wasn't paying attention to him. He leapt onto the coffee table, scattering some of the manuscript pages, then sprawled across the remaining papers.

Tyanne laughed. "Yep, he's a normal cat." She held her hand out for Hitchcock to sniff. After he did, she stroked his head. "I don't suppose you have any mystical feline powers to help Sabrina solve this case so she can get back to writing."

"Mrreow," Hitchcock said.

I got down on the floor to gather the fallen papers. My movement startled the cat, and he took off for the bedroom, sending more pages flying.

Tyanne helped me put them back in order. "You know, Luke Griffin is a better suspect for your list than his mother is." She paused and watched me.

I kept my attention on the paper and didn't meet her eyes until everything was organized. "I guess."

I realized Griffin might have the best motive of all. His mother was in love with Bobby Joe Flowers, who had likely swindled her out of a bundle of money. If Bobby Joe had convinced Marian to marry him, heaven forbid, he might have taken everything. But he'd left Marian for another woman. Claire Dubois? I would have loved to drag more information out of Marian. Aunt Rowe's outburst had squelched my interrogation. I wasn't out of people to interview, though. Chester Mosley might know about Bobby Joe's business dealings.

Tonight was the perfect time to visit The Wild Pony Saloon and talk to Bobby Joe's old friend.

Tyanne wouldn't see it that way because she, unlike me, was focused on tomorrow's meeting with Kree Vanderpool. I'd have to make the visit by myself. Fortunately, the night was still young.

"I need to take a break from real-life murder," I said. "Let's work on my book pitch and the make-believe kind."

Once I'd made up my mind to visit The Wild Pony later, I was miraculously able to focus on my fiction, much to Ty's delight. She gave me her oral critique of the synopsis, and I pulled the document up on my laptop to make edits as we discussed tightening the plot points and strengthening my protagonist's motivation.

When she left a little before ten, I finally had a synopsis I could use. I had skillfully avoided mentioning that the first three chapters of my book were still marked-up with red-pen edits yet to be made, but I did promise to massage my short pitch to make it as strong as possible. She planned to call me the moment she woke in the morning to hear the final version. Even though Sunday was another big day for tourist sales at the bookstore and she would have business on her mind, I knew I could count on that call.

After Tyanne's car pulled away, I dressed for my visit to The Wild Pony. I switched tennis shoes for Ropers, chose a white shirt, fastened turquoise multistrand beads at my neck, brushed out my scruffy ponytail, and added a pair of silver hoop earrings.

"No critiquing," I told Hitchcock, who watched me with interest. "The bar will be dim."

I swiped on a touch of blush, added lip gloss, said bye to the cat, and locked him in.

THE Wild Pony Saloon sat about two miles from the center of town. I loved reaching anywhere I needed to go within minutes, a huge contrast from Houston, where every destination seemed at least an hour away because of congested traffic.

Judging by the large number of cars lining the streets, The Wild Pony was Lavender's Saturday night hot spot. I found a parking space in a grassy lot near the water tower, and when I got out of the car, noticed that the metal bars bracing the structure were lined with buzzards roosting for the night.

Loud strains of "That's My Kind of Night" drifted on the breeze, live music that didn't do justice to Luke Bryan's original version, but was a decent attempt. White lights outlined the front porch, maybe to detract from the fact that the place could use a new coat of paint. The front railing allowed customers who arrived on horseback to hitch their rides. It was unused tonight, but it added a nice nostalgic touch. The windows and front door were covered with bumper stickers advertising everything from Miller beer to "Kinky Friedman for Governor."

A group of young women stood near the entrance, smoking cigarettes as if they'd never get another chance. I averted my gaze, but felt them check me out as I passed by and pulled open the door. Inside, the place was standing-room only. I managed to wind my way around the filled-to-capacity tables and chairs to reach the bar.

"Is Chester here tonight?" I asked when I finally had the attention of the bartender and had turned down a drink.

"Chester hangs by the pool tables," he replied.

I nodded my thanks and continued fighting the crowd until I heard the sound of balls clacking together. Before I could make any more progress in that direction, however, I spotted a man a couple of decades older than anyone else in the place. I recognized him, and he saw me at the same time.

Leo Dubois turned away, as if he didn't want me to notice him, but it was too late. When he looked over his shoulder a minute later, he found me standing next to him.

"Hi, Mr. Dubois," I said. "What brings you here?"

He wasn't holding a drink, and I couldn't imagine he came to hear the band, now doing a weak imitation of Kenny Chesney's "She Thinks My Tractor's Sexy."

"Looking for Claire." Mr. Dubois practically screamed in my ear to be heard over the music. "You seen her around?"

I shook my head. "Sorry, no."

His wife had insisted Claire wasn't missing. Mr. Dubois didn't believe her any more than I did.

I leaned close and said, "You have a reason for looking here?"

"Looked everywhere else I can think of," he said. "She's come here before, I'm told."

"With her boyfriend? I said.

"Maybe." He continued to scan the room, his expression very much that of the concerned father.

"What do you think happened to her?" I said.

He looked me in the eye. "Girl has a habit of doing things she shouldn't, then she's ashamed of herself and takes off. Like this her whole life. Should be over it by now."

"What do you think she's done?"

"No clue," he said. "Let me know if you see her before I do."

Leo Dubois headed away from me, steadily scanning the room. I didn't buy it for a second that he had no clue about Claire's disappearance, but I wasn't surprised he wouldn't admit anything to me, certainly not in this place where he had to shout to be heard.

Did he think she murdered Bobby Joe?

Something to pursue later, I decided as I watched Leo disappear into the crowd. Back to my original goal.

Toward the rear of the building, I found a room with four pool tables. I peeked into the larger space next to the poolroom, where the live band played onstage before spectators seated at long picnic tables. Dancers swarmed a small hardwood dance floor.

I turned my attention to the pool players, male but for a couple of women who leaned seductively over the table to take their shots. I surveyed the room and, remembering what Aunt Rowe said about Chester's eating habits, zeroed in on a fiftysomething guy who weighed upwards of three hundred pounds. He sat on a high stool against the wall and held a supersized beer mug.

The big man watched me approach and took a healthy swallow of his drink. He had buzz-cut gray hair and wore a neon green T-shirt that said Wild Pony on the front.

"Hi," I said when I reached him. "Are you by chance the owner?"

"'At's me," he said with a slurred voice. "Hope you ain't another broad from the health department."

"I'm not," I said quickly, then jumped when billiard balls clacked loudly behind me as someone broke them.

Chester frowned and looked down at me from his perch. His chin fell into multiple layers resting on his upper chest. "Told the last one to take her list of requirements, with a capital *R*, and shove it up her capital *A*—"

A man's tattooed arm shot between us, making a chopping gesture. "Cut it out, Chester. Be nice to the pretty lady."

The man connected to the arm was another older guy, but slim and in good shape. He wore too-tight jeans with a brown belt that had a buckle nearly the size of a pie plate. The grin he wore as he gave me a once-over made me look down to make sure my shirt was buttoned.

I gave the man a tight smile and wondered why he seemed familiar. "I'm *not* from the health department."

Someone hollered from the pool table, "Eddie, you're up," and Mr. Belt Buckle sauntered to the table and picked up a cue stick.

I turned to Chester. "I'm a relative of Bobby Joe Flowers, and I came to talk to you about him."

"Bobby Joe," Chester moaned, then took another swig of his beer. "That river's wicked, man. He shoulda never gone out there."

"Do you have any idea who might have wanted to hurt Bobby Joe?" I said.

"The river took him," Chester said, "and swallowed him up like it's done plenty of folks before."

That wasn't what happened, but Chester appeared so

inebriated that I doubted I could get anything useful from him.

"Eight tourists in the past twenty years," Chester went on. "River might look like fun, but I say look again, that sucker is danger with a capital *D*."

He chugged more beer.

"Bobby Joe was murdered with a capital *M*," I said. "Do you know who might have wanted to do such a thing?"

Chester looked at me with rheumy eyes and said, "Them Palmers been out to get Bobby Joe for thirty years, man."

"Palmers?" I said. "You mean Vicki Palmer's family?"

"Shoot, yeah." He nodded, and the motion sent his body teetering. I prepared to jump back if he toppled off his stool.

"He didn't do nothin' to her, but they talk crap about him ever' chance they get."

I felt an arm snake around my waist and turned to see Mr. Belt Buckle had come back.

"Hiya, sweetheart." He brought his face close to mine. "Whaddya say we leave Chester in his misery and have us a little dance. I wiped the table with those bozos." He glanced over his shoulder at the cleared pool table and the other players clustered at one end.

The band was playing a slow song now, and there was no way I was getting any closer to this guy than I already was.

"You're Ernie Baxter's twin brother," I said, realizing why he looked familiar.

"Guilty," he said. "I'm Eddie, and you must be Sabrina, the not-so-teenage witch I heard about from Mom. She told me I'd be runnin' into you sometime soon, and here you are." He gave me another appraising glance.

I twisted out of his grasp, uncomfortable with him and the eerie suggestion that Twila Baxter knew I'd show up at The

Wild Pony before I had any intention of doing so. "I came to speak with Chester."

"Best wait till he dries out." Eddie took my arm and started toward the dance floor. "He gets delirious when he's drunk. We have plenty of time to get to know each other better."

I tried dodging him, but Eddie moved closer and soon his arm was around my waist again, fingers twisted around one of my belt loops. I grabbed those fingers and said, "Let me go."

"Aw, sweetheart," he said, "I'm cool. Give me a chance."

I writhed and twisted as I tried to disconnect myself from him, but he stuck like glue.

"Why don't you show me some of your witchy moves," he said. "Bet you got some—"

Before he finished the thought, Eddie's knees buckled and his legs were swept out from under him. Someone ripped his hand away from my waistline and took my arm. Then I was hurtled along through the crowd and found myself outside, where light rain was falling.

"C'mon," the man next to me said. "Let's take cover."

I was grateful he'd separated me from Eddie Baxter, but did I want to go anywhere with this guy?

I turned to him and saw in the glare of the lights along the porch that Luke Griffin held my arm.

He pointed across the street to what looked like an abandoned service station with a roof over what used to be the pumping area.

We ran across the street together.

21

"I THINK IT'S A bad idea for you to visit this bar by yourself on a Saturday night," Luke Griffin said.

We sat on a decrepit wooden bench outside the gas station, protected from the wet weather by the narrow roof overhead. Raindrops splattered on the asphalt, and faint thunder rumbled in the distance.

I crossed my arms, feeling defiant. "I came to talk with the owner, *not* because it's a bar."

"What business do you have with Chester?" Griffin raised his eyebrows.

"That's personal, and what's any different about your coming to this bar alone? Or is Deputy Rosales still with you?"

Griffin frowned. "Still?"

"You were together this morning," I said.

"No, we weren't." He shook his head. "She may have had intentions, she often does, but I worked all day. I'm still working, officially. I'm on the clock."

"Huh." He didn't owe me an explanation, but he'd given me one anyway. I felt stupid for bringing up Rosales. "What kind of work? I didn't notice any hunting or fishing going on inside."

"Game wardens enforce the law," he said, "and doing that takes me to a lot of unexpected places."

"Oh." I was digging myself in deeper. I studied Griffin's face. His skin was tanned from long hours spent outdoors, and his dark whisker stubble only made him more appealing. I averted my eyes. "Thanks for interrupting that Baxter creep."

"Best steer clear of him," Griffin said. "He's the biggest womanizer around."

"Bigger than Bobby Joe Flowers?"

Griffin leaned forward and planted his elbows on his knees. He clasped his hands and looked at the ground. "Second thought, Flowers was a lot worse."

"You won't have to worry about him anymore."

Griffin turned his head to look at me. "What are you saying?"

"I met your mother earlier this evening. She's distraught about Bobby Joe's death."

"I know that," he said sharply. "And I'm sorry for her feelings, but I'm even sorrier he came into her life in the first place."

I nodded, but he must have seen my not-quite-satisfied expression.

"What?"

"Why were you on my aunt's property the night Bobby Joe died?"

He straightened and met my gaze directly. "I was patrolling the river. People fish without a license. I write citations."

"You always go out at night?"

"That's when criminals get busy." He paused. "You think *I* killed Flowers?"

I shook my head. "I don't want to think that."

"But you're not sure."

"How could I be?"

Griffin nodded and resumed his elbows-on-knees position. We sat there for a few minutes, thinking our own thoughts, watching the rain, and watching patrons coming and going from The Wild Pony. I thought about Bobby Joe's death, Aunt Rowe's attitude, and the fact that people believed she was guilty. She was getting a bad rap. I disliked how easily gossip swayed people.

Aunt Rowe was innocent, and the killer was totally free.

And here I sat next to Luke Griffin. If he was a killer, sitting with him was infinitely more dangerous than going into The Wild Pony alone. Yet I didn't feel one teensy speck of danger as I sat here next to this man.

"I wouldn't blame you if you're glad Bobby Joe is gone," I said.

"Good," Griffin said, "because I *am* glad."

"So is my aunt Rowe."

"Then she and I have something in common." His eyes met mine, and he smiled slightly. "Maybe more than one thing."

My heart lurched, and I looked away. "Hey, when you're out on your patrols, have you ever come across small traps set up to catch animals?"

"Sure," he said. "Why do you ask?"

"Before I explain, tell me you're not superstitious."

"I'm not superstitious."

"Seriously?"

"No. Yes, I'm serious. I'm *not* superstitious. Why?"

"There's this cat," I said, "and some people—"

He began nodding before I finished. "The bad luck cat?"

"Yes. I mean no. He's *not* bad luck."

"Definitely not." Griffin grinned.

"I'm serious."

"I know you are." He put on an exaggerated somber face, which made me laugh. "Go on. Tell me. I'll behave."

"It's just, I don't want anyone trying to trap him, the black cat. He's a sweetheart, and he doesn't deserve—"

"Uh-oh, she's bonded with the cat," he said, as if talking to an unseen observer.

"Stop it." I slapped at his leg, and my face heated at the too-familiar gesture.

He looked down at the spot I'd touched, then over to the hand I'd quickly moved to my lap. His gaze moved up to meet my eyes, and his lips curved into what might be the sexiest smile I'd ever seen.

"Hey," he said. "I'm a cat lover myself from way back. My dog even loves cats, and I sure don't condone trapping them."

"I wish everyone felt the same. Thomas Cortez, who works for my aunt, and don't get me wrong, he's a good guy, honestly he is, but he's afraid of black cats. He has this thing about 'El Gato Diablo.'" I made imaginary quote marks in the air. "He means to trap the cat and take him away. Is there some law to stop him?"

Griffin shrugged. "I'm afraid not. People set traps for various reasons, often to keep raccoons from invading their homes, ripping the shingles off their house, things like that. And cats get into those traps at times. No way to prevent that."

I blew out a breath.

"I *could* spring any cat I ever come across in a trap."

I grinned. "Would you?"

"Might get me into trouble with the spay-neuter-release group in town. Maybe I'll only set jet-black cats free."

"I'd appreciate that *so much*."

He smiled, and I smiled back, and I restrained myself from throwing my arms around Luke Griffin's neck to show him how much appreciation I felt.

While driving home a few minutes later, my face heated again as I thought about sitting so close to the good-looking game warden.

Keep your distance, Sabrina. He might be the most accomplished liar on the planet.

I forced my thoughts back to the book proposal. Dinner with Kree Vanderpool was set for six tomorrow night, cocktails at five. I was surprised Tyanne hadn't asked what I planned to wear. Not that I owned much of a wardrobe since all my old law-firm clothes went to Goodwill before I moved to Lavender. They always made me look older, and that's the last thing I wanted at this stage of my life. Tyanne had dragged me along on one Austin shopping spree where I'd purchased a few things she'd described as "young and hip." I was pretty sure the term "hip" dated us.

I would read that synopsis one more time when I got back to the cottage. Then I'd ad-lib my pitch. Hitchcock would be happy to listen to me, I felt sure. I had to make a great first impression on Kree Vanderpool—my spoken and written words as well as my appearance all needed to shine. I felt giddy thinking that tomorrow's meeting might be a giant step to my becoming a published mystery author.

I drove slowly along the stretch where deer often crossed the highway at night, and watched the trees alongside the road for any eyes glaring in the night. As I followed one hairpin curve in the road, my lights spanned the woods, and I saw something flash.

Not eyes.

I checked the rearview and saw no one coming, so I braked and backed up a bit.

Drove forward and saw the same glint.

I was about two football fields away from my cottage as the crow flies. I could go on home, then try to walk back and find this spot.

Nah. That would take too long.

I pulled as far off the road as I could and parked next to the woods. The rain clouds had already passed through, and I suspected the drips I saw came from the trees rather than another shower. I rustled in my glove box until I found a flashlight and flicked it on, glad to see the batteries had a good charge.

If that was a cat trap Thomas had set up in the woods, I was going to spring that sucker. Maybe even pick up the trap, if it wasn't too heavy, and take it back home to hide it from Thomas.

I turned on my hazard lights and left the car to tromp through the trees and find the mysterious, glinting object. Wet droplets hit me as I went. My nose itched from the moldy smell of wet leaves. There hadn't been enough rain to make the ground muddy, and for that I was grateful.

A commotion in the brush sounded off to my right and sent me into a panic until my light landed on three white-tailed deer crashing through the woods. One of them stopped and stared at me for a few seconds before following the others. I waited for my heart rate to slow down before proceeding.

I aimed my light through the trees ahead of me, and before long I spied the object straight ahead. It *was* a trap, no doubt about that. I squinted to make out the details. I was no expert, but it appeared to me that the door was open. I wouldn't find an animal trapped inside, thank goodness.

There was an animal nearby, though. I could see its eyes. Something small appeared to be sitting on top of the trap. It looked like—

That's not possible.

I rushed forward as the cat watched me approach. For goodness' sake, it *was* Hitchcock. How on earth did he get out of my cottage? I'd double-checked the locked door before I left. Then again, I wasn't the only one who had a key.

Worry about it later.

The important thing now was to reach Hitchcock and get him home before something happened to him. When I got close enough for him to hear me, I began scolding.

"Hitchcock, what are you doing out here? Get away from that trap."

Before I reached him, I tripped over something and fell face-first toward the leaf-covered ground. My arms shot out in the nick of time for my hands to break my fall.

I groaned, rolled onto my back, and brushed my hands together to get the dirt off. Hitchcock ran over and circled me, butting me with his head.

"I'm okay, buddy, I'm okay." I straightened my arms and tested my elbows. "I don't think anything's broken."

He meowed and sat beside me until I rolled over and pulled myself to a sitting position.

I had dropped the flashlight, but luckily it still shone and lay within arm's reach. I picked it up to illuminate the area behind me, looking for the cause of my fall.

"There," I said. "It's a—"

Pole?

I stood and went back a few steps to brush leaves away from the object with my boot. An old wooden handle—the type I'd seen on brooms, hoes, shovels. I shone the flashlight down the three-foot-long piece to a splintered, jagged end.

I remembered all too well hearing about Bobby Joe's wound that could well have been made by a shovel. What if this was part of the murder weapon?

I knelt to get a closer look, not wanting to touch anything. Judging by the worn wood, this handle was very old. It might have been left out here long ago. On the other hand, if it *was* connected to the murder, that was good news for Aunt Rowe. No way could she have driven her golf cart to this spot in the midst of all these trees to ditch a murder weapon. I needed to call the sheriff.

I patted my jeans, relieved that my cell phone had stayed put in my back pocket. I pulled it out and with shaking fingers turned the phone on.

Hitchcock was still going crazy over something in those dang leaves. What the heck was he doing?

I punched in Sheriff Crawford's personal cell number and walked over to the cat.

The phone rang once, twice.

Hitchcock was meowing nonstop now and pawing at the leaves.

"Shush, please." I toed the leaves he was concentrating on.

And uncovered the business end of a broken shovel—the blade marred by a rust-colored stain that could be dried blood.

22

SHERIFF CRAWFORD ANSWERED on the third ring, and my words seemed to trip over themselves as I hurriedly told him what I had found in the woods.

"You have a reason for calling me instead of 911?" he said, in a tone a teacher might use with a naughty student.

"I found a broken handle, for Pete's sake." I shifted from foot to foot, though I would have preferred pacing. If this became a crime scene, though, I didn't want to disturb things any more than I already had. "I found the broken piece, and it was only because I heard about Bobby Joe's shovel-like wound I called anyone at all. Otherwise, it was an old broken pole someone forgot to pick up."

"A pole in the middle of the woods along with a bloody shovel blade," he said.

"I hadn't seen the blade end yet when I dialed your number."

"And where did you hear about the wound?" he said. "Those details were kept quiet—or were supposed to be."

"I, um, I don't remember where I heard that."

"Uh-huh," the sheriff said.

"Seriously."

Was it Glenda? Tyanne? No, I'd heard that bit from Daisy McKetta, who'd heard it from someone else.

"You know gossip travels like wildfire around here," I told the sheriff. "It's likely everyone knows by now."

"I wouldn't doubt it. Tell me again where you are. Deputy Rosales and I will be there in two shakes of a rabbit's tail."

"Wait, what?" In a panic, I looked at Hitchcock, who needed to be back in my cottage before anyone showed up here.

"We're on the highway," he said, "coming your way. Your lucky night—we were out on a Crime Stoppers tip."

Luck. Right.

"I'm in the woods between—"

At that moment a distant siren split the still night air, and Hitchcock took off. The cat disappeared into the woods, and I could only hope he would head back to my place.

"You'll see my car parked beside the road with the flashers going," I said, "about a mile out from Traveler's Lane."

"Got it," the sheriff said and hung up.

I slumped against a tree and attempted to spot Hitchcock with my flashlight. He was out of sight, but I wouldn't put it past him to climb a tree and watch the action from above. The little dickens was smart enough to sit on a trap instead of being caught in one, and that was a good thing.

The happy realization wasn't enough to calm me, not after what I'd uncovered. The thought of the killer using this very shovel to bash Bobby Joe's head hard enough to break the handle had me feeling queasy.

I kept my flashlight turned on so the sheriff could spot me easily. A couple of minutes later the siren turned off. Two beams of light streamed through the woods in my direction. Just my luck Deputy Rosales was out with Sheriff Crawford tonight. Maybe she wouldn't be quite so testy in his company.

I straightened as they reached my position in the woods. The sheriff and Rosales were both in jeans and sheriff's department rain jackets, though the rain had stopped.

Sheriff Crawford tipped the bill of his Texas Rangers ball cap to me. "Evening, Sabrina."

Rosales said, "You again."

So much for hoping she'd be polite this time.

I pointed toward the place where I'd fallen. "That disturbance in the leaves is where I fell after tripping over the broken handle."

"So you messed with the scene," Rosales said.

The sheriff looked at her and said, "She stumbled onto the scene."

Rosales gave him a look, and I could tell she was itching to dispute him, but she didn't respond.

"Stay here," the sheriff told me, "while we look around."

I went back to my tree and ignored the glare Rosales sent my way before she followed the sheriff to the shovel.

They spent a good ten minutes inspecting the broken handle, the shovel blade, and every leaf and fallen limb around them without picking anything up. Then the sheriff sent Rosales to their car for crime scene tape and their evidence kit.

She headed toward the road, and Sheriff Crawford came over to me.

"Your instincts were right on," he said. "Chances are we have the weapon that killed Flowers."

I let out the breath I'd been holding. "How can you tell?"

"It's definitely blood on the blade, along with a few strands of hair."

I cringed.

"What brought you out into the woods tonight?" he said.

"I was driving home, and I saw that." I pointed to the trap.

"You saw it from the road?"

"I did. My headlights caught a glint of metal. Of course, I didn't know it was a trap until I got in here."

"It's a rainy night, and you got out of your car to traipse into the woods to look at a trap?" His tone grew more skeptical by the second.

"The rain had stopped, and I've been a little paranoid about traps the past few days."

"Why?"

"Because, um, well, you've heard about the bad luck cat, right?"

Sheriff Crawford's thick eyebrows drew together. "I don't pay such things any mind."

"I didn't either until people started talking about trapping this black cat, and that's wrong."

I could tell I sounded like a petulant child, but I couldn't help it.

"We're not out here because of the trap, Sabrina," he said. "Did you touch the handle?"

I frowned at him. "Of course not."

"Good. Then we won't find your fingerprints on it."

"No, you won't."

"How about the blade?"

"I didn't touch that either. I'm not stupid."

He smoothed his mustache with a thumb and forefinger. "Have you ever seen these items before?"

I shook my head. "What are you getting at?"

"Asking a simple question, that's all."

"Sounds to me like you're trying to make something more

of this than what it is. I came out here to look at the trap, tripped on the shovel handle, then I called you."

"Okay," he said.

"If you're thinking I had anything to do with putting these things out here before I called to alert you, then you're mistaken."

"I didn't say any such thing."

I huffed and crossed my arms over my chest. "Good."

"Actually, Sabrina, you can go home now if you like. Thank you for reporting this."

I wanted to go, but I sure wished I knew what the sheriff had on his mind. With this discovery, Aunt Rowe should be off the suspect grid, but where would that leave the sheriff's department investigation? Did they have any of the same information I'd uncovered? I couldn't trust that they did.

"I hope you're getting close to finding the killer," I said. "I've learned some disturbing things in the past few days."

"Like what?"

He wouldn't want to hear Chester Mosley's claim that the Palmer family was out to get Bobby Joe, especially since Chester was practically falling-down drunk when he'd told me.

I didn't want to mention Luke Griffin's mother. The sheriff had already warned me off discussing Griffin around Rosales, and I was hoping I'd never have to point any fingers in Griffin's direction.

Claire Dubois was fair game, so I asked the sheriff if he knew about Claire's disappearance or the fact that she'd dated Bobby Joe before his death.

"Her parents haven't reported her missing," the sheriff said. "Even if they had, I saw her myself a day or two ago. Not to mention she's a grown woman and entitled to leave town if she wants to."

"But she left right after Bobby Joe's death."

"Maybe she's mourning," he said.

"She'd have told her parents if that was the case."

"Maybe, maybe not."

He wasn't going for this, so I changed tacks and asked if he had talked to the man who called himself Adam Lee and was staying in the Venice cottage.

"I'd have to ask my deputy about him," the sheriff said. "She interviewed most of the guests."

Rosales's bobbing flashlight was almost back to us, and I wasn't too keen about discussing any of this in her presence. The sheriff didn't give me a choice.

"Deputy Pat," he said when she was in earshot. "You talk to a man named Adam Lee over at the cottages?"

"Nope," she said. "Don't remember anybody named Lee."

"He's renting the Venice cottage," he said.

Rosales reached us, and the sheriff took the paraphernalia she had lugged from the car off her hands.

She pulled a notebook from her pocket and flipped back several pages, using her flashlight to illuminate the notes.

"I talked to the dude in Venice," she said. "One Alvin Ledwosinski."

I gasped, and they both looked at me.

"What?" the sheriff said.

"He's using an alias," I said. "Adam Lee."

"No, he's not," Rosales said. "He showed me his ID."

"When he checked in, he told Aunt Rowe his name is Adam Lee. He's telling everyone that's his name, except for you."

"Is there some reason you'd rather he lied to me?" she said.

"No, but he's been lying all along. Did he tell you he's a private investigator?"

"He said he's on vacation."

I turned to the sheriff.

"PIs are allowed to go on vacation, Sabrina," he said.

I threw my arms out to my sides. "Am I the only person concerned that a PI is hanging around with my aunt and claiming he's a photographer? I know his real name is Alvin Ledwosinski, but he insists on calling himself Adam Lee. He could be Bobby Joe's killer for all we know."

Rosales and the sheriff exchanged glances.

"That's a big leap," the sheriff said.

I needed to tamp down my anxiety. I took a deep breath and blew it out. "I'm not crazy."

"Didn't say you were. I am curious about one thing, though."

"What?"

"If he's using the name Lee, how do you know his name is Ledwosinski?" The sheriff's dark gaze rested on my face.

I paused.

"And don't say you don't remember where you heard that," he added.

"Okay." I wondered how much trouble a person could get into for looking in someone else's truck, but I couldn't think quickly enough to come up with another plausible way to know the guy's real name. "He makes me nervous, always hanging around Aunt Rowe. He seems so suspicious, and I didn't believe he sincerely wants to help her create a new pamphlet to advertise the cottages, which is what she said they were working on."

Rosales said, "What's this got to do with anything?"

"Adam Lee is out there taking a bunch of pictures," I said.

"You mean Ledwosinski," Rosales said.

I ignored her. "Pictures of Aunt Rowe and the other guests. He cozied up to my aunt, and I don't trust him. I felt like I needed to find out more about him."

"So you checked out his license registration," Sheriff Crawford said.

"Something like that," I said in a low voice.

"Sabrina used to work in a big Houston law firm," he told Rosales. "Probably has plenty of tricks up her sleeve."

"I'll bet," Rosales said.

He'd given me an out, and I was grateful.

"Think I'll head back to my cottage now," I said. "One good thing came from tonight. Now you know Aunt Rowe had nothing to do with Bobby Joe's murder."

"How's that?" Rosales said.

Her snide tone sent a sliver of fear through me. "As you well know, Aunt Rowe has that broken leg and the crutches."

"And?" she said.

"She didn't come out here to leave this shovel."

Rosales continued to watch me. Sheriff Crawford had a weird expression on his face.

He's worried.

"She couldn't drive to this spot in her golf cart if she tried," I continued, "not with all these trees so close together. She wasn't here, period. Someone else was. The killer."

"Or . . ." Rosales paused dramatically. "Someone that your aunt sent to ditch her weapon."

23

I TRUDGED BACK TO my car and got inside. All the uncertainty was making me bone weary. I wished Bobby Joe had never gone out to the river that night. Or come to Lavender at all, for that matter. Which didn't mean he wouldn't be dead, because whoever killed him might have gone to the ends of the earth to do the deed. I wouldn't have tripped over the murder weapon, though, and Aunt Rowe wouldn't be on anyone's suspect list.

But Bobby Joe *had* come, and his murderer had likely crept around in the night very close to where I lay trying to sleep. For all I knew, I'd seen the killer in the flesh since then and didn't know it. I rubbed my upper arms to take away a sudden chill, then drove home.

It was after midnight when I pulled in at my place. Walking from the car to the cottage, I spied the glow of eyes on the front porch and picked up my step.

"Hitchcock, thank goodness you're here." I knelt by the

cat and stroked his back. His motor cranked into full purr, and I realized my cheeks were wet with tears. "C'mon, you, let's go inside."

I stood and unlocked the door, and he followed me in.

"Hey, how'd you get out of here in the first place?"

"Mrreow," he said.

I checked the cottage for an open window or a cat-sized opening I hadn't noticed before, but didn't find either. Everything looked exactly as I'd left it, so I didn't think anyone had come into the cottage in my absence. How the heck had the cat gotten out?

Hitchcock sprawled on the fireplace hearth clutching one of my balled-up manuscript pages between his paws. He'd decided they made great cat toys. I sat next to him. "Just so you know, I don't believe you're some Houdini cat any more than I believe you're bad luck, and if you're trying to make me crazy, you'll have to get in line."

For the moment, I shoved Hitchcock's comings and goings to the bottom of my worry list. I sure wished I hadn't mentioned Aunt Rowe out there in the woods, but it simply hadn't crossed my mind that Rosales would accuse her of involving an accomplice in her supposed murder plot. At least the deputy evidently didn't believe *I* was the accomplice, or she'd have happily cuffed me and thrown me in the back of the cruiser.

Sheriff Crawford had to be concerned about Aunt Rowe, but he wasn't in a position to allow his personal feelings for her to get in the way of a murder investigation. Too bad my information about Claire Dubois didn't interest him in the least. Her leaving town certainly made her a suspect in my eyes.

Unless someone came up with concrete evidence or a new suspect to steer the investigation away from Aunt Rowe, she was still in jeopardy. I thought about Chester's story of Vicki Palmer's family. They were excellent suspects, the whole lot of them. If a family member of mine was murdered and the case remained unsolved, I wouldn't *ever* let go. The same might be said about the Palmers. If no one else was going to take a closer look at them, I'd do it myself.

Hitchcock crawled up on my lap and reached with one arm to tap a paw softly against my cheek.

I patted his head. "I'm okay, buddy, and I have a plan. Tomorrow, I'll visit the Palmers and see what I can learn."

He crossed the room to the table and jumped up to take a seat on my closed laptop. "Mrreow."

I sighed. "I know. I'm supposed to be writing. Did Tyanne put you up to this?"

His whiskers twitched.

"I'll work on the pitch, promise, but I hear my sweet tooth calling. I betcha baking would put me in a perfect creative frame of mind."

The cat didn't reply, but I didn't care whether he agreed with me. I stood and headed for Aunt Rowe's big kitchen. I had a craving for Texas toffee cake that wouldn't quit.

THE next morning, I woke to whiskers tickling my cheeks. I opened my eyes and found Hitchcock standing on my chest, nearly nose to nose with me.

"Mrreow," he said.

I couldn't keep from smiling, though I felt groggy from too little sleep. "I suppose you want breakfast."

I raised my arm and squinted at my watch. Jeez, nearly ten. I never slept this late, and what the heck had happened to Tyanne? I'd fully expected a call from her to act as my alarm clock.

Hitchcock batted my chin with a paw.

I blinked a few times, looked around to get my bearings, and realized I'd fallen asleep on the couch. Printed pages were stuck between me and the cushions, and others had fallen on the floor. The cat jumped up to the back of the couch and looked down at me.

After baking two toffee cakes the night before—one to cut into immediately, one to take with me to Tyanne's dinner—I'd returned to the cottage, where Hitchcock supervised as I worked on my book till at least three in the morning. Afterward I moved to the couch, where I practiced my pitch on him until, apparently, I passed out.

I was only partially awake, but my mind was already racing. I needed to get on the road to Riverview soon to see the Palmers. First, I had to talk to Aunt Rowe. When I'd gone to the house to bake, she was asleep. I didn't see the sense in waking her to share disturbing news about the murder weapon found in the woods.

The screeching of a power tool interrupted my thoughts. "What the heck is that?"

I rolled off the cushions and used the coffee table to push myself to a standing position. I slipped into the flip-flops I'd shed the night before.

Hitchcock marched over to his empty food bowl, so I fed him before heating a leftover cup of coffee in the microwave for myself. Sorry excuse for morning java, but it was all I could manage. While Hitchcock was occupied with his breakfast, I took my coffee outside, careful to close the door behind me.

The weather felt like a hundred percent humidity under the bright sun. The scorching days of summer were almost upon us. I was still in my jeans from the night before, and they felt overwhelmingly hot. The tool screamed again. The noise was coming from the direction of the river, so I headed that way.

The water level was up after last night's rain. Watching the current and listening to birds singing in the morning usually puts me in a tranquil mood. Today, not so much.

Thomas was drilling holes into posts he had cemented into the ground alongside the river steps. He looked up when he noticed my approach and pushed the brim of his straw hat back. He wiped a shirt sleeve across his sweaty forehead and set his drill on the top step.

"Mornin'."

"Morning, Thomas." I walked closer and checked over my shoulder to make sure he couldn't see my cottage from where he stood. "What are you doing out here on a Sunday?"

"Alma took the kids to a play over in Emerald Springs," he said. "I feel better staying here to keep an eye on things. I'll go hang near the house after I make sure I have the right bolts for this project."

I brushed straggly hairs away from my face and scanned the tools Thomas had scattered around him. Boxes of screws, some supersized bolts, tape measure, and—

My gaze fixed on a shovel that looked nearly new.

"What's wrong?" Thomas said.

I hesitated, remembering his frame of mind the day he'd walked into the coffee shop to tell me Bobby Joe Flowers was coming.

Did I believe he got rid of the problem? No, surely not.

I shook my head to clear the unwelcome thought. "I'm having a hard time waking up, that's all. I'll go to the house with you. I need to see Aunt Rowe."

"She's gone to the play. Glenda, too. Said they'd be back by late afternoon."

"Oh." By the time I caught up with my aunt, I wouldn't

have to tell her anything about my discovery in the woods. She'd probably know more details than I did.

"If Aunt Rowe is gone," I said, "what are you keeping an eye on?"

"The Lee fella," he said. "Hoped he'd leave today. No such luck."

"Where is he now?"

"Downriver," he said. "Him and his camera."

"Watching birds, you think?"

"Nah," Thomas said. "There's more to him than that."

"You have good instincts. I checked him out. He's Alvin Ledwosinski, using the alias Adam Lee, and he's a private investigator."

Thomas shot me a look. "Where'd you get that?"

I told him about Rosales's interview with the PI who gave her his true identity and claimed he was visiting Lavender for purely touristy reasons.

"If that's true," Thomas said, "then why give Rowena a fake name when he checked in?"

I shrugged. "I don't know, but I'm glad you're here to watch him. I'm off in another direction today."

"Doing what?"

"Looking for any and all clues I can find to help the sheriff nail the killer."

"So long's you're not sabotaging my traps," he said.

"I haven't done a thing to your— Wait a second, did you say traps, plural?"

"I did." He frowned. "I figure you know about the crime scene tape strung up in the woods, and now the trap I had out there is gone."

"Well, I didn't touch it. I stumbled across some evidence and had to call the sheriff."

"So I heard," he said.

I breathed easier. Thomas wouldn't bring up the crime scene if he had anything to do with the murder, right? Or was he faking me out?

"You should tread careful," he went on. "This is not some book you're writing, and you could get yourself in a load of trouble."

"I'm searching for clues, and I'll keep it up until Bobby Joe's killer is found," I told him, then switched subjects. "How the heck do you have multiple traps? Judith Krane said the shipment wasn't coming in until Tuesday."

Good Lord, had he gone and built several traps because he couldn't wait a few more days?

Thomas raised his eyebrows. "Nosing into my personal business isn't going to solve anything."

I sensed that if I pushed too hard Thomas would only be more adamant about trapping Hitchcock and removing him from Lavender.

"I'm sorry you have a problem with cats, Thomas."

"Not all cats," he said.

"Okay, you have a problem with one black cat."

"That's right."

"Maybe you should see someone."

"What do you mean?"

"A psychologist, someone who treats people for anxiety, maybe a hypnotist, so you won't get so worked up about your fears."

"Maybe you're the one ought to be hypnotized, so you won't worry about El Gato Diablo." Thomas stooped to pick up his drill. "I need to work."

"I'm going to keep investigating, and I sure would appreciate it if you'd quit obsessing about an innocent cat, 'cause you're distracting me from what's more important."

Thomas didn't respond.

I stomped back to my cottage, frustrated with him and his stupid traps. What would he do if he *did* happen to spot Hitchcock at my window? Would he use his master key to go inside my cottage and take the cat?

Or maybe he was toying with me, and he *had* already gone into the Monte Carlo cottage last night in an attempt to capture the cat, only to have Hitchcock escape and run into the woods, where I'd found him sitting on the trap.

My worry list was growing unmanageably long.

I went inside and checked the clock. I'd have to speed up if I wanted to make it to the Palmers' place and get back in time for Tyanne's meet-the-agent dinner. I took a quick shower and dressed in a pair of denim capris with a yellow short-sleeved shirt.

Belatedly, I remembered my phone and found it buried beneath the couch cushions, where I hadn't heard it ring any of the three times Tyanne had tried. I dialed her number.

"Had a big writing night," I said when she answered, "and I have good news."

"Let me hear it," she said.

"My proposal is ready for Kree." I eyed the mess of papers around the couch and realized I needed to print a fresh copy. "And I baked a cake for tonight."

"All good," she said. "Let me hear the pitch."

With the events of the past few days tumbling around in my head, I wasn't sure if I remembered what I had recited for the cat in the middle of the night. Hitchcock ambled into the kitchen and jumped on a ladder-back chair. He kept his eyes on me as if waiting for a performance to begin.

I cleared my throat. "How's this? A young Niagara Falls mother receives a package intended for a neighbor, but when she attempts to deliver it, she finds the neighbor missing, a dead stranger on the living room floor, and a killer ransacking

the bedroom. Now Scarlett Olson is on the run, with her toddler in tow, and only the clues inside the package to help her
as she flees into Canada."

"Could be tighter," Tyanne said. "Keep working on it.
We're covered with customers. Any chance you can pick
up the wine I ordered on your way to dinner?"

"No problem," I said.

So long as I'm back in time from Riverview.

"Great. See you then."

"She didn't hate it," I told Hitchcock after I hung up. "Now
you be a good boy and stay away from the windows. I don't
want to come home and find you're missing, and I don't want
to go to Canada to track you down."

"Mrreow," Hitchcock said.

24

T HE ORANGE BLOOMS of Indian paintbrush and the last of the season's bluebonnets decorated the roadside between Lavender and Riverview, Texas. I easily located the produce stand Twila had mentioned, about an hour into the drive. I parked in front of the long lean-to-like structure where a dozen or more customers browsed the displays of fruits and vegetables. I got out of my car and homed in on the fresh-picked strawberries, my imagination already flitting to thoughts of strawberry cheesecake.

That's not why you're here.

I plucked a shopping basket from a stack and hung it over my arm. I'd have to buy *something* so the reason for my visit wouldn't seem so conspicuous. I placed two cartons of strawberries in the basket before moving toward the vegetables.

As I browsed the lettuce section, I watched the woman at the checkout and guessed her to be about Aunt Rowe's age. Unlike my aunt, this woman had opted to stick with her hair's natural gray color. A younger woman with chin-length brown hair and wearing a red gingham-checked apron was discussing the variety of onions with a customer.

In a field next to the market, a man and a couple of helpers loaded filled produce baskets onto a trailer. I made the rounds, admiring the green beans, squash, and new potatoes. When I'd come full circle, I heard the checkout woman say, "Vick, honey, could you bring Mrs. Green another peck of tomatoes?"

The younger woman—Vick—carried a container over to the cash register and spoke a few words to the customer. I wondered if someone in the family had named their daughter Vick after the girl who died, or if the Palmers had coincidentally hired a woman named Vick. When she headed toward the back of the market, I followed and made a show of inspecting the yams.

"Help you with something?" she said.

"Are you Vick?"

She nodded.

"Are you related to the Palmers?"

She smiled. "I'm their daughter."

Was I acting on rumors about Vicki Palmer's death that weren't even true? I didn't think so. My information about her had come from several different sources.

"You're Vicki Palmer?"

A shadow passed over the woman's face. "My name is Vick Sittler. Why do you ask?"

"I, um, I came to talk with Mr. and Mrs. Palmer about their daughter Vicki. Is that you?"

She hesitated for a second before answering. "Yes. Look, I need to get to work."

"Wait. My name's Sabrina Tate, and I've come all the way

from Lavender. There's been a murder, and I found the body in the river. I heard about Vicki Palmer dying there, too, but you're obviously not dead."

So much for acting inconspicuous.

Vick's eyes widened, and she made a keep-your-voice-down motion with her hand. She whispered, "We can't talk about this here."

"When can we talk? This is really important."

She looked toward the checkout before turning back to me. She kept her voice low. "Whatever you do, don't discuss Vicki around my parents. That would send them into a tizzy so huge we'd have to close down the market for the day. Maybe all week."

"*You're* not Vicki?"

She sighed. "It's a long story."

"I have time."

The woman studied my face for a few seconds before nodding. She called out, "Mom, I'm taking a short break."

The gray-haired woman waved an acknowledgment, then continued to check out the next customer in line.

Vick headed through a door at the back of the market and motioned for me to follow. We were on a covered cement patio that was open to the field behind the market. Two tables and a refrigerator stood by a door marked Ladies. Three baskets of not-so-fresh tomatoes sat next to one of the tables, along with a tower of empty baskets.

"Let's sit," she said. "You care for a bottled water?"

I accepted and she removed two bottles from the refrigerator. We sat at the table nearest the tomato baskets. After taking a long drink, Vick pulled one of the full baskets closer to her chair. She took an empty basket from the stack and set it to her right.

"Shame how thousands of tomatoes come in at the same time," she said. "Some of these will be good for sauce, some are garbage." She picked up a tomato and rolled it in her palm. Pressed the fruit with her fingers to test for firmness before placing it in the smaller empty basket.

"My sister Vicki died a very long time ago," she said. "Why are you asking about her now?"

I summarized Bobby Joe's death, ending with how and where I'd found his body in the river.

"You found him in the place where Vicki died?" she said.

"That's what I'm told."

She took another swig of water, stared at the field for a minute, then turned back to me.

"Has the sheriff solved my sister's case?"

"No. Sorry."

"Then why are you here?"

I heard the pain in her tone and was sorry I'd brought it to the surface.

"From the moment I heard about your sister, I can't get her off my mind. I live by the river, and it's a constant reminder."

"One of the reasons we left," she said.

"No one knows what happened to Bobby Joe Flowers either, but I've learned he knew your sister. Maybe *you* knew him, too."

"I was eight years younger than Vicki, and she sure didn't like me tagging along with her—ever. I didn't really get to know her friends."

"Maybe you've heard your parents mention him."

She thought for a moment and shook her head. "I don't think so."

Chester Mosley's comment about the Palmers had brought me here, but his memories of them bad-mouthing Bobby Joe were three decades old and he'd been drunk when he brought up the subject.

Someone knew more about the connection between Vicki and Bobby Joe, if there was one, but I didn't think Vick was that person. I sure was curious, though, about her name.

"So your sister was Vicki, and you're Vick?"

"Odd, I know," she said. "My legal name's Debbie Sue. Vicki was Vicki Lynn."

"But you go by Vick?"

She leaned over to pull three more tomatoes from the large basket and began inspecting them. Two went into the sauce pile, one got pitched into a nearby garbage can.

"My folks started calling me Vick shortly after my sister died. At first, they didn't realize they were doing it. I didn't object, so they kept it up. Relatives would look at us weird, but after a while they got used to it and now I'm Vick to most everybody."

"Did you change your name legally?"

"No, I'm Debbie Sue Sittler on paper. Vick Sittler in the flesh." She shrugged. "Small price to pay for my parents' peace."

"Do they touch base with the Lavender sheriff every so often to see if there are any new developments?"

"Heavens no. Most of the time, they think I *am* Vicki. Hell of it is, they don't seem to realize their daughter Debbie's been missing for the past thirty years." She gave me a rueful smile.

Sadness for this woman, for the little girl who'd never gotten a chance to grow up as herself, as Debbie Sue Palmer, washed over me. I didn't think she wanted my pity, though, so I asked another question.

"After all this time, has anyone in the family come to a conclusion about what they think happened to her?"

Vick shook her head. "Not really. She had trouble with an abusive guy for a while, but he moved away."

The boy the sheriff had run out of town, according to Twila.

"There was someone new," Vick went on, "but she hadn't introduced him to anyone. Her closest girlfriends didn't even know his name."

"And there were no clues as to his identity left behind after she died?"

"Only thing I ever saw that might have had a connection to the guy was a velvet necklace box. I hung out in her room all the time after she was gone. She never allowed me in there, and even though I was devastated by her death, I absolutely loved spending time in that special place."

I smiled. "What was in the box?"

"Oh, it was empty," she said, "and I never found any necklace of hers that would have come in such a fancy box."

"I'm sorry you didn't get the chance to grow up with your sister," I said.

"Thanks," she said. "I'm okay. Frank, my brother, is the one who won't let go."

"What do you mean?"

"We moved out here less than a year after Vicki died. Started the produce business, but Frank wanted nothing to do with it. He left the day after high school graduation and hasn't come back."

She continued sorting the tomatoes. Three in the garbage, one for the sauce basket.

"You haven't seen him in all this time?"

"I've seen him, but he won't come here. Every once in a while my husband and I pack up the kids and go back to Lavender. They love renting tubes from their uncle Frank and floating down the Glidden River."

"Your brother is Frank of Frank's Floats?" I said.

"That's him. The only person who still insists on calling me Debbie. Sure confuses my kids, but they go with the flow."

"Isn't it hard for him to live so near to the place where Vicki died?"

"Frank doesn't want to forget," she said. "He can't stand the fact that our parents blocked out the whole thing. My brother's the angry one in the family, and he's bound and determined to hang on to that anger for the rest of his life."

Maybe Frank was the Palmer that Chester remembered hearing talk about Bobby Joe. I wondered if something had happened recently to bring the brother's anger to the surface, but I'd rather question the man himself than take up more of Vick's time. Besides, I had the dinner at Tyanne's tonight, and I was already cutting it close.

I thanked Vick for talking to me, and paid Mrs. Palmer for my strawberries with her none the wiser about the real reason I'd come.

On the way home I mulled over the new information. Sheriff Crawford, I felt sure, would know that Frank Palmer, Vicki's brother, lived close to the site of Bobby Joe's death. I wondered if he or Rosales had talked to Frank, and how the man had responded. If he was generally an angry person, any type of discussion about his deceased sister might have set him off. If they hadn't talked to him, then I wanted to be the one to bring up the subject and see Frank's reaction firsthand.

I PULLED in at the cottages with the perfect amount of time left for reviewing my proposal, printing a fresh copy, and changing my outfit. It was hard to believe I'd soon be meeting with Kree Vanderpool, the agent I'd heard good things about from the time I began writing fiction. Butterflies danced in

my stomach at the thought. If she liked my work and agreed
to represent me, my writing career might finally take off.

I was considering what it would feel like to hold the first
copy of my published book as I rolled past Aunt Rowe's house
and noticed her golf cart parked in the driveway next to an
older-model Lexus. A woman in skinny jeans and high-heeled
sandals stood between the vehicles, talking with Aunt Rowe,
who was seated in her cart. The stranger flailed her arms as
she talked, and I got the impression she presented a problem.

Aunt Rowe noticed me and waved. Not a frantic I-need-
your-help wave, but I pulled in behind the Lexus and jumped
out of my car just the same.

As the other woman dropped her arms and turned to me,
I realized she looked familiar.

"Sabrina," Aunt Rowe said, "You remember Bobby Joe's
sister?"

I might not have connected this bleached-blonde with the
attractive brunette cousin I'd met years ago, but I smiled and
said, "Of course. Becky, right?"

"That's me, the broke baby sister," she said.

I glanced at Aunt Rowe, who said, "Why don't we go inside and make ourselves comfortable. You've been on the
road all day, Becky. I'm sure you could use a bite to eat,
maybe some tea."

"What I could use," Becky said, "is for someone to tell me
where Bobby Joe stashed his money."

"What money?" I said.

She cocked her head toward me and said, "The money my
brother said he'd be depositin' into the bank account. If that
doesn't happen right quick, I'll have checks bouncin' all over
hell and back."

I wondered how she expected us to solve that little problem

for her now that Bobby Joe was gone. It wasn't like he'd shared details about his finances with us.

"We'll help however we can," Aunt Rowe said.

That sounded like a nice safe promise, but if Becky wanted help, she'd have to give us a lot more information.

"Did Bobby Joe deposit money into your account on a regular basis?" I said.

"It wasn't exactly my account," Becky said, "but he gave me some of the money."

I frowned. "I don't understand."

Becky sighed. "Bobby Joe didn't want an account in his own name, so he came to me. 'Do me a favor, sis,' he says. 'Keep the money in your name and you can have a cut.' So I opened an account for him to use."

"When was this?" I said.

"Nine months? A year? I don't know what he's hidin' but I decided I'm better off not knowin' so I didn't ask."

Aunt Rowe said, "There's quite a bit of money in this account?"

"Used to be," Becky said, "before he went out and paid cash for a brand-new Jeep SUV. That was a fool move."

"What makes you think he'd be making a deposit soon?" I said.

"He told me the account would be up twenty thousand by the first of the week." She raised her eyebrows. "Then he goes and dies, so I had no choice but to come see if he left a check layin' around, 'cause I gotta get that sucker deposited by Monday morning or else."

25

AUNT ROWE GRABBED her crutches and climbed out of the golf cart.

"Becky," she said in the no-nonsense tone she'd used on me when I was a kid, "come inside and we'll figure this out. Grab your luggage. You can spend the night here."

Aunt Rowe started for the back door. Becky scowled and folded her arms over her chest.

Aunt Rowe stopped and gave her cousin the eye. "You *did* bring luggage?"

Becky wore the expression of someone who wanted to pick a fight, but the person she most likely wanted to fight with was dead. After a second, she went around to the driver's side of the car and popped the trunk.

I went to Aunt Rowe and asked in a low voice, "What are we going to do?"

"*I'm* going to collect some facts," Aunt Rowe said. "*You're* going to meet that agent."

"But—"

"No excuses," she said. "Tyanne's dinner is still on, isn't it?"

"Yes, but—"

"This is a big night for you," she interrupted. "And Becky's surprise visit isn't going to ruin it."

I looked back at Becky, who had a tote slung over her shoulder. She pulled a small suitcase from the trunk. I turned back to Aunt Rowe.

"The money might be the missing link to figuring out who killed Bobby Joe," I said.

"Sure as shootin'," Aunt Rowe said. "Another thing I learned from watching cop shows. Follow the money."

"I'm not leaving you alone with her," I said.

"I won't be alone when Jeb gets here." Aunt Rowe grinned. "He'll ask the right questions, and we'll get to the bottom of this."

"You're going to call the sheriff?" I said.

"Already texted him." Aunt Rowe patted her shirt pocket, and I could see the tip of her phone sticking out. "Should be here soon, so you go on. I'll fill you in when you get back. Deal?"

I wanted to hear what Becky had to say firsthand, but chances were the sheriff wouldn't let me stay in the same room while he questioned her. Aunt Rowe seemed to have everything under control, and Tyanne was expecting me.

"Okay, deal."

"Some might say break a leg." Aunt Rowe repositioned her crutches. "Or is that only used in theater? Whatever. I wouldn't wish this on anybody."

HITCHCOCK supervised as I booted up my laptop and queued it to print my proposal. While the printer hummed, I hurriedly changed into one of my Tyanneapproved outfits. Khaki ankle-length pants and a cream-colored tunic with a wide brown belt. I yanked an orange print scarf from a dresser drawer. Hitchcock pounced on the scarf and pawed the fringed end.

"Sorry. No time to play." I gently removed the cat from the fabric and looped the scarf around my neck. "I'm switching out of investigator mode and into writer mode. Send some of your good luck with me to the meeting."

Hitchcock attempted to rub some luck onto my light slacks, but I dodged his black fur as I placed my printed pages into a crisp new folder. I patted the cat on the head, grabbed my keys and the Texas toffee cake, and took off for town.

On the way there I couldn't keep my mind from racing. I should have asked Becky if she knew where Bobby Joe planned to get twenty thousand dollars. Whether he customarily made deposits of that size. If the money came from legitimate business dealings. What kind of business he was in. Surely the sheriff would cover all of that.

I needed to concentrate on my own business—the business of writing, of becoming a published author. That thought pleased me, and I worked at putting myself in the proper frame of mind by the time I pulled up in front of the bookstore.

The second I turned off the car, I remembered I was supposed to pick up the wine.

Not a problem with the wine shop right next door. Couldn't be more handy. Except that when I rushed up to the entrance, I spotted the Closed sign hanging prominently in the front window.

My watch read 5:01.

Jeez. I shaded my eyes with my hands to peer inside. The store was dark. I hurried around the building to the back. Forgetting the wine was not the first impression I wanted to make on Kree Vanderpool.

A Cadillac Escalade was parked in the back lot, and I took that as a good sign. Even better, the back door to the building stood ajar.

Yes.

I approached the door and lifted my hand to knock. My fist froze in midair when I heard a woman's voice coming from inside.

"Your father is having an absolute fit," she said. "He's liable to give himself a stroke and end up in the hospital. Then we'd be in a real pickle."

She's talking to Claire.

I listened to silence for half a minute and decided I was hearing a phone conversation rather than an in-person talk.

Felice said, "Roommates, yeah. I have a big picture of that."

A pause.

"I know you're doing what you have to do. Call me again in the morning. Don't worry about the store. We're handling it fine, and the books are locked up where he won't see a thing. You take care of you."

Felice Dubois had said from the beginning that Claire wasn't missing, and now I knew why. They were in touch all along. So where was she? Why had she left? Did it have anything to do with Bobby Joe's death?

I didn't figure it would work if I rushed inside and demanded Felice tell me her daughter's whereabouts, so I waited until she said good-bye before I rapped on the door.

I'd be a bit late, yes, but I *had* to get that wine. And if I happened to get information about Claire, too, all the better.

"Hello, anyone here?" I pushed the door in as I spoke and stepped inside. "Mrs. Dubois? Felice?"

"Who's there?" The woman crossed the back storage room and spotted me. She appeared more casual today in a shimmery white blouse over black trousers. I glanced at the cell phone she placed on a table that held packaging materials I presumed were used for mail orders.

"It's Sabrina," I said. "We met the other day."

"I remember you," she said, "but I'm afraid the store is closed."

"I'm running late, but I promised my friend I'd pick up the wine she ordered."

"Tyanne, yes." Felice smiled as she came over to me. "No worries. I took the wine to the bookstore. I knew she wanted it for a dinner meeting tonight with a writer friend of hers and an agent."

"I'm the writer, so thank you for delivering the wine. That was thoughtful." I smiled.

"You're welcome. Now, if you don't mind, I need to close the shop. My husband likes his dinner served promptly at six."

I glanced at my watch. It read 5:07. Not so bad. I might not get another opportunity this good to ask questions.

"I ran into your husband last night," I said. "I'm surprised he can think about food at a time like this."

"What do you mean?" Her scowl deepened the groove between her brows.

"He's beside himself worrying about Claire," I said. "I'd be surprised if he sleeps. You're probably just as worried, aren't you?"

Felice's back stiffened visibly. "I'm sure our daughter is fine," she said. "Leo is a control freak, and that gets so tiresome."

"He's afraid for Claire's safety," I said, "and I don't blame him."

"What are you talking about?" Felice said.

I pasted on a wide-eyed innocent expression. "Her boyfriend died, and the sheriff doesn't know who murdered him. Claire may be in danger."

Felice trilled a laugh. "Claire is not in any danger, and to call that Flowers character her boyfriend is a gross misstatement of facts."

I had the distinct impression she wanted to slam the door, but I stood in her way. My lateness weighed heavily, and it wasn't like back in Houston where I could blame the traffic.

I said, "What *are* the facts?"

"Unlike my husband, I don't discuss my daughter's personal life with strangers. Please leave now so I can go about my business."

"Okay, but first might I ask for one itsy-bitsy favor?" I was pressing my luck with this woman, but I had to try.

"What is it?" she snapped.

"I would *love* to give something special to the agent I'm meeting tonight." I racked my brain to think of something that would take her into the store for a minute. Long enough for me to peek at her phone. "May I buy two boxes of those liqueur-centered chocolates? I hate to be a burden, but this meeting is really important. I can pay you in cash now, or give you a check, or—"

Felice held up a hand and shook her head. "Spare me. I'll be right back."

The moment she disappeared, I rushed to the table and picked up her phone. Punched it on. Good, no password. I scanned the list of most recent calls. Tried to memorize numbers, but then had a better idea and pulled my phone out with shaking hands and snapped a picture of her screen.

I glanced at the doorway she'd gone through, my heart slamming against my chest. I scrolled to "Contacts" and found the entry for Claire that confirmed several of the recent calls were to and from her. Flipped over to texts and saw numerous messages from Claire. They didn't pinpoint her location, but they piqued my curiosity.

A few moments later, Felice's footsteps headed my way. I put the phone down and returned to the doorway. Sweat dampened my forehead, and I could barely hold my quaking knees still.

Felice handed me a gold gift bag stuffed with deep purple tissue and an invoice.

"Take this and go," she said. "Pay me later."

I thanked her and went back to the car for my proposal and the cake. At quarter past five, I burst through the bookshop's entrance, startling the cats, who had been lounging in the front window.

Ethan Brady glanced up from the money he was counting at the cash register. "Breathe, man," he said. "You look crazed."

"There's a lot going on." I walked over to pet Zelda and Willis, always a calming activity, and took several deep breaths for good measure.

Ethan came out from behind the counter to lock the front door behind me. "Kree Vanderpool is dope, man. You'll like her. She knows some of my favorite authors, like personally. They're having wine back there, so they might not notice you're late."

Tyanne would notice.

I pushed thoughts of Becky's surprise visit and the elusive Claire Dubois aside. All that existed here and now was this meeting and my fictional world. I conjured up a smile, crossed the store, and walked into the back room, where Tyanne had set a lovely table with a yellow-and-blue theme. She and the woman who must be Kree Vanderpool stood near the table, each with a wineglass.

"Hi, ladies. I brought cake."

Tyanne's gaze flicked to the wall clock and back to me. If it had been just the two of us, she would have said something. In front of Kree, she was the perfect hostess and introduced me to the other woman.

"Sabrina writes by day and bakes by night," she said.

I put my things down on a side table and took Kree's outstretched hand. The agent was tall and slim, fortyish, with shoulder-length auburn hair and dark-framed glasses. She wore a black-and-white geometric print sundress with a lime green shrug.

"Writing and baking—a fun combination," the agent said, "and this small town is the perfect setting. Is your novel set in a small town?"

I accepted a glass of wine from Tyanne. "No, it's actually set closer to your home. My protagonist lives in Niagara Falls and then flees into Canada."

"I see," Kree said. "It's a fem-jep?"

"That's not how I would describe it." I took a sip of wine. "Though I've felt a bit like a woman in jeopardy myself these past few days."

Tyanne gave me a look that clearly said, *Whatever you do, don't bring up the murder.*

Kree said, "I have plenty of those days myself, especially around my kids." She had an unusually loud and contagious laugh, and once she got going, we all laughed.

"Mine put themselves in jeopardy at times," Tyanne said.

"Children can be challenging," Kree said and looked at me. "Are you a mom, Sabrina?"

I shook my head. "Nope. Unless you count my cat."

"I *love* cats," Kree said. "Is there a cat in your book?"

"Afraid not. There is a child, though, and she's quite a challenge in the story."

I congratulated Kree on the new addition in her sister's

family—Kree's first nephew who, she joked, had the bad fortune of looking just like his father. We segued into a lively discussion about best-selling novels and well-known authors over an elegant dinner of herb-roasted pork, creamy baked Parmesan polenta that I recognized because I'd eaten it at Tyanne's once before, and asparagus.

When Tyanne excused herself to get the coffee to serve with our dessert, Kree asked me about my own book, and I presented my pitch. She took my proposal and scanned the pages as I finished my dinner. I'd been talking nonstop and hadn't eaten much. The food tasted delicious, and I didn't want to waste a bite.

Over cake and coffee, Kree looked from me to Tyanne. "You were right, Ty, this girl really can write. Right?" She giggled long and loud, and I attributed her rowdy laughter to the wine she'd consumed. Then she quieted and looked at me. "I love what you've put together."

"You do?" I said.

Kree grinned. "I do, and I'd love to represent you."

"That's great." I felt shaky with a case of sudden nerves. I couldn't believe this was happening.

"I have a publisher in mind that's specifically interested in stories like yours," she said. "One of their newer editors is actively looking for authors. I'd like to send your book out to him no later than June first. The timing is critical. We need to hit them with it before everyone takes off on summer vacation."

"You mean you'll send the editor this proposal?" I took a sip of wine.

Kree shook her head. "The whole book. I want you to send me the manuscript in two weeks, no later. If the rest of the book is as well written as this proposal, there's a good chance they'll make you an offer."

Two weeks? I nearly choked on the wine, but somehow

managed to swallow, and smiled. My chest constricted. I couldn't seem to get a full breath, like an asthmatic who needed a hit from an inhaler.

Tyanne turned to me. "Isn't this exciting?"

"Sure is," I said in spite of my panic about the deadline.

Two bottles of wine later, the majority of it consumed by Kree, we wrapped up our meeting. I thanked the agent profusely, and at the last minute remembered to give her the gift I'd picked up at the wine store. I had worked myself up from "concerned" to "terrified."

Two weeks? Is that even possible?

Before Tyanne left to drive Kree back to her hotel, my friend gave me her sternest look. "Go home and write. Now. Tonight."

Okay, I knew she had my best interests at heart. I needed to write at every possible moment. But how could I let go of the investigation and leave everything in the sheriff's hands? I lived at the scene of the murder, with my aunt on the suspect list, and the dead man's sister visiting us.

Night fell as I headed back to my car. I walked down the bookstore's sidewalk and punched the key fob to unlock the driver's door. A shadowy figure stepped out from behind the tree by my car, startling me. A short figure.

I inched closer and realized it was Twila Baxter. She was wearing the same type of high-collared dark dress she'd had on the day I visited her at the antiques store.

The woman approached me and stopped in the glow of a streetlight. "Miss Sabrina, good evening."

"Twila," I said. "What are you doing here?"

The shops in town were closed, and we were quite a distance from her place.

"I need to apologize for my son's boorish behavior last night," she said.

I frowned. "You mean Eddie?"

"Yes." She shook her head and tsk-tsked. "I raised him better than that."

"No harm done," I said. "Don't give it another thought." How did she know what had happened at The Wild Pony Saloon? Had someone seen Eddie hitting on me and reported back to his mother? Or had *he* told her? Either way, her feeling the need to bring this up was plain weird.

"Also," Twila said, "I wish to congratulate you on your good fortune."

I waited, wondering where she was going with this.

"Your book will be a hit," she said. "Your career as an author will take off."

"And you know this how?" I said.

"I see things," Twila said with a sly smile. "I see good, and I see bad. That was the good."

This woo-woo vibe of hers creeped me out even more than it had during our first meeting.

"I don't want to hear bad news, Twila. I need to get home and work on that book."

"You go home, Sabrina," she said, "but take care. Bad news will come very soon."

I couldn't stop myself from asking, "What bad news?"

"You will know when it comes."

I halfway expected her body to vanish right before my eyes, but the woman turned and shuffled down the sidewalk.

26

ON THE WAY home, I tried to forget crazy Twila's comments about fortunes, good news, and bad. I didn't care to hear from people who thought they could see into the future any more than I wanted to hear talk about a cat bringing bad luck. I refused to speculate on how Twila had learned the things she knew. I was too busy being overwhelmed about Kree's reaction to my book and couldn't wait to tell Aunt Rowe.

When I got to the house, a sheriff's department car was parked in the driveway next to Becky's Lexus. Funny that Sheriff Crawford would still be here, assuming he had arrived shortly after I left for my meeting. I hoped he'd come alone. The last thing I wanted tonight was a run-in with Rosales to kill my good mood.

I entered quietly through the back door so I could take off if I found Rosales was inside. I crept through the kitchen and down the hall. The murmur of low voices drifted to me from the living room. Rosales had a strident voice, and I decided she wasn't present. Thank goodness.

I walked casually into the living room, ready to greet Aunt Rowe with my book news, and froze when I saw Sheriff Crawford and Aunt Rowe seated intimately close on the sofa. The sheriff was turned toward my aunt and held one of her hands in his.

Holy moly.

I began to back out, but the sheriff caught sight of me and smiled.

"Hello, Sabrina," he said.

Aunt Rowe shifted and pulled her hand out of his grasp. Her cheeks seemed flushed. "How was your meeting? C'mon in. Have a seat. Tell us all about it."

I grinned at her. "I'm sure the sheriff is too busy to hear about my book news."

Aunt Rowe kept her expression bland.

The sheriff said, "Never too busy to share a friend's good news, or so I'm guessing by your happy face."

My expression had as much to do with finding Aunt Rowe in close proximity to him as it did about my news. Saying so would annoy Aunt Rowe, so I told them all about Kree Vanderpool's comments, including the deadline she'd given me.

"Atta girl," Aunt Rowe said. "I knew you had talent. You'd better get right to work so you finish on time."

Is she trying to get rid of me?

"How far along are you?" the sheriff said.

"My first draft is almost finished," I said, "but I won't be able to concentrate until you catch me up on what Becky said after I left."

The sheriff shook his head. "You know I can't discuss an ongoing investigation with you, Sabrina."

"For Pete's sake, Jeb," Aunt Rowe said. "If you don't tell her, I will. This is no state secret."

"Where *is* Becky?" I said.

"She turned in early. Glenda gave up the guest room for her." Aunt Rowe picked up a glass of what looked like tea and took a swallow. "Bottom line is Bobby Joe didn't tell his sister anything about where he got the money he deposited into that bank account. Far as she knows, he doesn't have a business. Worked at an appliance store for a while, but they fired him sometime last year. Could be he scammed a whole slew of women the same way he scammed Marian Kauffman and got the money that way."

Apparently, Aunt Rowe had shared Marian's visit the night before with the sheriff. I wondered how he'd interpret Marian's story and if he'd look closely at Luke Griffin as a result.

"Does Becky know the names of other women Bobby Joe dated?" I said.

"No such luck," the sheriff said.

Aunt Rowe said, "Another possibility is he hung on to part of the paltry sum he inherited when his daddy passed. Becky used her share for living expenses. She came into that money around the time her husband left her with next to nothing."

"You think Bobby Joe would share his money with Becky because hers ran out?" I said.

"Doubtful." Aunt Rowe shook her head. "Now that I'm thinking this through, it's more likely he burned through his in a month."

"Where does that leave us?" I looked from Aunt Rowe to the sheriff.

He stood. "That leaves the rest of the investigating to Deputy Rosales. Come tomorrow, she's taking the lead in this case."

My heart lurched. I knew we could trust Sheriff Crawford to do the right thing while keeping Aunt Rowe's best interests in mind. With Rosales in charge, all bets were off.

"You'll still keep an eye on things, right?" I said.

He shook his head. "Better if I distance myself. I'm too close to this." He looked at my aunt. "Rowe, it's been a lovely evening. I best call it a night."

"Goodnight, Jeb." Aunt Rowe made no move to get up. "Thanks for coming over."

I said, "I'll walk with you."

When we were out of Aunt Rowe's earshot, I said, "Are you going to take a look at Becky's bank account?"

"I'll report everything to my deputy," he said, "and that's all you need to know."

"I learned more about Claire Dubois tonight, and you should take a closer look at her, too."

He stopped walking and looked at me. "You learned this information at your meeting with the agent?"

"No." I filled him in on the conversation I'd heard between Claire and her mother. "One thing that struck me was her reference to keeping the wine store's books a secret from Claire's father. He and his wife own the vineyard and may own the store as well. Sounds like there's something fishy going on accounting-wise. What if their accounting issue is connected somehow with Becky's bank account?"

"As a mystery writer, you ought to know big leaps in logic are problematic," the sheriff said. "I'm going now."

Okay, that *was* a leap, but it wasn't impossible that Claire had siphoned money out of the wine business and given it to Bobby Joe to deposit into the account in Becky's name. Of course, I had no evidence of any such thing. I kept pace with the sheriff as he left via the front door and approached his car.

"Did you know Frank Palmer is still holding on to his anger about his sister's death?"

He sighed and stared down at me. "We already covered that ground. End of discussion."

"You're no fun," I said in an attempt to humor him.

"Nothing funny about this case." He looked at his feet and rubbed his chin before meeting my eyes. "I'm doing what I can, Sabrina, but none of it can hide the fact that Rowe has the best motive for wanting her cousin dead."

I struggled to swallow. "You can't know that until you know everyone else's motive. Besides, Aunt Rowe has no connection to Becky's bank account."

"The money may be a different issue," he said. "Deputy Rosales will follow the evidence. That's the way this thing needs to go."

He climbed into his car, gave me a wave, and backed out of the driveway.

I was busy reading between the lines of what the sheriff had and hadn't said. I knew he cared about what happened to Aunt Rowe. How could he simply step away from the investigation knowing that doing so placed her in danger?

He's an honorable man, that's how.

Crawford cared about truth and justice, and he didn't want the ultimate court case to be influenced by the fact that he and Aunt Rowe were friends. That made a lot of sense, but I wasn't a fan of the sheriff's straitlaced character under these circumstances.

This might be Twila's bad news.

With my heart pounding, I turned back to the house and was shocked to see Hitchcock sitting next to the back door.

"How on earth do you get out of that cottage?" I rushed over to the cat and picked him up. His purr was going ninety-to-nothing. "I guess now that you're here, this is a good time to introduce you to my aunt Rowe. We could use some pet therapy right about now."

I carried the cat into the living room with me and made the introductions.

"He's a good-lookin' fella," Aunt Rowe said as Hitchcock walked from the sofa to the ottoman to rub against her cast. "Does he happen to be *the* black cat that has Thomas practically fearing for all of our lives?"

"I'm afraid so." I sat beside her on the sofa and watched the cat as he stretched to sniff at Aunt Rowe's pink-polished toenails protruding from the cast.

She shook her head. "Sometimes Thomas doesn't have the sense God gave a billy goat."

"So you'll take my side and ask him to stop setting traps to catch Hitchcock?"

"I'll tell him I think what he's doing is a load of nonsense," she said, "but he got the superstitious streak from his mama. I'm afraid it's there to stay."

Hitchcock's fate was one problem, but not the biggest one at the moment. I sighed.

Aunt Rowe put her hand on my leg. "What's the matter, little girl?"

I smiled at her. "Many moons have passed since I was your little girl, but I've missed you calling me that."

"You grew up too fast," she said, "but I'll always feel the same way about you, Sabrina. Granted, I'm not the soul-baring type, and I'm hard on people."

"Not too hard."

"In case I've never told you," she said, "you have brought great joy to my life."

I rested my head on her shoulder. "And you to mine."

My eyes teared, and the lump in my throat was so big, there was no way I could speak around it. Even if I could, I didn't know whether I should voice my fear that Deputy Rosales was not compiling a list of suspects, that she was likely to show up on the doorstep with an arrest warrant.

"For the life of me, I don't know why Jeb's deputy continues to suspect me," Aunt Rowe said as if she'd read my mind. "It's insane for her to think I had anything to do with Bobby Joe's murder."

I blinked rapidly to clear my tears. "I know, right? It had to be someone Bobby Joe cheated out of money."

"Do you suspect Becky?"

I shrugged. "Didn't we watch some movie where a character said everything is suspect and nothing is what it seems? That sums up how I'm feeling about it all."

"Mrreow," Hitchcock said.

Aunt Rowe laughed. "Inspector Clouseau said 'I suspect everyone and I suspect no one.' Let's hope Jeb's department is a little more savvy than the Pink Panther detective."

"Surely they are," I said.

And that's what worries me most.

27

A CALL FROM TYANNE woke me the next morning. Hitchcock, amazingly still curled at the foot of my bed even though it was daylight, barely slitted his eyes to glare at the phone.

"Are you basking in the glow of impending publication," Tyanne said, "or are you writing?"

"Neither." I yawned. "I was asleep."

"That's not good."

"But I wrote until two in the morning."

"Better. I was hoping you'd say that."

"Something about the dire situation around here, with the murder investigation going on, put me in the mood for writing the critical black moment scene."

"I'm looking forward to reading it," she said. "Has something new happened with the murder investigation?"

"Bobby Joe's sister, Becky, showed up, and she shared

interesting facts about a bank account she kept for him because he didn't want the money in his name."

"Whoa," Tyanne said. "I didn't see that coming."

"Neither did we."

Hitchcock stood and stretched, then walked up the bed to
rub against my hand holding the phone. I filled Tyanne in on
what we'd learned since Becky's arrival, gave her a rundown
of my visit with Debbie Sue/Vick, then shared my conversation with Felice Dubois at the wine shop.

"All that when you could have spent the time writing,"
Tyanne said.

She was like a broken record, and I ignored her comment.

"I did a reverse lookup of the phone numbers from Felice's
phone," I said. "In the past few days, she's made several calls
to Claire's number, a couple to St. Joseph's Hospital in Austin,
and one to some guy named Colin Guidry, also in Austin."

"Guidry," Tyanne said. "That sounds familiar for some
reason."

"Doesn't ring any bells for me," I said, "and the text messages weren't very telling. They were brief, like 'all good'
and 'keep you posted.' Claire said 'we' a few times. Wherever
she is, she's not alone."

"Claire's probably not worth worrying about," Tyanne said.

"Unless she killed Bobby Joe before she took off."

"That doesn't feel right to me," she said.

"Nothing feels right, that's the problem."

"I wish they'd hurry up and solve the case so you could
focus."

"If Deputy Rosales has her way, it'll get solved all right,
but not the way I'd like." I swung my legs around to the side
of the bed and placed my feet on the floor. The cat jumped
down from the bed and ran toward the kitchen.

"What do you mean?" Tyanne said.

"They're not finding evidence pointing them to anyone except Aunt Rowe, who, according to the sheriff, has the best motive."

"That's frightening," she said.

I could tell by the long pause that she was struggling not to tell me to ignore everything else and write. In terms of priority, Tyanne knew Aunt Rowe's safety was always going to come out in the number one spot.

"What are you going to do?" she asked.

"Keep investigating. I'm going to talk to Frank Palmer later today. He's a good suspect the sheriff refuses to consider."

Another pause told me she knew better than to mention my book again.

"Good luck," Tyanne said and hung up.

AFTER breakfast, I dressed for a walk around the grounds. My late night had me feeling sluggish, and I needed to get my blood moving to think about how to approach Frank Palmer.

I told Hitchcock I'd be right back and that if he knew what was good for him, he'd stay inside, then set out into the glorious spring morning. It was after nine, but I'd made one lap around the cottages before spotting anyone else outside.

Molly Hartman sat on the front step at the Barcelona cottage. She looked pouty, so I stopped to say hi.

"You doing okay?" I said.

"I guess," she said. "I wanted to see that kitty and tell him bye before we go, but I can't find him anywhere."

"When are you leaving?"

"This afternoon."

I thought about taking the girl to my place and letting her play with Hitchcock for a while, but not without getting her father's permission first.

"Where's your dad?"

"He went to town," she said, "with Sophia."

"They left you here alone?"

"My brother's inside."

Molly's brother couldn't be more than ten years old, and I didn't like the kids being here by themselves.

"They'll be back soon," Molly said.

"You don't look happy about that." The girl seemed upset. "Is something wrong?"

"Dad and Sophia are getting *engaged*."

She stressed the word "engaged," making it sound like a fate worse than death.

"I take it you don't like the idea."

"I'd rather have Mom and Dad stay married."

"A lot of kids who go through this feel the same way," I said, "but it'll be fine."

She was looking past me toward the road. "Here they come. They're bringing breakfast. Don't tell them I told you. I'm not supposed to tell anybody."

I made a zipper across my lips.

Molly jumped up and ran to meet the adults, so I continued my walk.

My brain was deep into sorting out various motives people might have for killing Bobby Joe when I came up behind Aunt Rowe's house and saw that lying jerk—"Adam Lee"—sitting on the back deck beside my aunt. I was in no mood to keep up his charade.

I hurried over to the deck.

"Good morning, Mr. Ledwosinski," I said, loudly enunciating each syllable of his real name.

Aunt Rowe looked around to see who I was talking to while Ledwosinski met my gaze. He raised his brows, as if saying *touché*, then turned and said something to my aunt. He left the deck, taking the steps opposite the ones that I climbed up.

Aunt Rowe watched him go, then turned to me. "Were you talking to Adam just now?"

"You mean the man who calls himself Adam."

She looked confused. "What are you saying?"

"He's *not* Adam, that's what." I explained what I had learned about the private investigator. "I can't figure out what he wants, Aunt Rowe. What does he talk to you about?"

"You think he's here to investigate *me*?"

"I don't know. He always seems to be with you."

A blip of a police siren sounded, startling both of us.

"What the heck?" I said.

A car door slammed.

"Stay here," I told Aunt Rowe, as if she could race around the house on her crutches. "I'll see what's going on."

I felt a sense of dread as I rounded the house to find Deputy Rosales standing next to the cruiser. She and Ledwosinski appeared to be deep in conversation.

I hurried up to them. "Can I help you with something, Deputy?"

Rosales turned to me. "I need to see Thomas Cortez. Where is he?"

I frowned. "Thomas? I don't know. What do you want with Thomas?"

Ledwosinski said, "He's down by the river working on those steps."

I glared at the man. "Is this any of your business?"

Had Rosales hired the PI to investigate Thomas?

"I need to see Cortez," Rosales said, "and I need to see him now."

Aunt Rowe had not stayed on the deck. I heard the *click-clomp* of her crutches as she crossed the driveway behind me.

"Why are you asking to see my employee?" she said.

"Not that I'm obligated to explain," Rosales said, "but I'm sure you'll find out anyway, so I may as well tell you now. Thomas Cortez's fingerprints are on the shovel that killed Bobby Joe Flowers, and I'm arresting him for murder."

Aunt Rowe's good leg buckled, and I reached out to grab an arm before she toppled. Ledwosinski beat me to it and supported my aunt while she hollered at the deputy.

"Are you out of your mind? Thomas would never hurt anyone. This is my property, and I want you to—"

"Stop." I placed myself in front of Aunt Rowe, blocking her from the deputy's view. "Don't say another word. This will only make things worse."

"I'll say whatever I please," Aunt Rowe said through gritted teeth.

"Your niece is right," Ledwosinski said, still holding on to Aunt Rowe's arm.

"Did anyone ask you?" I said.

Behind me, a car door opened and then slammed shut. The engine started up and tires crunched on the gravel driveway.

"Rosales is headed for the river, isn't she?" I said without turning around.

"Good guess," Ledwosinski said.

"Let go of me." Aunt Rowe squirmed out of the man's grasp. "I'm getting my golf cart. I won't leave Thomas alone to face that woman."

"Would you rather she arrest *you*?" Ledwosinski said. "'Cause that could happen if you rub her the wrong way."

"I don't care what happens to me," Aunt Rowe said. "I have to get down there."

"No, you don't," he said. "You'd be more help to Thomas if you call a good criminal attorney. She'll probably take him to Riverview, and the Lawton County DA will arraign him there. I can get you some names if you need them."

I stared at the PI. "And pray tell, how does a photographer—wait, let me be more specific—a bird-watching photographer, know so much about the criminal justice system?"

"You're not helping the situation," he said.

I hated to admit he was right. Aunt Rowe's face was screwed up in pain, more mental than physical I guessed, but I couldn't be sure.

I took her hand. "I'll go to Thomas. I'll tell him you're contacting a lawyer. This will be okay. I promise."

It has to be okay.

"Go, then." She flung my hand away.

I yanked the garage door up and jumped into the golf cart. Following the road would take too long, so I cut across the yard with my foot to the floor. The cart bounced so hard over the grass that I might have flown out if I hadn't been gripping the steering wheel for all I was worth.

I could see Rosales and Thomas standing at the head of the stairs before I reached them. His arms were at his sides, so she hadn't handcuffed him, thank goodness. At least not yet.

Rosales was holding something, and I could hear her talking.

"You have the right to remain silent—"

I brought the cart to a skidding stop, jumped out, and ran toward them.

"Thomas," I yelled. "Don't say anything."

"I didn't kill Flowers," he said.

I glanced at Rosales, but she was focused on completing the *Miranda* warning and kept right on talking.

"Of course you didn't," I said. "We all know you didn't do anything."

"It *was* my shovel," he said. "I used it to plant rosebushes on Thursday."

"Thomas, keep quiet." I shook my head and held an index finger to my lips, but he wasn't finished.

"When I went back Friday morning to finish planting, the shovel was gone."

"Thomas, Aunt Rowe is going to get you a good attorney. The best attorney. Don't say one more word. Okay?"

"What I'm telling you is the truth," he said. "There is only one reason this is happening to me now."

Even though I had told him to be quiet, I couldn't help myself. "What reason?"

Deputy Rosales stopped speaking to wait for his answer.

"El Gato Diablo crossed my path not one hour ago," he said. "Now here I am, headed to jail."

28

DEFENDING THE CAT wouldn't help, so I waited while Deputy Rosales finished saying her piece.

She snapped handcuffs on Thomas, then opened the car door and guided him into the backseat.

"We'll get you out," I called to him right before she closed the door.

When Rosales looked at me with narrowed eyes, I said, "You're wrong about this, Deputy."

"The man's fingerprints are on the murder weapon," she said. "From what I'm told, he would do anything for Rowena Flowers. I'd watch what I said next if I were you."

Rosales got in her car and drove away. This was even worse than I had feared. She wasn't finished with us. Did she think she could interrogate Thomas and pressure him until he confessed? I knew she would use anything he said, no matter how innocuous, as an excuse to go after Aunt Rowe, to claim that Aunt Rowe had asked Thomas to take care of the Bobby Joe problem. My heart hammered as the dust kicked up by the deputy's car began to settle. If Rosales came back for my aunt, what would I do?

I turned toward the gurgling rush of the river, but found no calm from the soothing sound. Just as well, because it was time for action. I needed to start thinking straight. Aunt Rowe needed my support now more than ever. First, we'd find a lawyer for Thomas, then one for my aunt, no matter how much she protested.

I drove the golf cart, via the road this time, back to the house. Becky stood in the kitchen, wearing wrinkled pajamas and eating a peanut-butter-and-jelly sandwich. Her eyes were so swollen I wondered how she'd found the fixings for her breakfast. Either spring allergies had hit her hard or she'd cried herself to sleep. I didn't see her as the weepy type.

"What's going on?" she said. "Rowe's on the phone with a lawyer."

Aunt Rowe had beat me to the number one task on my list.

"The sheriff's department just made an arrest," I said, "but they have the wrong person."

Becky's puffy eyelids flew up. "They got the guy who took Bobby Joe's money?"

"I didn't say that. I said they arrested the *wrong* person, Thomas, and he has nothing to do with Bobby Joe or his money."

"How do you know? I'm gonna ask Rowe right now." She turned and flounced out of the room, trailing bread crumbs as she took another bite of her sandwich.

The fact that she cared more about the money than her brother's murder disgusted me. I looked at the ceiling and shook my head.

Glenda came in through the back door. "I hope you're praying, 'cause we need all the help we can get."

"I know. Poor Thomas."

"Him, too, but I was talking about the flood in the Madrid cottage."

I looked at her. "What flood?"

"I took fresh towels over and the floor was sopping wet. We have a bad leak under the bathroom sink. Had to shut off the water."

"Where are the guests?"

Glenda shrugged. "Out to breakfast, maybe. I left a note for them. Got to take more towels. Used the first batch drying the floor."

"Why do you look so calm?" I said. "We can't leave the people with no water, and I don't want Aunt Rowe dealing with any more stress."

"You look like you're about to stroke out yourself," she said. "I called Thomas's friend Wes to get a referral for a plumber."

"Mr. Krane?"

She nodded. "He offered to bring parts and fix it himself. Better than waiting Lord knows how long for a plumber to show up, so I accepted."

"Mr. Krane is coming here?"

"Said he'd be here in forty-five minutes." Glenda's brow creased. "Are you okay, hon?"

My head ached, but I nodded slowly.

In spite of my worry for Thomas and my aunt and the leak in the Madrid cottage, I needed to hide Hitchcock before Wes Krane arrived.

On the way back to my place, I rounded the Barcelona cottage and found Molly standing in the grass. She was playing with a yo-yo, or trying to, but spent more time rewinding the string.

"Did you find the kitty?" she said when she saw me.

I started to say no, because I certainly didn't have time for this distraction, but the girl looked so hopeful.

And lonely.

And bored.

"I might be able to introduce you to the cat, if you promise not to tell anyone about him."

"Why?"

"Because not everyone is friendly to cats like we are."

She shook her head. "I won't tell."

"Let's ask your dad if you can come with me for a little bit to see the Monte Carlo cottage. Is he here?"

"Yeah, he's packing," she said and disappeared inside.

Thirty seconds later she reappeared with her father, and he gave his permission for her to accompany me. Walking to my cottage, Molly skipped beside me, evidently cheered by the fact that she was going to see the cat.

I cautioned her to be quiet lest she frighten Hitchcock, but when I opened the door, he was taking a bath in a patch of sunlight near his food bowl and continued as if our intrusion was no big deal.

Molly knelt on the floor and waited for him to come to her, which he did without hesitation. He plopped down in front of the girl, and she started baby-talking to him and rubbing his belly. Not all cats are fond of belly rubs, and I watched closely to make sure he didn't look annoyed. From what I could see, Hitchcock ate up the attention.

My phone rang, and I pulled it out. Aunt Rowe.

"Where are you?" she said.

"My place."

"Glenda's taking me into town to meet with the lawyer," she said.

"I can do that. Do you need to leave now?"

"We already left," Aunt Rowe said. "Thomas's wife is

meeting us there. We're hoping to post a bond and get him out quickly."

Thomas hadn't been gone long enough to reach the jail, but that little fact wouldn't slow down my aunt. I wasn't surprised she had turned all aggressive-mama-bear when it came to Thomas. If I were in his shoes, she would do the same for me.

"How'd you get a meeting so fast?" I said.

"Pulled some strings," she said.

I wished she had pulled strings earlier and convinced the sheriff to keep his finger on the pulse of this case instead of turning it over to Rosales. I didn't think he would have made the rash decision to arrest Thomas.

I looked over my shoulder at Molly. She sat on the hearth, running the string from her yo-yo across the stone for Hitchcock to chase.

"I want to come and hear what the lawyer has to say," I told Aunt Rowe, "and tell him about my suspect list."

"There'll be time for that later. I need you to meet Wes Krane at Madrid."

I couldn't think of a better option for handling the plumbing problem, so I agreed, and we hung up.

Molly trailed her string on the floor, then around her back, then up on the hearth. Hitchcock cooperated fully, jumping up and down, running to and fro, and pouncing on the string. I could hear his loud purr across the room and had to smile at the fun they were having.

I checked my watch. Twenty minutes until Krane's arrival. I should wait by the Madrid cottage in case the guests returned before we had the problem fixed.

"Hey, look at this," Molly said.

I turned and saw her kneeling on the left side of the wraparound hearth. She held a piece of stone about the size of a tennis ball in her hand.

What the heck?

"There's a little hidey-hole back here," she said. "The kitty kept pushing this stone with his paw. It was loose."

I hurried over to them and saw Hitchcock had his paw stuck into the crevice where the small piece of stone had come out. Something was snagged on his claws.

I bent to look closer.

"It's a necklace," Molly said. "Cool."

"Let me have a look." I picked the cat up and unhooked a chain, more tarnished black than silver, from his paw. A small heart-shaped pendant hung from the chain.

I rubbed the heart with my thumb. "It's engraved, but I can't make out the initials. I'll have to get some silver polish and clean it up."

"This is like a movie," Molly said. "Will you find the owner of the necklace?"

"I can try." I unzipped one of the pockets on my cargo shorts and dropped the necklace inside. "Right now, though, I need to get you back. Your dad will be looking for you, and I have an appointment with a plumber."

Molly pouted and gave Hitchcock one last hug. "Bye-bye kitty. Maybe I can come and visit you again."

"I could e-mail you a picture," I said, then realized I didn't want any evidence on the Internet that Hitchcock existed. Which reminded me that I'd come here to hide the cat.

I walked Molly over to her place, then returned quickly to deal with Hitchcock.

"Sorry about this, boy, but I need to keep you out of sight."

I didn't think he could manage to get up on the high, narrow bathroom windowsill, so I put him, his bowl, and his litter box in there, where there was no way he'd be spotted, and closed the door.

When Wes Krane drove up to the Madrid cottage fifteen

minutes later, I was there to meet him. He wore his usual
frown along with navy work pants, a white short-sleeved shirt,
and a Krane's gimme cap.

"We sure appreciate your help with this, Mr. Krane," I
said.

He set his red toolbox down on the tile floor. I opened the
sink cabinet doors where Glenda had left a bucket under the
dripping pipes. I pulled it out of his way.

"Hell of a thing," he muttered as he opened the toolbox
and removed a wrench. "I'll tell ya, arresting Thomas con-
firms Deputy Rosales is out of her freakin' mind. She never
was one of my favorite people."

I wouldn't have thought the perpetually grouchy man had
any favorite people.

He grunted as he lowered his lanky frame to the floor and
shifted his body until his head was under the drain trap, his
shoulders crammed into the narrow door opening. He flicked
on a flashlight to inspect the pipes, then maneuvered his arm
to put the light down and pick up the wrench. He attached the
wrench to the pipe and started cranking it.

"There's only one consolation," I said. "They can't possibly convict Thomas simply because his fingerprints are on
a shovel. He used that shovel in his work, for crying out loud."

I didn't want to think about other witnesses Rosales might
have lined up. My own mother for one. This whole mess made
me more and more angry. There was no good reason for
Thomas to be going through this. An arrest? Making bail?
Hiring a lawyer? I would tell that lawyer everything I knew
first chance I got. I'd go talk to Frank Palmer today and decide
whether or not to add him to my suspect list.

Inside the cabinet, Krane muttered something I couldn't
make out.

I stooped to look at him. "Sorry, what was that?"

"The other wrench, the smaller one." He motioned with one hand toward his toolbox.

I found what he wanted and handed it to him.

"Mr. Krane, you've lived here a long time, haven't you?"

"All my life," he said.

"So you must have known Bobby Joe Flowers."

He grunted with the effort of twisting the wrench inside the small confines and didn't answer right away.

"Flowers? Yeah, he went to my high school. Small classes. Everybody knew everybody to an extent." He slid out of the cabinet, holding a section of pipe, then dug around in his toolbox and came up with two new pieces. He compared them to the old piece and chose one. Slid back into the cabinet. Krane was in pretty good condition for a man his age, which I guessed at late fifties.

"What's your take on who killed Bobby Joe?" I said.

"Don't know who did it," he said, "but it wasn't Thomas."

"What do you know about Claire Dubois?"

He lifted his head and peered out at me. "What about her?"

"Your daughter told me Claire and Bobby Joe were dating."

"He could have dated a dozen women. So what?"

I got the impression Krane lacked the patience to listen to my theories about Claire. No good reason to tell him what I knew anyway. I paced from the bathroom to the back door and peered out to see if the guests had returned yet. No sign of them. The Hartmans were still here, though. Molly and her brother kicked a ball around in the grass near the Barcelona cottage. I went back to the bathroom.

"Mr. Krane, do you know Frank Palmer?"

He lifted his head again, accidentally clunking it on the side of the cabinet. "Aw, dammit. Look, you want me to get this fixed today?"

"Sorry. Yes, I do."

I stooped again to see how the project was coming. It appeared that he had the new pipe in and was tightening it.

"Why are you asking about Frank?" he said. "I know him. He runs that tube rental place."

"Right. You know, Frank's sister died on the river, too, and I can't shake the feeling these two deaths are somehow related."

Krane put his wrench down, turned on his side, and slid free of the cabinet. "You got quite the imagination there. Guess that's why you're the book writer." He threw his wrenches into the toolbox, then closed and locked the lid.

"I suppose the writing contributes to my wandering mind."

"I'm going out to turn the water back on." He opened the sink faucet. "Keep an eye on that pipe and holler if you see a drip."

"Okay."

I knelt in front of the cabinet, and he went outside. I heard some thunks and squeaking on the other side of the wall before water rushed from the faucet.

I watched the pipes and held my hands under them for a little while with no sign of a leak. When Mr. Krane didn't return right away, I decided to turn the faucet off and closed the cabinet doors. I heard voices outside and assumed the guests had returned, so I went out to smooth things over with them. But the guests weren't back. I walked around the cottage and saw Molly chatting away to Mr. Krane. She was holding the ball she and her brother had been playing with a few minutes before.

Mr. Krane actually looked like he was enjoying the conversation.

Good grief. I hoped she wasn't telling him about the cat.

I hurried over to them. "Mr. Krane, could you take another look at that connection inside to be doubly sure there's no leak? Molly, I heard your dad calling you to come back. Sure was nice having you and your family stay with us."

When man and girl separated and headed in opposite directions, I fell against the side of the cottage and blew out a breath.

29

AFTER MR. KRANE left, I went back to Aunt Rowe's house to check on Becky. I hoped she didn't have a crazy notion to tell Deputy Rosales that Thomas stole money from Bobby Joe. She seemed to have a one-track mind when it came to the money. I guess I couldn't blame her. If the money I counted on to pay bills suddenly dried up, I'd be pretty darn worried. Still, I wanted to keep an eye on her.

The kitchen was empty, but as I neared the guest room I heard music playing. Hard rock music. I wouldn't have thought Becky was the Led Zeppelin type. I rapped on the closed door, got no response, and rapped again. Harder.

"Hold your horses," Becky yelled. "I'm comin'."

Ten seconds later, she flung the door open. Her hair was wrapped in Velcro curlers, and she held a mascara wand in one hand. I was stunned speechless for a moment as I studied her sparkly lavender eye shadow and thick black eyeliner.

"What is it?" she said. "I don't have all day."

"Where are *you* headed?"

I didn't think she was dressed for a visit to the sheriff's office in jeans tighter than the ones she had on when she arrived and a V-necked sleeveless white sweater.

"I'm going to meet with Al." She turned and walked back toward the bathroom. "Now before you say a word, I know good and well I could be the guy's mother. Doesn't mean I have to look like an old lady when I see him."

"Excuse me?" I followed her and stopped in the doorway to watch her apply mascara.

"That private eye," she said. "Al."

"You're going out with Alvin Ledwosinski while everybody else around here is worried sick about Thomas being arrested?"

"Cripes, we are not *going out*," Becky said. "I'm as concerned about Thomas as you are. What do you take me for?"

I wasn't sure how to take her. She was a heck of a lot *to* take. So far, I hadn't seen her grieving over the loss of her brother.

"How'd you find out about the PI?"

"Rowe mentioned him."

"Why are you meeting with a PI?"

Becky turned and looked at me like I'd told her Fort Worth was the capital of Texas. "He's an investigator, and I have to find Bobby Joe's money. I mean, how convenient is that to find a private eye practically on my doorstep?"

It wasn't *her* doorstep, but I kept the snide thought to myself.

"This might not be such a good idea," I said. "We haven't even begun to research where Bobby Joe got his money. More important, I don't know whether Ledwosinski can be trusted."

"Oh, I think he's perfect," she said. "He's like a gift from heaven, you know?"

The common sense gene must have skipped her branch of the family tree.

I tried a different tack. "How are you going to afford an investigator with your bank balance so low? Remember those checks you were worried about?"

She finished with the mascara and began removing the curlers. "Al said he just finished a good-paying job, and he could maybe give me a price break. Or wait until I recovered the money, or something. No biggie."

My brain stuck on the good-paying job comment. "What did he say about his last job? He didn't happen to mention who he was working for, did he?"

She raised her brows. "He's a *private* eye. They don't go around blabbing about their clients. Though you wouldn't know it from the last one I hired. What a loudmouth jerk that guy was."

"You've hired an investigator before?" I never had, but Becky was beginning to sound like she needed to keep one on retainer.

"Yeah, during my messy divorce." Becky removed the last curler and fluffed her hair. "That guy followed my husband for a week and got some right-nice pictures of him with his assistant in a *very* compromising position, if you know what I mean."

"Oh, I get it." My divorce from Elliott was more about us drifting apart than either of us being involved with a different partner. When we decided to end the marriage, the legal process was simply a dispassionate task to check off the to-do list. Things worked out for the best, I supposed, though it might be nice to have a partner again one of these days.

"Anyway, *that* PI gouged me," Becky said. "Followed Dennis for a week. Seemed more like he charged me for a month, but I gotta give him credit. He got the goods on ol' Dennis."

She prattled on while teasing her hair and dousing every little section with hair spray. I was thinking about something Molly had said. She'd rather her mom and dad stayed married. I had assumed Tim Hartman and his wife were already divorced, but if that wasn't the case—

I turned and hightailed toward the door. Behind me, Becky asked where I was going, but I didn't stop to reply. I jogged to the Venice cottage, relieved to see Ledwosinski's Tundra parked in front. The door stood open, and I could see straight through the small cottage kitchen and into the bedroom. The PI stood at the foot of the bed where a suitcase lay open.

I knocked on the door frame, and he looked up. He dropped something on the bed and approached the door where I stood.

"To what do I owe the pleasure?" he said, smiling.

"This is not a pleasure call," I said. "You can be sure of that."

"Okay," he said. "So tell me why you have a burr up your butt."

I grimaced. "Guess you're packing up to take off."

"Actually, I *was* packed. Now I'm unpacking. My departure got pushed back."

"Because of Becky?"

"For several reasons."

"It's no secret. Becky told me she's interested in hiring you."

He shrugged. "I agreed to talk with Becky, but she probably can't afford me."

"And Tim Hartman's wife could?"

Ledwosinski's lips curled into a smirk. "I'm not discussing her."

"You could have denied it." I held a hand to my chest and feigned an innocent expression. "'Who? I have no idea who you're referring to.'"

"Why bother?" he said.

The guy's smug attitude got under my skin. "I don't appreciate your staying with us under false pretenses. Our guests come here to get away from it all, not to be followed around by some dipwad."

Ledwosinski busted out laughing. "Dipwad?"

"If the name fits." I took a breath, attempting to regain my composure. "I guess you're ready to report back to the wife. Give her some pictures, I'm sure, of Tim and his friend."

He didn't respond.

"So your story was true all along," I went on. "You *are* a photographer, but you weren't here to take pictures of the birds."

"Nope," he said.

"The good news is you weren't working for Deputy Rosales either."

He raised his brows. "That's what you thought?"

"It crossed my mind," I said, "and I'm glad to know you weren't here to follow or investigate my aunt."

He chuckled. "Rowe would eat me up and spit me out."

"Why'd you bother using an alias?" I said.

"Trying to blend in," he said. "Can't do that with a name like mine."

"I guess not." I gnawed my lower lip.

"What's the matter?" he said.

"Guess you didn't come to Lavender to kill Bobby Joe Flowers."

"Nope."

"So I have to cross you off my suspect list."

"I made the list?" He chuckled. "Seriously?"

I wasn't amused, especially not today, with Thomas in jail. I wouldn't mind having an investigator to talk to, one that I could share my concerns with, but Ledwosinski wasn't the guy. When it came right down to it, he hadn't given me any straight answers.

"Earth to Sabrina." Ledwosinski snapped his fingers in front of my face. "Something else I can do for you? I'm kind of busy."

He looked past me, and I turned to see Becky flouncing down the path toward us.

"No," I said. "You've done plenty."

I approached Becky and stopped her on the path, out of Ledwosinski's earshot.

"Hope you're not tryin' to horn in on my time," she said.

"I wouldn't think of it." I leaned in and spoke in a low voice. "If you want this guy to investigate your brother and the money, fine. But if he starts asking questions about Aunt Rowe or Thomas, don't tell him anything."

"Why not?"

"I already told you I don't trust him. It's not his job to nose into the murder investigation."

She agreed without pointing out that it wasn't my job either. As she walked away, though, I figured she'd answer every little thing he asked, no matter how private. Nothing I could do about that, and I needed to check on Hitchcock. He'd be happier out of the bathroom, and I didn't want him to think he was being punished.

That thought was interrupted by my ringing phone.

I pulled it out and looked at the screen. I didn't recognize the number, but my cell phone was listed on a contact sheet in each cottage, along with Aunt Rowe's, Glenda's, and Thomas's. Since no one else was on the grounds at the moment, I answered.

"Sabrina, thank goodness, you won't believe what's happened."

"Glenda, chill. What is it?"

"They've taken Rowe in for questioning, and they say I'm next, and they plan on calling you, too. I'm afraid this isn't going to go well, and—"

"Wait," I said. "Back up. Where are you?"

"At the lawyer's office," she said. "Rowe went into a meeting with him. I think he contacted a bail bondsman to get the process started for Thomas, but then someone showed up from the sheriff's department. I guess he saw Rowe's car parked outside."

"Sheriff Crawford?"

"No, he's out of town," she said. "I think he left to keep his fingers out of this case. Because of his friendship with Rowe."

My shoulders slumped. "This isn't good."

"That's an understatement," she said. "It was Brent Ainsley who escorted Rowe to the sheriff's department. I've known him since he was a snot-nosed bully on the peewee football team playing against my nephew's team. Had a bad attitude that hasn't improved since he made deputy last year."

I had heard of Deputy Ainsley, but I didn't know him personally.

"What should we do?" I said.

"The attorney went with Rowe," she said. "I'm sure he won't let her spill her guts about everything that's ever gone down between her and Bobby Joe. 'Cause there's been plenty of that."

"Sounds like you know more than just the couple episodes I'm aware of." More than I wanted to know, probably. "What if they ask you? Can the attorney accompany you in your interview, too?"

"I haven't asked him yet," she said. "But I'm plenty nervous."

Glenda didn't rattle easily. The fact that she sounded so

panic-stricken sent my heart rate climbing. I remembered a case I had worked on years ago where a client told the authorities one little thing that wasn't precisely the truth and ended up in a federal prison.

"Either the lawyer will advise you, or maybe they can give you time to get your own lawyer if need be," I said. "If you answer their questions, make sure you tell the truth."

"I'm not a liar, Sabrina. You know that."

"I know, but I'm freaking out here."

"That makes two of us."

"This isn't right. I have so much information that no one will listen to. There are people who disliked Bobby Joe every bit as much or more than Aunt Rowe did."

"They need evidence," she said. "You have any of that?"

"Nothing good enough."

"Can you get some, quick-like? In the next couple hours?"

"How? It's not like I can pick some up at the grocery store."

She ignored my sarcasm. "Do what you can before Ainsley comes looking for you. Matter of fact, you might want to stay away from the cottages for a little bit."

"I can't leave here with no one to watch over the place. I certainly won't put Becky in charge." I purposely didn't mention Becky's plan to hire the PI. Glenda had enough on her mind.

"I'll send Lloyd," she said. "He's building some cabinets for the church kitchen, but that can wait."

Lloyd Kessler, Glenda's husband, was a cabinetmaker who helped Thomas with carpentry projects from time to time.

"I'll stay until he gets here," I said, "then I'll make myself scarce. And Glenda, if you talk to Aunt Rowe, tell her to stay calm. We'll figure this out."

"Calm? Rowe? Somebody's coming. I need to hang up."

The phone clicked, and I was left with a dial tone.

Staying calm was not in Aunt Rowe's DNA, especially not if some bully of a deputy backed her into a corner. She wasn't a stupid woman, though, and I could only pray she took the lawyer's advice and realized the gravity of the situation.

I sure did.

30

SPRINTED BACK TO my cottage and burst through the door, then remembered Hitchcock and hoped I hadn't scared the bejeebers out of him. I opened the bathroom door and found the cat sitting peacefully on the bathroom windowsill—the one I thought he wouldn't be able to reach.

He jumped down and wound figure eights around my legs. I picked him up and cuddled him to my chest.

"Boy, we have a terrible mess here. I could use an investigator's help, but I'll be darned if I'm going to that Ledwosinski for anything. He could be part of the reason for this catastrophe for all I know."

"Mrreow." Hitchcock squirmed to get down, so I let him go and followed him into the living room. He jumped up on the back of a chair by a window where he could watch doves pecking on the lawn outside.

I paced. What if they arrested Aunt Rowe? What if they thought Bobby Joe's threat to her was as much a threat to me and my possible future inheritance? They might decide *I* was the one who'd killed him. Good grief, we might all be booked for conspiracy to commit murder.

Glenda was right. I should get out of here before they jumped to the wrong conclusion and came to get me. I had things to do.

Sheriff Crawford might not see a connection between Bobby Joe's and Vicki Palmer's deaths, but I did. I was going to talk to Frank Palmer today, as soon as Glenda's husband showed up.

Just in case I didn't make it back to my cottage, I packed my computer and all of my manuscript pages into a tote. I cleaned out the cat's litter box and filled his water and food bowls. If I wasn't back, I'd have someone else come to make sure he was fed.

I said bye to Hitchcock with tears in my eyes and drove up to Aunt Rowe's to wait for Lloyd Kessler. I sat in a rocker on the porch and rocked hard enough to leave an impression in the concrete. Doing nothing was going to drive me bonkers, even if it was only for a few minutes until Lloyd arrived. I had to make a conscious effort to unclench my fingers from around my phone so I could pull up the picture I'd taken of Felice Dubois's phone screen.

I reviewed the phone numbers and decided to call the one labeled "The Shop."

"Taste of Texas Wines," answered a gruff male voice.

"Mr. Dubois?" I said.

"Speaking. Who's this?"

I gave him my name. "I saw you the other night at The Wild Pony."

"I remember."

"You were looking for Claire. I've been worried about her, too. Has she turned up yet?"

"No," he said. "Three days, and not a word."

"Does she know someone who's in the hospital?" I said.

"What? She's in the hospital? Which hospital?"

"No, no. She's not in the hospital." Jeez, now I'd gotten him all stirred up. "I thought I heard a friend of hers was in the hospital."

"What friend? I have no idea."

"I'm sorry I scared you," I said, "but I really need to talk to Claire. If you see her, please tell her to give me a call."

"If I see that girl, I'd like to whip her butt," he said, "but I couldn't even handle her when she was a kid. No reason to think I could control her today."

"She was a problem child?"

"She had one mean temper, I'll tell you. And not enough respect for her elders."

I'd witnessed Bobby Joe setting off Aunt Rowe's temper. Maybe he'd set Claire's off, too.

"One more thing," I said. "Do you know the name Colin Guidry?"

"Why are you asking about that sorry so-and-so?" he said.

"I thought he might be able to put me in touch with Claire."

"No way," he said. "That's the jerk who left her with a boatload of bills. Most of 'em for things he bought before their divorce. Bills I ended up paying."

"That certainly wasn't fair," I said. "She's lucky she had your help."

"You can say that again."

"Thanks for the information. I hope you find her soon."

"Yeah. Me, too."

I disconnected and rocked some more. Maybe Felice was calling Guidry in an attempt to recoup some of the money he'd taken from her daughter. If that was the case, he probably hadn't answered her calls. Guidry didn't know me, though, so maybe he'd take a call from me.

I tapped in his number and listened to the phone ring six times before a machine picked up. An automated voice answered. No way to know if I had Guidry's phone, but I left a message anyway.

"Mr. Guidry, I desperately need to get in touch with Claire Dubois. It's an emergency. If you know where I can reach her, please give me a call. My name's Sabrina."

I left my number, disconnected, and continued rocking.

I could imagine this as a novel with Claire playing the villain. She dated Bobby Joe. Maybe he'd swindled some of her money and she, the mean-tempered girlfriend, was still ticked off about the bills her ex had saddled her with. Bobby Joe's actions sent her over the edge, and she arranged to meet him out by the river.

I stopped rocking. More likely she killed him elsewhere, then transported his body to a place where she could dump it in the river. That didn't track either. I wasn't a small person, but I couldn't have accomplished such a thing if my life depended on it. Maybe Claire had help.

Much as I'd love to quiz her in person about all of these things, that wasn't going to happen unless I found the woman. I opted for the next best thing and dialed her number, but the call went straight to voice mail. I left my name and number, but I wasn't going to hold my breath waiting for a return call.

A pickup rumbled down the lane toward the house, and I stood to greet Glenda's husband. I appreciated Lloyd's willingness to spend the day watching over the cottages without asking a bunch of questions. Glenda shared pretty much everything with her husband, so he already knew all about Bobby Joe's death and Becky's arrival.

"You don't have any idea where I am," I told him before I left, "or when I'm coming back."

"Got it," Lloyd said with a little salute.

We exchanged cell numbers, and I input his into my phone. Then I drove away, wondering whether Glenda had told Lloyd that the authorities wanted to question her or if he thought she was only there as moral support for Aunt Rowe. That was between the two of them.

F RANK'S Floats sat inches from the road, about five miles out of town. The Glidden River flowed right past the run-down wooden structure that housed the business. Back when I was a kid, river-goers parked precariously along the narrow road. Frank had acquired land across the street and put in a nice parking lot. Smart move.

Spring was definitely in the air, but I figured the water was still plenty chilly. That didn't stop the dozens of people who stood in line to rent tubes. A few schools had already let out for the summer. Come June, thousands of water lovers would gravitate to the river. Frank must be making a good living here.

I took my place in the line, knowing better than to try cutting to talk to Frank. The chatter of excited kids mixed with Willie Nelson blaring over a loudspeaker. I watched as tubes were handed over to patrons and checked out the people working the counter. Looked like three or four teenagers, certainly no one the right age to be Frank Palmer.

Impatient to talk to the man, I decided to take a different approach. I got out of line and moved closer to the river, where I could see kids running down the bank to throw their tubes into the water and jump in on top of them. Took a certain amount of coordination, but everyone I watched eventually got control of their tube as the current swept them away.

I walked through a stand of trees to approach the building from behind, hoping to find a back entrance. I rounded the structure and came up short on the outside of a chain-link fence. A middle-aged man stood inside the fence, next to a mountain of inner tubes. He wore cargo shorts with ankle-high work shoes and a ball cap. Frank, if I had to bet. With his back to me, he flipped a switch on an air compressor and used a hose to air up a partially deflated tube. The hum of the compressor, along with the rush of the river, masked the sound of my footsteps. I circled the fence to stand where he would be able to see me and gave him a little wave when he looked up.

He switched the compressor off. "Yes, ma'am?"

He didn't look like an angry person. Better to take this slow, though.

"Hi, are you Frank?"

"Yup." He twisted the cap back on the tube's stem.

"I was out at the produce market in Riverview yesterday," I said. "Visited with Debbie Sue."

"Yeah? How is she?"

"She's doing well," I said. "We talked about you for a little while. You and your sister Vicki."

Frank threw the filled tube onto the pile. "Vicki's gone."

"I know."

He stalked over to the fence to stand inches from me. His complexion had gone from golden tan to flushed red in an instant, and I was glad the fence separated us. "Look, if you're another one of those damn reporters wanting to tell some sob story about my sister and Bobby Joe Flowers, you can shut your mouth right now."

Okay, here's the anger.

"I'm not a reporter. I live on the river at Around-the-World Cottages. Rowena Flowers is my aunt. I found Bobby Joe's body in the river."

"Don't look to me for sympathy." He removed the ball cap, baring his shaved head, and wiped his sweaty brow on the sleeve of his T-shirt.

"That's not why I'm here."

"Then why?"

I couldn't very well say I was hoping to pin the murder on him.

"What do you think happened to your sister?"

"Wrong place, wrong time," he said. "I don't want to talk about it. Not unless the sheriff decides to give the case the attention it never got."

"Sheriff Crawford told me they worked the case as long and hard as they could."

"What else is he gonna say? My sister's dead, and no one gives a damn."

"I do."

He pinned me with his stare. "Why is that? Did you know her?"

"No, but I think there's likely a connection between her death and what happened to Bobby Joe, no matter how many years have passed between the two events."

"So you *are* a reporter."

"No, I'm *not*. I'm a person who wants to find the truth. I understand Bobby Joe knew your sister."

"So what?"

"Did you ever suspect him of involvement with her death?"

"No."

"I heard your family gave him some trouble afterward."

"Yeah, 'cause he gave kids a place to go, to get away from it all and do the things they shouldn't have been doing in the first place."

"Did you suspect Vicki was doing those things with Bobby Joe?"

"No."

"Really? Because I would have. I heard he was a ladies' man back then."

"Vicki wasn't the type to fall for his line of bull," he said.

"You sound kind of angry," I said. "Here we are thirty years later, and I think you'd be pretty darn upset if you learned Bobby Joe Flowers had dated your sister."

"They never dated," he said, "and I *told* you I did *not* want to talk about my sister. Now I have work to do, and you need to leave."

Thoughts of the wrong path the deputies were taking in their investigation spurred me on.

"Why does talking about Bobby Joe get you so riled up?"

"I asked you nicely to leave my property." He walked toward a gate in the chain-link fence.

"Is it because you don't want anyone to know what you did to him?" I said.

Frank stopped walking and turned back to me. "I didn't do a damn thing to Bobby Joe."

"But you think he murdered your sister?"

He did a double take. "You have one twisted mind, woman. Bobby Joe wasn't one of my favorite people, but he didn't do anything to my sister."

"How do you know?"

"Because I was shooting pool at The Wild Pony the night she died. All night long, shooting pool, not a care in the world, while my sister was in trouble."

His face screwed up, and he looked like he might cry.

"How do you know Bobby Joe wasn't with your sister?"

"'Cause I was betting pretty heavy that night. Thought I could make some money. Instead, I lost every last cent to Bobby Joe Flowers."

31

FRANK'S REVELATION SHUT me up. I told him I was sorry about his sister and walked away. The man didn't have any reason to lie to me about where he and Bobby Joe were on the night Vicki died. Sheriff Crawford probably knew this information already, which could be one of the reasons he didn't want to hear my theories.

So now what? It wasn't a good idea to head straight for my car, because what I wanted to do more than anything was drive straight to the sheriff's department and tell everyone there how stupid they were.

Bad idea.

I hated to waste time, but I needed to calm down. Ditch the attitude and think logically about my next step. So I walked on the riverbank, upstream from the place where people jumped in with their tubes, to a peaceful area where I could think. Squeals of the river-goers sounded faint in the distance.

I thought about Bobby Joe as I climbed over rocks and sidestepped fallen limbs. He had done something that led to his murder. He had crossed, or cheated, or threatened the wrong person. How could I learn the identity of that person? A squirrel chattered in the tree above me. If he was trying to tell me something that would help, the clue escaped me.

If only the peacefulness of this place could seep into my bones and make my heart rate slow down. That probably wouldn't happen until the murder was solved once and for all. I stood, walked a little farther, and stopped when I noticed a couple of teenage boys fishing from the riverbank up ahead. They were laughing and seemed to be having a great time. A large light-colored dog pushed through nearby bushes and approached the kids. Trailing behind the dog, a man crossed the bank. I stopped short. Luke Griffin. He walked up to the boys and began a conversation.

Time to head for the car.

I turned and walked in the direction opposite the fishermen, dreading the long hike back to where I'd parked. I thought about Luke's mother, who obviously hadn't killed Bobby Joe. She was grief-stricken over his death. Luke, on the other hand, was glad to see the man dead. He'd admitted as much to me. I could understand why he'd want Bobby Joe out of his mother's life, especially if the bit about the business investment was a complete fabrication on Bobby Joe's part to take Marian's money. Did Luke know that Marian had handed off money to Bobby Joe? Was that the same money Becky expected to appear in the bank account?

I stopped walking. Griffin might have facts that could help me figure this mess out. No time like the present to ask him. I turned around and headed back. Before I'd gone ten feet, the dog trotted toward me and I realized it was the yellow Lab I'd seen riding in Griffin's truck.

"Angie," Griffin called out. "Come, Angie."

The dog's ears perked up, but she continued to watch me until her master came through the trees, saving me the extra steps in going after him.

Angie nudged my leg, and I reached down to pat her head.

"Hey," Griffin said, "you planning a dognapping?"

"Not me." I shook my head. "You give those kids a ticket?"

"Nope. They have their fishing licenses."

"Good." I didn't know where to begin with my questions.

"You look like you lost your last friend," he said.

"Not yet," I said, "but my friend Thomas and my aunt Rowe are being investigated by the sheriff's department for murder. It's absolutely ridiculous, but I'm afraid those deputies have their minds made up."

He looked thoughtful for a moment, then said, "I saw you talking to Frank Palmer. What's that about?"

Common sense told me not to share everything with Griffin, but I didn't see any harm in discussing events from thirty years ago. I told him what I knew about Vicki Palmer and Bobby Joe from back in the day.

"Once a scoundrel, always a scoundrel, I guess." Griffin leaned against a tree, and his dog circled two times before lying by his feet. "Bobby Joe might have aided and abetted Vicki's affair with the secret boyfriend, but Frank gave Bobby Joe an alibi for the night she died."

"That's about right."

"So you don't think Frank killed Bobby Joe."

"No."

"Who do you think did it?"

"I don't know."

"Well, it wasn't me," he said. "Just in case that crazy thought is running around in your head."

I studied his sincere expression and believed him. "Did

you know your mother gave money to Bobby Joe, purportedly as a business investment?"

He sighed. "She finally admitted that to me a couple days ago. If the guy hadn't been killed, you'd better believe I'd go after him to get the money back. Probably no use now."

"She's not the only woman he left high and dry." I stopped before mentioning Becky.

"Who else?"

"There might be a whole row of them," I said, keeping it vague.

"The jerk obviously thought Mom was rich. Went after her to get to her money. When she happened to mention that my stepfather's entire estate including the ranch was left to his children from a prior marriage, not to her, he dropped her like a rock."

"That sounds like something he would do."

I wondered where the money was that Bobby Joe had stolen from Griffin's mother. Might Claire Dubois have it? Should I mention her to Griffin? Before I could decide, my phone signaled an incoming text.

I pulled it out, read the message from Glenda's husband, and felt the blood drain from my face.

Monte Carlo broken into and ransacked. Called 911.

"I have to get home," I told Griffin and began running back toward where I'd left my car. The Lab ran along beside me, and I heard Griffin coming, too.

"Wait." He caught up with me and grabbed my arm. "My truck's right here. We'll take you."

32

I DIDN'T WANT TO waste a second, so we didn't stop to get my car. Griffin negotiated the curving road while I huddled in the passenger seat with one arm around his dog. The Lab leaned into me and drooled on my lap the whole way. I read Griffin the text message from Lloyd and appreciated the fact that he didn't ask a bunch of questions I couldn't answer anyway. I worried what had become of Hitchcock during the break-in and prayed he was okay.

We arrived in eight minutes flat, and I directed Griffin to my cottage, where a sheriff's department car was parked in front. Lloyd sat on the porch, and I immediately spotted the cat in his lap.

Hitchcock.

Griffin rolled down a window and ordered Angie to stay in the truck. We jumped out, and I ran over to Lloyd, concerned for the cat. The cottage door stood open, and one of the glass panes was shattered. All the intruder had to do was reach inside and turn the keyless deadbolt. We definitely needed to upgrade security around here.

I stroked Hitchcock, who seemed unperturbed by all the activity, and looked at Lloyd. "What happened?"

He shrugged. "Didn't see anything out of the ordinary. I was making laps of the grounds. On my third go-round, I heard this one." He indicated the cat. "Howling and meowing for all he was worth, making a terrible racket, so I came over to take a closer look."

"You could hear the cat from inside?"

Lloyd shook his head. "No, he was outside. I'd seen him earlier hanging around the birdbath by Rowe's deck, but when the ruckus started, he was on your porch. I don't think he was down here when the break-in happened, but he sure wanted me to know about it."

I'd have to make another search of the cottage for cat-escape hatches. The only time Hitchcock hadn't gotten outside while I was gone was when I'd locked him in the bathroom.

Griffin patted the cat's head. "This the little guy you told me about?"

"Yes, this is Hitchcock, but the break-in has *nothing* to do with bad luck. I don't care what anyone says." I turned my attention to Lloyd. "Any news about Aunt Rowe and Thomas?"

"Rowe rode back with Deputy Rosales." Lloyd tipped his head toward the open cottage door. "They're inside."

I groaned inwardly at the thought of dealing with Rosales, but I wanted badly to see my aunt. I rushed inside, and Griffin followed. The extent of the vandalism took me aback, but I went straight to Aunt Rowe, perched on a dining chair with her cast sticking out at an uncomfortable-looking angle. She held shards of a red glass vase I knew had belonged to my granny, her mother. The despair in her expression broke my heart. Rosales wasn't in sight.

I stooped next to Aunt Rowe's chair and touched her arm.
"Are you okay?"

"I'll live." Her gaze traveled around the cottage, taking in
the mess. "I ever find out who trashed this place, I'll—"

"What's going on with Thomas?" I interrupted to stop her
from making a threat while Rosales was on the premises.

"Glenda's waiting with Alma," she said. "He should be out
any minute."

"Out of where?" Griffin said. "You told me he was being
investigated."

Aunt Rowe peered at Griffin. "'Less we have a problem
with wild animals that I don't know about, Warden, I don't
get why you're here."

"He's with me, Aunt Rowe," I said. "Well, not *with* me,
but he drove me home."

"Your car break down?" she said.

"No, but—"

"Sabrina was upset when she heard about the break-in,"
Griffin said. "I thought it safer if I drove her."

Aunt Rowe eyed Griffin, then me, and nodded.

I looked at Griffin. "Thomas was arrested for murder this
morning. Sounds less frightening to say he's being investigated."

Griffin frowned. "Do they have any evidence?"

"Hardly," I said, "but Rosales is in some all-fired hurry to
get this done and—"

A throat cleared behind me, and I turned to see the deputy
coming from the bedroom. "Ms. Tate," she said tightly as she
looked from me to Griffin, "why don't you have a look around
and tell me what's missing. Seems your annoying habit of
asking questions about a murder has caused someone to re-
taliate."

"Questions I wouldn't have to bring up if you had asked

them before arresting the wrong person," I shot back. "I'm surprised you could pull yourself away from the case to come over here."

"You're part of the case," she said before turning her attention to Luke Griffin. "What are *you* doing here?"

"We were up at Frank's when Sabrina learned about the break-in," he said.

She propped a fist on one hip. "Doing what?"

He lifted his chin. "Talking."

I didn't want to get into the middle of their conversation, so I walked into the bedroom to survey the damage. Every dresser drawer was open and dumped, the contents strewn across the floor. The clothes from my closet had been thrown on the bed and rifled through. Aunt Rowe's artwork from Monte Carlo had been removed from the walls and laid on the floor. A framed photograph of my dad had fallen off the dresser. I took in the damage with a lump in my throat, not sure whether I wanted to scream or cry.

Griffin came into the room and put a hand on my shoulder. "Is there anything I can do?"

"Stay out of this, Luke," Rosales said, coming in behind him. "Ms. Tate, make me a list of everything that's missing, and I'll include it in my report."

"I can't tell if anything's missing," I said. "The TV's still here, and I had my computer with me."

"Check your jewelry," she said, "and cash. Sometimes they're after money."

"I don't have much jewelry, and if the perpetrator wanted cash, they were out of luck coming here."

Someone *was* looking for money, though. Becky. Had she searched my cabin to see if I was holding money for Bobby Joe? If she and Ledwosinski suspected me of being involved, why wouldn't they simply have come out and asked me? I thought of mentioning the two of them to Rosales, but if I sent her down a rabbit hole, she'd only have more to hold against me.

"Were any of the other cottages touched?" I said.

"No." Rosales shook her head. "But I'll be talking to everyone, looking for witnesses."

"You're going to tell our guests we've had a break-in?" I threw my hands in the air. "You can't do that."

Of course she had to question the guests. Alert them for the sake of their own safety. I realized that, but I was so dang frustrated.

"Sabrina," Griffin said in a warning tone, but I couldn't shut up.

"We have a right to privacy, you know," I said. "You better not say anything to ruin Aunt Rowe's business. And you better not talk to them about Thomas, because he's not guilty."

Rosales gave me a look that might strike a weaker person dead. "I'm going to do my job to the full extent of the law," she said, "which includes interviewing you down at the sheriff's department. I'll expect you in my office tomorrow morning at eight sharp. Got that?"

"Oh, I got it all right, and I'll be ready. 'Cause you know what, Deputy? I've got nothing to hide from you."

"Maybe you don't," she said in a low voice, "but your aunt might. We'll get a copy of her father's will. DNA testing to confirm the victim was her brother. That should nail everything down."

Rosales walked out, and I turned to Griffin.

He shook his head. "I tried to stop you."

"Whatever," I said. "She doesn't scare me."

He looked down. "Your jittery knees say otherwise."

I locked my knees to keep my unsteady legs still. The truth was Rosales scared the heck out of me. I didn't want to con-

sider what would happen if Bobby Joe's claim that he was
Aunt Rowe's brother turned out to be a fact.

Worry about that later.

I looked around the room. "Seems like whoever broke in
was searching for something. Too bad I have no earthly idea
what that might be."

33

Aunt Rowe stood and hobbled over to the kitchen counter on her cast after Deputy Rosales's car pulled away. I felt heartsick about the break-in and her damaged mementoes. She tossed what was left of her broken vase into the garbage and looked at me and Griffin.

"I don't know what you two did to tick off the deputy," she said, "but the highlight of my day was watching the hostility pour off that girl, thick as mashed potatoes, when she saw you together."

"We didn't *do* anything," I said.

"The deputy likes to act tough." Griffin righted a dining chair and pushed it up to the table. "It's a front."

His comment insinuated he'd seen a different side of Rosales, maybe a softer, more cordial side. I wasn't sure I wanted to know more.

"That woman doesn't even care who broke in here," I said. "All she's thinking about is closing the murder case, even if it means locking up an innocent person. At least you're back home where you belong, Aunt Rowe."

"For the time being," she said.

My heart rate kicked up. "What do you mean?"

"She's not finished with me. Asked me a passel of questions about our family and my past with Bobby Joe. You know I couldn't keep a straight face and say we were pals. He never deserved a second's respect, that's for dang sure."

"Shh, Aunt Rowe. Don't say that."

"What?" She looked around the room. "You think whoever broke in bugged the place?"

"Good grief, I hope not."

Griffin said, "You have any ideas about motive for the break-in?"

I shook my head. "Not a one."

"Rosales is doing her best to link me to the crime," Aunt Rowe said. "Real sly-like, as if I'm too dumb to realize what she's up to. Tomorrow she'll turn on you."

"Not the first time," I muttered under my breath.

Hitchcock wandered in from the porch and approached Aunt Rowe to rub the side of his mouth against her rough cast. She grimaced as she leaned over to scratch the cat's head.

Lloyd, who had stayed outside on the porch, stuck his head in. "Glenda called. Thomas and Alma went home, and she's on her way here. Said to be sure you've taken your pain meds, Rowe."

"Tell that wife of yours to quit harping on me," Aunt Rowe said.

"You need to take Glenda's advice," I said, "and get some rest, too. You look beat."

"Plenty of time for rest if I end up in the slammer," she said.

"Which is *not* going to happen." My stomach churned at the thought.

Aunt Rowe approached the door and motioned to Lloyd. "Help me up to the house, before your wife, or should I call her the drug police, makes it back."

After they left, Griffin said, "Want some help straightening this place up?"

"No, thanks, but I could use a lift to my car."

"Okay. Let's go."

While Griffin let his dog out of the truck for a quick potty break, I measured the broken window so I'd know what size replacement glass to get. We were both silent during the drive back to Frank's. It was near dinnertime when Griffin pulled up next to my car in the half-empty lot.

He looked over at me. "Take care of yourself. I don't think that was a random break-in."

"Neither do I. Thanks for the help." I gave Angie a hug, then climbed out and brushed dog hair from my shirt.

I fumed about my ransacked cottage as I headed back. I couldn't miraculously find and punish whoever was responsible, but I hoped I'd feel better after the place was cleaned up. A few minutes later, I pulled in at the hardware store to pick up the things I'd need to accomplish my mission. Business dwindled as closing time neared. Inside, Judith Krane worked one of the registers while Hallie straightened a display of work gloves near the front door.

"Hi there," the girl said. "Help you with something?"

"I need a piece of glass to replace a windowpane," I said, "and that goopy white stuff that holds the glass in." I'd never installed a new pane myself, but I'd watched Thomas replace one after a kid accidentally cracked the window with his baseball. It looked like a relatively easy task.

"Sure," Hallie said. "Follow me."

As we walked down an aisle, I grabbed a dustpan and brush, a package of sponges, and a bottle of Mr. Clean. Glenda kept a storage closet at Aunt Rowe's house filled with supplies, but I'd been meaning to pick up some things of my own. The dustpan would come in extra handy now that I had a litter box in my cottage.

"Dad taught me how to cut the glass, and he says I'm real good at it." Hallie reached her destination and turned around. She noticed the things I'd picked up. "You need a shopping cart?"

"I'm fine." I propped everything on a nearby shelf.

"Doing some spring cleaning?" she said.

"Not intentionally." I gave her the window dimensions, and she pulled out a fresh piece of glass.

"How can you be unintentionally cleaning, if you don't mind my asking?"

"Had a break-in," I told her, "and the place is in shambles. I'm gonna burn off some of my anger by cleaning."

"I get it." Hallie nodded. "Sorry to hear about the break-in."

"Thanks."

"This have anything to do with the murder?" she said.

"Probably."

"Maybe you shouldn't go back there. Is it safe?"

Good question. I drummed my fingernails on a shelf. I could always spend the night at Aunt Rowe's if staying in the cottage made me nervous, but I'd clean up first regardless.

"I'll be fine," I told Hallie.

The girl measured and marked the glass for cutting. "I heard a customer talking about a girl who died in the river by your place. Long time ago."

"Yeah. There's a connection between her and the murder. You hear anything about that?"

Hallie shook her head. "What's the connection?"

"Don't know yet, but I'm not gonna quit looking until I figure it out."

"Huh." Hallie picked up her glass cutter and leaned over to make a cut. "Mom told me you're a writer. Maybe you can use this in a book plot someday."

"That's a possibility," I said. "Real-life experience gives me plenty of ideas."

For all the good it did me. I already had more ideas than I could ever write about—what I needed was the time to write them. Now a murder investigation of all things was taking up my precious time while an agent waited for my completed manuscript. I hated to say the book had to wait however long it took to solve the case, even if it meant losing my big chance with the agent, but in this instance that was the hard truth.

Hallie finished cutting my glass and wrapped it in brown paper. Two minutes later, I was back at the car placing my things in the trunk. As I slammed the lid, an Escalade pulled up smoothly and stopped right behind me.

Now what?

I marched around to the driver's door and was surprised to see Felice Dubois behind the wheel as the driver's-side window powered down.

"I thought that was you," she said in an unfriendly tone. "I want you to stop harassing my husband."

I glanced around to see if there was someone else standing near me that she might be addressing.

There wasn't.

"What are you talking about?" I said.

"You keep asking Leo about our daughter, and he gets so worked up. You need to stop. Immediately."

"If Claire's being gone is so upsetting to him, why don't

you tell him where she is?" I wasn't taking any guff from this woman after everything that had happened today. There was only so much restraint in a person, and mine was used up.

Felice stared at me for a moment before responding. "My daughter is working through some personal issues," she said. "If Leo gets involved, things will become too emotional. You have no need to speak with Claire right now."

I had to give her credit for not lying and saying she didn't know Claire's whereabouts. "But I *do* need her now. There's a murder investigation going on."

"Murder?" Felice jerked back as if I'd spit in her face. "She has nothing to do with that."

"How do we know? She dated the dead man, didn't she?"

"She may have," Felice said slowly.

"You know she did, and several other people have mentioned seeing them together."

"So what? You're not a cop, and you shouldn't be investigating in the first place. I don't have to tell you anything."

"I suppose I could ask Mr. Dubois," I said.

"Don't you dare," Felice said.

"Then talk to me." I raised my eyebrows. "Claire dated Bobby Joe Flowers, then she disappeared, and he's dead. Now I understand some money is missing. Someone broke into my cottage. I want to know what the heck is going on."

Felice's eyes widened. "You're calling my daughter a thief?"

I shrugged. "Put together the fact that she's so elusive and bad tempered, and I think it's reasonable to suspect her of killing the guy before going into hiding."

"Are you out of your ever-loving mind?" Felice shouted, then glanced at customers leaving the store and lowered her voice. "If you must know, my daughter is with her ex-husband."

"What?" I felt like I'd missed a plot point and needed to go back and reread a chapter or two.

"Her ex-husband, Colin Guidry, is recuperating from open heart surgery. Claire's staying with him for a while, but don't you dare breathe one word of this to my husband, young lady. Not one word. Do you understand?"

I DROVE home feeling more agitated than ever. I had *wanted* Claire to be guilty. I'd hoped clues would fall into place once I got answers from her. But her mysterious whereabouts were only a deep dark secret from her father, who, according to Felice, detested the ex-son-in-law with a passion. The only reason they didn't want Leo Dubois inspecting the wine store's books was because Claire had paid some of her ex's medical expenses from the business account. Her agenda had nothing to do with Bobby Joe's death. She'd ditched him before he could do any damage to her life. Good for her.

Bad for the rest of us.

I went straight to my cottage and carried my purchases inside. Laid the new glass on the kitchen table to deal with later. I went into the bedroom and changed into my oldest, most comfortable sweatpants and T-shirt, then filled a bucket with soapy water and got to work. I started in the bathroom and rescued all of the toiletries that the burglar had thrown out of my medicine cabinet into the sink.

What the heck was this all about?

I cleaned the inside of the cabinet and replaced the products on the shelves, then attacked the sink and scrubbed until my knuckles felt raw.

Hitchcock sat on top of the mussed bedclothes, watching me. So far, I was getting more angry instead of ridding myself of tension. I tackled the tub, then scrubbed the tile floor. The cat played with the shorts I'd taken off, batting at the zipper pull on a pocket. Nice to see someone was having a good time. I left him to play and moved on to the kitchen. I was sweeping up the organic sugar dumped on the kitchen counter when I heard a knock.

I took two steps back to a point where I could see the door.

"Mr. Krane, what are you doing here?" I turned my head slowly to look toward the bedroom. I felt sure he couldn't see Hitchcock, and I didn't need to open the door since we could speak to each other through the broken window frame.

"That plumbing job I did earlier hold up okay?" Mr. Krane said.

"Yeah, fine, I guess." Odd that he'd feel the need to come over to check on the leak he'd fixed, but I knew he was concerned about Thomas's arrest, too.

"Thomas should be home by now," I said, "if you were wondering about him."

"That's good news." He peered through the window into the cottage. "Looks like you could use a hand."

"No, thank you." I wanted him to leave before Hitchcock decided to wander out to investigate our visitor. "Thanks for checking in."

"Hallie told me you bought some glass. I can put that in for you."

"No need," I said. "I'm sure you're tired after a long workday."

"It's no problem." He reached through the broken window and turned the knob, then opened the door and stepped inside. "I can fix that right quick."

I stared at the man. I didn't want him inside with the cat mere yards away. Why was he being pushy about this? More than pushy. Inviting himself into the cottage was seriously creepy.

Mr. Krane went to the table and unwrapped the glass. "This sure is a nice cabin. You like it here?"

I wanted the man to get out and leave me alone, but maybe I was overreacting. He'd helped us out earlier, and he was Thomas's friend.

"I love the cottage. It's a great place to live."

"Lots of nooks and crannies," he said. "Betcha there's lots of little secret hiding places in here."

Hiding places?

"Think whoever broke in was looking for something special?" he said.

I frowned. "There's nothing special in here."

"Sure about that?" He wiped his palms on the legs of his pants before picking up the piece of glass and holding it up to the window frame. I noticed large wet rings under the arms of his white short-sleeved shirt. The evening was a pleasant seventysomething with a light breeze, not the least bit humid.

"No little trinkets hidden away?" he said.

A chill ran down my back. I remembered the necklace Molly had found and the initials engraved on the tarnished heart. The girl had talked to Mr. Krane before he left. Was he personally familiar with the necklace?

I cleared my dry throat. "Mr. Krane, you told me you've lived in Lavender your whole life, right?"

"Me?" He glanced over his shoulder. "Yeah, my whole life. Sure have." He placed the glass back on the table and reached for the tube of caulk.

"And you knew Bobby Joe Flowers?"

"Yeah, sure."

"You probably knew Vicki Palmer, too."

The caulking tube slipped from his fingers, and he stooped to pick it up.

"Who?"

"Vicki Palmer. The girl who died near this very spot."

"Palmer, hmm, maybe I did."

"I believe you knew her very well," I said, on a hunch.

I waited for him to turn around. When he did, his complexion was strawberry red. Tears filled his eyes.

34

"I DON'T WANT TO talk about this," Wes Krane said.

If the man had killed Vicki Palmer all those years ago, I ought to race into my bedroom, lock the door, and call 911, but where had I left my phone? I turned my head slightly to scan the kitchen counter.

No phone.

"I didn't mean to upset you, Mr. Krane. What's the matter?" I moved my arms surreptitiously against my pockets to feel for a phone bulge.

Nothing.

"Things didn't work out the way I hoped they would," he said.

"They often don't." I took a minuscule step backward and hoped he wouldn't notice. "In a perfect world, I'd be celebrating my tenth wedding anniversary this year. My marriage didn't work out, though, and here I am all by myself."

Except for the cat.

"How long have you and Mrs. Krane been married?"

"Thirty-two years," he said, his tone flat.

"Wow, that's great." I took another step. "I don't know why you say things didn't work out. You have a great daughter and a successful business."

He walked over to the table and put the tube of caulking down. "Money's not everything."

"I totally agree. Otherwise, I'd still be living in Houston, working at a law firm." I could hear the panic in my voice. Krane still looked sad rather than threatening, but emotions could turn quickly. Would he chase me if I ran?

"I'm sorry you're unhappy, Mr. Krane. You should really discuss things and get your feelings out in the open."

"Always kept to myself, no reason to change now." He lowered his head and looked at the floor. "A wonder I haven't gone insane."

This was a certain cue for me to run, but I truly didn't believe the man meant to harm me. To be on the safe side, I moved into the living area and stood on the opposite side of the sofa. The bedroom door was less than ten feet from me if I decided to bolt. I could climb out the window with the cat in seconds, if necessary.

"You should never keep your emotions bottled up," I said. "You loved Vicki, didn't you?"

His chin quivered as he nodded slowly. "I can't think about her without losing it. So many years later, but it seems like yesterday."

"You were seeing her, weren't you, here at this cottage?"

He nodded again.

"Did you break in here today looking for something?"

His eyes met mine. "Her necklace. I need it back now. The girl said you found it."

"You could have asked me to give you the necklace without trashing my home." I couldn't help the hint of aggravation that crept into my voice.

"The necklace is very personal," he said, "and I want to keep it private."

Didn't want his wife seeing the engraved jewelry is what I figured he meant, but no sense riling the man up by putting it in so many words. I'd left the necklace in the pocket of those shorts Hitchcock was playing with on the bed. I wasn't going to risk Krane in his unstable mood seeing the cat.

"I'll look for the necklace," I said, "but you can't expect me to find anything this minute after the big mess you made in here."

"Sorry," he said. "Vicki only wore it when we were together, and I thought she hid it outside. She said under the stone. I thought she meant the steps, but I never could find it."

"What?"

"Those steps." He pointed halfheartedly in the direction of the river.

"You messed with the steps, too?" This guy was really ticking me off.

He shifted nervously. "I said I was sorry. This was a lot of years ago. A necklace could have worked its way into the ground."

"So you went digging around our steps?"

"How else was I gonna find it?" he said.

I could feel my blood pressure rising. Heat flooded my face. "You moved the steps and made them dangerous. My aunt took a tumble down those stairs and broke her leg because of you. She could have been killed."

"I didn't mean for anyone to get hurt."

"No woman would hide a cherished gift from her lover in

the dirt," I said, my voice rising. "Even if she had, did you ever once think it would be smarter if what Vicki buried thirty years ago stayed buried?"

He shook his head. "I had to find the necklace before someone else did."

Behind Mr. Krane, the door slammed open against the kitchen counter. Judith Krane walked into the cottage.

Her husband jumped nearly a foot. His jaw dropped when he saw her. "Judith. What . . . what are you doing here?"

I didn't care as much why she was here as I cared about the gun she held in her right hand.

"You idiot," she spat. "All these years, and you're still making dumb-ass choices."

"Judith, I— How did you know where I was?"

The woman's gun wavered between me and her husband, but her fierce expression was all for him. I almost felt sorry for the man. "I followed you, Wesley. Now go outside and wait for me while I take care of things."

My stomach sank. I should have run when I had the chance.

"Why are you here, Judith?" I said.

"I don't need to answer that," she said. "You already know way too much."

Mr. Krane didn't move. "What do you need to take care of?"

I swallowed. "I don't think she's here to retrieve the necklace, Mr. Krane. She looks like she's here to kill somebody, and I'm guessing this isn't the first time. She may be the one who got rid of your girlfriend."

He tried for a wide-eyed innocent expression. "What girlfriend?"

Judith snorted. "For pity's sake, Wesley, I know about you and Vicki Palmer. I've *always* known."

Mr. Krane's brow creased.

"So you killed Vicki?" I said. "Because you didn't want to share your husband? That's pretty drastic."

"Judith didn't do anything," Mr. Krane blurted. "She wasn't here when Vicki died."

I looked at him. "But you were?"

He hesitated for a few seconds, then said, "I can't live with this anymore. Ever since the bad luck cat came back, things keep getting worse and worse."

No way was he blaming this disaster on Hitchcock. "Dang it, Mr. Krane, no cat caused Vicki Palmer's murder."

Tears sprang to his eyes again. "It was an accident."

"She was accidentally murdered?" I said.

"No. Vicki fell and hit her head. We were fixin' to leave, but then a car was coming, and we ran along the river so they wouldn't see us." He paused, his expression sorrowful.

"And then what?" I said.

"Vicki tripped and fell in the dark. She tumbled, cried out. I heard a loud crack, then quiet. Her head." He lifted his hands and stared at them. "So much blood. I tried to save her, I swear."

I glanced at Judith Krane, who appeared to be following the story with interest.

"But you couldn't save her," I said. "So you moved her body to the river to make it look like she'd drowned?"

"I, I didn't know what to do." His voice collapsed into sobs. "I couldn't let anyone know about us."

Judith barked out a laugh. "Best dang news I ever had when that slut died. Didn't know how it happened, and I didn't care."

I edged toward the bedroom, but Judith wasn't about to let a move go unnoticed. "Stay put," she yelled.

"Why?" I said. "I don't care about your marital issues. I don't care about whatever happened thirty years ago. I don't even care that Mr. Krane broke in here to search for a damn necklace. It's no big deal, so why don't the two of you go on home now?"

"That's not gonna happen," Judith said. "We're leaving, but you're coming with us."

That's what she thinks.

"Why did you put up with your husband's affair in the first place, Judith?" I said. "That doesn't seem like your style."

A shadow crossed her expression. "I had Hallie to think about."

"Okay," I said, "that's a reason, but it sure as heck isn't a good enough one."

"Wesley's parents needed our help to run the store," she said. "Their business was growing fast."

"Ah," I said. "You wanted to inherit the cash cow."

Judith gave me a bitter grin. "I worked my butt off for that damn business."

Mr. Krane cocked his head. "You stayed with me because of the business?"

"Finally, the light dawns," she said. "Now quit being such a wuss, and help me fix this disaster you created."

I said, "If Vicki's death was an accident, all you need to do is admit the truth to the sheriff."

"We're *not* talking to the sheriff," Judith said. "No one is going to ruin our family name."

I swallowed. "I wouldn't do that."

"You would when you get this whole mess figured out," she said, "and you're too damn close. That's why you're leaving with us. It'd be too coincidental to find another body in the river, though. We'll have to take you on a little trip."

"Another body?" I said. "The only body in the river since Vicki Palmer's was Bobby Joe Flowers." I stopped talking, and my mind raced.

Bobby Joe had given couples access to the cottages. Odds

were Judith wasn't the only person who'd known about Wes Krane and Vicki Palmer all along. Bobby Joe wasn't above lying, cheating, or taking advantage of people to get what he wanted. Obviously, Judith would go to great lengths to protect what was hers. If the two of them had opposing goals—

I did my best to ignore Judith's gun and looked her straight in the eye. "What did Bobby Joe do to you, or should I say, what did he try to pull before you decided to get rid of him?"

Judith smirked. "I knew you'd figure it out."

Mr. Krane looked at his wife. "What's she talking about, Judith?"

She gave him a disgusted look. "Wesley, you don't have the sense God gave a rock. I wasn't going to sit by and let that man bleed us dry."

Mr. Krane's eyes widened. "You knew?"

"Of course, I knew," she hollered. "Get it through your thick skull that I know *everything*. You couldn't have paid out tens of thousands in blackmail money without my knowing about it."

"You killed Bobby Joe," I whispered.

"That's right." Judith walked past her husband, nearing me, and motioned with the gun. "Go on. We're leaving now."

Wes Krane watched with an expression of complete disbelief.

"I'm not going anywhere with you," I said. "And you don't want to shoot me here, because they'd find the blood even if you tried to clean it up, and they wouldn't quit looking until you were behind bars."

"They quit looking for Palmer's killer," she said. "You mean even less to the community."

I looked at Mr. Krane, but he was focused on something else. His expression had changed from incredulity to horror as he stared toward my bedroom doorway.

That's when Hitchcock shot into the living room like a rocket, charging between Mr. Krane and his wife.

Wes Krane jumped a foot and screamed, "It's him, the bad luck cat."

"Cut the crap, Wes," Judith shouted. "It's a damn cat."

But Mr. Krane couldn't be calmed and kept up his screaming as Hitchcock raced in circles around the sofa, cutting between me and Judith. Above the blood pounding in my head, I heard a weird jangling noise. The cat had something caught in his claws.

Vicki Palmer's necklace.

Wes saw it, too, but his fear of Hitchcock must have outweighed his desire to retrieve the sought-after piece of jewelry. He ran screaming from the cottage.

Judith aimed her gun at the circling cat, but he was moving too fast.

I couldn't let her get off a shot.

I whirled and grabbed the fireplace poker. Just as I was about to clobber Judith with it, Hitchcock took a flying leap over the sofa to land on the woman's back.

From her bloodcurdling scream, I knew he'd landed with claws fully extended.

The gun slipped from Judith's fingers, and I rushed to pick up the weapon.

"That's enough, Hitchcock." I trained the gun on Judith as she sank to her knees.

Thomas burst through the cottage door. "Wes Krane took off out of here like his pants were on fire. What's going—?" He froze when he caught sight of Hitchcock hanging on to Judith's back.

He pointed. "That's the—"

"The cat who saved my life," I interrupted, "and he's one heck of a good luck charm."

35

W HEN MAX OPENED Hot Stuff for business on
Thursday morning, he found me standing at the
coffee shop's entrance with my laptop.

Seven a.m.—an ungodly hour to be out and about, but I
had declared today do-or-die time for finishing the draft of
my book. I told Max so, and he cooperated by leaving me to
sit alone with my back to the other customers. Most important,
he kept the fresh-brewed Lavender's Sunrise coffee coming.

I had spent the better part of the past two days at the sheriff's office answering questions about the Kranes and Vicki
Palmer and dealing with phone calls. Today I was ready to
delve into fiction, preferably not in my cottage, where I
couldn't quite banish the image of Judith Krane and her gun.

Here at Hot Stuff, with background music by Kool & The
Gang, the Pointer Sisters, and Michael Jackson, my writing
zipped along. By eleven, Max couldn't stay quiet any longer
and took the seat across the table from me.

"I appreciate your keeping the public at bay," I joked, "so I can concentrate on my book."

"Everyone says you're a hero." He grinned. "You brought closure to the Vicki Palmer case that's been plaguing the community for thirty years. They understand you need some time, but you can bet there'll be a slew of questions from the gossipmongers when they catch up with you."

I nodded. "After this book is turned in."

Max tipped his head toward the window overlooking the shop's parking lot.

"Don't know if it's a good idea for your cat to sit out there in plain sight," he said.

I glanced out the window. My car was parked under a tree, and Hitchcock sat in a statuesque position on the hood.

"Don't worry," I said with a grin. "He's not going to bring you bad luck."

"I believe you, but I don't know about everyone else. Ethan Brady from the bookstore was out there taking pictures earlier."

"Yes, I know. Ethan had my permission to take publicity photos for our Love-a-Black-Cat campaign. He and I are teaming up with the vet's office to educate people about the endearing qualities and good luck that black cats can bring to families."

"That may be a bigger challenge than you expect," Max said. "Had a customer in here this morning who says her tomatoes won't turn red because the bad luck cat walked through her garden."

"Reasonable people know that's a bunch of baloney," I said.

"Of course," he said, "but you *do* have to deal with Thomas. How do you think he'll take to this campaign?"

I shrugged. "He knows Hitchcock lives with me now, and that the cat saved my life."

"Think that will keep him in line?"

"Believe me, I've threatened Thomas enough times that *his* life would be in danger from me if he even *thinks* about touching my cat."

"That might do the trick." Max nodded. "I'm glad Hitchcock was in the right place at the right time to help you. I need you to finish that book, 'cause I'm itching to read it."

"When it's published, Max, not before."

"Step in the right direction to hear you say *when* and not *if*." He stood and bopped away from my table in time with "Boogie Oogie Oogie."

I had Kree Vanderpool to thank for giving me the added confidence I needed to finish the manuscript. Her complimentary words had done wonders to silence my inner critic. I picked up my coffee cup and reread the passage I'd just written. Before I could decide what to type next, I heard a familiar *click-clomp* and turned to see Aunt Rowe on her crutches coming toward me with Glenda trailing her.

They didn't hesitate to join me at the table.

"Max is supposed to be protecting me from interruptions," I teased. "I'm trying to finish the Great American Novel here."

"How 'bout you take a break for some Great American Gossip?" Aunt Rowe propped her crutches against the side wall. "We went to see Abigail Stafford this morning."

"The woman Bobby Joe mentioned?" The one whose gossip had started this whole mess.

"Yup," Aunt Rowe said.

"I thought she lived in Austin."

"Used to," Glenda said. "She just moved into a retirement center in Mayfair."

"Huh." Mayfair was about forty miles away, a mere skip and a jump in terms of traveling the huge state of Texas.

"She may be eighty-nine years old," Aunt Rowe said, "but she remembers Bobby Joe's and Becky's mama having an affair clear as day."

"Oh no." I slumped in my chair. "With PawPaw?"

"Nope." Aunt Rowe beamed. "There was another Charles who lived down the street. Upon further questioning, it dawned on Abigail that she'd seen Charlie Yost and Eliza Flowers together that one summer. *Not* Charles Flowers after all."

"That's great news," I said. "I'm happy to keep my good memories of PawPaw intact."

"Me, too." Aunt Rowe grinned. "Bobby Joe might have been somebody else's half brother. Glad he wasn't mine."

Glenda stared out the window at my car with its feline hood ornament. "Why'd you bring that poor cat to town with you and put him on display in this heat?"

"Hey, don't blame me." I shook my head. "He has a mind of his own."

"What does that mean?"

"No matter how hard I try to get out the door without Hitchcock on my heels, if that cat wants out, he gets out. He's an expert at slipping past me without me even seeing him go."

Glenda rolled her eyes. "Are you saying he's a magical cat?"

"I don't believe in magic." I remembered Twila Baxter's claims that I had powers as a witch now that I'd been reunited with my black cat. That was crazy talk, and I refused to take it seriously.

"Hitchcock is talented, that's all," I said. "I didn't even know he was in the backseat of my car today until I pulled into the lot, and he meowed."

"If that don't beat all," Aunt Rowe said.

"And get this." I laughed. "I saw cat hair on the backseat of Thomas's Wrangler. I have a feeling Hitchcock has ridden to town with him a time or two, with Thomas never the wiser. Where is Thomas this morning anyway? Still home celebrating the fact that he's not in jail?"

"No," Aunt Rowe said. "He's at my house. I asked him to keep an eye on Becky. She's headed up to Dallas in the morning for Bobby Joe's memorial service. Meanwhile, I want to make sure she doesn't steal the silver."

"You seriously think she would steal from you?" I said.

"She's Bobby Joe's sister," Aunt Rowe said. "Wouldn't surprise me if she learned a trick or two from him. Last I heard, she still has that private eye looking high and low for money that probably doesn't exist. Bobby Joe hardly had two nickels to rub together."

I shook my head. "He sure made some bad choices."

"If any money *is* found, won't it have to be returned to the Krane family?" Glenda said.

"I think Wes Krane is too emotionally damaged to take action on getting the money back," I said. "With his wife in prison, who knows what will happen to the family and their store."

"I could never have held my temper like that woman did," Aunt Rowe said. "If Wes Krane was my husband, and I found out about his fling, I'd've had his nuts in a vise so fast—"

"And that's why you're divorced, Rowe." Glenda giggled.

"Guess Judith's temper finally got the best of her," I said. "Bobby Joe only thought he was at the river to meet Mr. Krane and get another twenty-thousand-dollar payment."

"The money Becky expected to see in the bank account that never showed up," Aunt Rowe said.

"That's right. Instead, Judith showed up with a gun that she didn't even need when slamming Bobby Joe with the shovel did the trick."

Aunt Rowe said, "Is that how Jeb says it went down?"

"He doesn't like giving details to civilians," I said, "but I heard enough to get the gist. Speaking of Sheriff Crawford, when are you going to give in and start accepting his invitations, Aunt Rowe? You'd make a cute couple."

"Whenever you hitch up with that handsome game warden," she said with a glint in her eye.

I wasn't ready to admit my interest in Luke Griffin. "Life is complicated enough without adding a man to the mix."

"You'll rethink that one of these days," Aunt Rowe said.

"Maybe." I shrugged. "Today I'm thankful Judith Krane didn't get the chance to use her gun on me because Hitchcock was there to save the day."

Aunt Rowe reached across the table and put her hand on mine. "I'll bet you would have figured a way out of that jam all by yourself," she said, "but if Hitchcock helped you, then I owe him big-time."

"At least everyone has stopped freaking out when they see the cat." I turned to look at my car again, but Hitchcock was gone. I scanned the parking lot and spotted him as he jumped up on the shop's front windowsill.

A woman sitting nearby saw him, too, and leapt out of her chair, screaming, "It's the bad luck cat!"

The clatter of a falling tray and breaking dishes came from the kitchen.

I turned to Aunt Rowe and Glenda and shrugged. "Well, almost everyone."

RECIPES

Pecan Tarts

CRUST
1 stick butter
1 three-ounce package cream cheese
1-¼ cup flour

FILLING
1 egg
¾ cup brown sugar
2 tablespoons softened butter
1 teaspoon vanilla
¾ cup chopped pecans

For the crust, soften the butter and cream cheese. Mix them together, then add flour. Chill for 2 hours. Roll into small balls, then press into tart pans.

For the filling, beat together egg, brown sugar, butter, and vanilla. Stir in pecans. Spoon one teaspoon into each crust. Bake at 350 degrees for 25 minutes. Makes 24.

P.O. 0003355266

Texas Toffee Cake

1 box devil's food cake mix
1 can sweetened condensed milk
1 container caramel topping
1 container Cool Whip
Toffee bits

Prepare and bake the cake according to package directions. Allow to cool, but while still warm poke holes in top of cake and drizzle with one can of sweetened condensed milk and ¾ container caramel topping. Frost with Cool Whip and sprinkle with toffee bits. Refrigerate.

Easy Peach Cobbler

2 cans peach pie filling
1 package yellow cake mix
2 sticks butter, melted
1 cup chopped nuts

Spread pie filling on bottom of greased 9x13 pan. Sprinkle cake mix over top. Pour melted butter over cake mix. Sprinkle top with nuts. Bake for 45-50 minutes at 350 degrees. Serve with whipped cream or ice cream.

P9-DMP-701

PRAISE FOR PAUL LEVINE
and
THE DEEP BLUE ALIBI

"A smart, enjoyable page-turner . . . Levine once again supplies plenty of quirky characters and witty banter between Steve and Victoria." —*Publishers Weekly*

"Courtroom drama has never been this much fun. A cross between *Moonlighting* and *Night Court*, *The Deep Blue Alibi* takes off with crisp writing and sharp dialogue that will delight readers. Levine captures the essence of the Key West characters at their quirkiest and gives the added bonus of a solid mystery. I loved it!" —*Fresh Fiction*

"A delicious, fun read . . . Sometimes hilarious, always amusing, *The Deep Blue Alibi* is highly recommended." —*Oakland* (MI) *Press*

"A smartly plotted and often funny novel . . . Levine again shows his acumen, skewing the law and showcasing Florida scenery while delivering an action-packed plot." —*Fort Lauderdale Sun-Sentinel*

"Wonderfully entertaining (think TV's *Moonlighting*), the blue blood lawyer from Miami and the Coconut Grove beach bum attack each case with vigor and wit. Don't miss this series."
—*Mystery Lovers Bookshop News*

"A must read for those who are familiar with the Florida Keys and enjoy thrilling intrigue, mystery, humor and sexual tension . . . You can't put the book down." —www.floridaboatersguide.com

"A delightful mystery to enjoy."
—www.armchairinterviews.com

"A worthy sequel to the winsome *Solomon* vs. *Lord* . . . The laughs keep coming in this furiously fast paced, rollicking good read." —www.bookbitch.com

"An entertaining, witty comedy caper . . . Sparkles with promise, humor, and more than a dash of suspense." —www.blogcritics.org

"Always enjoyable . . . A novel fans of legal thrillers and Jimmy Buffet can enjoy together." —Craig's Book Club

SOLOMON *VS.* LORD

"The legal thriller *Solomon* vs. *Lord* not only delivers a humorous yet solid tale about lawyers, it also proves how much Paul Levine's novels have been missed. . . . Authentic dialogue, rich characterizations, complicated relationships and even pathos bolster *Solomon* vs. *Lord*. Unique plot twists and well-paced humor help, too." —*Fort Lauderdale Sun-Sentinel*

"A delightful mix of legal thriller and romantic comedy . . . Terrific legal entertainment." —*Connecticut Post*

"A hilarious, touching and entertaining twist on the legal thriller that makes Levine's return a welcome one . . . Levine's book is remarkably fresh and original, with characters you can't help loving, and sparkling dialogue that echoes the Hepburn-Tracy screwball comedies. *Solomon* vs. *Lord* is the first in what we hope will be a long and successful series." —*Chicago Sun-Times*

"*Solomon* vs. *Lord* . . . provides lots of pleasure and promise."
—*Chicago Tribune*

"Paul Levine has written a terrific courtroom drama that's also funny as hell. It's as if John Grisham wrote a book with . . . well, me. (John, if you're interested, call!)" —Dave Barry

"*Solomon* vs. *Lord* is a howl. Not since *Moonlighting* has such a funny, combative, romantic relationship been depicted. Paul Levine uses his extensive gifts as a novelist to give us two battling lawyers who are destined to delight you. This book is a winner!" —Stephen J. Cannell

"*Solomon* vs. *Lord* is a beauty. A fast, hilarious, and suspenseful tale with juicy characters and an insider's knowledge of the court system and legal hijinks of every kind." —James W. Hall, author of *Forests of the Night*

"*Solomon* vs. *Lord* is a terrific courtroom thriller, a wonderful comedy, a delightful love story, and one of the best books I've read this year."
—Phillip Margolin

"A funny, fast-paced legal thriller . . . Levine keeps things fresh by injecting the story with interesting subplots and a full roster of quirky, lovable characters. . . . Fans of Carl Hiaasen and Dave Barry will enjoy this humorous Florida crime romp."
—*Publishers Weekly*

"This is what Tracy and Hepburn would have been like if they were allowed to show skin."
—Jeff Arch, screenwriter, *Sleepless in Seattle*

"If you love the courtroom and legalese,
you can't miss this book. If you love to laugh,
you can't miss this book, whether you like legalese
or not. If you appreciate an extraordinary mind,
this novel is a must. If you enjoy good writing,
sharp humor, and the twists and turns
of a good mystery, you've got to read
Solomon vs. Lord."
—www.whodunnit.com

"A laugh-out-loud funny legal thriller with wit and
energy."
—www.internetwritingjournal.com

"Had I known that Levine could make murder so
funny, I would have made him editor of the *National
Lampoon*." —Jim Jimirro, Chairman of the Board,
National Lampoon

"As the old adage claims, 'opposites attract,' and
Paul Levine's funny and quick-moving courtroom
mystery *Solomon vs. Lord* proves that it makes for
good reading too. . . . The writing makes me think of
Janet Evanovich out to dinner with John Grisham."
—*Mystery Scene*

"An entertaining read, perfect for a day at the beach
or a long plane trip. The two principals do evolve and
the cast is inventive and their antics amusing."
—*Books on Review*

"*Solomon vs. Lord* is a hoot." —*Connecticut Times*

"The words explode like fireworks. A raucous &
amusing tale . . . a whirlwind affair."
—*Rambles Cultural Arts Magazine*

THE VERDICT IS IN ON PAUL LEVINE'S LEGAL THRILLERS

"Paul Levine is guilty of master storytelling in the first degree." —Carl Hiaasen

"Irreverent . . . genuinely clever . . . great fun." —*New York Times Book Review*

"Delicious." —*Los Angeles Times*

"Take one part John Grisham, two parts Carl Hiaasen, throw in a dash of John D. MacDonald, and voilà!" —*Tulsa World*

"Cracking-good action-mystery . . . funny, sardonic, and fast paced." —*Detroit Free Press*

"A blend of raucous humor and high adventure . . . wildly entertaining." —*St. Louis Post-Dispatch*

"Mystery writing at its very, very best." —Larry King, *USA Today*

"First-rate . . . The prose is as smooth as a writ for libel." —*Boston Globe*

"Highly readable and fun." —*USA Today*

"Tense, sexy, and sublime." —*Philadelphia Legal Intelligencer*

"A rip-roaring read. Vivid, funny and tense . . . Twice as good as Turow and Grisham and four times the fun." —*Armchair Detective*

Also by Paul Levine

SOLOMON VS. LORD

THE DEEP BLUE ALIBI

Kill All
the Lawyers

A
SOLOMON

Lord
Novel

Paul Levine

BANTAM BOOKS

KILL ALL THE LAWYERS
A Bantam Book / September 2006

Published by
Bantam Dell
A Division of Random House, Inc.
New York, New York

This is a work of fiction. Names, characters, places, and incidents
either are the product of the author's imagination or are used
fictitiously. Any resemblance to actual persons, living or dead,
events, or locales is entirely coincidental.

All rights reserved
Copyright © 2006 by Nittany Valley Productions, Inc.
Cover illustration © 2006 by Tom Hallman
Cover design by Jae Song

If you purchased this book without a cover, you should be aware
that this book is stolen property. It was reported as "unsold and
destroyed" to the publisher, and neither the author nor the
publisher has received any payment for this "stripped book."

Bantam Books and the rooster colophon are registered trademarks
of Random House, Inc.

ISBN-13: 978-0-440-24275-8
ISBN-10: 0-440-24275-4

Printed in the United States of America
Published simultaneously in Canada

www.bantamdell.com

OPM   10   9   8   7   6   5   4   3   2   1

To the memory of Margaux Renee Grossman
(1986–2001)

www.margauxsmiracle.org

ACKNOWLEDGMENTS

Thanks again to fellow wordsmith and friend Randy Anderson for his criticism and suggestions. Another round of drinks to my Florida crew: Rick Bischoff, Roy Cronacher, and Paul Flanigan for their nautical advice; Ed and Maria Shohat for their criminal law expertise; and Angel Castillo Jr. for brushing up my *español*.

Thanks to Kate Miciak for her editing; Sharon Propson for her publicizing; and Al Zuckerman for his agenting. Much appreciation to everyone at Bantam Books for their support.

Gratitude, too, to Carol Fitzgerald, Sunil Kumar, and Wiley Saichek for masterminding www.paul-levine.com.

One

FISH OUT OF WATER

Wearing boxers and nothing else, eyes still crusty with sleep, Steve Solomon smacked the front door with his shoulder. Stuck. Another smack, another shove, and the door creaked open. Which was when Steve noticed the three-hundred-pound fish, its razored bill jammed through the peephole. A blue marlin. Dangling there, as if frozen in midleap.

He had seen alligators slithering out of neighborhood canals. He had heard wild parrots squawking in a nearby park. He had stepped on palmetto bugs the size of roller skates. But even in the zoo that was Miami, this qualified as weird.

Steve glanced up and down Kumquat Avenue, a leafy street a mile from the brackish water of Biscayne Bay. *Nada*. Not a creature was stirring, not even a crab.

He checked the front of his bungalow, the stucco faded the color of pool algae. No other animals lodged in windows or eaves. No pranksters hiding in the hibiscus hedge.

A squadron of flies buzzed around the marlin's head. The air, usually scented jasmine in the morning

dew, took on a distinctively fishy smell. A trickle of
sweat ran down Steve's chest, the day already steaming
with moist heat. He grabbed the newspaper, sprinkled
with red berries from a pepper tree, like blood spatter
at a crime scene. Nothing on the front page about a
late-night tidal wave.

He considered other possibilities. Bobby, of course.
His twelve-year-old nephew was a jokester, but where
would he have come up with a giant fish? And who
would have helped the kid hoist it into place?

"Bobby!"

"Yeah?"

"Would you come out here, please?"

"Yeah."

Yeah being the oxygen of adolescent lungs.

Steve heard the boy's bare feet padding across the
tile. A moment later, wearing a Miami Dolphins jersey
that hung to his knees, Bobby appeared at the fish-
sticked front door. "Holy shit!"

"Watch your language, kiddo."

The boy removed his black-framed eyeglasses and
cleaned the lenses with the tail of his jersey. "I didn't
do it, Uncle Steve."

"Never said you did." Steve slapped at his neck,
squashing a mosquito and leaving a bloody smear.
"Got any ideas?"

"Could be one of those he-sleeps-with-the-fishes
deals."

Steve tried to remember if he had offended anyone
lately. Not a soul, if you didn't count judges, cops, and
creditors. He scratched himself through his boxers,
and his nephew did the same through his Jockeys, two
males of the species in deep-thinking mode.

"You know what's really ironic, kiddo?"

"What?"

"My shorts." Steve pointed to his Florida Marlins orange-and-teal boxers, where giant fish leapt from the sea.

"You're confusing irony and coincidence, Uncle Steve," the little wise guy said.

* * *

Twenty minutes later, Victoria Lord showed up, carrying a bag of bagels, a tub of cream cheese, and a quart of orange juice. She kissed Steve on the cheek, tousled Bobby's hair, and said: "I suppose you know there's a marlin hanging on your front door."

"I didn't do it," Bobby repeated.

"So what's up?" Victoria asked.

Steve shrugged and grabbed the bagels. "Probably some neighborhood kids."

He had showered, shaved, and put on jeans and a tropical shirt with pictures of surfers on giant waves, his uniform for days with no court appearances. Before Victoria came into his life, he would have moseyed into the office wearing shorts, flip-flops and a T-shirt reading: "*Lawyers Do It in Their Briefs.*" At the time, Steve's cut-rate law firm had the embellished name of Solomon & Associates. In truth, Steve's only associates were the roaches that crawled out of the splintered wainscoting.

Now it was Solomon & Lord. Victoria had brought a touch of class along with furniture polish, fresh lilies, and an insistence that Steve follow at least *some* of the ethical rules.

Today she wore a silk blouse the hue of a ripe peach, stretchy gray slacks, and a short jacket woven with intricate geometrical shapes. Five foot eleven in her velvet-toed Italian pumps. Perfect posture. Blond hair, a sculpted jaw, and bright green eyes. An overall package that projected strength and smarts and sexiness.

"You listen to the radio this morning?" Victoria asked.

Steve poured her a thimbleful of café Cubano, syrupy thick. "Sure. Mad Dog Mandich's sports report."

"Dr. Bill's talk show."

"That quack? Why would I listen to him?"

"He was talking about you, partner."

"Don't believe a word he says."

"Why didn't you tell me you were his lawyer?"

Steve took his time spreading cream cheese on a poppyseed bagel. "It was a long time ago." Evading all questions about Dr. William Kreeger. Pop psychiatrist. Mini-celebrity. And now ex-con. "What'd he say?"

"He called you Steve-the-Shyster Solomon."

"I'll sue him for slander."

"Said you couldn't win a jaywalking case if the light was green."

"Gonna get punitive damages."

"Claimed you barely graduated from a no-name law school."

"The Key West School of Law has a name; it just doesn't have accreditation."

"He said you botched his trial and that he'd sue you for malpractice, except he has no faith in the justice system. Then he ranted about O. J. Simpson and Robert Blake and Michael Jackson."

"I saw O.J. at Dadeland the other day," Bobby said, munching a bagel. "He's really fat."

"So did you screw up Dr. Bill's case?" Victoria asked Steve.

"I did a great job. The jury could have nailed him for murder but came back with manslaughter."

"Then why's he so mad at you?"

"Aw, you know clients."

"I know mine are usually happy. What happened between you and Dr. Bill?"

If he told her, Steve knew, she'd go ballistic. *"You did what? That's unethical! Illegal! Immoral!"*

"Nothing happened. He did time, so he blames me."

"Uh-huh." She sipped at the Cuban coffee. "Bobby, you know how I can tell when your uncle's lying?"

"His lips are moving," the boy answered.

"He speaks very quietly and puts on this really sincere look."

"I'm telling the truth," Steve said. "I don't know why the bastard's mad at me."

Technically, that was true. Steve knew exactly what he did wrong in Kreeger's case. He just didn't know what Kreeger knew. On appeal, the guy never claimed ineffective counsel. He never sued for malpractice or filed disbarment proceedings. Instead, he went off and served six years, worked in the prison mental health facility, and got early release.

Before he was indicted for murder, William Kreeger had a clinical psychiatry practice in Coral Gables and had achieved notoriety with a self-help book, *But Enough About You*. He peddled a simplistic me-first philosophy, and after a puff piece on *Good Morning America*, he landed his own syndicated TV show where he dispensed feel-good one-liners along with relationship advice. Women adored the guy, and his ratings shot into *Oprah* territory. "You ever see Kreeger on TV?" Steve asked.

"Caught his show when I was in college. I loved the advice he'd give those women. 'Drop the jerk! Drop-kick him out of your life right now.' "

"Ever notice his eyes?"

"A killer's eyes?" Bobby sneaked a sip of the café Cubano. It only took a thimbleful to turn him into a whirling dervish. "Like Hannibal Lecter. Or Freddy Krueger. Or Norman Bates. Killers, killers, killers!"

"They're fictional characters, not real killers," Steve corrected him. "And put down the coffee."

The boy stared defiantly at his uncle, hoisted the cup, and took a gulp. "Ted Bundy. Ted Kaczynski. John Wayne Gacy. Real enough, Uncle Steve?"

"Cool it, kiddo."

"David Berkowitz. Dennis Rader. Mr. Callahan . . ."

"Who's Mr. Callahan?" Victoria asked.

"My P.E. teacher," the boy replied. "He's a real dip-stick."

Bobby's rebellious streak had started with the onset of puberty. If it were up to Steve, his nephew would have stayed a little kid forever. Playing catch, riding bikes, camping out in the Glades. But the kid had become a steaming kettle of testosterone. He was already interested in girls, dangerous terrain for even the well-adjusted. For a troubled boy like Bobby, this new frontier would be even more treacherous.

"Last warning, and I mean it." Steve poured some molten steel into his voice. "No more coffee, no more murderers, or you're grounded."

Bobby put down the cup, and drew a finger—*hush, hush*—to his lips.

Steve nodded his thanks and turned to Victoria. "What were you saying about Kreeger's eyes?"

"Hot," Victoria said. "Dark, glowing coals. The camera would come in so close you could almost feel the heat."

"Turned women on," Steve said.

"What about that woman in his hot tub? Did he kill her?"

"Jury said he did, in a manslaughterly kind of way."

"What do you say?"

"I never breach a client's confidence."

Victoria laughed. "Since when?"

"Dr. William Kreeger is out of my life."

"But you're not out of his. What aren't you telling me?"

"Wil-liam Kree-ger," Bobby said, drawing out the syllables, his eyes narrowing.

Steve knew the boy was working up an anagram from Kreeger's name. Bobby's central nervous system deficit had a flip side. Doctors called it "paradoxical functional facilitation." The kid had a savant's capacity to memorize reams of data. Plus the ability to work out anagrams in his head.

"William Kreeger," the boy repeated. "I EMERGE, KILL RAW."

"Nicely done," Steve complimented him.

"So you do think he's a murderer?" Victoria cross-examined.

"The jury's spoken. So has the judge and the appellate court. I respect all of them."

"Hah."

"Don't you have to get to court, Vic?"

"I've got lots of time."

"But I don't. Bobby, let's go to school."

"I'd rather watch you two fight," the boy said.

"We're not fighting," Steve said.

"Yet." Victoria studied him, her eyes piercing green laser beams. "This morning, Dr. Bill challenged you to come on the air and defend yourself."

"Forget it."

"I thought you'd leap at free publicity."

"Not on some third-rate radio program."

"Aren't you the guy who bought ads on the back of ambulances?"

"Ancient history, Vic," Steve said. "I've decided to become more like you. Principled and dignified."

"Uncle Steve's speaking softly again," Bobby said, "and trying to look sincere."

* * *

Thirty minutes later, Steve was headed across the MacArthur Causeway toward Miami Beach. He had kissed Victoria good-bye and dropped off Bobby at Ponce de Leon Middle School. Now, as his old Mustang rolled past the cruise ships lined up at the port, Steve tried to process the morning's information. What was this feeling of dread creeping over him? The last time he'd seen Kreeger was at the sentencing. It had been a messy case with just enough tabloid elements—drugs, sex, celebrity—to attract media attention.

A woman named Nancy Lamm had drowned in three feet of water. Unfortunately for Kreeger, the water was in the hot tub on his pool deck. That wouldn't have been so bad, except for the gash on Nancy Lamm's skull. Then there was the tox scan revealing a potent mixture of barbiturates and booze. The pills had come from Kreeger, which was a big no-no. He was a court-appointed expert in Nancy's child custody case, so he shouldn't have been playing footsie with her in a Jacuzzi. In an unseemly breach of medical ethics, Kreeger and Nancy had become lovers. The state claimed they'd had a spat, and she was going to blow the whistle on him with the state medical board. Armed with proof of motive, the state charged Kreeger with murder.

Steve could still remember his closing argument. He used the trial lawyer's trick of the loaded rhetorical question.

"Is Dr. William Kreeger a stupid man? No, he has a near-genius IQ. Is he a careless man? No, quite the contrary. He's precise and meticulous. So, ask yourselves, if Dr. Kreeger were inclined to kill someone, would he do it at his own home? Would he be present at the time of death? Would he admit to police that he had provided a controlled substance to the victim? I think you know the answers. This was an unfortunate accident, not an act of murder."

The jury returned a compromise verdict: guilty of involuntary manslaughter. Not a bad result, Steve thought—but then, he didn't have to serve the time. Now he dredged up everything he could remember about the moment the jury came back with the verdict. Kreeger didn't even wince. Not one of those clients whose knees buckle and eyes brim with tears.

Kreeger didn't blame Steve. Thanked him, in fact, for doing his best. Kreeger hired another lawyer for the appeal, but nothing unusual there. Appellate work was brief writing. Steve was never much for book work, and footnotes gave him a headache.

He never heard from Kreeger again. Not a call or postcard from prison. And nothing when he got out.

So what's with all the insults now? Why is he call-ing me a shyster and challenging me to debate him on the air?

Steve didn't like the answer. Only one thing could have changed.

He found out. Somehow, he found out exactly what I did.

Meaning Kreeger also figured out that he would have been acquitted if any other lawyer on the planet had defended the case. And that marlin on the door? It had to be a message from Kreeger, something they both would understand.

A marlin.

Not a grouper or a shark or a moray eel.

A marlin had significance for both of them.

So what's Kreeger want?

Steve tried the loose-thread approach, something his father taught him. *"Whenever you're stumped and feeling dumb as a suck-egg mule,"* Herbert T. Solomon used to drawl, *"grab a loose thread and pull the cotton-picking thing till you find where it leads."* Now Steve pulled at the idea of Kreeger suddenly attacking him on the radio and jamming a rotting fish into his front door. Where did that thread lead?

Probably not to a lawsuit or disbarment proceed-ings. No challenge for Kreeger's towering ego to seek redress through official channels. No chance to show his obvious superiority. Steve pulled at the thread some more. It kept leading back to a dead woman in a hot tub.

"The bitch betrayed me."

That's what Kreeger had told Steve, even while denying that he'd killed Nancy Lamm. Kreeger's hot eyes notwithstanding, there was an icy coldness to the man that could make you shiver. And now the answer Steve was seeking emerged with chilling clarity.

The bastard doesn't want to sue me. He wants to kill me.

Two

THE FACE IN THE WINDOW

Walking down the noisy corridor at school, dodging bigger kids with Mack truck shoulders, Bobby tried to remember the dream.

It was a dream, right?

The face in his bedroom window. He tried to picture the face, but it was lost in the fog of sleep. Dammit, his brain was letting him down. All that stuff in his head, but where was the face?

When I close my eyes, why does all this useless 411 pop up?

In one corner of his brain, floating letters, constantly rearranging themselves into new words. In another corner, the periodic table of elements, 118 of them, from hydrogen to ununoctium. *So where did the face go?*

He hadn't told Uncle Steve about the face in the window because it was just a dream.

Or was it?

Bobby decided to put his brain in reverse and logically consider the events of the past twelve hours. The same night someone stuck a giant fish on the front door, he dreamed of a face in the window.

Okay, think! What else do you remember?

A noise! There'd been a noise in the backyard. A palm frond falling, maybe? No, different than that.

Someone bumping into the old windsurfer propped against the house? Maybe. And a second sound. Metallic. The mast clanking against the boom? Could be.

Noise. Face. Fish.

The words flashed in his brain. Just like the warning sign in front of the school.

Slow Children. Slow Children. Slow Children.

Which could be rearranged to spell SIN HELL CROWD.

A raging river of words cascaded through his brain. He could shatter the words with a hammer, the letters scattering then re-forming, an endless scrawl of graffiti. Sometimes Bobby thought he could hear the synapses in his brain, crackling like a power line he once saw in the street after a storm, throwing off sparks, dancing like a thick black snake. Sometimes, listening to the sounds grow louder, watching the letters multiply, he would walk into walls or get lost heading home from the bus stop. When that happened, Uncle Steve would teach him the concentration game. That's how his uncle stole all those bases when he played baseball at U.M. Focusing on the pitcher, studying every twitch, knowing whether he would go to the plate, or try to pick him off first base.

"You're gonna be even better than me at the concentration game, kiddo, because your brain's a Ferrari and mine's an old pickup truck."

But it didn't feel that way. Sometimes Bobby thought there was too much floating around in his head, like

Grandpop's stews where he tossed in snapper heads and mackerel tails and called it bouillabaisse.

Bouillabaisse. USE A SLOB ALIBI.

The letters ricocheted inside his skull.

Noise. Face. Fish.

He tried to clear out all the other images and draw a picture of the face in the window. For several moments, nothing. Then . . .

A woman!

What else? Bobby played cop, like on the TV shows. What color hair? How old? Any identifying marks?

She looked familiar.

She looked like Mom!

Only cleaner. Bobby remembered the way his mother had looked on the farm. She was carrying cold soup into the shed where he was locked up. Her face streaked with soot from the fireplace, her eyes watery and far away. Totally zonked on stuff she smoked or inhaled or injected. That night, Uncle Steve broke into the shed to take him away. Lots of images there.

The bearded man with the walking stick.

The man smelled like wet straw and tobacco. Sometimes he slept in Mom's bed, and sometimes, after they yelled and hit each other, he would spend the night on the floor of the shed, farting and cursing. Bobby had watched the man carve the stick from a solid piece of wood. It was as long as a cane, but thicker, with a curved top like a shepherd's staff. The man had polished it and painted it with a shiny varnish.

Whoosh! Ker-thomp!

The sounds from that night. The man had tried to hit Uncle Steve with the staff. But Uncle Steve was very quick and strong, too, stronger than he looked. He wrestled the staff away and swung it like a baseball bat. *Whoosh*. Then, *ker-thomp*, the stick struck the man's head, sounding like a bat hitting a ball. Home run.

Bobby remembered Uncle Steve carrying him through the woods, slipping on wet stones, but never falling. Bobby could feel his uncle's heart beating as he ran. Instead of slowing down, he ran faster, Bobby wondering how anyone could go so fast while carrying another person, even someone as skinny as him.

Ever since that night, Bobby had lived with Uncle Steve. They were best buds. But Bobby couldn't tell him about Mom in the window. Uncle Steve hated Mom, even though she was his sister.

"My worthless sister Janice."

That's what he called her when he didn't think Bobby was listening.

There was another reason to keep quiet, too. It might only have been a dream.

* * *

Bobby spotted Maria kneeling at her locker, her shirt riding up the back of her low-rise jeans, revealing the dainty knobs of her spinal column, like the peaks of a mountain range. He caught a glimpse of her smooth skin, disappearing into the top of her black panties.

Black panties. PACK A SIN BELT.

Maria was the hottest hottie in the sixth grade. Caramel skin, hair as black as her panties. Eyes as dark as the obsidian rock Bobby handed her in earth science class, their hands touching.

Maria Munoz-Goldberg.

16 Paul Levine

Bobby crouched down at his own locker. He wanted to say something, but what?

Maria had taped photos of Hillary Duff and Chad Michael Murray to the inside of her locker. Bobby had seen them in that dipshit movie, *A Cinderella Story*, but maybe slamming Maria's favorite actors wasn't the way to go.

What could he do? Maria lived only a block away on Loquat, 573 steps from his front door. Should he tell her that?

No, she'll think I'm a stalker.

"Hey, Bobby," she said.

"Hey." He turned too quickly and bashed his elbow into his locker door. *Owww!* His funny bone, the pain so intense it momentarily blinded him.

"You read the history junk?" she asked.

He mumbled a "yeah" through the pain.

"The Civil War has too many battles," she complained. "I can't remember them all."

Bobby thought about saying he'd memorized the battles alphabetically from Antietam to Zollicoffer. But that would sound so dorky. "For the quiz, just know Gettysburg and both Bull Runs," he said.

"There's so much to read." A faint whine, but coming from her parted lips, it sounded musical.

Antietam, Bachelor's Creek. Chickamauga, Devil's Backbone, Ezra Church . . .

He couldn't help it. His brain was reciting Civil War battles from A to Z.

"Do you think you could help me?" she asked.

"You mean . . . study together?"

"I could come over to your house after school."

He tossed his shoulders, as if that would be okay, but no big deal. "Sure. Cool. You know where I live?"

She smiled, perfect teeth, the orthodonture having been removed at the beginning of the school year. "I know it's gotta be close. I've seen you outside my house."

Busted!

"I, uh . . . walk . . . sometimes. The neighborhood. Kumquat. Loquat. Avocado . . ."

Shut up already! You sound like a total wingnut.

"My hood, too." She stood up, and so did Bobby, miraculously managing not to drop his books or bang his shins into the locker.

"Give me your address," she said. "I'll come over around four."

Bobby wrote the address on a slip of paper. He knew that some people couldn't remember things the way he could.

"I'll bring some DVDs," Maria said. "If we get done early, maybe we can just hang and watch a movie."

"Great. Have you ever seen *A Cinderella Story*? It's pretty cool."

"Are you kidding! I *love* that movie. I've seen it like a zillion times."

Another smile, and she spun on her heel and headed off, breathing a "See ya later" over her perfect shoulder.

Holy shit.

Maria Munoz-Goldberg was coming to his house with her history book, her DVDs, and her black panties. He watched her walk toward home room, the symphony of her voice still echoing in his brain, along with . . .

Fredericksburg, Gettysburg, Harper's Ferry, Irish Bend, Jenkins' Ferry, Kennesaw Mountain . . .

The names wouldn't stop. But they were so soft, he could still hear Maria's voice and could still see her parted lips, warm and sugary in his brain.

Three

GAFF FROM THE PAST

Steve parked the car and admired the twenty-foot-high likeness of himself. It was a part of the day he always enjoyed.

The two-story mural was painted on the chipped stucco wall of Les Mannequins, the modeling agency where Solomon & Lord maintained its offices. There was Steve, sitting on the edge of a desk, wearing a charcoal gray suit, reading a law book. Something he never wore, something he never did. Standing next to him was Victoria, in a ruby red knit suit with a two-button, ruffled-trim jacket, her breasts fuller, her hips rounder than in real life.

Artistic license.

Then the caption, in fancy script:

Solomon & Lord, Attorneys-at-Law
The Wisdom of Solomon, the Strength of the Lord
Call (555) UBE-FREE

Victoria had been appalled, of course. "Cheesy" and "blasphemous" were two of her kinder adjectives. The mural was the handiwork of Henri Touissant, a

sixteen-year-old Steve had represented in Juvenile
Court. One of the best graffiti artists in Little Haiti,
Henri was busted while tagging an overpass with a
drawing of President Bush having intimate relations
with a goat. "Profound political satire," Steve argued
in the lad's defense. The judge gave Henri probation,
and Steve hired him to paint the mural, in lieu of attorney's fees.

Now, heading into the building, Steve was plagued
by a question that had been bothering him all morning.

Just how much should I tell Victoria?

It was one of the recurring issues of their relationship, both professional and personal. He'd been more
open with Victoria than with any other woman he'd
ever known. Of course, he'd never cared for any other
woman with the depth of feelings he had for her.

But she can be so damn judgmental.

Steve remembered the fireworks in Bobby's guardian-
ship case. Faced with the possibility that the state would
take his nephew away, Steve had secretly paid Janice, his
drug-addled sister, to change her testimony. When
Victoria found out, she exploded.

"You can't bribe a witness."

*"I'm paying her to tell the truth. If I don't, she'll lie
and we'll lose."*

"It's still illegal."

*"When are you gonna grow up? When the law
doesn't work, you've got to work the law."*

Smack. Vic slapped him. Hard. Sparring partners
instead of law partners.

So just how would Victoria react if he told her the
truth?

*"Oh, by the way, Vic. State versus Kreeger. Forgot
to tell you. I tanked the case."*

She'd clobber him with his Barry Bonds rock-hard maple baseball bat. Or his Mark McGwire, Jose Canseco, or Rafael Palmeiro models. Steve favored bats by baseball's most notoriously juiced players.

Or maybe not. Would she even believe him?

"You took a dive? You, the guy who cheats to win?"

As he walked through the front door, Steve decided to tell Victoria everything about the Kreeger case. What he did and why he did it.

Women appreciate honesty. He'd read that in one of Victoria's magazines, a relationship column tucked away in the ads for overpriced Italian footwear. Expose your doubts, express your fears, confess your weaknesses, and she'll be understanding and forgiving.

Okay, he'd bare his soul. He'd do it today. He made that promise to himself. He wished he had a Bible to swear on, wondering what happened to the one he lifted from a hotel room in Orlando.

* * *

"Ste-vie! Ste-vie!" A high-pitched whine.

"Wait up!" A second voice. Louder and more insistent.

The shouts came from somewhere between the photo studio and the wardrobe room.

Damn. If I don't hustle, they'll cut me off at the stairs.

"Stevie, wait!"

Steve heard the *clackety-clack* of leather hoofbeats, and in a second there they were. Lexy and Rexy. Pale blond twins. Models, six feet tall. As litigious as they were leggy.

One wore florescent orange spandex shorts and a white halter top. The other was in Daisy Duke cutoffs with a leopard-print halter. Both wore strappy sandals with stiletto heels that could take out an eye.

"You gotta help me," Lexy demanded. Or maybe it was Rexy. Who could tell?

"Got to," her sister agreed.

"What now, Lexy?" Taking a shot at the name. "I'm really busy."

"I'm Rexy! My belly button is an inny."

"And mine's an outy," Lexy confirmed.

"Everybody on South Beach knows that." Rexy shook a long index finger at him, the lacquered nail festooned with gold stars. "Margaux says you have to represent me. It's in your lease."

Margaux being the owner of Les Mannequins. Solomon & Lord got free office space under the litigate-for-rent clause he'd thought was such a great idea. Now he was spending half his time handling *mishegoss* for the models.

"Haven't I done enough for you two?" he asked.

"Hah." Rexy again.

He'd already gotten them handicapped parking stickers, successfully arguing that bulimia was as much a disability as paraplegia. He'd skated Lexy out of a RWI case—Rollerblading while intoxicated—even though she'd plowed into a group of tourists on Ocean Drive, knocking them over like bowling pins. And he'd beaten back a lawsuit against Rexy by an angry suitor who had spent two thousand bucks on dinner, drinks, a limo, and a Ricky Martin concert, only to have her go home with a member of the band.

"A man who dates a South Beach model takes the risk she'll be a rude, inconsiderate airhead," Steve had argued to the judge. Rexy thought he'd been brilliant.

Now the sisters blocked his path to the stairs, bony elbows akimbo, like wooden gates at a railroad crossing.

"Look at this!" Rexy waved an eight-by-ten flyer at him. An advertisement for a South Beach plastic surgeon with before-and-after shots of a woman's breasts. She pointed at the photo. "Can you believe *this*?"

"Boobs. What about them?"

"Don't you recognize them?" She yanked down her halter, exposing two coconut-size, gravity-defying breasts with pointy nipples.

"Ah," he said. "The afters." Suddenly, Steve was happy Victoria was across the causeway in the courthouse. Not that he kept his past a secret from her. Still, sleeping with a room-temperature IQ model wasn't something he'd post on his résumé. "They're your boobs, right?"

"You gotta sue that quack for my mental anguish." Rexy kept the top pulled down and stood, hipshot in model pose, as if Richard Avedon might record the moment for a coffee-table book. "A million dollars, at least."

Steve was about to say: "*A million bucks of mental anguish seems excessive for a twenty-dollar mind,*" then realized he'd told her that every time she wanted to sue someone.

"They're handing these out in the clubs," Rexy wailed, shaking the flyer in his face.

"I don't know, Rexy. Your face isn't even in the photo. What are your damages if you're the only one who knows it's you?"

"Are you nuts? You know how many guys already called me, saying they saw my tits on the way to the men's room?" She pulled her top back up, and Steve took the opportunity to brush past her and hightail it up the stairs.

"I'll go to the library, research the law," he called out, with as much sincerity as he could muster.

"Like you know where the library is," Rexy shot back.

At the top of the stairs, Steve was just about to open his reception room door when he heard a *thump,* followed by a woman's scream. Another *thump,* as if someone had bounced off a wall, then a woman's angry voice: *"No me toques, idiota!"*

Cece's voice!

Steve threw open the door and saw a jumble of images. His secretary, Cece Santiago, in red panties and bra. A man hoisting her into the air, swinging her left and right, her feet sailing off the floor.

"Hey, put her down!" Steve thundered.

"Fuck you!" The man was bare-chested and big, with a watermelon gut. Mid-forties, face lathered in sweat. He wore suit pants with suspenders and was barefoot.

Steve crossed the room in two steps. The man let go in midswing, and Cece flew across her desk, knocking files to the floor.

Steve grabbed the man by the suspenders.

"Hey! I don't do guys," the man protested.

"Steve, *no te metas!*" Cece shouted, just as he uncorked a straight right hand. It caught the man flush on the chin, and he fell to the floor like a sack of mangoes.

"Jesus! You knocked him out," Cece wailed. "I'll never get paid."

"What are you talking about? This guy was trying to rape you."

Cece stepped into a pair of spandex workout shorts. "Rape me? That limp-dick pays me two hundred dollars to *wrestle*."

"But you screamed. I thought—"

"I let him think he's gonna win, then I pin him."

"Here? In my office? You're running a sex service *here*?"

"Not sex, *jefe*. Fantasy wrestling. Some guys get off on it."

She tugged a sleeveless T-shirt over her head, her deltoids flexing, and the tattoo of a cobra coiling on her carved right bicep. Cece spent more time lifting than typing, and it showed, both in her ripped physique and in Steve's typo-laden legal briefs.

The guy moaned and tried to get to his feet.

"You all right, Arnie?" Cece asked.

"Gonna sue," the man mumbled, rubbing his jaw.

"Sorry I hit you, Arnie," Steve told him. "I didn't know."

"Yeah. Well, I know all about you, Solomon. I heard on the radio. You're that shyster who couldn't win a jaywalking case if the light was green."

"Aw, jeez."

"Gonna file criminal charges." Arnie grabbed his shirt from a corner of Cece's desk, picked up his socks and shoes from the floor, and hurried out the door.

"Are you gonna get in trouble, *jefe*?" Cece asked Steve.

"Me? What about you? This violates your probation."

"Doubt it. Arnie's my probation officer."

"No way."

"*Verdad, jefe*. On his reports, he says I enjoy competitive sports as a hobby."

Cece Santiago had been Steve's client before she became an employee. A little matter of beating the stuffing out of a cheating boyfriend, then driving his car off the boat ramp at Matheson Hammock.

Steve walked to his desk. "Do you think we can do a little work this morning, assuming it doesn't interfere with your hobby?"

"What work? Nobody called. Mail's not here yet. But you did get a personal delivery." She nodded toward the corner of the reception room.

Propped against the wall was a graphite pole, maybe eight feet long with a stainless-steel hook at the end.

"Fishing gaff," Steve said. "Who sent it?"

"*No sé*. It was outside when I opened up the store."

Steve picked up the gaff, hefted it, ran his hand over the sharp, lethal hook. "For landing big fish. Like marlin."

Kreeger on the radio. The marlin in the door. And now the gaff. It was all coming together, Steve thought, and he didn't like where it was heading.

Kreeger's telling me he's killed before, and he can kill again.

Steve felt a chill run up his spine. He sensed a presence behind him, whirled around, but no one was there.

The bastard's getting to me.

Which had to be part of Kreeger's plant, too. It would give him pleasure to inflict fear as well as pain.

"Deep-sea fishing?" Cece said. "Didn't you get seasick when you took Bobby on a paddle boat at Water World?"

"The gaff's not for me to use. It's to remind me of something."

"Of what, *jefe*?"

"Of the time a client of mine went fishing with someone else and only one of them came home."

SOLOMON'S LAWS

1. I'd rather lie to a judge than to the woman I love.

Four

LOGICAL LOVE

I hate lying.
   Strike that. I hate lying to someone I love.
   Some lies were worse than others, Steve thought. In court, lies come in all shapes and sizes. Outright false-hoods, cautious evasions, clever prevarications. Lies are as plentiful as the silk-suited lawyers mouthing them. Not to mention clients, cops, witnesses, and the guy peddling stale empanadas on the courthouse steps. Judges and juries do not expect to be told the truth, the whole truth, and nothing but the truth. And their ex-pectations are always fulfilled.
   But you should not lie to the woman you love. This morning, Victoria had asked what happened with Kreeger, and Steve had skated around the thin ice of the truth. Now, headed to meet Victoria at a condo open house, he tried to work up the courage to tell her everything. Just as he passed Parrot Jungle on the MacArthur Causeway, his cell phone rang.
   "If you been tuned to the AM dial, you ain't got no cheery smile."
   Steve recognized the mellifluous voice. "Good morning, Sugar Ray."

Seven years earlier, when he prosecuted Kreeger, Ray Pincher was just another deputy in the major crimes unit. Now the ex–amateur boxer, ex–seminary student, ex–rap musician was the duly elected State Attorney of Miami-Dade County. "Too bad the dude got out the clink. That crook, that bum, that shady shrink."

"I didn't listen to the show," Steve said. Figuring he was the only one in town who hadn't heard Dr. Bill torch him.

"Said you were more crooked than a corkscrew. Lower than a rattlesnake's belly. As rotten as week-old snapper. And those were the compliments."

"So what? The man's a convicted felon. He's got zero credibility."

"You figure he knows what came down?"

Steve felt a chill. Why the hell bring that up? And on the phone yet? "You taping this call, Sugar Ray?"

"Now, that gives me pause."

"And probable cause?" Steve completed his rhyme.

Pincher laughed. "Golly, Solly. You must have a guilty conscience."

On Biscayne Boulevard now, Steve passed Freedom Tower, the Mediterranean Revival building some called Miami's Ellis Island. Hundreds of thousands of Cuban refugees were processed there in the 1960s. Now a developer planned to envelop it with a sky-scraper.

"As I recall, Sugar Ray, your hands aren't exactly clean."

Pincher exhaled a breath that whistled through Steve's earpiece. "My job was to prosecute the dude. Yours was to defend him. I did *my* job, Solomon."

The conversation had taken a nasty turn. Was Pincher threatening him? "Why you calling me, Sugar Ray?"

"To say I can't protect you. If I'm subpoenaed, I'm gonna tell the truth. Only way I can get screwed is by covering for you. Malfeasance. Obstruction. Perjury."

"Hell, you do that before breakfast."

"Ain't gonna be funny, dude after your money."

"I don't have any, and Kreeger'd know that."

"Then he'll get excited to see you indicted."

Steve stayed silent. The conversation was sailing in rough waters. Approaching the Brickell Avenue Bridge, he beeped the horn at a lane-changer, a PT Cruiser with rental plates. *Damn tourists. Why don't they all stay at Disney World and let us clog our own streets?*

Running late, he could picture Victoria impatiently tapping the toe of her hand-stitched pump on the marble floor of the high-rise condo. Steve's mood had dipped. His desire to buy overpriced real estate was waning by the minute.

"I never asked you to do anything wrong," Pincher continued. "You remember that, don't you, Solomon?"

Sure, he's recording this. Making exculpatory statements and trying to get my corroboration.

"Only thing I remember," Steve said, "when your wife was out of town, you asked me to fix you up with the Les Mannequins girls."

"You prick, Solomon."

"And now that I think about it, I seem to recall you asking where you could score some crystal meth."

Play that for the grand jury, Sugar Ray.

"You're just like your old man, you know that, Solomon?"

"Leave him out of this."

Pincher laughed, the sound of a horse whinnying. "Both of you hold yourselves above the law. And you're both gonna end up the same way. Wouldn't that be something, father and son, both disbarred?"

"Dad wasn't disbarred. He quit the Bar. That's one difference between him and me, Pincher. I don't quit anything."

But the State Attorney had already hung up.

* * *

Victoria stood on the balcony of the high-rise condo, forty-one stories up, staring at the bay, where a dozen sailboats were rounding buoys in a triangular race. To her right was Rickenbacker Causeway, the sky bridge to Key Biscayne. The MacArthur Causeway was to the left, connecting the mainland with Watson, Palm, and Star islands on the way to Miami Beach. In the distance beyond, the greenish-blue waters of the Atlantic.

Not bad. She pictured herself waking up each morning at sunrise, carrying a glass of orange juice onto the balcony. Peaceful. Relaxing. Quiet. Until Steve put on *Sports Center* to get the late scores from the West Coast.

A breeze from the southeast kicked up, wafting perfumed scents. A gorgeous apartment, a spectacular view, a Chamber of Commerce day.

So why am I so irritated?

Because of Steve, of course. He was late, as usual. But that wasn't what was bothering her. When you love a man, you accept his annoying idiosyncrasies.

Hogging the remote.

Drinking milk straight from the carton.

And Irritating Habit Number 97, sending me to the

courthouse to take the heat in a crummy case he brought in the door but didn't want to handle.

All of that came with the territory, the territory being the sometimes enchanting, often exasperating land of relationships. A far more important issue was on her mind today. They were shopping for a place to live—together—and that raised scary questions of its own.

Is this the man I want to spend my life with? Can two people so different somehow make it work?

She tried to answer logically, but could matters of the heart ever be determined by reason? Once she had thought so. Marriage was a partnership, right? She'd aced Mergers and Acquisitions as an undergrad, then gotten the book award for Partnerships and Corporations in law school. Business arrangements were based on cooperation between like-minded individuals with a common goal. So why shouldn't love be similarly logical? Why shouldn't marriage be a synergistic partnership of two people with similar interests and tastes? That calculated reasoning had led her into the arms of Bruce Bigby, real estate developer, avocado grower, Kiwanis Man of the Year. An All-American, all-around good guy. She believed their mutual interests—opera, Impressionist art, and summers on Cape Cod—represented a balanced life relatively free of stress. But once engaged to Bruce, she discovered that life was devoid of excitement and fun and . . .

Electricity.

Which is what she found with Steve. Perhaps too much electricity. Is that possible? She supposed it was. Electrocution, for example.

What was it about Steve, anyway? He had dark hair a little too long and a little too messy. He tanned easily and looked great in shorts with his strong runner's legs. Then there were his eyes, a liquid brown, and his half smile, flashing with mischief.

"You're what my mother would call Mediterranean sexy," she once told him.

"You mean a handsome Hebe?"

"There's just something about your whole look. Those full lips. That aquiline nose. Like a Roman emperor."

"You sure you don't mean a kosher butcher?"

Now, waiting for him, she wondered if moving in together was a good idea. And *she* was the one who had suggested it.

She had taken a roundabout route, starting with Bobby, worried about his reaction. They had a great relationship. Still, being the girlfriend who slept over was different than being the full-time surrogate mom. A few weeks ago, she asked Bobby whether he was okay with her moving in. Bobby thought for a second, then grinned and high-fived her.

"All of us racking together? Cool."

Steve signed on, too, without any apparent reluctance. But she could tell he hadn't given it much thought. Maybe she should have waited for *Sports Center* to be over before bringing it up.

"Good idea," he had said, during the NFL highlights. *"We'll save money, cut down on driving time."*

Mr. Romance.

Then came the housing dilemma. Steve's bungalow on Kumquat Avenue was too small. Ditto, her condo. So today, Victoria had rushed from the downtown courthouse to the high-rise canyon of Brickell Avenue to check out this three-bedroom, three-bath beauty.

She liked it and hoped Steve would, too. Problem

was, he wanted a house with a yard; she wanted an apartment with a balcony.

He says po-tay-to, and I say po-tah-to.

She'd been irritated with Steve at breakfast when he sidestepped her questions about Kreeger. On the drive to her hearing, she listened carefully to Dr. Bill's tirade, trying to determine if it was just a shtick or part of something deeper and more menacing. Kreeger, after all, had been charged with murder and convicted of manslaughter.

Underneath the wisecracks, Kreeger sounded deadly serious. Aggrieved and angry. Just what was Steve hiding from her?

So typical of him. It was, she decided, Irritating Habit Number 98. Always thinking he could shield her from unpleasantness. Protecting the little woman, as if that were his job. Not understanding that she could handle anything he could.

I'm a trial lawyer. I can stare murderers in the eye and never blink.

"So where's the bad boy, Tori?" Jacqueline Tuttle walked onto the apartment balcony, the curtains trailing behind her in the breeze. "If he's not here soon, you won't have time to try out the bed."

"Or the inclination," Victoria said.

Jackie Tuttle, real estate broker, was Victoria's best girlfriend. A tall, buxom bachelorette with a curly mane of dyed red hair and a penchant for Spicy Nude lipstick, she drove a Mercedes convertible and worked the king-of-the-jungle market, high-rise condos where she hoped to find a wealthy, single man just dying to marry a tennis-playing, water-skiing party gal. Unlike Victoria, Jackie was uninhibited, with a loud laugh and a bawdy sense of humor.

There didn't seem to be a filtering device between Jackie's brain and her mouth. No subject was off-limits. Orgasms: number and intensity. Penises: shapes, sizes, and proficiency. Credit ratings: guys lacking a seven-figure net worth should not bother calling. She cataloged potential mates on a sliding scale she called "Minimum Husband Standards." Two extra points for the man who puts the toilet seat down. Two-point penalty for the guy who keeps his Rogaine next to the skim milk in the refrigerator.

Sometimes she would recite the names and attributes of her former beaus by creating a song to the tune of "Do-Re-Mi."

"Jack, a jerk, a cheapskate jerk. Dick, a drop of worthless scum . . ."

When she could no longer remember the names of all the men she'd slept with by counting on her fingers, Jackie peeled off her Jimmy Choos and computed on her toes. When she'd run out of toes, she created a spreadsheet on her computer.

"Do you think Steve will like the place?" Jackie asked, fingering a button on her silk and cashmere cardigan, which was purposely one size too small.

"Doubt it. He hates elevators."

"So why are we here?"

"It's a partnership." Victoria looked to the north where the drawbridge began to open on the Venetian Causeway, a sailboat with a tall mast waiting to pass through. "He doesn't get to choose where we live."

"Ooh. Assertiveness raises its well-coifed head."

"I mean, why should Steve call all the shots?"

"You go, girl."

"If we're going to move in together, shouldn't I have equal say?"

"If?"

"What?"

"Vic-a-licious. You just said 'if' you move in to-gether. I think you have cold feet and sweaty palms."

"What are you talking about?"

"You're a commitment phobe."

"That's absurd. I'm committed to Steve."

"How many men have you lived with?"

"You know the answer. None."

Jackie belted out a laugh that made her breasts jiggle underneath the Calvin Klein cardigan. "I've lived with three in one year."

"You call that commitment?"

"I call it courage. Tori, you're a scaredy-cat."

"Am not."

"Are too. You love Steve. You have from the day you met him."

"I hated him the day I met him."

"Same difference."

"Sometimes, Jackie, you're as exasperating as Steve is."

"Really? Well, if you ever dump that bad boy into the recycling bin, have him page me."

Jackie laughed again, Victoria joining in. A moment later, Steve came through the open door and onto the balcony. "What's so funny?"

"Men," the women said simultaneously.

Jackie looped an arm around Steve's elbow. "Have you seen the master bath? The Jacuzzi? The marble floors?"

"All I've seen are the damn elevators. You have to take one from the parking garage and another from the lobby."

"But did you check out the pool?" Victoria chimed

in. "Bobby will love it. You know how swimming soothes him."

"Swimming with dolphins soothes him. I didn't see any in the shallow end."

"C'mon, handsome," Jackie said. "Keep an open mind."

"There's no land. No grass." Steve gestured toward the ground, forty-one floors below. "It's all concrete down there. Where am I going to play catch with Bobby? And what's with that sign on the seawall? *No Fishing?*"

"You hate fishing," Victoria said.

"I hate rules. I love fishing. I come from a long line of anglers."

"You come from a long line of liars."

"Shows what you know. My *zayde* Abe Solomon caught a record herring off Savannah."

"There are no herring off Savannah."

"Grandpop Abe must have caught them all."

"Don't be difficult," Jackie intervened. She put both hands on her hips in a motion that pushed her breasts higher. "Steve, you have a few things going for you in the husband sweepstakes. You're single, straight, and self-supporting. But frankly, I've pulled your credit report, and you're not exactly Donald Trump."

"I'll dye my hair orange if that'll help."

"You drive a ratty old car, you dress like a Jimmy Buffet roadie, and except for what I've been told are your talents in the bedroom—"

"Jackie!" Victoria blushed.

"You're not all that great a prize," Jackie continued, "and my best bud deserves the best. So why not just chill and let Tori choose a place to live?"

"Hey, I get a vote here, Jack-o," Steve said.

She dismissed the notion with a wave of her fingernails, painted the pinkish color called "Italian Love Affair." "I've seen your house, Steve. You obviously have *no* sense of design or style."

"You mean I have no pretensions like those trust-fund boys you run around with."

"Stop it, you two," Victoria ordered. "Steve, don't be mean to Jackie."

"Me? She's the one who wishes you'd married Bigby."

"True," Jackie admitted. "But I told her to keep you on the side." She gestured toward the interior of the apartment. "Now, why don't we look at the master suite?"

"I hate this place," Steve said.

Sounding like a child, Victoria thought. A petulant child.

"I'm wasting my time here," Jackie said. "Toodles." She waved and headed back through the balcony door.

Victoria gave Steve one of her piercing looks.

"What? What'd I do, besides tell the truth?" he asked.

"You walked in throwing hand grenades. Why didn't you just call and say there's no way you'd live here?"

"I wasn't sure until the concierge spoke French to me."

"I'm serious, Steve. It's unfair to Jackie. She's doing us a favor."

"Not unless she kicks back half her commission." Steve took a deep breath. "Look, Vic. We need to talk."

"I know. You want a house with a yard and crab-grass."

"It's not that." He cast a long look toward the sail-boats, as if he wanted to be on one. "I need to tell you about Kreeger."

"You do?" She didn't even try to hide her surprise.

"This morning, I wasn't entirely truthful with you. Now I want to tell you everything."

"You do?" Sounding as skeptical as she felt.

"I've been too closed off. I'm going to share more of myself."

She studied him a moment. "Are you gaming me?"

"Jeez, when did you get so cynical?"

"When you taught me that everybody lies under oath."

"Look, I'm not saying I'm gonna become Mr. Sensitive. I'm as scared as the next guy to show weakness, but what I did this morning wasn't fair. I answered your questions about Kreeger like I was before the Grand Jury. So I'm gonna tell you what happened with him and maybe use that to open up on other stuff, too."

She threw both arms around his neck and drew him close. "You're a wonderful man, Steve Solomon, you know that?"

"Before you make that final, you might want to hear me out."

SOLOMON'S LAWS

2. Thou shalt not screw thy own client . . . unless thou hast a damn good reason.

Five

SURVIVAL OF THE HOMICIDAL

A pelican sat on a coral boulder, scratching its feathery belly with its beak. Steve and Victoria walked along Bayfront Drive, a wall of condos on one side, the flat, green water of Biscayne Bay on the other. Her sunglasses were perched on top her head and her long stride tugged her Sunny Choi pencil skirt tight at the hips. Steve didn't know Sunny Choi from chicken chow mein, but he'd started picking up slivers of fashion information by listening to Victoria's end of phone conversations with Jackie.

They headed in and out of shadows cast by the high-rises, the sun slanting toward the Everglades. In the light, Victoria's hair glowed with butterscotch highlights. In the shadows, her green eyes gave off their own light. She seemed happy, already forgiving Steve for being late, for being obstreperous, for being . . . Steve.

"I did something in Kreeger's case I'd never done before and haven't since," he said. "And I'm not proud of it."

"Tell me. Tell me everything, Steve."

Her nurturing tone. That was it. Women were born

nuterers. Cling to their warm bosoms, and everything will be all right. This would be easy. Victoria was, by nature, supportive and caring. And forgiving.

"The case against Kreeger was purely circumstantial," he said. "I thought I could win."

"You always think you can win."

"Yeah, but this was different. I thought Kreeger was innocent."

He didn't have to say, *"as opposed to not guilty."* Victoria knew the difference. In criminal cases, you seldom defend a person who is truly I-didn't-do-the-crime innocent. But you'll often defend someone who almost certainly did the crime; the state just can't prove it. That's the difference between *innocent* and *not guilty.*

As everyone knows who watches blabbermouth lawyers on TV dissecting the latest trial of the century, the state must prove guilt beyond every reasonable doubt. The prosecutor is the sturdy workman at the center of a storm, carrying sandbags to the dike, staving off the flood that will swamp the state's case. The defense lawyer is the vandal, poking holes in the sandbags, pissing in the river, and praying for even more rain. Steve believed he was second to none in the hole-poking and river-pissing departments. He took seriously the lawyer's duty to zealously defend his client. And he always had. Except once.

"Kreeger had no criminal record," Steve continued. "He was wealthy, well known, respected. He was the court-appointed expert in a nasty child custody fight. At the same time, he was having an affair with the mother."

"Not nice."

"A woman named Nancy Lamm. Not only does

Kreeger seduce her, he gives her bushel baskets of pills, overprescribing antidepressants and sedatives. They have a falling-out, and she threatens to file a complaint with DPR, go after his license."

"Sounds like the state had its motive. Kill her. Shut her up."

"That's what Pincher argued to the jury, but think about it, Vic. If Kreeger planned to kill her, would he do it at his house, in his hot tub, with his drugs in her system?"

"If criminals were smart, we'd be out of business."

"Kreeger has a genius IQ. If he wanted to kill Nancy Lamm, it would have been a lot cleaner."

"Unless he snapped."

"He's not given to rages. He's a smart, calculating man who just happens to have a woman drown in his hot tub after mixing booze and barbiturates."

"Any signs of trauma?"

"Excellent question, Counselor. Laceration on the skull. Pincher's theory was that Kreeger bashed her with something, then tossed her into the hot tub. Kreeger told me he was in the house mixing a pitcher of daiquiris. When he came out, he found her in the tub. My theory was that she was zonked out of her mind, slipped on the wet pool deck, hit her head on the rounded edge of the tub, and tumbled in."

"Sounds pretty far-fetched to me."

"I had a human-factors expert who backed me up. Said it was within the realm of reasonable probability. We also put together a video animation that looked pretty convincing."

"So you made the slip-and-fall argument without blushing?"

"I never blush."

"Right. Not even when you claimed your client shouldn't have to return the engagement ring she accepted when she was . . . what was the term you used?"

" 'Temporarily unavailable for matrimony.' "

"Right. Solomon-speak for 'already married.' "

They walked past the Sheraton Hotel and neared the bridge to Brickell Key, once an undeveloped island, now a concrete jungle of high-rises, with barely a tree or shrub that wasn't potted on a condo balcony. A heavyset shirtless jogger plugged into an iPod lumbered past them.

"What did the coroner say about the laceration?" Victoria asked.

"Inconclusive. Could have come from impact with the tub or something else with a rounded edge."

"Such as?"

"The skimmer pole used to clean the pool."

"Did they test it, match up the marks?"

"Couldn't. The pole was missing. Never found."

"Oh, isn't that convenient?"

"Yeah, Pincher ranted and railed about that. Suggested to the jury that Kreeger smacked the woman with the pole, then got rid of it before he called nine-one-one."

They approached the small park at the point where the Miami River pours into Biscayne Bay. Off to one side was Miami Circle, the archeological site that dates back two thousand years. Long before Brickell Avenue was populated with lawyers and investment bankers and CPAs, a hardwood hammock stretched along the bay, a prairie ran inland, and Native Americans camped on the banks of the river, cooking their wild game over open flames and making carvings in the limestone.

"You already know what the jury did," Steve said. "Acquitted on murder and convicted on manslaughter."

"The curse of the lesser included offense."

"Exactly. A no-guts compromise verdict. They should have either convicted Kreeger of murder or acquitted him. But forget that for a second, Vic. You be a jury of one. What's *your* verdict?"

"I hope you don't think I'm being critical," she began. Her feminine way of softening whatever might follow, couching her criticism in terms as comfy as bedroom slippers. "I'm surprised the jury didn't acquit. Without a murder weapon, with a reasonable alternative scenario for the head wound, your guy should have walked."

"I thought you'd say that. But it wasn't a fair question. I left something out."

"Something incriminating?"

"You tell me. Let's go back almost twenty years. Kreeger's just finishing med school at Shands. To celebrate, he takes a weekend trip down to Islamorada with a couple classmates. One's his best friend, a guy named Jim Beshears. The other is Beshear's girlfriend."

Victoria seemed puzzled. "What's a trip to the Keys have to do with the dead lady in the hot tub twenty years later?"

"Like I always say to the jury, please wait until my entire case is presented before reaching any conclusions."

Victoria shrugged and he continued. "The three of them—Kreeger, Beshears, and the girlfriend—charter a boat to go after marlin. Now, they've been drinking all weekend, and everything they know about fish they learned at Red Lobster, but somehow Beshears' girlfriend manages to hook a marlin and fight the thing till it's alongside the boat. Not a huge one as marlins go, but still a couple hundred pounds or so. The captain's on the fly bridge, and Kreeger and Beshears are like Abbott and Costello trying to land the fish. Kreeger's waving a gaff and Beshears is leaning over the gunwale, and somehow the fish lands in the cockpit and Beshears lands in the drink."

"Okay, so he went overboard. They haul him aboard, right?"

"The girlfriend throws him a life ring but he can't reach it. Beshears is swallowing water and panicking. Kreeger leans over the side, holding the gaff for Beshears to grab on to. But the boat's rocking and Beshears is riding up and down on the waves, and somehow in the confusion, Kreeger brains him with the gaff. The captain's trying to maneuver the boat and they lose sight of Beshears until he's dragged into the props and chopped into sushi."

"Oh, God. You're not saying Kreeger intended to kill him? I mean, there's no proof of that, right?"

"No more than with Nancy Lamm in the hot tub."

"Meaning what?"

"All weekend long, Beshears had been busting Kreeger's balls about some paper he wrote, claiming Kreeger'd phonied up research to justify his conclusions about evolutionary psychology. Kreeger believed that murder is a natural consequence of our being human, that evolution favored those who kill their rivals."

"Survival of the homicidal."

"Exactly. Kreeger wrote that killing is programmed into our DNA, rather than being aberrational conduct. He did some studies with undergrads, measuring their propensity for violence. Beshears needled him the way guys do, calling him a fraud. Kreeger warned him to shut up, and it just kept getting uglier."

The sun had angled lower in the sky and was shooting daggers into their eyes. Victoria slipped her sunglasses down from the top of her head. "Pattern conduct," she said softly, as if thinking aloud. "Beshears and Lamm. Two people who pose threats to Kreeger. Each one gets clobbered on the head and knocked into the water. Both end up dead. Each time it looks like an accident. Similar facts under the Williams Rule."

"Which is how Pincher got the Beshears story into evidence, crippling my defense."

"Pincher's usually so lazy, I'm surprised he discovered the earlier case."

"He didn't."

"So how'd he find out about the fishing trip and the guy dying?"

"I told him," Steve said.

"No. You didn't."

"I did, Vic. I gave Pincher all the evidence he needed to convict my client."

Victoria's lower lip seemed to tremble. Then she shook her head, as if trying to cast out the memory of what she just heard. "You violated your oath?"

"I had a good reason."

"There's never a good reason," Victoria said, turning away.

Six

THE LOVE CHILD OF
AYN RAND AND TED BUNDY

Victoria tried to process what she had just heard. Just yards away, students at the dig site worked on hands and knees with trowels and whisk brooms, searching for archeological treasures.

She could hardly believe what he'd told her. Steve never rolled over and played dead for anyone. In court, he always fought hard and sometimes dirty. More than once, he had spent the night behind bars for contempt.

"A lawyer who's afraid of jail is like a surgeon who's afraid of blood."

He'd told her that the day they met. At that moment, they were ensconced in adjacent holding cells. He had provoked her in the courtroom. She'd lost her cool and they'd been held in mutual contempt. Which is the way they felt about each other. In the lockup, he had ridiculed her propriety; she'd railed about his ethics, or lack thereof.

"You make a mockery of the law."

"I make up my own. Solomon's Laws."

She knew that Steve cut corners to win. But breaking the law to *lose?* That was a new one. And perhaps even more frightening because it cut to the heart of the lawyer's oath. A lawyer was supposed to zealously defend—not double-cross—his or her client.

"Come on, Steve. You didn't give incriminating evidence to the state."

"Yes, I did."

"Why?"

"Kreeger lied to me, and I caught him at it."

"Then you should have withdrawn from the case."

"Then he would have lied to his next lawyer, and he would have gotten off. Like you said, without evidence of the earlier death, the state had a weak case."

"That's the system. The net has holes in it. Sometimes the guilty fall through so the innocent won't be snared. You, of all people, must know that."

Here she was, a former prosecutor, telling Steve-the-Shyster that it's okay for murderers to walk. She couldn't believe the role reversal at play.

"Somebody had to stop him," Steve said. "Kreeger killed Jim Beshears and Nancy Lamm."

"Dammit, Steve! You don't know that."

"I felt it in my bones. I was dead-solid certain."

"Even if you're right, a defense lawyer can't be a secret agent for the state."

She glared at the man she loved, the man she planned to live with, might even someday marry. But this was just astonishing. Something her mother once said came back to her.

"Men's deceptions are always the tip of the ice cube."

"You mean iceberg, Mother?"

"Not if they're drinking Scotch on the rocks. My point, Princess, if you catch them in one lie, others will surely follow."

In her chosen career as a glamorous widow, Irene Lord, The Queen, had developed a healthy cynicism about men. Victoria had picked up some of that. But it never seemed to apply to Steve. Most men put on a front and hide their aggravating traits. Like the archeology students at the dig site, you have to scrape with shovel and trowel to find their true nature. Not so with Steve. He hid his softer, caring side—his love for Bobby, his pro bono work, his passionate commitment to justice—under an exterior that could be both overbearing and unbearable.

She forced herself to speak to him in even, measured tones. "I understand your motive, but you stepped so far over the line, I have to question whether you're fit to be a lawyer."

"Jeez, why are you taking this so personally?" Sounding hurt.

"How am I supposed to take it? I'm your partner. And your lover."

"You weren't either one when this went down."

She clenched her teeth so hard, she felt her jaw muscles ache. "Would you like to restore the status quo ante?"

"Aw, c'mon, Vic. I didn't mean it that way. More like, you weren't around to influence me, so I did some things I wouldn't do now."

"Nice recovery, Slick. But what you did was still unethical and illegal."

"Okay, already. I've gotten over it. You should, too."

"Just like that! Could you give me a few minutes first?"

One of the students at the dig site, a young woman in khaki shorts, stood and yelled. She held something in her hand and waved to the others. From this distance it was impossible to make out the item. A shard of pottery, an arrowhead, some artifact of the Tequesta Indians? Scratching away to learn secrets of the past.

Victoria went into her lawyer mode. Speaking softly, as if thinking out loud, she said: "Kreeger probably can't sue you because the statute of limitations has run. But there's no limitations period on ethical violations. He could have you disbarred."

"Or hit me with a marlin gaff."

He told her then about the gaff delivered to the office. "The marlin on the door. The gaff. Kreeger's way of saying he knows I torpedoed his case."

"But why tell you?"

"To let me know he can do the same thing to me he did to Beshears and Lamm."

"So selling out your client wasn't just blatantly illegal," she said, shaking her head in disbelief. "It was also unbelievably stupid."

* * *

Her anger surprised him. What happened to that warm and comfy nurturing he'd expected?

What happened to clinging to her warm bosom?

Steve thought back to the day he'd discovered Kreeger's secret. He'd been looking for helpful witnesses, not damning ones. Kreeger had become a bit of a celebrity. The psychiatrist had done work with the FBI's Behavioral Science Unit and gained some credibility as an expert on serial killers. Turn on CNN or Court TV, and he'd pop up every time some freak was loose. Then he moved into personal relationships, which Steve figured wasn't all that different than homicide. Relaxed in front of the camera, Kreeger got his daytime TV show, dispensing wisdom to women fed up with their men, an inexhaustible and ever-growing audience.

Steve traveled to the med school in Gainesville, trying to find character witnesses. He spoke to a professor who remembered Kreeger and told a murky story about a fishing trip gone bad. A few more calls turned up the former girlfriend of the late Jim Beshears. The girlfriend told Steve that Kreeger had been enraged by Beshears' charges of academic fraud. The two men had argued, and from her vantage point in the cockpit of the boat, she thought Kreeger might have pushed Beshears overboard, then intentionally hit him with the gaff. But everything had happened so fast and she'd been so shaken, she couldn't be sure. Officially, the death was declared an accident without a full criminal investigation.

Then Steve read Kreeger's bestselling book: *Looking Out for Numero Uno*. The man's views of human nature were downright macabre. In chapter one, "Screw Thy Neighbor," Kreeger posited that greed, hedonism, and selfishness are good. Altruism, charity, and sacrifice are stupid. Self-interest is the only interest. Be the screwer, not the screwee. The more he read, the more concerned Steve became.

He went back to Gainesville and puttered around in the Shands Hospital library. He found Kreeger's monograph, *Murder Through the Eons: Homicide as an Essential Element of Evolutionary Biology*. While a hospital resident on the psychiatry staff, Kreeger had argued that human beings were bred to be murderers. Homicidal instincts, he wrote, are survival tactics dating from prehistoric times. By historical practice, it is rational and sane to kill anyone who threatens your cave, your mate, or your dinner. Our DNA carries those instincts today.

"Murder should not be considered a perversion of human values. Murder is the essential human value."

Then Kreeger went even further. To kill rationally, he declared, does not require one to be engaged in self-defense. Setting aside man-made notions of right and wrong, it would be logical to kill a rival for a promotion at work or for the love of a woman or even for the last seat on a bus.

Suddenly, preparing for the man's trial, it had all become clear to Steve.

William Kreeger, MD, was the love child of Ayn Rand and Ted Bundy.

A man so possessed of narcissism and self-interest and so devoid of feelings for others that he would eliminate anyone he believed was a threat.

His classmate. His lady friend. Or his lawyer.

Sure, Victoria was right. Not only was it illegal to turn over incriminating evidence to the state, with Kreeger as a client, it was also dangerous. So what now? Kreeger wouldn't be satisfied with pranks involving dead fish, marlin gaffs, and trash talk on the radio. Those were just preludes.

Kreeger could be planning his attack right now.

Which meant Steve needed a counterattack. Or better yet, an offensive. A way to bring down Kreeger *before* he took his shot. But how?

Storm into the radio station, jack Kreeger up against the wall, and rattle his fillings.

Nah.

Steve was a lawyer. A schmoozer. He could bob and weave in front of a jury and play rope-a-dope with opposing counsel. But violence? Not his style. Sure, he'd taken one swing with a stick that cracked a man's skull, but that had been necessary to rescue Bobby. What else?

Punching that probation officer in dubious defense of Cece's virtue? Not very impressive. Starting a brawl years ago by spiking the Florida State shortstop while breaking up a double play? Nah, nobody even got bruised.

But Kreeger? The man had a track record of deadly violence. So Steve needed a plan. But a problem there, too. How do you outsmart a man who is both brilliant and a killer, when you are neither?

SOLOMON'S LAWS

3. When you don't know what to do, seek advice from your father . . . even if he's two candles short of a menorah.

Seven

KING SOLOMON AND THE
QUEEN OF SHEBA

Steve needed advice. He needed to talk to the man who had once peered down at assorted miscreants, pronouncing them guilty, dispatching them to places where the only harm they could inflict was on one another. The Honorable Herbert T. Solomon had a feel for this sort of thing.

What do I do, Dad, when some nutcase is after me?

Steve walked out the kitchen door into his backyard. His father and nephew sat cross-legged on the ground, in the shade of a bottlebrush tree. Pieces of plywood and two-by-fours were strewn on the grass, along with a hammer, a saw, and an open toolbox.

"*Shalom,* son," his father called out. Chin stubbled with white whiskers, long silvery hair swept straight back, flipping up at his neck. With a bottle of sour mash whiskey within arm's reach, Herbert T. Solomon looked like Wild Bill Hickock in a yarmulke.

Or maybe a biblical prophet. He held a weathered copy of the Old Testament in one hand and a drink in the other. "The Queen of Sheba," Herbert intoned in his Southern drawl, "having heard of Solomon's fame, came to test him with tricky questions."

"Get to the sexy part," Bobby said. "Where Solomon slips it to Sheba and all the concubines."

Herbert took a sip of the whiskey. "In due time, boychik."

"What's going on, Dad?"

"Ah'm teaching Robert the good book." Herbert flipped a page. " '*The Queen of Sheba gave Solomon gold and spices, and*—' "

" 'Spice' is Bible talk for nookie," Bobby interrupted, grinning at Steve. "Grandpop taught me that."

"Grandpop's a regular Talmudic scholar."

Bobby went on, excitedly: "In the first book of Kings, it says that Solomon gave Sheba '*everything she desired and asked for.*' You get it, Uncle Steve?"

"I think I can figure it out."

"Did you know King Solomon had seven hundred wives and three hundred concubines?"

"No wonder he wanted to get out of the house and conquer Mesopotamia." Steve turned to his father, who was pouring whiskey over ice. "Dad, why are you filling Bobby with this nonsense?"

"Our roots are not nonsense." Herbert took a noisy pull on his drink and turned to his grandson. "Robert, our ancestors were warriors in the court of King Solomon. We're direct descendants from His Honor's own wise self."

"Oh, for God's sake," Steve groaned.

"Don't you blaspheme in mah presence."

"And what's with the yarmulke? You covering a bald spot?"

"Ah pray for you, Stephen. You've become a Philistine."

"And you've flipped out. Going orthodox at your age is just plain weird."

Herbert shook his head. "Cain't believe mah son's a heathen and mah daughter's a whore."

"Hey, Dad. Cool it in front of Bobby with that stuff, okay?"

"*Nu?* What's the big deal? You think the boy doesn't know his mother's a junkie and a tramp?"

"Dad, that's enough." Not that it wasn't true, Steve thought, but you don't smack a kid in the face with that kind of talk.

"It's okay, Uncle Steve." Bobby fiddled with a two-by-four, showing no apparent concern. But Steve knew that look. A blank, neutral mask. It was how the boy hid the pain. What the hell was wrong with his father, anyway? Didn't he realize how sensitive Bobby was? Probably not. When Steve was a kid, his father treated him just as callously. Hadn't he called him a "wuss" when four *Marieltos* at Nautilus Middle School beat him up for his lunch money?

Without looking up, Bobby said: "The other day in the cafeteria, one of the kids asked about my parents."

Steve held his breath. Kids can be so cruel. Little predators preying on the one who's different.

"I told them I didn't know my father, and my mom was in prison," Bobby continued.

"You take some heat over that, kiddo?"

Bobby shook his head. "Everybody thought that was way cool. Manuel said he wished he didn't know his old man. Jason asked if I ever visited Mom in prison."

The boy let it hang there. His way of asking Steve why they never drove down to Homestead Correctional. So hard to understand the boy's longing. Janice had neglected and abused him. Locked him in a dog shed, starved him while she got stoned. And

Bobby, what . . . *missed* her? Steve decided to let it go.
What could he say, anyway?

*"If you visit your Mom, those nightmares will come
back, kiddo."*

No, he would rather stay clear of the subject of
Janice Solomon, junkie, tramp, and utterly worthless
mother.

"If mah son won't go to *Shabbos* services with me,"
Herbert declared, "maybe mah grandson will."

"I have to study," Bobby said.

"On a Friday night? You oughta be praying, then
chasing tail. Maybe praying you catch some."

"Dad, what the hell's going on? You haven't been to
synagogue in thirty years."

"The hell you say. When ah was a practicing lawyer,
ah went to High Holy Days every year."

"Right. You handed out your business card on Yom
Kippur. What's up now?"

"Mah grandfather was a cantor, you know that?"

Steve had heard the stories since he was a child.
Herbert claimed to have traced the family tree back
nearly three centuries. Ezekiel Solomon was among
the first English colonists to settle Savannah in the
1730s. The Solomons grew and prospered, and over
the generations the family sprawled to Atlanta and
Birmingham and Charleston. According to Herbert,
who specialized in the tradition of exaggeration em-
ployed by lawyers, peddlers, and Southerners, the tree
that sprouted from old Ezekiel produced farmers and
weavers, stone masons and mill owners. Even an occasional rabbi and cantor. Not to mention a stock
swindler and a bookie who went to prison for fixing
college football games in the 1940s.

But what was this crap about the court of King

Solomon? It was one thing to trace your ancestors back to James Oglethorpe. But quite another to lay claim to a royal name three thousand years old.

Until recently, Herbert hadn't cared much about spirituality. So, why now? He was getting older, of course. Probably sensing his own mortality.

Then there's his fall from grace.

Nearly fifteen years ago, snared in a bribery and extortion scandal, Herbert had protested his innocence but nonetheless quit the bench and resigned from the Bar in disgrace. That had to be it, Steve thought.

Lost and found. My old man found religion to make up for what he's lost.

Career and status, gone. Wife—Steve's mother, Eleanor—dead of a vicious cancer. Daughter Janice in and out of jail and drug rehab. A touchy relationship with Steve.

Herbert picked up a hammer and a handful of nails and grabbed a two-by-four. "Gotta get to work, son."

"On what?"

"Gonna make a scale model of the Temple of Solomon," Herbert said.

"You got a building permit for that?"

"Got the blueprints. How long's a cubit, anyway?"

Steve doubted his father could drive a nail straight. When Steve was Bobby's age, Herbert couldn't glue the wings of a balsa airplane to the fuselage.

"Robert, the temple is where King Solomon kept the Ark of the Covenant," Herbert said, "the very tablets the Lord gave to Moses."

"I know, Gramps. I saw *Raiders of the Lost Ark*."

Enough was enough. "Bobby, I need to talk to your grandfather for a few minutes," Steve said.

"So?"

"There are fresh mangoes on the counter. Go make yourself a smoothie."

"You can't order me around. I'm descended from King Solomon." Bobby squeezed his eyes shut. "King Solomon. SOLO GIN MONK."

"Fine, kiddo. Now, give us a few minutes."

"Okay, okay." The boy got to his feet and slouched toward the kitchen door.

"I've got a problem, Dad. I need advice."

"Then you damn well came to the right place," Herbert Solomon said.

* * *

Just as he had done with Victoria, Steve told his father everything. How he learned Kreeger's philosophy by reading his monograph on rational murder. How he uncovered Beshears' death, then sold Kreeger out in the murder trial by tipping off Pincher. How he found the marlin on his door and the gaff in his office, symbols of Kreeger's homicidal fishing trip. And how upset Victoria became when he confessed his lawyerly sins.

When he was finished, Herbert exhaled a long, low whistle. "Jesus and Magdalene, David and Bathsheba."

"I don't think those two couples are equivalent," Steve said.

"Then you didn't read *The Da Vinci Code*. Son, when you stroll through the cow pasture, you best not be wearing your wingtips."

"What the hell's that mean?"

"You stepped in deep shit. So what is it you want? Girlfriend advice or Florida Bar advice? 'Cause if it's girlfriend advice, ah'd say it's high time that shiksa converts. A dip in the *Mikvah,* the gateway to purity. Miriam's well in the desert."

"Jeez, Dad. Can you focus? I'm telling you this guy's coming after me."

"You mean to do you harm?"

"No, to wish me happy Chanukah. Don't you get it? Kreeger killed two people. I was supposed to defend him, and I double-crossed him. He's out of prison and he's pissed. It's a *Cape Fear* deal."

"Cape Fear, cape schmere. Ah heard him on the radio today. Talking about what a shitty lawyer you were. Some of it was damn funny."

"Glad you enjoyed it."

"He was riding you hard, sure. But it didn't sound mean. More like joshing."

"So what's the message he's sending?"

"The way Ah figure, he's saying he knows what you did. Confirming you were right about him being a killer. Boasting about it. Thinking maybe you would appreciate the artistry of it."

"Why would I appreciate him killing two people?"

"From what you say, he admires men who break the rules. That's you, son."

"But not by killing. Not like him."

"Dr. Bill probably considers you just a step or two up that slippery slope from where he stands."

"And what do you think he wants from me?"

"Take the man at his word. He said he wanted you to come on his show. Maybe he thinks he's Johnny Carson and you're his Ed McMahon. His sidekick. Ah don't believe Kreeger wants to kill you, Stephen. Ah believe he wants to be your pal."

"That's crazy."

"Just listen to the man flap his gums. He's a talker.

But who's he gonna talk to about killing those people? You, son. In his head, you're the only one who understands."

"I don't want to talk to him. I want him off my back."

"Okay, go tell him that. But what if he won't let up?"

"Then I'll bring him down. I don't know how, but I will."

"You best be careful about that."

"You saying I should do nothing, let him smear me?"

"Ah'm saying, you call me if you plan to take him on. That sumbitch ain't a one-mule load."

* * *

Bobby sliced the mangoes, taking care to cut around the pit so it would pop out, the way Uncle Steve had taught him. He could hear the two men talking in the yard. On the farm, when Bobby had been locked in the shed in the dark, his sense of hearing had sharpened. At night, he'd listened to the coyotes until he could tell one from another as they sang their songs. He could hear the horses shuffling in the barn, their rumps smacking the wall. Could almost feel the hot breath of their snorts and whinnies. During the days, he'd heard the trucks, their doors slamming, men cursing. When he was let out to work in the fields, he would listen to the birds chirping and the bees buzzing.

He'd liked it outside, even if the men would sometimes hit him for not working hard enough. The men smelled funny, and their beards were tangled and yucky. The women worked in the vegetable garden, bent over, greasy hair falling in their eyes.

Mom said they were organic farmers, but Bobby

saw drums of insecticide and bags of artificial fertilizer. And he knew the leafy green plants were marijuana. On moonless nights, he heard the trucks pull in, heard the men grunting as they hoisted bales, heard them yelling at the moon, whooping after their women, guns blasting empty liquor bottles to smithereens.

Now Bobby listened as Uncle Steve told Grandpop about the psychiatrist named Kreeger. Uncle Steve sounded worried, which was weird. He was always getting into trouble but it never seemed to bother him. But this was different. Was Uncle Steve scared?

Bobby tossed the mango slices into the blender with a sliced banana, a handful of ice, and two scoops of protein powder. He wanted to gain weight so he didn't look like such a weenie, but it wasn't working. Despite the smoothies and ham paninis and all the pistachio ice cream he could eat, his body still was all wires and bones. With the blender whirring, he could no longer hear the men. Were they talking about his mother?

Uncle Steve doesn't understand. He thinks just because Mom messed me up, I don't want to see her. But she's still my mom.

There was something he needed to tell Uncle Steve, but didn't know how. His mother had called him yesterday. She cried on the phone, and he did, too. Said she loved him and was sorry about everything and she had completely changed.

"*I'm a new woman, Bobby. I'm clean and sober.*"

"*That's great, Mom.*"

"*I'm never going back to those old ways. I have a new purpose. A guiding light.*"

"*What's that, Mom?*"

"*I found Jesus. I let Jesus Christ into my heart.*"

Wait till Grandpop hears, Bobby thought.

But that wasn't what Bobby needed to tell Uncle Steve. What he needed to tell him was the last thing Mom had said.

"I'm coming to get you, Bobby, honey. I'm coming back to be your mother again."

Eight

WAXING NOSTALGIC

Without really intending to, Victoria Lord was staring straight into The Queen's crotch. "Maybe this should wait, Mother."

"Nonsense. It's your duty to relieve my insufferable boredom." Naked from the waist down, Irene Lord lay on her back, her hands under her butt, her legs raised and spread. "Benedita, you will be quick about it, won't you, darling?"

"I will be *queek* so your lover can be slow," Benedita vowed in a thick Brazilian accent. A young woman with cinnamon skin and flaming red lipstick, Benedita wore pink nylon shorts, a crimson sequined wrestler's singlet, and knee-high suede boots.

They were in a private booth at the Salon Rio in Bal Harbour for The Queen's monthly bikini wax. Already, Victoria regretted coming here, but she was desperate for personal advice.

Should I move in with Steve? Why is the thought of All-Steve, All-the-Time, so terrifying?

Victoria hadn't expressed her fears to him. How could she? Moving in together had been her idea. Of course, if Steve were more attuned to the subtleties of her moods, he would have picked up the vibes. Instead, she had asked: *"Are you absolutely sure you're ready for this?"*

He quickly said yes, not realizing she had been expressing her own doubts. Typical tone-deaf male.

Now she was in full-blown crisis mode. Could she really work with him all day, then come home to the same house? Was 24/7 simply too much?

Something else, too. After that bombshell today, Steve nuking the ethical rules by turning on his own client, could she even work with him?

Then she wondered if she was overreacting. Or even worse . . .

Am I subconsciously using what Steve did years ago as a reason not to advance our relationship?

She wanted to ask her mother all these questions. After all, The Queen's experiences with men crossed several continents over several decades and were exponentially greater than her own. But her mother, as usual, was engrossed in her own affairs.

"You really must meet Carl," Irene said, peering over her pubic region. "He's a dreamboat and a dead ringer for George Clooney. They could be twins."

"Which would make him how much younger than you, Mother?"

"Actually, I haven't told him my age, but I implied I was too young to remember Neil Armstrong landing on the moon."

"Which means you gave birth to me when you were, what—ten?"

"It's been known to happen, dear."

"Stop moving," Benedita ordered as she dusted Irene's private parts with perfumed puffs of baby powder. Snow falling on pubies.

"Princess, you really should get waxed," Irene said.

"No thank you, Mother."

"I've seen that bush of yours. You could use a weed whacker."

"Mother!"

Benedita hoisted one of Irene's legs over a shoulder.

"I'm just trying to help, dear. Men love those bare, smooth loins. Probably the Lolita fantasy."

"I'm not having this discussion."

"Just trying to help, dear." The Queen studied her daughter a moment, pursing her lips. "And what have you done to your hair? Your *other* hair."

"Nothing."

"You've tinted it. I can tell."

"I haven't done anything except wash it."

"I liked it better the other way."

"What other way! Dammit, Mother, you're impossible."

"Don't raise your voice. Men can't stand a woman who's shrill."

Victoria sighed. "God, why did I come here?"

"Why, to keep me company, of course."

Victoria blurted it out: "I'm not sure about moving in with Steve."

"Well, I am. It's a terrible idea. Why you ever suggested it is beyond me. A man won't buy the cow if he's getting the crème fraiche for free."

"I thought you didn't want me to marry Steve."

"Oooh," The Queen sighed as Benedita slathered the warm beeswax concoction over her crotch. "I don't, Princess. The man is totally unsuitable for you."

"Why? Because he's not Episcopalian or because he's not rich?"

"Ouch!" A tearing sound and The Queen yelped. "Jesus, Benedita . . ."

Benedita smiled as she examined the glob of hardened wax she'd just yanked from The Queen.

"I'm not a bigot and I'm not *that* materialistic," Irene said. "But I can't help wondering, dear. If you're going to be with a Jewish man, why couldn't it be one with some wherewithal? Goodness knows, there are enough of them."

"I knew this would be useless."

Another rip. Another *"Ouch!"*

"I'm just worried that we're too different, Mother."

"Of course you are, dear."

As if it's a given. As if there's no need to discuss it.

"Keep the landing strip narrow, Benedita," Irene instructed as the Brazilian woman plucked stray hairs with tiny tweezers. "It makes the man look bigger."

More concerned about the aesthetics of her private parts than about her only child's happiness.

Victoria decided to try once more. One more stab at drawing her mother away from her own sybaritic pleasures. "Steve did something incomprehensible, and I just can't come to grips with it."

"He cheated on you?"

"Of course not! It involves a case."

"You know how legal talk bores me, dear."

But still, Victoria told her the story of Steve handing over evidence that helped convict his client. By the time Victoria finished, The Queen was left with a landing strip the width of a popsicle stick. The surrounding skin was flaming pink.

"I don't know, dear. What Stephen did doesn't sound that terrible to me. His client's a murderer who was going to get away with it. At least Stephen took him off the streets for a few years."

"But that's not his job. You don't understand, Mother. It cuts to the essence of the profession. A lawyer who'll do that . . . who knows what else he might do? If Steve represents a corporation, will he give away trade secrets if he decides the company's behaving badly? In a divorce, if his client tells him she's been cheating on her husband, will he tell the judge? Once you break the rules, where does it stop?"

"Did I mention that Carl is a fantastic golfer?"

"What?"

"He wants to take me to Scotland, play all the great courses."

What a breathtaking leap, Victoria thought, her mother vaulting to her own love life without breaking stride.

Of course, she already devoted nearly five minutes to my problems. How much more could I expect?

Victoria decided to surrender. What else could she do? "That's fascinating, Mother."

"Carl's family came over on the *Mayflower*. Personally, I never cared for cruises, though the S.S. *France* had foie gras to die for. Which reminds me. Are we going to the club for my birthday?"

"It's up to Steve, Mother. He's picking up the check."

"If he mentions that chili dog place on the causeway, tell him to forget it."

"Will you be bringing the fantastic golfer?"

"Of course. It will be the perfect time for our announcement."

"What!"

"Don't furrow your brow, dear. Little lines today,

deep ditches tomorrow. And don't worry. Carl and I are not getting married." She smiled mischievously. "Yet."

"I had no idea the two of you were so serious."

"Because you don't listen to your mother. All wrapped up in your own problems. My life drifts along, unnoticed and unadorned."

"Hardly, Mother. Don't project your personality onto me."

"Nonsense. You're my only child, Victoria. My entire *life*."

There was no way to win the argument, Victoria knew.

"As for Carl," Irene continued, "I haven't been drawn to any man this way since your father died. We fit together so perfectly. He has such a—*je ne sais quoi*—I find almost indescribable."

Something felt out of kilter, Victoria thought. The Queen made men swoon, not the other way around. "So what exactly is the big announcement?"

"Sur-prise," Irene sang out. "You'll have to wait. But I'll say this. I haven't been this happy in years. Just look at me. Am I glowing?"

"Your crotch certainly is, Mother."

* * *

Well, that was useful, Victoria thought ruefully as she crossed the Broad Causeway on her way back to the mainland. Indian Creek Country Club was to her left across a narrow channel. She had played tennis there as a child, had consumed gallons of root beer floats in the clubhouse restaurant, had learned to sail in the calm waters of the bay. She hadn't envisioned an adulthood filled with complications, both professional and personal. When her father was still alive, when her mother seemed to care for more than just herself, the future promised rewards that thus far eluded her.

I have to make decisions. About Steve. About me. About life.

Ten minutes later, she was on Biscayne Boulevard, stopped at a police barricade. A parade passed by. A steel band from one of the islands. Marchers carrying signs that either celebrated some holiday or protested conditions in their native land. From five cars back in line, she couldn't tell which.

She decided to go with her gut. Wasn't that what Steve always taught her?

"Throw away the books, Vic. Go with your gut."

Okay, so he'd been talking about jury selection, but didn't the advice apply to mate selection, too?

Her gut told her she loved Steve. But did that mean they should live together? Then there was Bobby to think about. Bobby kept talking about "family," and she was included. The boy'd had so many disappointments. She didn't want to add to them.

So, as the parade passed and the police barricade gave way, Victoria hit the gas. She decided to plunge ahead. Her gut was telling her to move in with Steve, to give the relationship every chance, to see if they would have a *je ne sais quoi* that would be almost indescribable.

SOLOMON'S LAWS

4. If you're going to all the trouble to make a
   fool of yourself, be sure to have plenty of witnesses.

Nine

THE SHRINK AND THE SHYSTER

"You gotta look out for *numero uno*. You gotta do what gives you pleasure, not what others want you to do. Hedonism is good. Selfishness is good. Greed is good. No, I take that back. Greed is great!"

The voice was deep, rhythmic, and spellbinding. Wearing a headset and a beige silk guayabera, Dr. Bill Kreeger crooned into a ceiling-mounted microphone. Steve stood in the control room, looking over the shoulder of the board operator, watching through the window. So far, Kreeger, his mouth close enough to the microphone to kiss the cold metal, hadn't seen him. Steve had come here to deliver the message that would get Kreeger off his back.

"Self-interest is the highest morality," Kreeger prattled on, "and selflessness is the deepest immorality. You can't make another person happy, so don't even try. Give a hundred bucks to a charity at Thanksgiving, they'll hit you for two hundred at Christmas. Bake a tuna casserole for the neighborhood shut-in, next week she'll expect filet mignon. The people you sacrifice for won't appreciate it, so forget them. Wait, you say. That's cruel, Dr. Bill. Wrong!

Don't be a sucker. The moral life is one of self-interest. If everyone pursued his or her own happiness, there wouldn't be a bunch of losers who always need help. And what a beau-ti-ful world it would be."

Putting a tune to it. Then laughing, a deep rumble. Kreeger had gone a little gray around the temples since Steve had seen him last. But he looked remarkably healthy and fit. Wavy hair combed straight back revealed a widow's peak. A firm jawline that never even sagged when he looked down at his notes. No more than five-nine, he had a square, blocky build and seemed to have put meat on his chest and shoulders. Prison weight lifting, maybe.

"After a short break," Kreeger said into the microphone, "my seven tips for living the life of self-fulfillment. Tip number one. The word 'invincible' starts with 'I.' And *I'll* be right back."

Kreeger hoisted his coffee cup and turned toward the window. He spotted Steve on the other side of the glass and smiled broadly. For an instant, the smile seemed genuine, a look of pleasant surprise at seeing an old friend. Then the corners of his mouth dropped a bit, as if Kreeger just remembered the old friend owed him money. A second after that, the smile turned chilly, a frozen mask.

* * *

"To what do I owe this honor?" Kreeger asked, waving Steve into the seat next to him.

"I came here to tell you just one thing: I'm not scared of you."

"Why would you be?"

"If you come after me, I'll land on you like a ton of concrete."

"That's two things, actually. You're not scared and you're a ton of concrete."

"I'm not some stoned woman in a hot tub."

"Not sure I know where you're going with that, Counselor. Are you saying you'd *like* to be a stoned woman in a hot tub? Some gender confusion issues?"

"What I'm saying, Kreeger, is I can handle myself."

"Interesting choice of words. 'Handle myself.' Did you masturbate excessively as a child? Or do you now?"

"Fuck you, Kreeger."

A mechanical *beep* came from the speaker mounted on the wall.

"Whoa, Nellie," Kreeger laughed. "Good thing we're on a seven-second delay."

Confused, Steve looked toward the control room. A red light illuminated the words: "On Air."

Oh, shit. Is this going out on the airwaves?

Kreeger leaned close to the microphone. "You're listening to Dr. Bill on WPYG, broadcasting live from South Miami, with our special guest, Steve-the-Shyster Solomon. Phone lines are open from Palm Beach to the Keys, from Marco Island to Bimini."

Steve was halfway out of his seat when Kreeger punched a flashing button on his telephone. "Jerry in Pinecrest, you're on the air."

"Gotta question for the lawyer."

"Shoot, Jerry," Kreeger said. "But don't make it too tough. It took Solomon four times to pass the bar exam."

"Three," Steve corrected him.

"What's the difference between a lawyer and a catfish?" Jerry asked.

"Aw, c'mon," Steve said.

"One is a scum-sucking bottom feeder," Jerry answered. "The other is a fish."

Kreeger bellowed as if Jerry in Pinecrest were the new Robin Williams.

"I said what I had to say." Steve headed for the door.

Kreeger hit the cough button, silencing the mike. "Stick around, Solomon. At the break, I got something good to tell you."

Steve stood in place a second. Kreeger looked at a monitor and punched another button on the phone. "Lou in Miramar, you're on with Dr. Bill."

"I'm a big Hurricane baseball fan and I remember when Solomon played."

"Hear that, Solomon?" Kreeger asked, motioning Steve back into his seat. "You got a fan here. Obviously, he's never been a client."

"What I remember best," Lou in Miramar said, "was Solomon getting picked off third base in the College World Series."

Steve groaned.

Why did I come here, anyway? To show some toughness. To warn Kreeger off. And what do I get? Ridicule on talk radio, the cesspool of broadcasting.

"I was safe," Steve protested, moving toward the microphone. "Ump blew the call."

"No surprise, Lou. When Solomon loses a case, he always blames the judge." Kreeger punched another button. "Lexy, on South Beach, you're on the line."

Lexy? No. It can't be.

"Why don't you get off Stevie's case, anyway?" A young woman's whiny voice. Yep, Lexy.

Whatever you do, Lex, don't try to help.

"He's a terrific lawyer and he's cute, too."

Kreeger flashed Steve a smile. It was the same smile a barracuda shows to a porkfish. "So Solomon has represented you, has he?"

"He got me out of like a zillion dollars in parking tickets."

"Traffic court. Now, that's Solomon's speed."

"You don't understand, Doc. The tickets were all for parking in a handicapped zone. But Stevie found a chiropractor who said I had bulimia, so I got off."

"Fabulous," Kreeger enthused. "With Solomon, the guilty go free and the innocent do six years in prison." The psychiatrist lowered his voice, as if letting his listeners in on a secret. "Now, friends, you won't believe this, but Steve-the-Shyster Solomon once sued a surfer for stealing another surfer's wave. And who says we don't need tort reform?"

"Surfers consider waves their property," Steve said. But music was already coming up, and the board operator was pointing an index finger at Kreeger from the other side of the window.

"We'll be right back after this news update," Kreeger said. The *On Air* sign went dark, and he slipped off his headset. "That was great. We should take this on the road. *The Shrink and the Shyster.* Maybe get a syndication deal. Satellite radio within a year."

Maybe his father was right, Steve thought. Maybe Kreeger just wanted a sidekick.

"I'm vox populi," Kreeger continued. "The voice of an aggrieved populace that hates lawyers. You keep playing the dunce."

"I wasn't playing."

A newsman's baritone voice came over a speaker. The stock market was up. The water table was down.

City fathers were shocked, *shocked* to discover that prostitution was rampant along Biscayne Boulevard. Kreeger turned a dial and lowered the volume a notch. "You know, I really admire you, Solomon. What you did to me took balls."

Steve stayed quiet.

"You're not curious how I found out?" Kreeger asked.

Steve took a long breath, said nothing. On the speakers, the news anchor was giving the fishing report. Mackerel were running. Snapper, on the other hand, were merely swimming.

"Right in the middle of my trial," Kreeger continued, "the State Attorney files a notice about a so-called similar incident. What's it called?"

"Williams Rule material," Steve said. "The state can introduce similar incidents from a defendant's past to show a pattern of conduct."

"Yeah. Poor Jim Beshears drowns down in the Keys. And years later, wretched Nancy Lamm drowns in my hot tub. Kind of a stretch tying those two together, don't you think, Counselor?"

"Not when each person got hit on the head with a pole you happened to be holding. The judge thought the first incident was similar enough to be admissible."

"My quibble's not with the judge, Solomon."

In the background, Steve could hear a commercial for a local dating service for overworked and horny executives.

"One day, when the appeal was pending," Kreeger went on, "I looked through every piece of paper in the file. You know what I found? Two copies of the police report of the boat accident. One attached to the State Attorney's brief and one in your file."

"So what? Pincher was required to give me a copy when he filed his Williams Rule notice."

"Right. Except your copy had an earlier time stamp. *You* had the police report first and you gave Pincher a photocopy. You dropped the dime on your own client."

Steve didn't say a word. There could be a tape recorder rolling. They were, after all, in a recording studio.

The damn time stamps. He'd been sloppy, Steve realized. Well, what could you expect? He'd never sold out a client before.

"At first," Kreeger said, "I was mad enough to kill you. And you, of all people, know I'm capable, right? Then I realized you do whatever it takes. You live by your own code. You violated your attorney's oath in order to put your own client away." Kreeger rumbled a laugh. It sounded like coal pouring down a chute. "I get goose bumps just thinking about it. You put my theories into practice, Solomon. We're like long-lost brothers, you and I."

"I don't kill people."

"Not yet." Another laugh. Then, with what seemed like dead-earnest sincerity, Kreeger said, "We're gonna be great friends. We're gonna spend some quality time together."

"The hell we are."

"C'mon, Solomon. You owe me that much. In fact, you owe me six years. There I was, eating all that starchy food, living in a cell with a metal toilet, and you were out here enjoying the good life. You've got yourself a lady. What's her name? Victoria, right? I look forward to meeting her. And you have your nephew with you. Robert. Has some medical problems, doesn't he?

And you had a bit of a dustup with the state over custody. Well, you'd better keep your record clean. Wouldn't want to upset those hard-asses at Family Services. And how's your father, by the way? Judge Solomon drinking too much these days?"

There are lots of ways to threaten someone, Steve thought. At one end of the spectrum, your lawyer can send a letter, advising that you intend to use all lawful means to enforce your legal rights. At the other end, you can jam the barrel of a gun into someone's mouth, breaking off teeth and yelling you're going to blow their brains all over the wall. Or you can take a middle ground. You can mention everyone in the world the person loves and just leave it at that. Steve felt his face heat up, and his stomach clenched itself into a fist.

"Stay away from them, Kreeger. Stay the hell away or I'll cut you into little pieces and feed you to the sharks."

"Doubt it. Like you said, Steve, you're not a killer."

"And like you said: Not yet."

"Pardon me for not peeing on my socks, but I've just spent six years in a rattlesnake nest and never got bit."

"Maybe your next stay, you won't be so lucky."

"Now, why would I go back to prison?"

"It's just a matter of time before you feel wronged by someone. You'll use that bullshit philosophy of yours to justify your actions, and before you can say, 'Man overboard,' there's another body floating facedown. So maybe I will stick close to you, Kreeger, because I want to be there the day the cops come knocking on your door."

No one knocked, but the cushioned door to the control room popped open and two City of Miami

Beach cops walked in. Weird, Steve thought. But life is like that sometimes. You think of a woman you haven't seen in three or four years, and that day she comes knocking on your door, with a little boy at her side who looks alarmingly like you. Not that it had ever happened to him, but he'd heard stories.

So what were the Beach cops doing out of their jurisdiction? Had Kreeger slashed some tourist's throat while waiting in line at Joe's Stone Crab?

"Are you Stephen Solomon?" The cop wore sergeant's stripes and had a mustache. He was in his forties, with a tired look.

"Guilty," Steve said. "What's this about?"

He was vaguely aware that Kreeger was leaning close to the microphone, his voice a portentous whisper. "Exclusive report. Breaking news here at WPYG. You're live with Dr. Bill. . . ."

"You're under arrest, Mr. Solomon," the sergeant said wearily.

"For what! What'd I do, curse on the air?"

"Steve-the-Shyster Solomon *arrested*, right here in Studio A," Kreeger rhapsodized.

"Assault and battery."

"I haven't hit the bastard yet." Steve nodded toward Kreeger.

"Not him. A guy named Freskin."

"Who the hell is that?"

The younger cop took a pair of handcuffs from his belt. "Please place your hands behind your back, sir."

Damn polite, just like they teach them in cop school.

"I don't know any Freskin."

"I have to pat you down, sir," the younger cop persisted.

"The excitement builds," Kreeger announced, sounding like Joe Buck doing a World Series game. "They're putting the cuffs on Solomon."

"Goddammit. Who's Freskin?" Steve felt a mixture of anger and humiliation.

"State probation officer," the sergeant answered. "Arnold Freskin. You assaulted him in your law office."

Oh, him!

"That freak? He was getting off wrestling with my secretary."

Even as he spoke, Steve knew he was violating the advice he gave to every client he'd ever had.

"Never talk to the cops. You'll only dig yourself a deeper hole."

"You have the right to remain silent," the sergeant reminded him. "You have the right to an attorney. If you cannot afford an attorney—"

"I know. I know."

"They're taking him downtown," Kreeger sang out cheerfully. "Is Steve Solomon not only a shyster, but a violent thug, too? Stay tuned."

Ten

EVEN MURDERERS NEED PALS

Steve stood at the kitchen sink, scrubbing the ink off his fingertips. He'd been booked and processed, finger-printed and photographed, and generally ridiculed by cops and corrections officers who knew him from court. He had spent two hours in a holding cell where the walls were covered with yellowish-brown graffiti. Generations of inmates had used mustard from their state-issued bologna sandwiches to leave their mis-spelled profanities to posterity. Perhaps not as im-pressive as Paleolithic cave drawings, the graffiti nonetheless provided a sociological snapshot of our un-derclass, as well as an indictment of our public schools.

Judge Alvin Elias Schwartz released Steve without bail on the grounds that His Honor used to play pinochle with the defendant's father. Steve would be required to show up in a week to be arraigned on charges of assault and battery and obstructing a state official, to wit: Mr. Arnold G. Freskin, in the perfor-mance of his duties. According to the criminal com-plaint, Freskin's duties included an "on-site interview with a probationer," which Steve figured sounded better than an "erotic wrestling match with an undressed secretary."

Steve had taken a sweaty taxi ride home, the Jamaican driver explaining the A/C was on the blink, but Steve figured the guy was just saving gas. Steve's pants and shirt stuck to the vinyl seats, though the heat didn't seem to bother the driver, who was sitting on one of those beaded back supports.

"You sounded like a horse's ass on the radio today." Herbert Solomon sat at the kitchen table, sipping kosher red wine and eviscerating his son. "A real *putz.*"

"Thanks for the support, Dad." Steve was not up for his father's abuse. It had been a shitty day, and it wasn't over yet. In an hour, he would have to put on a smiley face and brush-kiss Irene Lord. The Queen. Victoria's mother. A woman so cold and imperious she made Martha Stewart seem warm and cuddly.

"Ah bailed you out, didn't ah?"

"I was released on my own recognizance. All you did was call the judge."

"That's a helluva lot."

"You could have driven downtown and picked me up from the jail."

"Not after sundown, boychik."

"Why, you got night blindness?"

"*Shabbos,* you *shmoe*!"

"What is it, open-bar night at temple?"

"Wouldn't hurt you to come along. Say a *Sh'ma* or two."

So that explained his father's outfit. A double-breasted blue blazer, rep tie with khaki walking shorts and sneakers. Ever since the old man went ortho, he began adhering to the rule of not driving between sundown Friday and sundown Saturday. Now, looking like a demented Englishman in the midday sun, he was ready for the three-mile trek to Temple Judea.

"It's Irene's birthday," Steve said. "Otherwise, I'd be right there with you in the front row."

"Hah. You don't even know where the shul is."

"On Granada, right across Dixie Highway from the ball field." The *ball field* being Mark Light Stadium at the University of Miami, where Steve couldn't hit a lick but semi-starred as a pinch runner and base stealer. He also occasionally attended class, majoring in theater and minoring in the swimming pool. Herbert had wanted Steve to study political science or pre-law, something that might lead to the legal profession. But the word in the dorm was that the hottest girls were in theater. Enough said. Steve brushed up his Shakespeare and headed for the Ring Theater, which was conveniently located next to the campus Rathskellar.

Only later did Steve realize that the acting skills he accidentally learned would be useful in court. As an undergrad, he played the cynical reporter E. K. Hornbeck in *Inherit the Wind*, a role that came easily. Then he was Teach in *American Buffalo*, a part he enjoyed mainly because he got to say a lot of fuck you's. His senior year, Steve played the older brother, Biff, in *Death of a Salesman*. A jock with early promise, Biff's life crumbled when he discovered that his father was a fraud.

"Pop's going to kill himself! Don't you know that?"

At virtually the same time Steve cried out that line, his own father—Herbert Solomon, not Willy Loman—was being hauled before the Grand Jury. Looking back, Steve knew his onstage tears were real.

For much the same reason he studied theater—hot coeds—Steve joined the campus chapter of the ACLU. The prevailing wisdom then was that liberal chicks were easier to bag than, say, the Young Republican Women for Chastity. The ACLU meetings gave him a feel for the underdog. All considered, the acting lessons and liberal politics provided solid, if unintentional, training for the life of a solo practitioner in the mystical art of the Law.

"So what's your plan?" Herbert asked.

"For Irene's birthday? We're going to Joe's for stone crabs."

"For Kreeger!"

"I'm working on it, Dad. He claims he wants to hang out with me."

"What'd Ah tell you? Murderers need pals, too."

"Except it sounded more like a threat. Be my pal—or else."

"So what's your plan?" Herbert pressed him.

Steve didn't know how much to tell his father. His father's parenting had swung between benign neglect and caustic criticism. And now, that old fear resurfaced. Ridicule and rejection. Not measuring up.

"I need to get down to the Keys. Find a witness."

"What for?"

Steve decided to go for it. His ego had pretty much survived all the welts and bruises his father could dish out. "That fishing trip I told you about. Kreeger and his classmate Jim Beshears."

"Old news. You think Kreeger pushed the guy overboard and clobbered him with a gaff."

"It's all I've got. I can't nail Kreeger for killing Nancy Lamm."

"Double jeopardy. They already convicted him of manslaughter."

"Exactly. But Kreeger was never charged with murdering Beshears. I need someone who was there. A witness. Beshears' girlfriend is too vague about what happened. But there was one more person on the boat."

"The charter captain."

"Oscar De la Fuente. He was on the fly bridge, holding the boat steady, yelling instructions. He had the angle to see everything. But I never found him."

"Shouldn't be hard. The state would have his charter license."

"The computer records only go back ten years. The incident was nineteen years ago. If De la Fuente had a license then, he doesn't anymore."

"County property records?"

"Doesn't own anything in Miami-Dade, Monroe, or Collier. No business license. No fictitious-name license. No phone, listed or unlisted."

"At least you've done your homework."

The compliment sounded grudging, but Steve took it just the same. "Now I'm gonna pound the pavement. Or maybe the sand."

"What? Wear some lawyer's suit down in the Keys, poke around asking questions?"

Actually, he'd been planning on wearing cutoffs and a T-shirt that read: "*Practice Safe Sex. Go Screw Yourself.*" But his father was on a roll, so Steve let him go.

"The Conchs will think you're DEA," Herbert warned him. "No one will talk to you. And if anyone knows this De la Fuente character, they'll warn him to stay away from you. Problem is, you don't know the territory, son."

There it was, Steve thought, his old man hauling out the knives to carve him up. "What choice do I have?"

"You got me, you *shmoe*! Who knows the bars and marinas better than me?"

True. When Herbert wasn't crashing on a sofa in Steve's spare bedroom, he was fishing off his leaky houseboat on Sugarloaf Key. "You'd do that for me?"

"I'm your father. You gotta ask?" Pleased with himself, Herbert grabbed a white straw hat he would wear over his yarmulke for the walk to the synagogue. The hat had a small, upturned brim. Steve thought it was called a porkpie, but maybe not. That didn't sound kosher.

"Thanks, Dad. I really appreciate it."

"Don't mention it. By the way, how much are P.I.'s charging these days?"

"Good *Shabbos*, Dad."

Herbert started for the door. "Bobby's dinner is in the fridge."

"Where is the Bobster?"

"In his room with that gypsy girl."

"What? Who?"

"That harlot-in-training with the jewelry in her belly button. The Juban girl from a block over."

"Not polite, Dad. We don't describe people by their religion or ethnicity."

"That so, matzoh boy?"

"Very old-school, Dad."

"Well, kiss my kosher *tuches*. Ain't my fault the girl's both a Yid and a Cubana. Tell her to change her name if she's so ashamed of it. Like some of our chickenshit *landsmen*. Cohen becomes Kane, Levine becomes Landers. *Schmendricks.*" Herbert gave a snort of disapproval.

"Her name's Maria Munoz-Goldberg, and I doubt she's ashamed of it," Steve said.

"Fine by me, but if I were you, I'd go peek in Robert's bedroom. Or next thing you know, there'll be a little tyke named Munoz-Solomon running around the house."

Eleven

THAT JUBAN GIRL

Steve finished off the glass of kosher wine his father had left on the table. It tasted like liquified grape jelly. Bobby was in the bedroom with Maria, and Steve needed to fortify himself before moseying down the hall. He planned to knock on the door before entering. If it was locked, he'd batter it down like a SWAT team at a meth lab.

Just what were the rules with pubescent kids these days, anyway? Only recently had it occurred to him that Bobby, on the hazardous precipice of puberty, might need a fatherly lecture on the birds and bees. When he talked to his nephew about it, the boy said he knew all about STDs and condoms and even told Steve about a girl at Ponce de León Middle School who got pregnant.

"After that, none of the girls would, you know, do it, but there were a lot more rainbow parties, not that I've ever been invited."

"Rainbow parties?"

"C'mon, Uncle Steve. Where the chicks all put on a different color lipstick and the guys drop their pants, and the idea is to get as many different colors on your—"

"Jesus!"

Now Steve paused outside Bobby's door, sniffing the air like a bloodhound. No tobacco, no pot. But something odd. A citrus scent. Oranges or tangerines.

Steve knocked once and headed inside.

Both kids had textbooks open. Wearing baggy shorts and a Hurricanes football jersey, Bobby was slouched in his beanbag chair. Maria was sprawled across Bobby's bed. She wore low-riding jeans with enough holes and shreds to give the impression she'd stepped on a land mine. A sleeveless mesh T-shirt revealed a lacy bra underneath. Her complexion was a rich caramel, and her bright red lipstick was as slick as fresh paint. A shiny rhinestone peeked out of her twelve-year-old navel.

Bobby waved at Steve but kept talking to Maria, sounding like a little professor. "The Battle of Gettysburg was a big-time accident. Lee and Meade never said, 'C'mon, let's meet in this little town in Pennsylvania and have a big battle.' That's just where the Union decided to stop the Confederate advance. I mean, if they hadn't, Lee's army could have taken Philadelphia, and then maybe Washington, and the South would have won the war."

"That'd suck," Maria said. "Hey, Mr. Solomon."

"Hi, Maria. So what are you guys studying?"

"Duh. Like calculus," Bobby said. Showing some spunk for his little hottie.

"American history, Mr. Solomon. Bobby knows everything that ever happened."

"It's no big deal," Bobby said.

"It is to me." Maria smiled at Bobby. An inviting

come-hither smile. The citrus aroma was stronger here.

"What's that smell?" Steve asked.

"Oh, probably my perfume, Mr. Solomon."

Perfume! Bobby doesn't have a chance.

"Boucheron," Maria continued. "My mom's."

First they take their mothers' perfume. Then their birth control pills.

Steve knew Maria's parents from a Neighborhood Watch committee. Eva Munoz-Goldberg, the proud daughter of an anti-Castro militant, frequently roamed the neighborhood, passing out flyers that called for bombing Venezuela and assassinating Hugo Chávez. As a child, Eva spent weekends with her father and a pack of cousins, trekking through the Everglades, shooting Uzis at cardboard cutouts of Fidel Castro. Later, they would all head home to grill burgers, drink Cuba Libres, and watch the Dolphins on TV. Recently, Steve had seen Eva piloting her black Hummer through Coconut Grove, an NRA bumper sticker pasted on the rear bumper.

Maria's father, Myron Goldberg, was a periodontist with an office on Miracle Mile in Coral Gables. Myron's hybrid Prius sported bumper stickers for Greenpeace and Save the Manatees, and the most dangerous weapon he owned was a titanium root-canal shaft. The Munoz-Goldbergs were Exhibit A in South Florida's paella-filled melting pot of cross-cultural multiethnicity.

Looking at the two kids lounging in the bedroom, Steve was certain he should lecture his nephew about exercising self-control in a time of raging hormones. Another thought, too. A contrary one. Could this little vixen be just using Bobby to pass her courses? As much as Steve adored his nephew, he had to admit the kid was not exactly a candidate for the Abercrombie & Fitch catalog. Basically, Bobby was a skinny, loveable loner in thick glasses who didn't fit into any of the cliques.

"What's this about the high-water mark?" Maria asked, thumbing through the textbook. "It sounds like something that'll be on the test."

"The High-Water Mark of the Confederacy," Bobby said, confidently. "It's where the tide turned the Union's way at Gettysburg."

"Ooh, right." She scribbled a note.

"Pickett's Charge," Bobby continued. "Fifteen thousand Confederate soldiers. Some made it to the Union line, but they were cut to ribbons. A frontal assault moving uphill never works. When the enemy's holding the high ground, you gotta outflank him. Fake an attack on one flank." Bobby threw an imaginary left hook. "But really attack the other flank." With a *whoosh,* he tossed a roundhouse right. "When your enemy zigs, you zag."

"You're so smart." Maria rewarded the boy with another twinkling smile, then turned toward Steve. "We heard you on the radio today, Mr. Solomon."

"Yeah," Bobby added. "Never thought that shrink could school you like that."

"Are you going to jail?" Maria asked Steve.

"Uncle Steve's been to jail lots of times," Bobby declared, a touch of pride in his voice. "Judges make him stay overnight because he gets rowdy."

"Everything's gonna be okay," Steve said. "What I did was only technically illegal."

Bobby snorted. "Yeah, you *technically* beat the shit out of some guy."

"Watch the lingo, kiddo."

"Are you gonna let that shrink keep cracking on you?"

"Nope. I've got a plan to shut him up."

"Ph-a-a-t! How you gonna do it?"

Steve shook his head. What could he say? *"Your uncle and grandfather are trying to nail a killer, but don't worry about it."* No. He wouldn't spook the boy.

"Highly confidential," Steve said.

"Just so you're not doing what that woman in the hot tub did. Because if Dr. Bill killed her . . ."

Bobby let the words hang there, then turned back to his book.

* * *

Half an hour later, Bobby scooted deeper into the beanbag chair. Maria was still sprawled on his bed, leafing through the pages of the history book. Moments earlier, Bobby did a trick with his brain, purposely dividing his conscious thoughts in two. Going split screen, he called it, something that let him think two unrelated thoughts at once.

I want to kiss Maria. And . . .

Why does Uncle Steve treat me like a baby?

It was really Bobby's only complaint.

Most of the time Uncle Steve was really cool. Always spending time with him. Tossing the ball, teaching him to dig in at home plate and not bail out even when the pitch was inside. Taking him to court and even to a couple of autopsies, which was way cool, except for the smell.

But he hides stuff from me, afraid I can't handle it.

Uncle Steve was planning to go after Dr. Bill. Which was scary.

But why can't he tell me?

Above him, on the bed, Maria draped a leg over his shoulder. She wiggled her toes, the nails painted some color that looked like flames.

The brain waves carrying thoughts of Dr. Bill suddenly flatlined. Bobby felt a pleasant buzz in his undershorts. But this was awkward. His butt was sunk into the beanbag chair, his back was toward the bed, and he couldn't even see her. To kiss her, he'd have to scoot around, get to his knees, and crawl onto the bed, and then what? It would take several seconds and would seem premeditated and dorky, instead of casual and cool.

Another problem: *to tongue or not to tongue?*

He heard more pages rustling. She couldn't be reading that fast. Could she be getting bored? Was she waiting for him to make a move? He wished he could ask Uncle Steve for advice right now.

Or Mom. Yesterday, she told me she first had sex at twelve. My age!

Now his brain opened another screen. There was Maria on the bed, her flame-toed foot dangling in his face. And there was Mom, talking about sex.

Bobby could never tell Uncle Steve what Mom said. Or even that he'd seen her. Uncle Steve thought Mom was still in prison.

She had shown up at the park, picked him up, just like a regular mother, not an ex-con. They'd gone to Whip 'N Dip for pistachio ice cream. She started talking about her life, the stuff just spilling out, and a lot was pretty icky. The guys—sometimes, she didn't even know their names. The drugs—they'd messed her up bad, and that's why she stole and got in trouble, but now she'd kicked the habit. She thanked Jesus for his help, the Son of God being the true messiah and all, and maybe it was time for Bobby to be baptized.

Sure, Mom. Right after my bar mitzvah.

Bobby had told her about Maria and how much he liked her. She seemed interested, especially in Maria's family, the mother being Catholic and the father Jewish.

"She sounds like a good candidate for Jews for Jesus," his mother had said.

Now Maria draped a second leg over his other shoulder. She pressed her thighs together, squeezing his ears, knocking his glasses sideways. He could smell her perfume, orange and vanilla, like a Creamsicle. He wanted to lick her face.

"I'm tired of studying," she whispered.

All right!

Time for action. But how?

If he could turn around and somehow stand up, his crotch would be at her eye level. Ordinarily, no big deal, but right now, he had a world-class boner. What if she didn't want to kiss him? Would she tell everyone at school he was a horn-dog perv?

A third screen opened in his brain, and Uncle Steve was saying: *"Always show respect for girls. Sometimes you even have to show more respect for them than they have for themselves."*

And Mom was saying: *"Like Jesus said, if you look at a girl with lust, you've committed a sin. But the cool thing about the Savior, Bobby, is that he's very forgiving. So my motto is to do what feels right at the time. You can always repent later."*

Twelve

REPORT AND RAPPORT

Why is Steve so quiet?

Victoria pondered the question as they drove across the causeway on their way to The Queen's birthday dinner. Of course, Steve wasn't exactly crazy about her mother, who treated him as she did so many people: like hired help.

The thought of Steve marrying into the family really curdled the cream in The Queen's demitasse.

"Steve has many qualities, dear, but is he really the one for you?"

Translation: *"I hate him, and you can do better."*

It probably didn't help his cause that Steve would sometimes wear a T-shirt with the logo: *"If It's Not One Thing, It's Your Mother."*

Irene Lord considered Steve déclassé. Steve considered Irene Lord a gold digger. Victoria loved them both but, like the lion tamer at the circus, had to occasionally crack the whip to keep them apart.

Taking The Queen and her new beau, Carl, to dinner—and getting stuck with the check—probably wasn't high on Steve's list of favorite things. But still, Victoria wondered, why did he seem so distant? Okay, so getting humiliated on the radio and arrested for assault might throw a guy off his game. But Steve was used to verbal combat and was no stranger to jail, so what was really bothering him?

Thinking back over recent events, it seemed as if Steve had been out of sorts for a while. When they'd looked at the condo, he'd been almost hostile to the idea of moving in together. They were supposed to see other properties with Jackie, but did Steve really want to do it? In his typical male fashion, he wasn't talking, so she had no choice but to ask.

"So what's your plan?" she said as they passed Fisher Island.

The question seemed to startle him. "Wow, that's something." With one hand on the steering wheel, he playfully shook a finger at her. "You're reading my mind."

"Good. Tell me about it."

"I'm not sure I can."

"Who would you tell if not me?"

"It's dangerous," he said, "and I don't want you to worry."

She was lost. "Moving in together is dangerous?"

"What? Who's talking about moving in together?"

"We are. Or at least I am. I'm trying to figure out what you're planning. House or condo? Move in together now or maybe wait a bit?"

"Oh."

"So what are you talking about?"

"Kreeger. How I'm gonna nail him."

Wasn't that just like Steve? Or any man, she decided. Your guy is sitting there, quietly stewing, and you think he's worried about the relationship. Turns out he's wondering if the Dolphins can cover the spread against the Jets. And when men do talk, it's like dispensing the news on CNN. Hurricane in Gulf. Dow Jones up twenty. I-95 gridlocked. Just the facts, ma'am.

She had studied psychology and linguistics at Princeton, and she knew that men and women communicate differently. It sounded clichéd, but it was true. Women talk about feelings, what academics called "rapport talk." Men dispense information, what's called "report talk." When they talk at all.

"Both Dad and Bobby asked me about my plan for Kreeger," Steve told her, "so when you asked 'What's your plan?' I just naturally thought—"

"It's okay, Steve. But maybe you should just let Kreeger go. It didn't work out that great on the radio."

Her feminine mode of communication. She could have said: *You really got your ass handed to you today, partner.* But with a lover, it was best to cloak your criticism in lamb's wool, not lash it with barbed wire.

"I was just getting warmed up when the cops came in."

"It seemed like he enjoyed tormenting you. And if he's as dangerous as you say . . ."

"Exactly. That's why my plan will work."

Steve swung the car off the causeway and onto Alton Road. They'd be at Joe's in three minutes. There'd be a line of tourists snaking through the bar and into the courtyard. But between Dennis the maître d' and Bones the captain, Steve would manage to have his party seated within ninety seconds.

"I'm almost afraid to ask," Victoria said.

"Kreeger killed two people, right?"

"Two you know about."

"Right. Each one posed a threat. Jim Beshears was gonna blow the whistle on his phony research. Nancy Lamm was gonna report Kreeger's ethical violations. Suppose someone else poses a threat to him now?"

"What kind of threat?"

Victoria listened as Steve told her about Herbert trying to track down the charter boat captain who would have seen Kreeger brain Jim Beshears with the gaff.

As he went over the details, she began analyzing the plan in her logical way. Then she said, "Even if you found the captain, even if he says, 'Yeah, I think Kreeger shoved the guy overboard, then purposely hit him,' a defense lawyer would slice him up. Why'd it take you all these years to come forward? Why doesn't the other witness, the girlfriend, corroborate your story? And all this assumes you can get an indictment, and the chances of that are—"

"Slim to none."

"Right. So why do it?"

"If I tell you, take a deep breath and think it over before unloading on me."

"So it's got to be illegal."

"I told Dad to make sure he handed out my card everywhere he went, from Key Largo to Key West. Tell every drinker and fisherman and old salt that Stephen Solomon, Esquire, of Miami Beach, will pay a reward for finding Oscar De la Fuente, missing charter captain. Then I took an ad in the *Key West Citizen* and posted some notices on websites, saying the same thing."

It only took her a second. "You don't care if you find the guy! You just want Kreeger to know you're looking for him."

"You're getting warmer. Keep going."

"You're going to tell Kreeger you found De la Fuente, whether you do or not. You're going to say you have solid eyewitness evidence against him. You might even come up with a phony affidavit, De la Fuente swearing he heard Kreeger threaten Beshears, then saw Kreeger push him overboard before clobbering him."

"Hadn't thought of the affidavit. Nice touch."

"So this is your brilliant plan? To use yourself as bait. To get that psycho to try to kill you."

He had a grin on his face that managed to be both childish and clueless. Like a boy who catches a viper and shows it to a girl in the misguided belief she will immediately want to start necking. "I can't get him for either of the two murders he's committed, Vic. But I can get him for attempting a third."

"Has it occurred to you that Kreeger might be better at committing murder than you are at preventing it?"

"I'll have an advantage Beshears and Lamm didn't have. I'll be sober, and I'll know what's coming."

This time, she didn't try to cushion her words. "You are utterly irresponsible. Even worse, you don't care about the people who love you."

"Don't see how you can say that."

"What about Bobby? What about your father? What about me? If you get hurt or killed, what about us?"

"Vic, I'm not scared of Kreeger. The guy's a coward who murdered a stoned woman in a hot tub and a drunk on a boat."

They were the fifth car in line as they pulled up to valet parking in front of the restaurant. Patrons spilled out the doors and clogged the patio. On the outdoor speakers, they heard Dennis the maître d' announce: "Grossman party. Stuart Grossman. Party of eight."

"Now, as for that other thing," Steve said.

"What other thing?"

"The living-together thing. House versus condo."

Wait a second, she thought. *We're not through discussing your asinine plan. You can't move on to the next subject just because you've done your über-male report-talk.*

"I have this great compromise." Steve sounded proud of himself. "You like condos. Low maintenance. Lock and leave. And I respect that. But I like houses. Privacy. Mango tree in the backyard. So how about a townhouse?"

This isn't communication. This is the male of the species setting a brush fire, scorching the earth, and moving on.

"Steve, the townhouse can wait. We're not done here."

Now they were second in line for the valet. She didn't have much time. "You didn't even ask my opinion about your crazy plan, which, by the way, I think is suicidal. And now, what? Subject closed? Now we're supposed to talk about a townhouse and a hibiscus hedge?"

"I was thinking bougainvillea—"

"I'm serious. I'm really unhappy about this, and you'd better deal with it."

Steve's eyes widened. Getting hit with a two-by-four will do that. He chewed at his lower lip a moment. Over the loudspeaker, "Berkowitz party, Jeff Berkowitz. Party of six."

"Okay, Vic. Here it is. There are three people in the world I dearly care about. Three people I love with all my heart. You and Bobby and my crazy father. You're the ones I'd take a bullet for."

His words startled her. "Is that *literally* true?"

He seemed to consider it a moment. "Well, I'd take a bullet for you and Bobby. For my old man, I'd take a punch."

He seemed sincere, she thought. No man had ever said anything like that to her, that her life was more important to him than his own.

"There are some concepts I care a helluva lot about, too," he continued. "That vague, shadowy thing we call justice. Seven years ago, I really screwed up. Everything you said the other day was right. I tried to convict my own client, and I was wrong. Now it's come back to haunt me. But I was right about one thing. Bill Kreeger is a killer. When I was at the radio station today, he mentioned Bobby and Dad by name. And he mentioned you, too, Vic."

She felt a shiver go through her. "Why?"

"Because he wanted me to know he could get to the three of you."

"Did he make any threats?"

"He says I owe him for the six years he spent in prison. He's come back to collect the debt. Six years isn't something I can repay in cash, so I figure he wants to hurt me by going after someone I love. I can't sit back and do nothing. To keep him from coming after one of you, Vic, I need him to come after me."

What could she say? Sure, he was being reckless, but it was a recklessness born of love and care and obligation. That was another aspect of the male of the species. Man, the protector.

"I still hate the idea of you doing this," she said. "Will you at least promise to be careful?"

"Hell, yes. I'll promise that and anything else you want."

"Deal." She gave Steve a soft smile just as the attendant opened the door. "Promise to be nice to my mother tonight."

Thirteen

THE QUEEN AND THE PIRATE

"You're looking lovely, Irene," Steve said, on his best behavior.

"Thank you, Stephen," Irene Lord replied with a smile as brittle as an icicle.

"And your dress." Steve let out a whistle. "What can I say?"

"I'm not sure, Stephen. What *can* you say?"

"Why don't we order?" Victoria interjected. Steve was on his third tequila, and she had no desire to watch him spout ribald limericks, one of his irksome habits when tipsy.

"Bright, Irene," Steve decided, after a moment. "Your dress is very bright."

It was an ankle-length number in flowing turquoise silk and chiffon. A trifle dressy for Joe's, Victoria thought.

"I thought we were going to the club," Irene said, with a tone of disappointment. "Hence, the gown."

"Hence, the frown," Steve added, draining his Chinaco Blanco.

"One would never know from your own wardrobe

that you paid such close attention to fashion," Irene said. Her smile was permafrosted in place.

Victoria tried again. "Mr. Drake, are you ready to order?"

"Call me Carl," the distinguished-looking man said. He was the much-ballyhooed new beau. Forty-five, tops, with shiny dark hair going gray at the temples. Face a little too tan, smile a little too bright. He wore a navy blazer with gold buttons, a blue striped shirt, and a rep tie. His fingernails were manicured and polished to a fine sheen. He had a trim mustache a bit darker than his hair. Victoria thought it might have been dyed, and was trying not to stare at it. He spoke with the faintest of British accents, as Americans sometimes do if they spend time in the U.K. All in all, Drake conveyed the impression of a successful investment banker and a gentleman, an extremely presentable accoutrement for an evening at the opera or country club.

"Might I propose a toast?" Drake inquired.

"By all means, Carl," Irene said. "Perhaps after another drink, I won't hear all the racket." She motioned in the direction of the hungry hordes.

"Loosen up, Irene. We're at Joe's. Center of the culinary universe." Steve leapt to the defense of his favorite restaurant.

"A fish house," she sniffed. "Filled with sweaty tourists." Again, she waved a dismissive arm toward a table of ten. Sunburned faces, aloha shirts still creased from the packaging. "What's going on there, an orthodontists' convention?"

"Is that an ethnic remark, Irene?" Steve fired back.

"What?"

"Orthodontist equals Jew? That it, Irene? Does that table of Israelites offend you?"

"Oh, for God's sake."

Not this again, Victoria thought. For a nonpracticing Jew, Steve could be extremely prickly about ethnic cracks, real and imagined.

The Queen leveled her gaze at Steve. "I have no idea if those loud men with the mustard sauce on their faces are Jewish. I have no idea if most orthodontists are Jewish." She flashed an exaggerated, toothy smile. "I have never required the services of an orthodontist, thank you very much."

True, Victoria thought. But much later, there had been staggeringly expensive periodontal work, and her mother's flawless smile now reflected two rows of glimmering white veneers.

"A toast?" Drake tried again. He hoisted his gin and tonic, forcing the rest of them to join in. "To the lovely Irene, a shimmering diamond in a world of rhinestones, a shooting star in a galaxy of burned-out asteroids, a woman of poise and purpose—"

"My nephew Bobby swims with a porpoise," Steve said.

"I beg your pardon?" Drake appeared puzzled.

"You said Irene had a porpoise."

"*Purpose.* I said she's a woman of poise and *purpose.*"

"Stephen, I'm beginning to wish they hadn't let you out of jail so quickly," Irene said.

"Jail?" Drake echoed. He had the startled look of a man who unexpectedly wakens to find himself in the monkey cage at the zoo.

"Stephen spends more time behind bars than his clients. Don't you, dear?"

"To a lawyer, that's a compliment," Steve said. "Thank you, Irene."

Drake shot looks around the table. "Perhaps I should finish my toast . . ."

Twirling a diamond earing between thumb and forefinger, Irene cocked her head coquettishly. "Please do, Carl. I love a man who's good with words. Which reminds me. Stephen, I heard you on the radio today. So surprising that a trial lawyer of your experience would become so flustered."

"Mother, can we just call a truce?" Victoria decided to intervene before the party of the first part attacked the party of the second part with a jagged crab claw. Steve had already violated his promise to be nice, and her mother wasn't doing much better. "On your birthday, can't we all just get along?"

"Yes, darling. Let's enjoy ourselves at Stephen's favorite, noisy restaurant." She glanced toward the diners who might have been Jewish orthodontists or Protestant stockbrokers, but who were undeniably loud. An overweight man in canary yellow Bermuda shorts was tossing stone-crab claws across the table, where they *clang*ed into a metal bowl. His friends applauded each score.

"If it were up to me," The Queen continued, "we would have gone to the club."

"If it were up to you," Steve counterpunched, "your club wouldn't accept my tribe as members."

"Oh, that's rubbish," Irene said. "My accountant is Jewish. My furrier is Jewish. *All* my doctors are Jewish."

"Yeah. Yeah. Yeah."

"It's true. Do you think I'd go to some *medico clinica* in Little Havana?"

Desperately, Drake *clink*ed his water glass with a spoon and cleared his throat. "A toast to Irene. May this birthday be better than all the ones that came before."

"*All* of them?" Steve prodded. "How will she even remember?"

"To Irene!" Drake repeated, then took a hard pull on his gin and tonic.

"Happy birthday, Mother." Victoria sipped at her margarita and glared at Steve, conveying a simple message: *Behave!*

"*L'chaim.*" Steve drained his tequila, then recited: "There once was a girl named Irene—"

"Steve!" Victoria warned.

"Who lived on distilled kerosene. But she started absorbin' a new hydrocarbon. And since then has never benzene."

Steve chortled at his own joke, a cappella, as nobody joined in. "Bobby made that up for you, Irene."

"How sweet of the child," The Queen replied, her smile now cemented into place.

Steve signaled the waiter for a refill on the drinks, and Victoria felt the beginning of panic. She had hoped to keep the evening civil, at least until the Key lime pie. "Steve, are you sure you want another drink before we eat?"

"C'mon, Vic. You know me. I'm half Irish and half Jewish. I drink to excess, then feel guilty about it."

"Two lies in one sentence," she replied. "You're not half Irish and you never feel guilty about anything."

* * *

Victoria felt like a referee.

In one corner, six feet tall and 180 pounds, the base

stealer from the University of Miami and the unaccredited Key West School of Law, the Mouth of the South (Beach, that is), Steve Sue-the-Bastards Solomon.

In the other corner, five feet ten in her Prada heels, 130 pounds (net, after liposuction subtractions and silicone additions), the woman known both for haute couture and her own hauteur, Irene The Queen.

Here was Steve, spouting his dogma for the underdog, railing against the Establishment, materialism, and Republicans. And there was her mother, who once remarked: *"Diamonds aren't a girl's best friend, darling. A diversified portfolio, including both growth and value stocks, is much friendlier."*

Her mother's economic fortunes hadn't been as bright as the remark indicated. After the suicide of Victoria's father, Irene had been left to fend for herself. She fended fine for a while, attaching herself—like a remora to a shark—to a number of exceedingly wealthy men. There were rides on private jets, tips on stocks, and quite a few diamonds, too. But The Queen never attained the status she both desired and believed herself entitled to. These days, Victoria knew, her mother felt the sand was running out of the glass. Wealthy men cast their nets for younger, perkier fish. Maybe that was why Carl Drake seemed so important to her.

The platters of shelled claws had been removed from the table. The mountains of cole slaw topped with tomato slices had disappeared, the bowls of creamed spinach were empty, and the spears of sweet potato fries had been consumed. Waiting for dessert, The Queen daintily dabbed her lips with a napkin, then turned her crystalline blue eyes on Drake.

"Carl, darling, why don't you tell Victoria our little secret?"

"While you're at it, tell me, too," Steve instructed.

Victoria stiffened. She'd already had enough surprises for today.

The waiter delivered three slices of Key lime pie—mother and daughter would split theirs—and Drake straightened in his chair. "Well, Victoria, it seems your mother and I are related. Distant cousins, you might say."

"Not quite kissing cousins," Irene chirped. "See, dear, my grandmother's maiden name was Drake and if you go back far enough, our Drakes were related to Carl's family."

"Fascinating." Steve was using his fork to spread the whipped cream over the pie filling.

"I haven't gotten to the best part," Irene prattled. "If you go back four hundred years to England, both Carl and I are descended from Sir Francis Drake."

"The pirate?" Steve asked. "That explains a lot, Irene."

"Privateer," Carl Drake corrected. "Queen Elizabeth issued official papers that allowed Drake to plunder Spanish ships."

"Like the Bush administration and Halliburton," Steve said, agreeably.

"Isn't it exciting, Victoria?" Irene said. "We're descended from a famous sea captain."

"My old man thinks we're descended from King Solomon," Steve said. "Of course, he's off his rocker."

"Captain Drake enjoyed an especially close relationship with Her Majesty," Carl said. "So close that the name Virgin Queen might have been a misnomer."

Irene chuckled and Steve burped at the risqué little joke.

"Drake amassed millions in gold and jewels. When he died in 1596, the Crown confiscated his fortune. Now, you might think all that loot went to the royal family. But it didn't. Elizabeth still carried the torch for that handsome rascal. She created the Drake Trust, later administered by the Royal Bank. Well, the money was never spent and never disbursed. It was invested and just kept growing and growing for four centuries. It's now worth north of thirty billion dollars."

"You're quite the expert on the subject," Victoria observed.

"It started as a hobby," Carl confessed. "Once I learned I was related to Captain Drake, I started constructing the family tree. It's quite a task, mind you. All those generations. I didn't even know about the money until the trustees contacted me and offered quite a tidy sum for my research."

"A tidy sum," Steve repeated. "I always wondered what an untidy sum might be."

"My work could save them years of going through musty documents in libraries and museums."

"Why do they want the family tree?" Victoria asked.

"To locate the heirs," Irene answered. "Isn't that right, Carl?"

"Precisely. By a secret ballot, the trustees recently voted to disburse the monies to all known blood relatives of Captain Drake. They want to close the estate."

"I know probate takes a long time, but four hundred years?" Steve questioned.

"It's quite unprecedented; but then, there's never been a case like this," Drake said. "I've located two thousand nine hundred and twelve descendants. The trustees estimate there are another six hundred or so. Thirty billion dollars going to thirty-five hundred heirs. As the kids say, do the math."

"I don't know, Drake. You tell me." Steve's eyes were closed as he savored a huge bite of the tart pie.

"About eight and a half million for each heir," Drake said.

Steve's eyes popped open. "You're saying Irene is going to get *eight million bucks*?"

"Give or take, once she's a certified descendant."

"Irene, have I told you how exceptionally lovely you look tonight?" Steve said.

The Queen rolled her eyes.

"And how much I've always admired you for your . . ." He seemed stumped. "Poise and porpoise," he finished triumphantly.

"Stop being so silly, Stephen," Irene said. "What do you think of my good fortune?"

Steve turned back to Drake. "What's it gonna cost her?"

"Cost?" Drake seemed bewildered. "What do you mean?"

"All these heirs. They've gotta fill out forms, right? Affidavits. Birth certificates. Lots of clerical work before you get your slice of the pie."

"Of course there's paperwork."

"So what are you charging these lucky souls? Ten thousand? Twenty thousand apiece? That's the scam, isn't it? People will gladly pay that if they think they're getting millions. Because I gotta tell you, Carl, this is what my old man would call a *bubbe meise,* a grandmother's story. And it's what I would call a load of crap."

"Ste-phen!" The Queen hissed his name.

"Steve, that's very insulting," Victoria said. "Apologize this instant."

Drake smiled and waved off their protests. "No problem. A savvy attorney should be skeptical. There are no fees, Steve. No charges. I'll help Irene fill out the forms, and if it is her desire, I hope to be by her side the day the trustees disburse the money to all of us."

Three sets of eyes bored into Steve, who was licking the last of the graham cracker crust from his fork. "Perhaps I misspoke."

"That's not much of an apology, Stephen," Irene said.

He gave his lopsided grin, and Victoria tensed; Steve was preparing to misspeak again.

"So, if it's not a big con," he said, "there must be public records in England that'll back up your story."

Drake shook his head as he stirred his coffee. "It's a private trust and is quite confidential. You see, there is no lawful requirement that the trustees disburse these monies to the descendants. They could have just as easily escheated the money to the government or conveyed it to charity. And to prevent phony claimants from climbing out of the woodwork, there's to be no public announcement at all. It's to be all extremely hush-hush."

"If I were you, Irene," Steve advised, "I wouldn't spend that money yet."

"Oh, don't be such a spoilsport," The Queen snapped.

* * *

They were waiting for the check when a voice sounded: "What a surprise. Hello, Solomon!"

Steve didn't have to turn around. He recognized the resonant tones at once. Now, what the hell was *he* doing here?

Dr. Bill Kreeger sidled up to the table. He wore a dark, tailored suit with a yellow silk shirt, open at the neck. A handkerchief the same color as the shirt blossomed from his jacket pocket like a daffodil. Standing a half step behind him was a young woman wearing a stretchy pink top with holes cut out to reveal the contours of her breasts. The top stopped a foot above her hip-hugging slacks, giving a view of a nice set of washboard abs. Strawberry blond hair, wavy and shoulder length. She couldn't have been more than twenty.

"Solomon, this is my niece, Amanda."

Niece?

Steve refrained from laughing. Sure, the girl was Kreeger's niece. And Irene was the heir of Sir Francis Drake. And Steve was a direct descendant of King Solomon.

Hellos were exchanged and Kreeger flashed his smile toward Victoria. "You must be the lovely Ms. Lord." He swept his gaze toward The Queen. "And I'll bet you're her sister."

Irene beamed. "People are always saying that."

"Where?" Steve asked. "At the Lighthouse for the Blind?"

More introductions, a shaking of hands, The Queen saying she listened to Dr. Bill every day and found herself agreeing with him, especially about Steve. The young woman—niece Amanda—stood shyly in place, her eyes darting across the restaurant.

Bored, maybe. Or ill at ease. Steve couldn't tell which. Just who was she, anyway?

"Whoops, that's mine," Steve said, reaching into a pocket for his cell phone.

"That's so rude," Irene said.

"I didn't hear anything," Victoria said.

"It's on vibrate." Steve flipped the phone open and punched a button. "Hey, Bobby. No, Maria may not spend the night. Why not? Because her mother owns automatic weapons."

Steve noticed Victoria staring at him. Was there just a hint of suspicion in those green eyes? Man, he couldn't get anything past her.

"See you later, kiddo." Steve flipped the phone closed.

Bobby had not called. No one had. But Steve had clicked three photos of Amanda, from her strawberry blond hair to her six-pack abs.

SOLOMON'S LAWS

5. When a woman is quiet and reflective, rather than combative and quarrelsome, watch out. She's likely picturing the bathroom without your boxers hanging on the showerhead.

Fourteen

THE SERPENTINE PATH

One week after the birthday bash, a cold front was pushing down from Canada. The orange groves up-state braced for freezing temperatures. The TV re-porters wore their colorful parkas and warned people to bring their dogs and cats and ferrets indoors. And an even deeper chill settled over the offices of Solomon & Lord.

Driving to the office, Steve reviewed the events of the past week. The deep freeze started on the way home from dinner with The Queen. They had just passed the port where the cruise ships were lined up in a neat row like the fleet at Pearl Harbor. Then, out of the blue, a sneak attack. "You were absolutely horrid to my mother," Victoria said.

"Not once I learned she's gonna be rich."

"You promised to be nice. Then you went out of your way to be horrid."

"Horrid" being the word of the day, Steve figured. A word doubtless passed down from The Queen to The Princess like an heirloom necklace.

"And you were monstrous to Carl Drake," she con-tinued.

" 'Monstrous' is a little strong, Vic."

"All right. Ill-mannered and boorish."

"Often boorish. Seldom a bore. That's me. As for Drake, I don't trust a guy with polished nails and a phony accent."

She glared at Steve long enough for him to stage a strategic retreat.

"Okay. Okay. If I offended anyone, I'm sorry."

Even a semi-apology didn't placate Victoria, so now, a week later, he waited for both cold fronts—the Canadian and the Episcopalian—to pass.

Driving the old Mustang solo across the causeway with the top down despite the chill, listening to Jimmy Buffet ask "Jamaica Mistaica," Steve took further inventory of the past seven days. He and Victoria had spent the time running back and forth to court, going through the motions of looking for a new abode . . . and not making love. Victoria hadn't slept over once, a world record *schnide*. Steve had dropped a few casual mentions about having a quiet dinner, and got shot down three nights in a row. Victoria had other things to do—dinner with Jackie Tuttle, shopping with her mother, even legal research, of all the lousy excuses.

He had called his father for company, but the old man was in the Keys on his fruitless search for the missing boat captain, Oscar De la Fuente. Steve just hoped Herbert was making a fuss everywhere he went so word would get back to Kreeger.

Feeling lonely, Steve wanted to spend time with Bobby. Maybe they'd rent a pitching machine at the park, hit some balls. But the kid was hanging out with Maria. Girls will do that, split up guys and keep them from taking their practice swings. At least Bobby had helped download the photos of Amanda-the-Niece from Steve's cell phone.

"A hottie," Bobby had proclaimed as he printed out the pictures.

"How old, you think?"

"Old. Twenty, maybe."

Just yesterday, Steve had tried to engage Victoria in a discussion about Kreeger and Amanda. "So what do you think? Niece or girlfriend or something else?"

"What difference does it make?"

"I need to gather everything I can on Kreeger. Knowledge is power."

"Uh-huh."

"C'mon, Vic. I'm asking for help here. You're really good at sizing up people. The way you pick juries, it's amazing."

"Oh, please. You're so transparent."

"See what I mean? You knew I was gaming you. But it's still true. You're better in voir dire than I am. So tell me, when you looked at Amanda, what did you see?"

She sighed and seemed to give it some thought. "The top she was wearing. It's right off the rack at The Gap or Victoria's Secret. But the jeans were True Religion. Expensive. And did you notice her shoulder bag?"

"Should I have?"

"I don't know how you could miss it. Kiwi green. Alligator skin. Probably a Nancy Gonzalez. At least fifteen hundred dollars."

"I know a poacher who'll get you the whole gator for a hundred bucks."

"And those sandals with the hundred-millimeter heels . . . ?"

"You measured them?"

"I can tell. They're Blahniks. You don't want to know the price."

"This is good, Vic. Very good."

"Why?"

"Because all those dollars add up to a girlfriend of a guy with money."

"What an unbelievably sexist statement. Maybe Amanda earned the money. She could be a model. Or a personal shopper at Saks, where she gets a discount. Or she could work for her uncle Bill."

"Bill Kreeger has one sister with two sons. And he's never been married. He doesn't have a niece."

"So if you already knew . . ."

"I needed to know what you picked up. I've been looking for a way to get inside Kreeger's head."

"And you think his girlfriend will help you?" Sounding skeptical.

"What if I proved to her that he was a killer?"

"She'll never believe you."

"Maybe I can get close to her, establish my credibility."

"How?

He gave her his best lounge lizard smile. "Using all my charm."

"That and a baseball bat ought to do it."

"Have a better idea?"

"All I'm saying, Steve, even assuming you can find Amanda, and you start trying to hang out with her, the first thing she'd do would be tell Kreeger."

"Maybe that's not such a bad thing. Especially if it puts more heat on him."

Victoria gave Steve one of those looks that would wilt petunias. "So, now you're going to hit on Kreeger's girlfriend, hoping he finds out. At the same time you want him to believe you're building a murder case against him. Why not burn down his house while you're at it?"

"I've got to do something. From the day he stuck that fish on my door, I've been on the defensive. All that trash talk on the radio. Those veiled threats about you and Bobby and my father. Even his showing up at Joe's. He's worming his way into our lives and I want him out. I need to knock him off his stride, force him to make a move he hasn't planned."

"When Kreeger makes a move," Victoria reminded him, with an air of exasperation, "people tend to die."

* * *

Tourists clogged the causeway as Steve neared the Fisher Island Ferry terminal. He wove in and out of lanes, trying to find the quickest route across the bay. His mind drifted back to the dinner at Joe's, the source of the skirmish with Victoria. Okay, he hadn't been on his best behavior, but The Queen was partly to blame. Her very presence brought out his sarcastic side.

The Queen and The Princess.

Guys always say to study a girl's mother to see just what your girlfriend will look like in thirty years or so. Well, no problem there. Even without her artificial enhancements, The Queen was still a dish, to use another one of her expressions.

But what about personality traits? Does a daughter pick up those, too? Victoria seemed to have rejected her mother's values. She had ditched filthy rich Bruce Bigby and she had rejected the advances of lethally handsome and equally rich Junior Griffin. Her devotion and selflessness toward Bobby nearly matched Steve's.

But something troubling had come up in the search for a place to live. Why was Victoria steering him toward seven-figure penthouse condos and mini mansions? If they bought something beyond their means, Solomon & Lord would have to start wooing banks and insurance companies and other well-heeled clients.

Is this her secret plan? Maybe in cahoots with The Queen?

Was there some mysterious genetic factor at work here? An invisible time bomb, a materialism gene embedded in her family's DNA. Maybe it went all the way back to Sir Francis Drake, plundering Spanish ships for their gold doubloons.

A minivan with Michigan plates swerved into his lane, cutting him off. Steve banged his horn, then sped around the doofus. In five minutes, he'd be at the office, sidestepping anorexic models and dashing for the stairs. He wondered if Victoria was already there. Usually, she arrived before him, and there'd be coffee brewing and fresh lilies in a vase by the time he arrived.

But the past week, she'd been the tardy one. Not only that, she'd been unusually quiet. She hadn't been giving him grief, another bad sign. The other day, he'd worn an old T-shirt, with the logo *"Please Forgive Me; I Was Raised by Wolves."* No reaction from The Princess. The next day, he wore one reading, *"Oh, No! Not Another Learning Experience."* Still nothing. This morning, he'd actually put on a suit and tie. The suit was friendly brown, not powerhouse navy or gray. The duds were not for Victoria; he was due in Criminal Court later. The arraignment in the case of *State* v. *Solomon.*

But now, all his thoughts were stuck on Victoria. Should he be alarmed at her silence? Where were the sparks? Where was the heat? Sound and fury, he could deal with. Stillness and indifference, he could not. In Steve's experience, when a woman was enmeshed in quiet reflection, best be prepared for oceanic change, a reversal of tidal flows. What was going on? Just what the hell was she thinking?

* * *

Driving her Mini Cooper across the causeway, Victoria spotted Steve just ahead in his Mustang convertible, hair blowing in the wind. Why was the top down on such a chilly day? Why did he have to be such a contrarian? She heard a horn blare, knew it was his, watched as he cut hard to the left and passed a minivan with Michigan plates.

Here they were, Solomon and Lord, headed the same direction but traveling in different lanes. At different speeds. About to take different routes.

Is this some sort of metaphor for our lives?

She would stay on Fifth Street all the way to the beach and swing right on Ocean Drive. One simple turn and the Les Mannequins building would be two blocks away. Steve would sail south on Alton, hang a left on Fourth Street, a right on Meridian, and a left on Third.

Why does he always choose the serpentine path?

Presumably, their destination was the same . . . but was it really? She loved Steve, but sometimes she truly wondered why. He could be so aggravating. Ordinarily, his churlishness with her mother wouldn't have bothered her. God knew, Irene brought a lot of it on herself.

And The Queen enjoyed needling Steve as much as he enjoyed returning the favor.

But it was her birthday!

And what about the way he'd treated Carl Drake? Her mother really cared for the guy, and Steve practically called him a crook. As for the booty of Sir Francis Drake, sure, it all sounded a little fanciful. But Drake said he had some confidential paperwork he was going to give The Queen that should resolve any questions. And she wasn't laying out any money. So what was the harm? And maybe it was all real. Some people go to a garage sale and buy a Jackson Pollock for ten bucks.

Just ahead of her, she saw Steve's Mustang swing onto Alton, just as the light turned from yellow to red. Yep, taking his circuitous shortcut. She decided not to go to the office. Instead, she would drive to Lummus Park, walk along the ocean, think for a bit.

Did Steve even understand the problem? Or was he totally unaware of just how precarious their relationship was?

Fifteen

THE CASE OF THE
OVERBOOKED RABBI

"Let me get this straight," Steve said. "The rabbi was late for your wedding."

"Causing us emotional distress," piped up Sheila Minkin.

"And costing us like a thousand bucks in extra liquor charges," added Max Minkin, newly minted groom. "We had to start the reception before the wedding. Do you know how much the Ritz-Carlton charges per bottle?"

Steve didn't know and didn't care. He just wanted to get the basic facts of this *farshlugginer* case, then head to court for his own arraignment. It wouldn't hurt if his lawyer—Victoria Lord, Esq.—showed up so she could go along, too.

Where the hell is she?

In the past two minutes, Steve had learned that Max was a stockbroker downtown, Sheila a personal shopper for Neiman Marcus in Bal Harbour. Bride and groom were in their early thirties and well dressed. Steve figured the case was worth fifteen minutes of his time, twenty if he liked the couple. So far, he didn't.

They were sitting in the interior office of Solomon

& Lord on this chilly day. A northwest wind had definitely replaced the soft Caribbean breezes, and the windows rattled in their panes. Across the alley, on the balcony of an apartment occupied by a Trinidad steel band, wind chimes banged against one another, loud as cymbals. Still, that was preferable to half a dozen bare-chested men with dreadlocks beating sticks against metal pans. In the reception room, Cece Santiago did her bench presses, her grunts interspersed with the clang of the bar dropping into its brackets.

"Three hours late," Sheila Minkin was saying. "Rabbi Finsterman showed up three hours late, and he smelled of liquor."

"He got our names wrong during the ceremony," Max Minkin tossed in. "That's got to be worth something, right?"

Steve tried to pay attention. It was a shit case, no doubt about it. But sometimes you can write a demand letter. . . .

My clients have suffered grievously as a result of your negligence.

And the guy coughs up five grand to make you go away. One-third of which was $1666.67. Not a bad day's pay, even if he had to listen to the newly wedded Minkins piss and moan, kvetch and noodge.

"First the rabbi said traffic was blocked getting over the Rickenbacker because of the tennis tournament. Then he said a Purim festival in Aventura ran late. But I did a little sleuthing."

Sheila Minkin paused, as if waiting for applause. "The big *k'nocker* triple-booked. He had another wedding at the Diplomat in Hallandale and a third at the Church of the Little Flower in the Gables."

"A Catholic church?"

"A mixed marriage," Sheila explained. "Finsterman's reform."

"A thousand bucks in extra booze," Max Minkin repeated. "My uncle Sol got so *shikker* he pinched Aunt Sadie instead of a bridesmaid."

"I have to tell you," Steve said, "this isn't a big-money case. Not much in hard damages."

Working his clients. Preparing them for pin money. And hoping to get them out of his office as quickly as possible.

Just where the hell is Victoria, anyway?

"What about my emotional distress?" Sheila insisted. "I broke out in hives when the band played 'Hava Nagila.' "

"A lot of brides experience tension and stress." Steve played devil's advocate, the devil being the opposing lawyer.

"There's more. Tell him, Max."

Her husband reddened but didn't say a word.

"Okay, I'll tell him. Max couldn't get it up that night. A six-hundred-dollar suite at the Ritz-Carlton, and he couldn't get it up. A groom, on his wedding night! There's a name for that in the law, right?"

Buyer's remorse, Steve thought, but what he said was: "Lost consortium."

"Right. We didn't consort for two days. That's hard damages, right?"

Or soft damages, as the case may be.

"It's a cognizable claim," Steve said, trying to sound like a lawyer. "I just don't want you to think we're talking big money here."

The door opened, and Victoria walked in. Cheeks pink. Her fair complexion showing the effects of the wind. Meaning she hadn't just gotten out of her car.

She'd been walking. Alone. As she did when troubled. Not a good sign. He needed Victoria on so many different levels, and here she was, going all introspective on him.

"Sorry to interrupt," Victoria said softly. "Steve, don't you have to go to court?"

"*We* do."

"Do you need me? It's all worked out, right?"

True, the hearing would take all of five minutes. The state had agreed to lower the charges to a misdemeanor; Steve would plead nolo contendere and take an anger management course. Adjudication would be withheld, and when Steve got his certificate saying he was gentle as a pussy cat, all records would be expunged. In a strict legal sense, he didn't really *need* Victoria to stand alongside him in court, but he *wanted* her there. Saying that was something else. He wasn't going to beg.

"Nah. You don't have to go, Vic. Why don't you finish up here?"

He introduced her to Max and Sheila Minkin and described the facts, which he termed "a shocking case of rabbinical malpractice."

"Shocking," Victoria agreed, with just a smidgen of sarcasm. She turned to the lovebirds and said, "I'm sure we'll be able to achieve a fair and just result for you."

"Fuck that," Sheila Minkin said. "I want you to put that rabbi's nuts in a vise and make him squeal."

Sixteen

DISORDER IN THE COURT

Harry Carraway, a young Miami Beach cop, was riding his Segway down Ocean Drive, looking like a complete dork in his safari shorts and shades.

"Morning, Steve," he called out, above the hum of the machine.

"Dirty Harry," Steve called back. "Catch any jaywalkers?"

"No, sir. You walk any felons today?"

"Day ain't over yet."

The cop waved, gave the Segway some juice, and buzzed down the street.

The bicycles were bad enough, Steve thought, the Beach cops pedaling up and down Lincoln Road in their tight shirts and canvas shorts, flirting with sunburned coeds. But the sissified Segways were just too much. Cops should be straddling Harleys or driving big ugly Crown Vics.

Steve hopped into the Mustang and headed to the Criminal Justice Building.

Alone.

Victoria had jumped ship. Not that he couldn't handle this himself. But he never would have left her alone if the situation were reversed. Of course, it never would be reversed. Victoria would never have to step into a courtroom to enter a plea to a crime. *But that aside,* he wondered, *what's going on here?* Approaching the civic center, listening to "Incommunicado," Jimmy Buffet singing about driving solo on a road with a hole in it, Steve asked himself yet again: *Just what the hell is going on?*

* * *

"What's cooking, Cadillac?" Steve said as he crossed the courthouse patio.

"Baby backs, oxtail soup, ham croquettes," answered Cadillac Johnson, an elderly black man with a thick chest and a salt-and-pepper Afro.

Steve stopped at the counter of the Sweet Potato Pie, a trailer permanently parked on the patio. Cadillac, former blues musician, former client, current owner emeritus of the Pie—he was officially retired—slid a cup of chicory coffee across the counter to Steve. "You want me to save you a slab of ribs, Counselor?"

"Nah. I've become a vegan."

"Sure. And I've become a Republican." Cadillac poured a cup of coffee for himself. "You hear Dr. Bill on the radio this morning?"

Steve shrugged. "I listen to Mad Dog Mandich talk football and Jimmy B sing about tequila."

"The doc was talking about you."

"I know all about it. Solomon the Shyster. Steve the Snake."

"Not anymore. Today he said you had psychological issues you needed to deal with, but underneath, you were a good person."

"You're kidding."

"If I'm lying, I'm dying."

Five minutes later, Steve walked along the fourth-floor corridor, sidestepping cops and probation officers, court clerks and bail bondsmen, girlfriends and mothers of the presumably innocent hordes who were being led in shackles from the jail tunnel to the holding cells.

"Hey, *boychik*! Hold your horses!"

Marvin the Maven Mendelsohn toddled up. A small, tidy man around eighty, Marvin had a neatly trimmed mustache and a gleaming bald head. His black eyeglasses were too large for his narrow face, and his powder blue polyester leisure suit must have been all the rage in the 1970s. "What's your hurry, Stevie? They can't start your arraignment without you."

"You still reading the dockets, Marvin?"

The little man shrugged. "State versus Solomon. Assault and battery. In front of that *alter kocker* Schwartz."

At eight A.M. each day, Marvin the Maven could be found thumbing through the printouts attached to the clipboard outside each courtroom. As unofficial leader of the Courthouse Gang, a group of retirees who preferred trials to television, Marvin chose which cases to observe.

"So where's Ms. Lord?" Marvin asked.

"Don't need her," Steve said.

"What *mishegoss*! Of course you need her."

"I've got a plea all worked out."

"You gotta know, a man who represents himself has a *shmendrick* for a client."

"And a *shlemiel* for a lawyer?"

"Exactly."

As they neared the door to Judge Schwartz's courtroom, Marvin said: "So did you hear Dr. Bill today?"

"Apparently, I'm the only one in town who doesn't listen to the guy."

"He was saying nice things about you. That you have a lovely girlfriend. And in his experience, a man must have some good qualities if a fine, upstanding woman sees something in him."

"He's talking about himself, Marvin."

"I don't get it."

"He's sending a message that the two of us are alike somehow."

Steve headed into the courtroom, Marvin in tow. Inside, it was "shoot-around time," Steve's term for the chaos of a motion calendar. Lawyers and cops, clerks and clients drifting all over the courtroom, defendants filling the jury box, everyone talking at once. A basketball team's shooting practice, a dozen balls launched toward the rim at the same time. Presiding over the disorder was the Honorable Alvin Elias Schwartz, the only person in the courthouse older than Marvin the Maven.

Judge Schwartz was propped on two pillows, either because his hemorrhoids were flaring up or because, at five foot three, he couldn't see over the bench. Known as King of the Curmudgeons when he was younger, his disposition had gotten even worse with age. He now had the title of "senior judge," meaning he was somewhere between Medicare and the mortuary. No longer permitted to preside over trials because of lousy hearing, a weak bladder, and chronic flatulence, he nonetheless handled bail hearings, motions, and arraignments.

At the moment, Judge Schwartz was peering through his trifocals at a teenager in baggy, low-slung pants. Skinny and round-shouldered, the kid had the vacant, openmouthed look of the terminally stupid. From what Steve could gather, the kid had just pleaded guilty to possession of marijuana and was getting probation.

"You're getting a second chance, you understand that, José?" Judge Schwartz said.

"My name's Freddy, Judge," the kid said. "You know, short for Fernando."

"Hernando? Like the county? I own thirty acres up by Weeki Wachee."

"*Fer*-nando!" the kid repeated.

"I don't give a flying fandango what your name is, José. You come back here for spitting on the sidewalk, I'm sending you straight to Raiford, where some big bucks are gonna use your candy ass for a piñata. You *comprende*?"

"*Viejo comemierda,*" the kid muttered.

Either the judge didn't hear him or didn't know he'd just been called a shit-eater, because he started absentmindedly thumbing through his stack of files.

Steve worked his way to the front row of the gallery and took a seat on the aisle. It took a moment to realize he was sitting next to Dr. Bill Kreeger.

"What the hell . . . ?"

"Good day, Steve."

"What are you doing here?"

"Surely you know that I testify on occasion. I'm considered quite an effective witness."

"Pathological liars usually are."

It couldn't be a coincidence, Steve thought. First, Kreeger popped up at Joe's. Then he started saying nice things about Steve on the air. Now he showed up in court, looking spiffy in a dark suit and burgundy tie. What was the bastard up to?

"And how's the gorgeous Ms. Lord?"

"Fine. How's your niece? Amanda, right?"

"Lovely young thing, isn't she?"

"*Woman*," Steve said. "Lovely young woman. Only psychopaths see people as things."

"It's only an expression, Solomon. I assure you that no one in the world appreciates Amanda's qualities the way I do. She has an intelligence and understanding far beyond her years."

"What did you say her last name was?"

"I didn't."

"And just how is she your niece?"

"Too many questions, Solomon. Don't you know that curiosity killed the cat burglar?"

"State of Florida versus Stephen Solomon!" the clerk sang out.

Steve popped up and headed through the swinging gate into the well of the courtroom.

"Is the state prepared to proceed?" Judge Schwartz asked.

"The People are ready and holding steady, Your Honor."

The voice came from the back of the courtroom. Bouncing on his toes, a trim African-American man in a double-breasted pin-striped suit strutted toward the bench. Silver cuff links shaped like miniature handcuffs clinked as he walked. The man was in his mid-forties and still looked like he could fight middleweight, as he did in Golden Gloves when growing up in Liberty City.

What the hell? Pincher only showed up for cases that could get him face time on television.

Dumbfounded, Steve whispered to Pincher: "Sugar Ray, what's going on?"

"A special case that time won't erase."

"What the hell's so special about it?" Steve hissed at the prosecutor. "Are you backing out of the plea?"

"Relax, Solomon." Pincher turned his politician smile on the judge. "Your Honor, we've reached an agreement, but nothing vehement."

"You mean a plea deal?"

"Which now I'll reveal."

"Stop that damned bebop and get to the point."

Pincher gave a courteous bow to the judge, as if he'd just been complimented on the cut of his suit. "Your Honor, the state is prepared to dismiss the felony charges, and Mr. Solomon will plead nolo to simple assault with adjudication to be withheld pending completion of anger-management therapy."

Steve let out a breath. Okay, that was exactly what he'd agreed to with one of Pincher's deputies. But why was the boss here? What was so damn special about the case?

"Mr. Solomon?" The judge seemed to focus on Steve for the first time. "Aren't you that lawyer I throw in the clink every now and then?"

"I plead nolo to that, too, Your Honor."

"Okay, then. Let's put the stuffing in this turkey."

The judge started running through the plea protocol. Did Steve understand the charges against him? Did he know he had the right to a trial? Was he entering the plea freely and voluntarily?

Steve gave all the right answers, and in less than three minutes, the judge had checked off the boxes on his form and signed the order Pincher handed to him. Judge Schwartz leaned close to the document, showing the courtroom the crown of his bald head as he read: "The Court finds that the defendant is alert and intelligent and understands the consequences of his plea, which is accepted for all purposes. Adjudication of guilt is withheld pending completion of anger-management therapy under the auspices of William Kreeger, MD, board-certified psychiatrist."

What!? Did the judge say what I think he said?

"Dr. Kreeger will file a written report with the Court at the conclusion of said therapy."

Yes. He definitely said it. But that's nuts. There must be some mistake.

"At which time, charges will either be dismissed and all records expunged, or in the event of the failure to satisfactorily complete said therapy, the defendant shall be sentenced in accordance with his plea of nolo contendere."

"Hold on, Judge!" Steve shouted, loud enough for the old buzzard to hear. "Kreeger's a convicted felon."

"Not anymore," Pincher shot back. "His rights have been restored. Dr. Kreeger received commendations from the Corrections Department for his work with violent offenders, and the DPR restored his medical license. He's a model of rehabilitation."

"He's a model nutcase," Steve said.

"You heard my ruling," the judge rasped. "Now stop your bellyaching and go get your anger managed."

The judge hammered his gavel. "Clerk, call the next case."

"No fucking way," Steve said.

"What'd you say?" the judge demanded.

"No fun this way, Your Honor."

"It's not supposed to be fun. You're a criminal, aren't you?"

"No, sir. I'm a defense lawyer."

"Same difference. You're accused of assaulting

one . . ." The judge licked his index finger and thumbed through the court file. "Arnold Freskin, an employee of the great State of Florida." Judge Schwartz used his feet to pedal his chair away from his desk and toward the flagpole a few feet away. He grasped the edge of the state flag and pulled it taut. "What do you see, Mr. Solomon?"

"I see the state seal, Your Honor. A Native American woman is scattering flowers on the ground."

"Damn right. These days the squaw would be raking in chips at the casino." The judge dropped the flag and rolled back to his desk. "My point, Mr. Solomon, is that you offended the dignity of the great State of Florida, and Mr. Pincher has magnanimously decided to cut you a break."

"Yes, sir, but—"

"No 'but.' I just disposed of this baked turd of a case."

"I'm being set up, Judge. By Mr. Pincher and Dr. Kreeger."

"You're talking in riddles, Mr. Solomon. I called the next case, and by God, I'm going to hear the next case."

The clerk called out: "City of Miami Beach *versus* Weingarten Delicatessen. Violation of Kosher Food Ordinance."

Pincher grabbed Steve's elbow and whispered: "Just chill. See Bill. Ain't nothing but a fire drill."

"You sold me out, Sugar Ray." Steve turned to the judge. "Your Honor, I move to withdraw my plea."

"Are you still here?" Judge Schwartz was scowling. "I'm going to charge you rent, Counselor."

Steve felt a presence beside him. Kreeger had come through the swinging gate. "Your Honor, Mr.

Solomon's recalcitrance is a normal manifestation of his behavioral type. I'm sure he'll do fine with therapy."

"Like I give a rat's *tuches*," the judge said. "Where's that butcher who's selling *trayf* as kosher?"

"Judge, there's a motion pending," Steve insisted. "I've moved to withdraw my plea. I want to go to trial."

"Motion denied. It's time to clear my calendar, Mr. Solomon, and not the one with the Playboy bunnies on it."

"Your Honor, I have an absolute right to—"

Bang! The judge smacked the gavel so hard, Steve could feel his teeth reverberate. "I'm driving the Studebaker, Mr. Solomon, and you're the greasy speck of a horsefly on my windshield."

Steve had no intention of giving up or backing down. "Judge, I once represented Kreeger in a case. State Attorney Pincher prosecuted for the state. They've cooked this up. If Kreeger doesn't clear me, you'll sentence me to jail. Can't you see it, Judge? It's a conspiracy."

Judge Schwartz turned his bleary gaze on Kreeger, and for a moment Steve thought maybe he'd made an impression.

"Let's hear from the headshrinker," the judge said. "Doc, what do you say about these accusations?"

"Nothing to be alarmed about, Your Honor," Kreeger replied in his soothing baritone. "While I'm working on Mr. Solomon's anger, I'll check out that paranoia, too."

SOLOMON'S LAWS

6. A creative lawyer considers a judge's order a mere suggestion.

Seventeen

THE UNFINISHED BUSINESS
OF PARENTING

"What did you do to make the judge so furious?" Victoria demanded.

"Nothing," Steve said. "Nada. Bupkes."

"You must have done something."

"Why?" Steve had come home hoping for comfort and support. Instead he was being cross-examined in his own kitchen. "Why do you automatically assume it's my fault?"

"Because you have a knack for driving people crazy."

"Judge Schwartz was crazy decades before I met him. Can you believe I'm supposed to be counseled by that psychopath Kreeger?"

"Sociopath," Bobby corrected him. "With narcissistic tendencies and omnipotent fantasies." The kid had been reading psychology texts and checking out various medical websites. At least that's what he said when asked why his computer had bookmarked nymphomaniacs.com. Now Bobby gave the adults his wiseguy look from underneath the bill of his Solomon & Lord ball cap. Steve had formed a team in the lawyers' softball league, but desperately short of players, he recruited clients to play. Purse snatchers turned out to be excellent base runners; pedestrians knocked down by taxicabs were a little slow off the bag.

Outside the windows, fronds from a sabal palm swatted the stucco walls of the house. Inside, Steve was defending himself from Victoria's torrent of criticism.

"I didn't do anything wrong," Steve insisted. "Kreeger set me up, and Pincher was in on it."

"Why? What's Pincher have to gain?"

"More like what he has to lose. Kreeger threatened to go public, tell everyone our esteemed State Attorney used tainted evidence to convict him."

"Pincher told you that?"

"I figured it out. Pincher's up for reelection next year. Who'd he rather have pissed off at him? A defense lawyer or a guy with a radio show?"

"Aw, why make a big *tsimiss* out of it?" Herbert Solomon walked into the kitchen, carrying a tumbler filled with ice. "Do the therapy and get the charges dismissed."

"Not that easy, Dad. Having Kreeger as my therapist is like having a burglar in my bedroom."

Herbert had filled his glass so high with bourbon, he needed to slurp it out. "So don't flap your gums about family secrets. Stonewall his ass."

"Then he files a report with the court saying I'm hiding my lunatic impulses."

"If the judge ordered you to go to Kreeger," Victoria said, "you have no choice."

"That's the difference between you and me, Vic," Steve said. "I consider judges' orders as mere suggestions."

"That's the difference between civilization and anarchy. And in your life, anarchy rules."

"Anarchy rules," Bobby repeated. "ANY CRUEL RASH."

"No reason to be all tore up, son," Herbert said. "Maybe the more time you spend with that shrink, the better."

"How you figure, Dad?"

"Ah couldn't find hide nor hair of that boat captain. You need a new plan."

Victoria shot Steve a look. He hadn't told his father everything, and she knew it.

"Dad, it doesn't matter if you found De la Fuente or not. I just want Kreeger to know I'm looking."

Herbert's bushy eyebrows seemed to arch higher. "So you send your old man on a wild-goose chase. Fine son you are."

"But you're right, Dad. There's an upside to spending more time with Kreeger. His girlfriend, too, if I could get her alone."

"You still think you can convince her Kreeger's a killer?" Victoria said.

"No!" He slapped his forehead to signify what an idiot he was. No one disagreed. "I've got it backwards. I think she *already* knows his past."

"And you base this on what?" Victoria asked.

"Something Kreeger said to me about how much he appreciates Amanda's qualities. That she has an intelligence and understanding beyond her years. That sort of thing."

"Yeah?"

"She's the one he feels safe with, the one who comforts him. Kreeger could have told her about Beshears and Lamm. And who knows? Maybe there's—"

"A third murder," Victoria said.

"Exactly. If Amanda knows Kreeger's secrets, and I can drive a wedge between them, maybe I can get her to help me nail him."

"This 'wedge' of yours? How's that going to work, exactly?"

"I don't know yet, Vic. I'm just riffing here."

"And you don't think a guy as smart as Kreeger will catch on?"

"So he's smart. What am I? Chopped liver?"

"You don't exactly bend spoons with your mind, Uncle Steve." Bobby unscrewed two halves of an Oreo cookie and used his teeth to scrape off the vanilla filling.

"Thanks, guys," Steve said. "But Kreeger's got his weaknesses. He's so damn cocky, he'll figure there's no way I can take him down."

"The omnipotence fantasy," Bobby added. "Freud wrote about it."

"And if Kreeger wants to hang out, like Dad says, that's fine, too."

"Keep your friends close but your enemies closer," Bobby recited.

"Freud?" Steve asked.

Bobby winced. "Al Pacino. *Godfather, Part II.*"

"Don't you have homework to do?" Steve said.

"Nope."

"And where were you last night?"

"Nowhere."

"Physically impossible."

The boy tossed his shoulders, the adolescent symbol for "so what" or "whatever" or "who gives a shit?"

"You violated curfew, kiddo."

"Jeez, this is like a prison."

"Ease up on the boy," Herbert said. "When you and Janice were kids, Ah—"

"Was nowhere to be found," Steve interrupted.

* * *

Bobby wanted to tell Uncle Steve the truth.

"I was with Mom. We sat in her car down by the bay and talked for hours."

But he couldn't do it. Uncle Steve thought she was a really bad influence. But she didn't seem that way at all. She seemed kind of lost, like she needed Bobby more than he needed her.

Mom seems so lonely, like there's nobody for her to talk to.

So Bobby had listened as she talked about growing up in a house with a sick mother and an absent father, Grandpop always being off somewhere, and Steve out playing sports. Mom had been the outsider, or that was how she felt, anyway.

When Mom was talking about the man who picked her up hitchhiking—she couldn't remember his name, even though he might be Bobby's father—Bobby tried to decide whether he loved her. Yeah, he probably did in some weird way. But he was certain he felt sorry for her.

Now Bobby listened as Uncle Steve and Grandpop argued for the zillionth time about the past.

"Don't tell me you're still mad because I didn't come to your Little League games," Grandpop said.

"Or to my spelling bees, my track meets, or the hospital when I had my tonsils out."

"For crying out loud, you were only there a few hours."

"Because you wouldn't pay for a room. The doctor wanted to keep me overnight."

"Highway robbery."

Sometimes Bobby wished the two of them would grow up.

* * *

Victoria tried to decide who was more immature, Steve or his father. Clearly, they were equally argumentative and pugnacious. She tried to picture the Solomon home during Steve's childhood. It didn't seem to be a happy place. Certainly, it was not a quiet place.

They railed at each other another few moments, Herbert calling Steve an "ungrateful grumble guts," Steve calling Herbert a "tumbleweed father, gone with the wind." Then they seemed to tire, and Steve turned back to Bobby. "You still haven't said where you were last night."

"Probably with his little shiksa," Herbert said.

"Dad! That's a derogatory term."

"The hell it is."

Here we go again, Victoria thought. *These two could argue over "Happy Chanukah."*

"A shiksa's a gentile gal," Herbert continued. "Nothing derogatory about it. As for little Miss Havana-Jerusalem, her mother's a Catholic and that makes her a shiksa."

"So I'm a shiksa," Victoria said.

"Hell, no. You're Jewish by injection." Herbert laughed and took a pull on his bourbon. "Unless you two haven't played hide-the-salami yet."

"Dad, put a lid on it," Steve ordered.

Herbert grinned at Victoria. "How 'bout it, *bubele*? Stephen been slipping you the Hebrew National?"

Herbert cackled again and headed toward the living

room without waiting for an answer. "Hold mah calls. Ah'm gonna watch a titty movie on Cinemax, then take a nap."

Victoria whirled toward Steve. "Why do you have to bait him?" she demanded.

"I could tell you, Vic, but I'm not sure you'd understand."

"Try me, partner. I've been to college and everything."

"It's a Jewish thing. We love arguing, complaining, talking with our mouths full. You're Episcopalian. You love—I don't know—drinking tea, wearing Burberry, the Queen of England."

Victoria was not particularly pleased about being reduced to a stereotype. She would talk to Steve about it later. But right now Bobby was still there, fishing into the Oreo bag. "Steve, don't you have some unfinished parenting to do?"

"Parenting's always unfinished." He turned to the boy. "So, kiddo, was your grandpop right? Were you with Maria last night?"

"Jeez, it's like the Inquisition in here." Bobby pried off the top of a cookie. "No, I wasn't with her. Maria's stupid dad won't let me see her anymore."

Victoria spoke gently. "Bobby, what's happened?"

"Nothing, except Dr. Goldberg thinks I'm weird." The pain was audible in the boy's voice.

"You're weird?" Steve said. "He's a periodontist."

Victoria ran a hand through Bobby's hair. "Why would he say something like that?"

Bobby hunched his shoulders. "Lots of reasons, I guess. Dr. Goldberg's always cracking on me. Like, he hates the T-shirt Uncle Steve got me."

"What T-shirt?"

Steve shook his head in Bobby's direction, but the kid either didn't pick up the sign or didn't care. " 'If We Don't Have Sex, the Terrorists Win.' "

Victoria shot a look at Steve. In the household of the three Solomon men, she now concluded, Steve clearly was the most childish.

"And Dr. Goldberg hated the poetry I wrote for Maria," Bobby continued. "I made anagrams of every line of 'The Rubaiyat of Omar Khayyam.' "

"Why, that must have been beautiful," Victoria said, trying to boost the boy's ego.

"Dr. Goldberg said the whole poem was smutty."

"Smutty!" Steve smacked the countertop.

Why was it, Victoria wondered, that men always needed to throw things, hit things, and make noise to express displeasure?

"Who uses words like 'smutty' anymore?" Steve railed. "What else did this tight-ass say to you?"

"Nothin'." The boy licked another open-faced Oreo.

"C'mon, Bobby. Don't hold out on Uncle Steve."

Without looking up from the table, Bobby said: "That I was a klutz. That he didn't want me hanging around Maria. And in case I thought she liked me, she didn't. She just wanted me to do her homework."

Steve smacked *both* hands on the countertop. "That asshole! I'm going over there and kick his butt."

"That would be very smart," Victoria said evenly. "Give Kreeger ammunition for the judge."

"Forget Kreeger. This jerk's got no right to talk to Bobby that way."

"It's okay, Uncle Steve."

"The hell it is!"

"Steve," Victoria cautioned. "Settle down. You're not going over to the Goldbergs'."

"Vic, this is between Bobby and me, okay?"

She stiffened. "What does that mean?"

"Nothing."

"Are you trying to put distance between us?"

"I have no idea what you're talking about."

"Then answer this. Am I a member of this family or not?"

Steve hesitated. Just a second. Then he said, "Sure. Sure, you are."

Victoria remembered an early boyfriend once saying he loved her. She had thought it over a couple seconds—one-thousand-one, one-thousand-two—and finally agreed, *"I love you, too."* But if you have to think about it, well, the feeling just isn't there.

"So you don't consider me a member of the family?"

"I just said I do."

"Let's examine the instant replay," Victoria demanded, "because you looked like you were moving in slow motion."

"I just like to think before I speak."

"Since when? You have an intimacy problem, you know that, Steve?"

"Aw, jeez, don't change the subject. Name one good reason why I shouldn't go over to Myron Goldberg's house and call him out."

"Because it's juvenile, illegal, and self-destructive," Victoria said. "Three reasons."

That seemed to silence him. Then he said: "Okay, I get it. I'm going to take care of my stuff first. Go to Kreeger. Get my head shrunk, get the case dismissed.

Then I'm going to see Myron Goldberg and ask politely but firmly that he apologize to Bobby."

"And if he doesn't? What then?"

"I'll kick his ass from here to Sopchoppy," Steve said.

SOLOMON'S LAWS

7. When you run across a naked woman, act as if you've seen one before.

Eighteen

SKIN SHOW

Halloween had come and gone, Thanksgiving was around the corner, but the air was washcloth thick with heat and humidity. The palm fronds hung limply on the trees, no ocean breezes drifted inland. Driving through the winding streets of Coral Gables, Steve wore green Hurricanes shorts and a T-shirt with the logo *"I'm Hung Like Einstein and Smart as a Horse."* On the Margaritaville station, Jimmy Buffet was singing "Off to See the Lizard."

Steve parked next to a pile of yard clippings in a cul-de-sac off Alhambra, next to the Biltmore golf course. Halfway down the block was the home and office of Dr. William Kreeger.

Steve hopped out and headed down the street on foot. He could hear a power mower churning away behind one of the houses, could smell the fresh-cut grass. Around the corner, on Trevino, the sounds of sawing and chopping, a city crew cutting back the limbs on neighborhood banyan trees.

He wasn't quite sure why he parked so far away. Kreeger's place had a driveway, and there was parking at the curb, too. Maybe it was the embarrassment, going to visit a shrink. Or was Steve more like a burglar, stashing the getaway car out of sight? Didn't matter. The walk through the neighborhood of Mediterranean homes with barrel-tile roofs gave him a chance to plan. Should he bring up the subject of the boat captain? He could try bluffing, tell a big, fat lie.

"Say, Kreeger. I found the guy who was driving the boat when you killed your pal Beshears. Oscar De la Fuente. He's got some interesting things to say."

No. Too obvious. Let Kreeger bring it up. By now, he should know that Steve had been looking for the guy. Herbert had dropped off Steve's business card at every saloon and boat-repair yard in the Keys, lingering longer in the saloons, no doubt. Steve had placed ads in newspapers and on the Internet, promising a reward for anyone finding De la Fuente. No one came forward.

Kreeger lived in a stucco house that dated from the 1920s. The walls had been sandblasted, giving them the pallor of a dead man. Kreeger's office was around back. Steve followed a path of pink flagstones between hibiscus bushes and emerged in a yard surrounded by a ficus hedge. A waterfall gurgled between coral rock boulders and spilled into a rectangular swimming pool.

Steve had been here before. A lawyer always visits the scene of the crime. At the far end of the pool was the hot tub where Nancy Lamm had drowned.

Nothing had changed since Steve was here seven years ago, except that day, best he could recall, there was no naked woman on a chaise lounge. But today, reclining on a redwood chaise with thick patterned cushions was a very lithe young woman wearing sunglasses and nothing else. Her body was slick with oil, and the scent of coconut was in the air.

"Hello there," he said jauntily.

She sleepily turned her head toward him. "You don't recognize me, do you?"

"Sure I do." In truth, he hadn't been looking at her face. "Amanda, right? The niece. But I don't know your last name."

"Is that important?"

"I was just wondering how Dr. Bill is your uncle."

She rolled onto her side. "It's an honorary title. But I think that makes Bill even more special, don't you?"

The random fortuity of life struck Steve just then. One sunny day, you're walking on the beach and a bird shits on your head. Or if you're really unlucky, a tsunami swamps you and drags you out to sea. But another day, you're going to see a homicidal guy who hates you, and *poof,* a naked woman appears directly in your path. A woman who could alter the course of several lives. Could do justice where justice has failed. And there she is, like the gatekeeper at a bridge in a Greek myth.

It's almost too coincidental. Okay, strike the "almost."

Kreeger always seemed to be one step ahead of him. If Steve had plans for Amanda, surely Kreeger did, too. Steve just wasn't sure what they were.

"Wanna go for a swim?" Amanda asked.

The question threw him.

"Uncle Bill's still with a patient," she continued. "We've got time."

She cocked her head in the direction of Kreeger's office, a converted Florida room facing the yard. Slatted wooden shades appeared to be closed, but it was possible someone on the inside was watching them.

"I don't have a swimsuit."

"Me, either."

"I see that."

Dumb. "I see that." Of course you see it, schmuck.

"Nice day for a swim, though," he said. "Hot."

"I love hot days," Amanda purred.

"I see that."

Again? "I see that"? Act natural. Act like you've seen a naked woman or two.

She stretched her arms over her head, yawned, and pointed her toes. The motion was graceful and catlike. Her breasts were small, round, and tan, the nipples the color of copper. She was thin but strong, with developed calves that flexed as she straightened her legs. Carved abs. Farther south, a thin triangular strip of pubic hair ran between two small tattoos, but he couldn't make them out from this distance.

"An arrow and a heart," she said.

"What?"

"The tats you're staring at."

"Oh. Well. I wasn't. Staring, I mean. Exactly."

In retrospect, "I see that" sounded more intelligent.

"I mean, I was looking at your . . . uh . . . landing strip. That's what you call it, right? My girlfriend asked me if she should get one. I guess, technically, you don't 'get one.' It's not like buying a purse, right?"

He was aware he was babbling. What was it about a naked woman that discombobulated a man?

Her nakedness, idiot! Right. I see that.

What happened to his plans? He had wanted to find out everything about Amanda. How long had she known Kreeger? Did he ever talk about Nancy Lamm or Jim Beshears? Would she help Steve? But confronted with a naked woman, logical questions tend to evaporate faster than coconut oil.

"You were Uncle Bill's lawyer, weren't you?" Amanda asked.

"Right."

Wait a second. I'm supposed to be asking the questions.

"You double-crossed him."

"He tell you that?"

"Uncle Bill tells me everything."

"I thought he might. Maybe we can get together and swap stories."

"Uncle Bill wouldn't like that."

"Not a date or anything. I just want to talk."

Amanda gave him a patronizing smile with just a hint of an eyebrow raised above the sunglasses. "That's what he wouldn't like. Talking about private stuff. Having sex with you he wouldn't mind. If that's what I wanted."

Oh.

"But I haven't made up my mind about you yet," she said. She swung her legs out of the chaise and walked toward him. It wasn't a seductive walk. More bouncy and athletic, like a cheerleader, her small breasts not even jiggling. She came up to Steve, as if daring him not to move out of the way. He took the dare, and she stopped six inches in front of him. She took off the sunglasses. Her eyes were a greenish gold. "I don't know if you'd be as good to me as Uncle Bill. He always puts me first. My pleasures. My desires. That's how he got his honorary title."

"That's some uncle," Steve allowed.

"Uncle Bill loves me. And he has for a long time."

She took a half step toward him, stood on her tippy-toes, and kissed Steve lightly on the lips. He didn't kiss back, but he didn't pull away, either. "But a girl can always have *two* uncles," she whispered.

She moved past him, one breast brushing his arm, giving him a last look at her from behind. Bouncing toward the house, calves undulating, her butt high and firm. And just above the crack between her cheeks, another tattoo: an iridescent jellyfish, beautiful and deadly, its tentacles streaming down each buttock.

Nineteen

SHRINK WRAPPED

Ten minutes later, Steve was settling into a brown leather chair in Dr. William Kreeger's home office. The floor was Dade County pine, the stucco walls painted a grayish-green color Steve didn't care for. He once read that shrinks used earth colors to calm their troubled patients. But no beige walls, no corn plant in the corner, no gurgling fish tank with parrotfish and lionfish frolicking through coral caves.

The only personal items were several framed photos on a credenza. Kreeger on a power boat, a big-ass sport fisherman in the fifty-foot range. Best Steve could tell, there were no bodies floating in the water. Then there were a couple of grainy shots taken from videotape: Kreeger on CNN, opining why husbands kill their wives or mothers kill their children, or maybe even why clients kill their lawyers.

"Did you see Amanda on your way in?" Kreeger sat in his own leather chair.

"All of her." Steve looked toward the wood-slatted windows. Now he was sure Kreeger had been watching them, had planned the whole thing.

"She's a remarkable young woman," Kreeger said.

"Tell me about her."

"We're here to talk about you, Solomon. Not her."

"Hey, you brought it up."

"All I'll say is this: When I was in prison, Amanda was the only one who wrote me, the only one who cared. And when I got out, she was waiting for me."

"Seems a little young to be one of those wackos who fall for murderers."

"You have much to learn, Solomon. And so little time to learn it." He used a handheld sharpener to grind a fine point on a pencil, then continued. "Now, what should we discuss first? Your violent temper or your sleazy ethics?"

"That's sweet, Kreeger. You lecturing on ethics is like the Donner Party talking about table manners."

"I detect antagonism in your voice. Still having difficulty controlling your anger?"

"Aw, shit."

Kreeger crossed his legs and balanced a leather-bound notebook on his knee. An open leather briefcase, the old-fashioned doctor-bag variety, was at his feet. A rattan table with a green marble ashtray sat between the two men, and a paddle fan whirred silently overhead. They had barely started, and already Steve felt like bolting. If the bastard asked if he'd ever wanted to kill his father and sleep with his mother . . . well, there'd be a second assault-and-battery charge in his file.

"Tell me about your childhood," Kreeger instructed, his voice clinical and distant. "Were you a happy child?"

"Screw you, Kreeger."

"Did you have a good relationship with your father?"

"And the horse your rode in on."

Kreeger scribbled something in his notebook.

"Let me guess," Steve said. " 'Patient is obstreper-ous, uncooperative, manifests antisocial tendencies.' "

"Let's get something straight, Solomon. You're not my patient. I'm not here to treat you. I'm here to teach you how to manage your anger. It's up to you whether you take my advice. My report to the court will state whether your penchant for violence is under control or whether you should be incarcerated as a danger to the community. Understand?"

"Yeah."

"Splendid. Now, you still want to fuck with me?"

Steve took a breath and tried to relax. This wasn't going the way he had planned. He'd intended to be cooperative, maybe drop a comment or two about Nancy Lamm, maybe something about Jim Beshears, see if Kreeger brought up Oscar De la Fuente.

"Okay, Doc. Let's get this over with."

Kreeger reached into the open briefcase. He pulled out a photograph and slid it across the rattan table. "When you look at that, how do you feel?"

Steve picked up the photo and laughed. It was black-and-white and grainy, but there he was, in his U.M. baseball uniform, bareheaded. He'd already tossed his cap to the ground. His arms were thrown out to the sides, frozen in an awkward position as if he were attempting to fly. His face was contorted into an expression that seemed to be equal parts anguish and anger. A vein in his throat stood out, thick as a copper-head. He was screaming at an umpire, whose face was just inches from his own.

"Championship game of the College World Series," Steve said. "Bottom of the ninth. Two outs. I was on third, the potential tying run, and I got picked off. At least, the ump said I did, but I got in under the tag." He shook his head. "How do you think I felt?"

Kreeger scribbled something on his pad. "You tell me."

"Angry. Cheated. Humiliated. Angry."

"You already said that."

"I was *really* angry, but I didn't hit anyone. Write *that* down."

"What about this?"

Kreeger slid a photocopied newspaper clipping toward Steve, who immediately recognized the story from the *Miami Herald*. The headline read: "Judge Quits Bench, Dodges Indictment." A photo—a prize-winning photo, as it turned out—showed Herbert T. Solomon, in shirtsleeves, carrying a cardboard box down the steps of the Criminal Justice Building. Clearly visible in the box were miniature scales of justice, tilted to one side, the chains tangled. The look on Herbert's face: abject shame.

"Dad on the worst day of his life. What about it?"

"How does that picture make you feel?"

"It hurts. A lot. Happy now?"

"Let's analyze your pain. Which was greater? Pulling a bonehead play and losing the championship? Or seeing your father disgraced?"

"That's easy. Watching Dad go down was way worse."

"Why do you suppose you hurt so much, when the disgrace wasn't your own?"

"Because I love my father. Is that concept a little tough for you to understand, Kreeger?"

"And if he were guilty, if your father had taken those bribes, would you still love him?"

"Sure. But Dad was innocent. He was falsely accused."

"Then why didn't the Honorable Judge Solomon fight the charges?"

"Maybe he was afraid of a bad call from the umpire, too."

"Fair enough. He'd lost his faith in the system. Like father, like son-of-a-gun."

"What are you getting at, Kreeger?"

Again Kreeger reached into his briefcase. Another photo. A police mug shot. The woman was in her thirties. Round, pasty face. The tattoo of a snake peeked out of her tank top. Greasy ringlets of hair seemed to be glued to her forehead. And the eyes, glassy and staring into some distant universe.

How long ago must it have been, Steve wondered, that she was a pretty, well-mannered girl living in an upscale house on Pine Tree Drive? With a posse of girlfriends that elicited remarkable electrochemical reactions in a fifth grader named Steve Solomon.

"My sister Janice. What's she have to do with this?"

"Your sister the thief. The drug abuser. The abusive mother."

"All of the above."

"Do you love her, too, Solomon?"

"I'm not doing this, Kreeger." Steve got up and walked to the windows. With an index finger, he lifted one of the wooden shades. Clear view of the pool, the hot tub, and the chaise lounge, now empty. Not a nude young woman in sight.

"I'm afraid you don't have a choice. You kidnapped your nephew from your sister, didn't you?"

"I *rescued* Bobby."

"You hit a man, crushed his skull with a stick of some kind. What was it?"

"A piece of oak. A shepherd's staff."

"Not quite as heavy as a gaff, I would think."

Ah, so there it was, Steve thought. The boat in the Keys. Beshears overboard. De la Fuente at the wheel. *Okay, now we're getting somewhere.* "We talking about my hitting a guy named Thigpen or you hitting a guy named Beshears?"

"You'd agree there is some similarity. Except, of course, I was trying to rescue poor Jim Beshears."

"Funny. I didn't kill Thigpen. But you killed Beshears."

"Tell me about Thigpen, and I'll tell you about Beshears. Nancy, too."

Steve didn't know whether to believe him, but there was very little to lose. "Janice kept Bobby in a dog cage, fed him gruel. She would have sold him for half a dozen rocks of crack. I got him out of there, and I had to hit somebody to do it."

Remembering a snowy night in the Panhandle. A commune where Janice and her brain-dead friends grew marijuana in the summer and ingested all manner of illicit substances the rest of the year. Remembering swinging the staff, fracturing a man's skull, and carrying Bobby to safety. Bringing him home, the boy's first real home.

"Your turn," Steve said. "Did you push Beshears overboard? Did you intend to bash him with the gaff?"

"Police report said it was an accident."

"That's it, Kreeger? That's all you have to say?"

"Jim Beshears was an oaf and a boor and insanely

jealous of me. He ruined a perfectly fine fishing trip with his incessant pestering."

"Sounds like he deserved to be killed."

"Draw your own conclusions, Solomon."

"You're boasting, aren't you? Letting me know what you're capable of."

"We should go fishing sometime, you and I, Solomon."

Steve laughed; he couldn't help himself. "Why? So you could use me for chum?"

Kreeger gestured toward the photos on the credenza. The big sport fisherman tied up at a dock, then another shot, the boat powering through a channel, a mangrove island visible in the background, and a third photo, a closeup of Kreeger at the helm. "I love my boat. Brings me peace in times of trouble. You know its name?"

Steve shook his head. He hated cutesy boat names. Once, in a divorce, he got the wife her husband's boat, which she promptly renamed *Ex on the Beach*.

"*Psycho Therapy*," Kreeger said. "Two words. You like it?"

"It fits."

"So anytime you want, call me. We'll take the boat down to Elliot Key."

"Not without a Coast Guard escort."

"With your history of violence, I should be afraid of you, not the other way around. Hypothetical question: Would you kill Janice to save your nephew?"

"What!"

"If your sister posed a threat to young Robert, would you kill her to save him?"

"If I say yes, you'll tell Judge Schwartz I'm a

homicidal maniac, a danger to the community. At least the community of worthless junkies."

"I can tell the judge anything I want. This is just between you and me. Now, there's such a thing as justifiable homicide, isn't there?"

"Yeah. Self-defense. Defense of others."

"So who could blame you if you resorted to deadly force to protect an innocent child? What difference should it make if the person is your sister?"

"What's Janice have to do with anything? She—" Steve stopped. Suddenly, it became clear. "You're not talking about me. You're talking about you."

Kreeger smoothed out a fold in his silk guayabera, then laced his fingers together on his stomach. "How so?"

"That bit about the umpire and me. And my father quitting the bench. *You're* the one who doesn't trust judges or the legal system."

"Keep going, Solomon. It's always rewarding to a teacher when a slow child gets the hang of things."

"All your questions about whether I would kill Janice to protect Bobby. You're saying you killed Nancy Lamm because she was a threat to someone. And you're implying that I would do the same thing."

"We all would kill to protect someone we love. You and I are in the mainstream there, but it goes deeper than that. We're a lot closer than you'd like to admit."

"You still stuck on that blood-brothers shit?"

"Where's your sister now?"

"Prison. She's got another eighteen months. But if I know Janice, she'll beat up an inmate or attack a guard and get more time."

"Nope. She's out."

"What are you talking about?"

"She's detoxed and rehabbed and ready for civilian life."

"You're shitting me."

"I examined her myself for the Corrections Department. Volunteered my services. Janice was quite credible when addressing the commissioners."

"You helped her get out. Why?"

Kreeger smiled. "To see how far you'll go to protect someone you love. Did I mention that your sister's goal is to start over? What did she call it? 'Form a new family unit. Me and my boy.' Not very grammatical, but extremely moving."

"I don't believe this. You helped her so she can come after Bobby."

"Is there anything as powerful as a mother's love?"

"You son-of-a-bitch. You killed Nancy Lamm. You killed Jim Beshears. And you want me to kill my sister to prove I'm just like you. Well, you're nuts! I'm not like you, Kreeger."

"We'll see about that, won't we? And why do you keep bringing up poor Jim Beshears? Is it because you've been looking high and low for that boat captain?"

So he does know!

But if Kreeger was concerned, he didn't show it. A bemused smile played at his lips. "Find Señor De la Fuente yet, Solomon?"

"As a matter of fact, I have. He's signed one hell of an affidavit. Maybe you'll get a chance to see it."

"You'll give it to the State Attorney, I suppose. No statute of limitations on murder. Get him to indict me, that your plan?"

Kreeger slid open a desk drawer, and Steve caught

his breath. If he came out with a gun, Steve would fly across the desk. Like sliding into third headfirst.

"If anything happens to me, my office is under strict instructions to deliver that affidavit to Ray Pincher."

"Strict instructions, are they?" Kreeger laughed heartily, like coins *ka-ching*ing out of a slot machine. A second later, he pulled an emery board from the drawer and began filing his nails. "So how is the good captain? I haven't seen him in a long time."

"Retired. Living a quiet life. But he's got a great memory."

Kreeger showed Steve a patient smile. "I'm sure he's retired. And I'm sure it's quite quiet. The 'great memory' bit, not too convincing. Last time I saw Oscar, he wasn't doing that well."

Steve felt a chill, even though it was warm in the small office. Suddenly, he knew exactly where Kreeger was headed.

"Oscar had quite a drinking problem, you know," Kreeger continued. "And when he drank, he talked nonsense. Kept telling tales about these two med students who'd had a fight on his boat and one of them ended up dead. A fight! Oscar must have been drunk that day."

"You say you saw him?"

"Floating facedown. Must have slipped hopping from the rail to his dock. Could happen to anyone."

"And I'll bet he had a dent in his skull, too."

"That'll happen if you hit a concrete dock on the way into the drink."

So there it was, Kreeger delivering a message. *Threaten me and I'll kill you.* Just like he killed Beshears, Lamm, and De la Fuente. Steve felt his jaw muscles tighten. Yeah, *Psycho Therapy* was the perfect name for this freak's boat.

"Three bodies in the water," Steve said, shaking his head.

"Is there a better place to die?"

"Meaning what?"

"I've never really believed in ashes to ashes and dust to dust. We all crawled from the swamp, so how fitting to return to a watery grave. From the swamp to the sea, Solomon. That's our journey. From the swamp to the sea."

Twenty

TALKING STUPID

"You kissed a naked woman?" Victoria said.

"No. Yes. Not exactly." Steve realized he was ker-flumping. He opened the stainless-steel refrigerator door and looked inside. Empty, but the cool air felt great. They were in the model kitchen of a model townhouse on a model block three hundred yards from the ocean. Casa del Mar. Or Mar Bella. Or El Pollo del Mar, for all Steve knew. He hadn't bothered to read the sign.

"You kissed a naked woman!" Her voice had taken on the accusatory tone of a sentencing judge: *"You strangled a helpless kitten."*

"You're focusing on that?" Steve couldn't believe it. He had scarcely started telling Victoria about his visit to Kreeger, and she couldn't get past the suntanned nude in the backyard. "What's important is that Kreeger pretty much admitted killing De la Fuente. That makes *three*!"

"Is she pretty?"

"How many does it take to be serial killer?" Steve mused.

"I'll bet she has a nice body. That night in the restaurant, she looked very fit."

"More than two killings, for sure. But are three enough?"

"The way she stared at you, I knew something was going on."

"You know what this means, Vic?"

"You're cheating on me."

"What! What are you talking about?"

"You kissed a naked woman."

"Actually," Steve said, wishing there were beer in the model refrigerator, "*she* kissed me."

"But you didn't resist."

"What was I supposed to do? Clobber her?"

"No. I'll do that."

"She says Kreeger tells her everything. I was working her."

"I bet you were."

Steve kept opening and closing the refrigerator door, just to have something to do with his hands. The kitchen had a thirteen-foot ceiling, black granite countertops, and a teak work island the size of a racing sloop. The townhouse also had a seven-figure price tag that Steve knew they couldn't afford. But Victoria had wanted to look at the place, so here they were. He knew that women often shopped for items they had no intention of buying. He didn't know why this was so, but just last week Victoria had dragged him to Bal Harbour, where he sat patiently while she tried on a variety of exotic outfits by Italian designers. Each flimsy little frock had a price tag somewhat north of a flat-screen TV, and, of course, Victoria didn't buy a thing. Men would never do that, though he could remember once taking a test drive in a Ferrari, just for the hell of it.

"Anyway, it was all business," he said, closing the refrigerator door. And, hopefully, the subject of the naked Amanda.

Victoria studied him a moment, her brow furrowed. Steve had seen the look many times, though usually when she approached a hostile witness on the stand. "For the record," she said, "did you become aroused?"

Man, she just won't let up.

"Nope. It was way too quick for that."

"So, had there been time for a second kiss, you would have become aroused. Isn't that true?"

"Jeez, why did I have to fall for a trial lawyer? Here I am, being honest, telling you everything, and you're like Ken Starr in front of the Grand Jury."

"You must have flirted with her."

"I just stood there, being my irresistible self, but you're missing the point, Vic. This gives me a great chance to try to flip her."

"Your choice of words is absolutely Freudian."

"Maybe she wants to break away from him. If I help her do that, maybe she'll help me nail him."

"So you and your irresistible self will have to spend time with her, I suppose."

"Amanda shares Kreeger's bed. Who better to get close to if I want to bring him down?"

"I liked your first plan better. The one where you get Kreeger to kill you."

"*Try* to kill me." Steve checked out the built-in microwave. It had more gauges than the control panel of a jet. "C'mon, Vic. I'm gonna need your help with her."

"How many hands does it take to lube a woman with suntan oil?"

"You can give me tips on how to get her to open up."

"What can I tell you?" Victoria said, so airily Steve thought she might float away. "You've already gotten her naked."

"Hiya, lovebirds!" Jackie Tuttle burst into the kitchen from the patio, armed with her BlackBerry and soft leather briefcase. Her shoes and blouse shared something in common, Steve thought. Both were see-through. The shoes seemed to be made of Lucite. The blouse was a flimsy black material. And her gold hoop earrings were so big, you could toss a basketball through them. "Did you see the Jacuzzi, Vic? I can picture the two of you sipping spritzers and watching the sun set over the ocean."

"The sun sets over the Everglades," Steve said.

"Hot tubs give me yeast infections," Victoria said.

"Ooh. You two are fighting."

"No we're not," they said in unison.

"Great," Jackie replied. "Did you see the his-and-her closets?"

Steve ran a hand across the cool granite countertop. "Jackie, we can't afford this place."

Jackie glared at him. "Did I mention the windows exceed the hurricane specs? Won't shatter, even if Tori throws something heavy at you and misses."

"Jackie, Steve's right," Victoria said. "It's too much money."

Shaking a two-tone fingernail in Steve's face, Jackie said: "This is *your* fault."

"Now what'd I do?"

"If you'd let Tori upgrade the practice, you could buy a place in Gables Estates or at least Cocoplum."

"We're not gonna whore for banks and insurance companies."

"I suppose defending strip clubs is a high calling," Jackie shot back.

"First Amendment issues always are."

"And those sweaty migrant workers and illegal aliens you represent for free?"

"When the Pilgrims landed at Plymouth Rock, they were illegal aliens."

Jackie scowled at him. "You don't get it, Steve. Unless you two start making some real money, you'll never be able to afford a decent pup tent. Not in this market."

"I won't compromise my principles. Vic knows the rules."

"Rules?" Victoria pounced. "Like you're laying down the law? Like you're the Chief Justice of this relationship?"

"I didn't mean it that way, Vic. But it's Solomon and Lord, not the other way around."

Victoria folded her arms across her chest. "Maybe it would be better if it was just Steve Solomon, flying solo."

"C'mon. I'm senior to you. You have to acknowledge that. I've tried more cases in more courts and—"

"Been held in contempt more times."

"But we're equal partners in everything else," he said.

Jackie Tuttle gathered up her briefcase and started for the door, pausing only for one last shot. "Steve, let me tell you what Tori won't. You've got a very thick skull."

"You're wrong, Jackie. She's already told me."

"Has she told you this? Sometimes you're a real jerk, and if you don't watch it, you're gonna lose the best woman in the world."

Steve turned to Victoria, waiting for her to disagree. He waited five seconds, or was it five years? Nothing. Then he said something stupid. No, stupid wouldn't begin to describe it, he thought later. Maybe it was that idiotic male need to appear cool and unconcerned. He didn't know the reason. But instead of professing his love and care for Victoria, he said, "Hey, we're all free agents. Vic can do whatever she wants."

Jackie headed straight for the door, and Victoria turned her back on him.

* * *

Victoria stayed silent on the drive down Collins Avenue. Steve tuned the radio to the Margaritaville station, all that annoying island music he loved and she found so juvenile. When Jimmy Buffet began singing, "Beach House on the Moon," Victoria leaned forward and turned the volume down. She'd been processing their latest conversations, starting with the other day when Mr. Sensitivity had basically told her to butt out, that he would decide what was right for Bobby, and if he wanted to go down to the Goldberg house and swing on the chandelier like a deranged chimpanzee, then by God, he would. Then, just now, Steve's "rules" for "his" firm. Followed by his invitation to take a hike. Even though she knew he didn't mean it, she was fuming. His interest—professional or otherwise—in Amanda the Naked Tramp wasn't helping, either.

So irritating. So aggravating. So condescending.

And he doesn't even know it.

He can hurt my feelings and put distance between us without even realizing what he's done.

As they passed through the dingy burg of Surfside,

she shot a look at him. "Steve, are you sure you really want to move in together?"

"Sure. Haven't we discussed this already?"

Shutting off discussion again.

"What are you saying? The court has ruled?"

"Still with that? I'm not ruling on anything. We made a mutual decision, and—"

"Face it, Steve. You're not ready for a real relationship." Then she was silent again.

* * *

Steve figured the best way to get out of the personal relationship funk was to talk business. With Victoria staring straight ahead, he summarized his session with Kreeger. Back at the townhouse, Victoria had gotten so hung up on Amanda, he hadn't fully debriefed her. Now he told her about the doc's hypothetical admission that *if* he'd murdered Nancy Lamm, he did it only to protect someone else. And then the news that Steve's larcenous and drug-addled sister Janice, a shoo-in for Worst Mother of the Century, was a free woman, thanks to Kreeger's intervention.

"Kreeger tried to bait me about Janice. Said I'd kill my own sister if she was a threat to Bobby. You think that's what he wants? To set me up to kill Janice?"

No response.

"Or maybe he kills Janice and pins it on me. That would appeal to the freak."

They passed the Eden Roc and the Fontainebleau, both undergoing major renovations, neither Frank Sinatra nor Sammy Davis, Jr., anywhere in sight. Traffic was backed up at the bridge leading to Arthur Godfrey Road, and Steve eased to a stop.

"What I can't figure," Steve rambled on, "is who

was Kreeger supposedly protecting when he killed Nancy Lamm? He doesn't have any kids. Who's this mythical person who's analogous to Bobby?"

"What did Kreeger say, exactly?" Victoria asked, breaking her silence.

Great. She can't resist a mental challenge.

"Best I remember, he said, 'Who could blame you if you resorted to deadly force to protect an innocent child? To protect the one you love?'"

"He's talking about you and him both. You see that, right?"

"Sure, he's saying I would kill to protect Bobby. But who's his kid? Kreeger doesn't have any children."

"Technically, neither do you."

"I have a nephew I love, and Kreeger knows that."

The light turned green and Victoria said: "You really don't see it?"

"No. That's why I'm asking for your help."

"If you'd stop looking for serpentine paths, you'd see how simple and straightforward it is."

"Okay, already. Tell me before the Everglades disappear."

"You're Bobby's uncle."

"Yeah?"

"So who calls Kreeger 'Uncle Bill'?"

"Amanda!"

"She'd have been what, about thirteen when Nancy Lamm was killed. A child."

Questions flashed through his mind, and he spoke them aloud. "But why'd Amanda need protecting? Who is she, anyway? And is Kreeger even telling the truth?"

"I'm sure you'll figure it out, Steve." She motioned toward the curb. "Drop me off on Lincoln Road."

"What! We're finally cracking this case here."

"I need new shoes."

"C'mon. This isn't about shoes. What's going on?"

"I choose to go shopping. Just the way you choose to reject a beautiful condo on Brickell and a beautiful townhouse in Bal Harbour."

"So you're pissed at me? That's why you're buying shoes?"

"Let's just say the Jimmy Choos are on the other foot now."

Twenty-One

A WOMAN'S RIGHT TO SHOES

Victoria didn't really need new shoes. What woman really *needs* hot pink Jimmy Choo strappies or black patent leather Dolce & Gabbanas? Or even gunmetal Via Spiga slides and a pair of beige snakeskin Miu Mius?

But *need* is a relative term, Victoria knew. Maybe she didn't require shoes the way she required oxygen. But just now, she needed to get away from Steve for a few hours to think. And trying on purple velvet Manolo Blahniks was free, even if the shoes themselves were not. She had no intention of buying something she couldn't afford, but just why the hell couldn't she afford them?

Was Jackie right? Was Steve holding her back? Jackie didn't put it that way, exactly. But isn't that what she'd meant?

After Steve dropped her off, Victoria began walking west along Lincoln Road, passing the shops and cafés. Tall, willowy young women sat with suntanned men, sipping lattes and whiling away the afternoon.

Who are these people? Don't they ever work?

The more she thought about the current state of her

relationship with Steve, the more upset she became. Moving in together now seemed like an idiotic idea. Where would it lead? Steve hadn't even mentioned marriage. And was that even what she wanted? Could they get along over the long haul? Was love enough to carry a relationship? Didn't there have to be some commonality in personalities?

So many questions.

Her thoughts returned to the house they couldn't afford and the shoes that were ridiculously expensive.

Why shouldn't I be able to splurge on some wafery Italian footwear that costs nine hundred bucks?

She thought about it a minute. Wasn't there a constitutional right involved here? A Woman's Right to Shoes. Ha!

Her thoughts kept returning to Steve. Right now, he was so embroiled with Kreeger, he'd let the practice slide. The key in any law firm is to keep the faucets flowing. It's not enough to just work on the cases already in-house. You have to prime the pump, constantly bringing in new clients. And what was Steve, the self-appointed rainmaker, hustling up these days?

City of Coral Gables v. *Fiore.* Defending a homeowner who, having been ordered to cut his lawn, mowed "FUCK YOU" into the three-foot-tall grass. Then there was the DUI case for the Zamboni driver at the Florida Panthers hockey games. And let's not forget Sheila and Max Minkin, suing their rabbi for showing up late to their wedding. Steve tried one of his old tricks with those two whiners.

He brings in a lousy case with obnoxious clients, then tries to palm it off on me.

She was so angry at Steve right now, she wished she knew one of Herbert's Yiddish curses. The one about having an onion grow in your navel. Yes, that would do quite nicely. Lacking that, she silently cursed her lover and partner in English, conjuring up the most wicked voodoo she knew:

Dearest Steve. May you have to spend the afternoon with Max and Sheila Minkin.

Then she said the hell with it and whipped out her American Express card. She was going to buy some damn shoes.

Twenty-Two

MOTIVE FOR MURDER

Steve walked into his reception room to find the Minkins waiting.

Oh, shit. They didn't have an appointment.

What lousy luck is this?

Cece Santiago was there, in Lycra shorts and halter top, lying on her back, bench-pressing a buck fifty-five, the bar *clank*ing into its brackets. And here were the Minkins, thumbing through copies of *Coastal Living* and *Architectural Digest* that had been a year old when Steve pilfered them from a doctor's office.

"Hey, Max! Hey, Sheila!" Steve pumped as much pleasure into his voice as he could fake. "How are my favorite newlyweds?"

"How's our case?" Sheila shot back. Max kept his face buried in a magazine.

"Rabbi Finsterman won't settle, at least not yet. His lawyer filed an answer to the complaint, so the issue is joined."

The issue is joined.

Trying to sound like a lawyer. Trying to justify his fee. It was not entirely bad news that Finsterman refused to settle. Now that they were in court, Steve's fee

KILL ALL THE LAWYERS

had just been hiked up from one-third of the recovery to forty percent.

"When do we go to trial?" Sheila demanded.

"There are pleadings to file and discovery to take," Steve said, trying to justify whatever fee might be at the end of this faded rainbow. "And it's no slam dunk. Finsterman's lawyer has filed several affirmative defenses."

"What the hell are they?"

"The usual. Assumption of the risk. Comparative negligence. Plus he claims the rabbi was delayed because a thunderstorm snarled traffic. Says it was an act of God."

"It was August! It rains every frigging day," Sheila said.

"I'll probably have to go to the expense of hiring an expert witness."

"Like who?"

"A Talmudic scholar." Thinking Herbert might be up for it, now that he'd started going to synagogue.

The phone rang, and Cece picked it up. "Solomon and Lord. Felonies and misdemeanors. Torts of all sorts." She listened a moment, then said, "*Jefe*, it's for you."

"Ah, probably Justice Brandeis returning my call." Steve gave Cece a sideways glance so she wouldn't say: "*No, it's the collection agency for the rented copier.*" Then he headed for his inner office, thanking the Minkins for dropping by.

* * *

Ten minutes later, Steve sat cross-legged on the floor, pawing through the file of *State of Florida* v. *William Kreeger*. The death of Nancy Lamm. He'd had

the criminal file pulled out of storage and started by
going through the autopsy report and medical records.
So far, he hadn't found anything relevant. The witness
statements didn't help, either. He plowed back in time,
poring over the notes of his first meeting with Kreeger.

It all started with a divorce and child custody case.
In re the Marriage of Leonard and Nancy Lamm.
Leonard claimed that Nancy abused cocaine and was
an unfit mother. The judge appointed Kreeger to serve
as court-appointed psychiatrist. He was to interview
both parents and their child and file a report with the
court.

Some details started coming back to Steve. The
Lamms had a single child. A daughter. He remembered
her name. *Mary.* Steve recalled Kreeger saying he'd
told Nancy her daughter better not have a child out
of wedlock or she'd be teased: "Mary had a little
Lamm." Steve didn't think it was funny at the time,
and it hadn't gotten funnier with age.

Riffling through the files, Steve found a copy of
Kreeger's written report. The doc soft-pedaled Nancy's
addictions and seemed to blame Leonard for her
problems. Her husband was cold and distant and un-
communicative. Nancy was sensitive and lacked self-
esteem, a problem exacerbated by Leonard's verbally
abusive conduct. There was even a hint of abuse
toward Mary. Kreeger phrased this part very carefully.
Without ever accusing the father of making sexual
overtures, he referred to the man entering the bathroom while Mary was showering. Another episode involved Leonard asking his daughter to sit on his lap,
something Kreeger deemed "age inappropriate."

Leonard's lawyer filed a blistering set of objections
to Kreeger's report. The lawyer called the claims fabri-

cated and scandalous and asked that they be stricken.
There was one objection—a huge one—that could
have been made but wasn't because Leonard was unaware of it at the time. Kreeger had become Nancy
Lamm's lover and should have been disqualified from
the case on that ground.

The custody hearing was two weeks away when
Nancy Lamm drowned in Kreeger's hot tub. At virtually the same time a Grand Jury was indicting Kreeger
for murder, the family judge granted Leonard custody
of the girl.

Steve went through the Family Court pleadings one
at a time. With Nancy Lamm dead, the custody hearing had been moved to the uncontested calendar.
Nothing fancy. Just a form order: "It is therefore ordered and adjudged that the Respondent Leonard
Lamm be hereby granted permanent custody of the
minor child, Mary Amanda Lamm."

Mary Amanda Lamm.

Amanda.

"Uncle Bill loves me. And he has for a long time."

Suddenly, it all became clear. The state had gotten
the motive wrong. Pincher had told the jury that
Kreeger murdered Nancy Lamm because she threatened to file a complaint about the shrink seducing her.
But shrinks get involved with their patients all the
time. Sure, it was unethical, but it was slap-on-the-
wrist material, hardly a reason to kill the accuser.

The truth—the secret, ugly truth—was far worse.
Nancy must have found out that Kreeger had seduced
her daughter, Mary Amanda. *That* was what she
threatened to disclose, maybe to the State Attorney as
well as the medical board. Kreeger was facing prison
time for statutory rape. He couldn't let that happen.

He *didn't* let that happen. He killed Nancy Lamm and kept her daughter for himself. Even if he had to wait a while. Amanda went to live with her father, and Kreeger went off to prison.

"Amanda was the only one who wrote me, the only one who cared. And when I got out, she was waiting for me."

When Kreeger told him that, Steve thought Amanda was one of those wacko pen pals murderers sometimes attract. But that wasn't it. They had a history.

Steve tried to picture what went on during the years Kreeger was in prison. Amanda Lamm should have been hanging out at the mall, going to cheerleader practice, and buying a prom dress. But her development had been stunted at age thirteen by the half man, half goat named Kreeger.

Steve imagined the girl sitting at home, writing notes on pink stationery, carefully folding them into scented envelopes, sealed with lipsticked kisses. Dreaming sweet thoughts of the man who stole her childhood and replaced it with whispered lies. Living in some perverted fairy tale where two lovers are pried apart by the dragons of fate.

Sure, Kreeger loved her. Loved her in a way both twisted and vile. And she loved him right back. Loved the man who had murdered her mother. And that, Steve thought, seemed as sad and tragic as the murder itself.

SOLOMON'S LAWS

8. Love is chemistry and mystery, not logic and
   reason.

Twenty-Three

WE ARE WHO WE ARE

Women don't sweep into a room anymore, Steve thought. There are no more Scarlett O'Haras, their dresses hoisted by hoops and petticoats, whooshing into a room, putting on airs.

But then there was Irene Lord.

The Queen burst through the door of his office, her eyes taking in the police-auction furniture, her glossy, collagened lips pursing as she contemplated whether it would be safe to sit down, lest a palmetto bug crawl up her panty hose.

"We must talk," Irene breathed, those puffy lips barely moving.

"Vic's not here," Steve said.

"I'm not blind, Stephen. Old and decrepit perhaps, but not blind."

Steve knew the remark was intended to elicit the obligatory denials, and he semi-complied. "Irene, you're not decrepit or blind."

"And . . . ?"

"And you're not old. You're gorgeous and vibrant and men still come sniffing after you like skunks after sunflowers."

"Thank you, Stephen. I've always been quite fond of you."

That stopped him. "A little early in the day for your gin and tonic, Irene."

"I haven't been drinking. I've come to see you, not my daughter, and I'm making pleasant small talk. Haven't you one iota of decorum?"

"Now, there's the Irene I love."

"And the truth is, I am somewhat fond of you, despite how damned aggravating you can be."

"Thank you."

"I know you say things just to get a rise out of me, but sometimes you're so aggressive and pushy."

"Pushy? Dammit, Irene, that's an anti-Semitic slur."

"Oh, for heaven's sake. Not that again."

"We wanted to join your country clubs. We were being pushy. We wanted to attend Princeton. We were being pushy. Damn pushy Jews!"

"Don't raise your voice, Stephen. It's very unbecoming."

"Ah, so I'm loud, too. 'Loud' is another ethnic slur."

"Some of my favorite fiancés were Jewish, so please cease this harangue. It's becoming tedious."

"You never hear about those pushy Episcopalians, do you? Those loud Lutherans? Don't think so. What's next, Irene. How about 'greedy'?"

"You're not greedy. God knows, I wish you cared more about money. Now, would you please calm down and give me some legal advice?"

"Ask Vic. She knows more law than I do."

"I need someone who's more . . ." Irene clucked her tongue as if ticking off words until she found the right one. "*Flexible.* And forgiving. My darling daughter is somewhat . . ." *Cluck-cluck-cluck.*

"Rigid?" Steve helped out.

"Exactly. Can I count on your discretion?"

"Lawyer-client privilege trumps boyfriend-girlfriend. Who'd you kill?"

Irene rolled her eyes and reached into a soft leathery purse that seemed to be made of the belly skin of a baby alligator. She pulled out a document, slid it across Steve's desk, whisked invisible dirt from the cracked leather client chair, and sat down. Her hair, the color of corn silk, was swept up in a style that reminded Steve of Princess Grace of Monaco.

"First Dade Bank versus Irene Lord," Steve said, reading aloud. "Mortgage foreclosure?"

"They're after my condo, Stephen. You must help me."

"Says here you're five months behind on payments."

"At the moment, I'm cash strapped. What can I do?"

"What about those old boyfriends with all the money? Call that Australian shipping magnate who said you were his favorite ketch."

"He moved on to a sleeker sloop."

"What about the gold-bullion trader? He's loaded."

"Last year, when I turned fifty, he traded me in for two twenty-five-year-olds."

"C'mon, Irene. Last year you turned fifty-seven."

"So he traded me for three nineteen-year-olds. The point is, I'm with Carl now, and he doesn't have a dime."

It hit him then. Carl Drake. Alleged heir of Sir Francis Drake. Smooth talker with a trim mustache and a gold-buttoned navy blazer. "Is that where your money went, Irene? To Drake?"

"It's for my share of the expenses in the trust. I had to put up my money to stake my claim."

"The son-of-a-bitch. When I grilled him at Joe's, he said you didn't have to put up a cent."

"I know. I know."

"And you kept quiet."

"The way I was brought up, Stephen, a woman does not contradict her man."

"Too bad you didn't pass that along to your daughter." Steve shook his head. "Jeez, Irene. Drake's a con man."

"Expenses came up. It happens, Stephen."

"Oh, come on, Irene. Sir Francis Drake's money hasn't been sitting around for four hundred years waiting for you to claim it. It's a scam. A flim-flam. A con job."

"When it pays off, don't expect an invitation to my yacht."

But she said it with such a lack of conviction that Steve immediately sensed something else. Irene *knew* she'd been swindled. Maybe she even knew it when she was writing the check. And this from a woman who was always the recipient of money and jewelry and designer duds. Which could only mean one thing, and that was scariest of all.

"Irene, please don't tell me you're in love with this guy."

Her eyes, unnaturally wide open thanks to lid surgery, now brimmed with tears. "With all my heart, Stephen. The man fills me with wonder."

"Oh, jeez." Steve stood up. "C'mon, Irene. It's not too early. I'm gonna buy you a drink."

* * *

They sat at a sidewalk table at an Ocean Drive café. A woman lost in the deep and treacherous ocean of love, Irene Lord rejected every logical suggestion Steve made.

No, she wouldn't break up with Carl Drake; no, she wouldn't sue him and freeze his accounts; and no, she certainly wouldn't file charges with the State Attorney.

Steve said he would do what he could to slow down the foreclosure litigation. He'd hit the bank with endless discovery. He'd claim fraud and usury and violations of banking regulations, and anything else he could think of, including the Treaty of Versailles and the Nuclear Test Ban Treaty. He'd obfuscate and distort, muddle and confuse. He'd buy time with dilatory tactics, and if all else failed, he'd have Irene enlist in the army and seek protection under the Soldiers and Sailors Civil Relief Act. That was where The Queen seemed to draw the line, but otherwise she seemed to approve his strategy. And with each sip of Tanqueray, she appreciated Steve even more.

"I feel we're bonding here, Stephen."

"Aw, c'mon, Irene. The only bonds you know about are tax-free municipals."

She laughed. "I'm not going to pretend I'm your biggest supporter. Many is the day I've wished Victoria had found a man who was more traditional and less . . ."

"Pushy?"

"Reckless." She smiled at him, her veneers snowy white. "But you do have something going for you."

He waited to see if a zinger was attached to the compliment, like a stinging cell on a jellyfish.

"Victoria loves you. She loves you in a way she's never loved any other man. And that goes a long way with me."

Wow. The Queen had never said anything to him like that before.

"Stephen, this is where you say you love her, too."

"I do, Irene. A lot. More than I ever knew was possible. I fell for Vic when we were on opposite sides of a case, and it just grew from there."

"So. If there's anything I can ever do for you . . ."

It was an offer she'd never made before and might never make again. "To tell you the truth, I could use some advice right now. About Victoria."

"If you're worried, that's a good sign. Some men are so dense they never see it coming."

"It?"

"The three-inch heel of the Prada pumps as they're walking away."

Steve let out a sigh.

"Of course you have problems, Stephen. Every couple does. Nelson Lord was the love of my life, but boy did we fight." She used her fingertips to squeeze the lime into her gin and tonic. "With you and Victoria, it's even more difficult because you're so different."

In the next seventeen minutes, Steve summarized the current state of his relationship with Victoria, admitting that, yes, he had some second thoughts about moving in together, and sure, she'd picked up on it. Now she didn't seem to want to share a Coke with him, much less live under the same roof.

"She needs to know where the two of you are headed," Irene said.

"Why can't she just relax, go with the flow, see where it takes us?"

"Someone as highly organized as my daughter

needs certainly in her life. Let's face it. Spontaneity isn't her strong suit and predictability isn't yours."

"I can change."

"How's that, Stephen?"

He thought about it. On the sidewalk, the usual collection of wannabe models sashayed past their table. In the street, teenage boys drove by in their parents' SUVs, gawking at the girls, their CD players blasting unintelligible reggaeton, something with a lot of drums from Tego Calderon.

"I'm gonna tell Vic to choose where we should live," he answered. "I'm gonna go to the ballet with her. I'm even gonna join the Kiwanis."

Irene's laugh was a bit louder than necessary. Three gin and tonics will do that. "If The Princess wanted a man like that, she would have married Bruce."

Meaning Bruce Bigby, Steve knew. Real estate developer. Avocado grower. Chamber of Commerce Man of the Year.

Irene signaled for another drink. But the waiter must have been an out-of-work actor, because he seemed to be posing for a table of teenage girls in shorts and tank tops. "Victoria dropped Bruce for you," Irene continued. "Why do you suppose she did that?"

"Temporary insanity?"

"She loves you the way you are, despite your many peccadillos. So don't you dare try to change. Besides, it wouldn't work. We are who we are. You, me. Victoria. Carl. All of us. Our true natures will come out, no matter what we do to disguise them."

"That's your advice, Irene? Don't change?"

"That's it. Although . . ."

Here it comes, Steve thought.

"What's the Jewish word for money?" she asked.

"Yiddish word. 'Gelt.' "

Irene smiled at him and did her best impression of a Jewish mother. "Would it hurt you, Stephen, to bring home a little more gelt?"

Twenty-Four

DANCE FOR ME

It was dark, but the moon was three-quarters full—the waning gibbous, Bobby knew—so the yard was illuminated. Myron Goldberg spent a fortune on outdoor lighting, so the house was lit up, too. Bobby heard a whirring sound, followed by a *whoosh*. Below him, sprinkler heads popped out of the lawn like those aliens in *War of the Worlds*. A second later, water shot out, the spray chilling his bare legs. A dozen feet above the ground, Bobby was wedged into the crevice between the trunk and a gnarly limb of a mango tree.

Maria's mango tree. Bobby could smell the peachy aroma of the fruit, still green and hard. A wasp sat on one of the mangoes, antennae wiggling. Could the wasp smell it, too? It annoyed Bobby that he didn't know if wasps had a sense of smell.

Maria. Where are you?

While he waited, Bobby whispered to himself the names of the shrubs and flowers surrounding the Goldberg home. Even their gardener wouldn't know the real name of the honeysuckle with the flowers that looked like purple trumpets.

Lonicera sempervirens!

Then there was the bougainvillea vine with flowers so red, if you crushed them, the liquid would look like wine.

Maria! Where are you?

The wind picked up, rustling leaves. Bobby shivered and felt goose bumps on his legs.

If a goose gets cold, does he say to his mate: "Hey, take a gander at my people bumps"?

It was nearly midnight. Any minute now. The Goldberg house was dark except for the outdoor lighting that cast an eerie glow over the tree and the shrubs.

"When the clock strikes twelve, be there."

That was what Maria had said. As if he would be late. He'd been in the tree for at least an hour, and his butt hurt from the way he was wedged against the trunk.

"Should I throw pebbles against the window?"

"Totally old school, Bobby. At midnight, call but don't say who it is. Just say, 'Dance for me.' "

"What if your parents hear the ring?"

"I'll have the phone on vibrate, and I'll keep it between my thighs."

"Wow."

The conversation had pretty much left him breathless. Now he rehearsed his line several times, trying to lower his voice into a manly baritone, emphasizing the word 'dance' a few times, then the word 'me.'

"Dance for me." Definitely hit the "me."

The hottest hottie in the sixth grade was going to dance for him. She hadn't said "naked," but he had his hopes.

It seemed fair, Bobby thought. He had taught Maria how to divide decimals by whole numbers and how to change fractions into decimals. She had asked him if the quotient becomes larger or smaller as the dividend becomes a greater multiple of ten.

Duh.

He checked the time in the cell phone window. Oh, jeez, 12:03. He speed-dialed her number, listened to the *brrring,* heard her whisper, "What do you want?"

"Dance for me!" His voice cracking, but he got it out.

A light flicked on in the second-story window. Maria's bedroom. Bobby could make out a lamp near the window, probably on Maria's desk. A moment later, the light took on a reddish glow as Maria draped a red cloth over the lampshade. Ooh. This was gonna be good.

She stood in front of the window, her silhouette tinged reddish-black from the lamp, and she started dancing, moving her thin arms overhead in a motion that made Bobby think of someone drowning. If there was music on, he couldn't hear it. She slipped out of her top and turned sideways, her boobies the size of eggs.

Bobby heard his breathing grow deeper, and suddenly he wasn't cold anymore. He shifted his position between the trunk and the limb because of the tightness in his pants. But then new thoughts emerged, intruding thoughts, flowing like a river, breeching the dike his mind had erected.

That cloth over the lampshade. Is it cotton or polyester? What is its flammable rating?

And the lightbulb. He hoped it wasn't a halogen. Those babies throw off 250 degrees Celsius, which he calculated in about three seconds to be 482 degrees Fahrenheit.

Maria slithered out of her shorts, and judging from the angle of her elbow, her hand seemed to be in her crotch, but Bobby couldn't concentrate. He was certain that, any moment, the cloth would burst into flame. The curtains, the bedcovers, the wallpaper—everything would be ablaze. Would Maria even have time to run from the room? Was their A/C hooked up to natural gas? If so, he was sure it was leaking. The house was about to become a fiery inferno, and it was all his fault. In the window, Maria writhed from side to side and swiveled her hips. But in Bobby's mind, all he could see was an orange fireball exploding, tearing the house apart at the beams, incinerating Maria, her mother, and her father.

And that was when he screamed as loud as he could, "Fire! Fire! *Fire!*"

Twenty-Five

MOTHER LODE

Steve ran full speed along Kumquat Avenue, took the bend to the left, then another left on Loquat. The only sounds were his Nikes hitting the pavement and his own breathing.

The phone call had come just after midnight, waking him from a dream that involved stealing home in the College World Series—instead of being picked off third base—and getting carried off the field on his teammates' shoulders.

"This is Eva Munoz-Goldberg. My husband is Dr. Myron J. Goldberg . . ."

Doctor. As if I might confuse him with Myron J. Goldberg, garbage collector.

"Get over here and pick up your sicko nephew before I call the police."

Oh, shit.

Steve had grabbed the closest T-shirt—*"I'm Not Fluent in Idiot, So Please Speak Clearly"*—pulled on a pair of orange Hurricanes shorts, and took off down the street.

What now, Bobby?

As he ran, Steve envisioned his nephew being

caught in Maria's bedroom. What was it Herbert had called her? A harlot-in-training. But maybe they were doing homework and just fell asleep on Maria's bed. Thinking like a defense lawyer.

The yard lights were blazing when Steve huffed to a stop. Spots embedded in planters illuminating the sabal palms, floodlights under the eaves of the barrel-tile roof, Malibu lights lining both sides of a flagstone path, and matching lanterns on bronze posts at the front door. All in all, as bright as the Orange Bowl for a Saturday night game.

Swaying from side to side, Bobby stood with his shoulders hunched and his arms hugging himself. Steve wrapped an arm around the boy and whispered in his ear. "It'll be all right, kiddo. Uncle Steve's here."

Myron Goldberg, a small man in his forties, wore a bathrobe and bedroom slippers and a look of consternation. His wife, Eva, her long black hair asunder, wore a white silk robe that stopped at midthigh. She was a petite but large-bosomed woman around her husband's age, and even without X-ray vision, Steve could tell she wore nothing under the robe. Cradled in the crook of her right arm was a short-barreled automatic weapon.

"Mrs. Goldberg, tell me that's not an Uzi," Steve said.

"This is America. I've got the right."

Maria appeared in the doorway behind them. "Bobby didn't do anything!"

"Back in the house!" Eva ordered. *"Ahora mismo!"*

The girl muttered something Steve couldn't hear, then disappeared behind the front door.

"The thing is," Myron began hesitantly, "your

nephew is a peeper. We caught him in the tree outside Maria's bedroom."

His head pressed against Steve's side, Bobby whimpered.

"Doesn't sound like my Bobby," Steve said, giving the boy a squeeze.

"Ask him!" Eva insisted with a wave of her arm and the Uzi.

"Would you mind putting that gun down?" Steve said.

She gave a dismissive little snort. "Second Amendment. You're a lawyer. Look it up."

"I'm gonna take Bobby home and talk to him there," Steve said evenly. "I'll call you in the morning and we'll sort everything out."

"Not good enough," Eva said. "I want a police report."

"Let's not overreact," Myron said, so softly he could barely be heard over the neighborhood crickets.

"Overreact!" She swung around to face her husband, and for a second, Steve thought she might unleash a quick burst with the Uzi and cut him in half. "You want this little pervert to do it again?"

"Hey," Steve said. "Everybody's a little excited. Maybe we should all just go to sleep and—"

Screeching tires interrupted him. Steve turned toward the driveway, expecting to see a police cruiser, figuring Bobby's future had just turned to a pile of crud. His nephew was about to become his client. A date in Juvenile Court. Psychiatric testing followed by sex-offender registration.

But it wasn't a cop. It was a muddy green Dodge pickup truck, at least ten years old. A woman got out and headed their way. She wore a granny dress that came to her ankles and two-strap Birkenstock sandals. She was tall and stout, with a round face and hair pulled straight back and tied with a band. Even before she got into the light, Steve recognized her and immediately wished it had been the police.

"What the hell are you doing here?" Steve said.

"Bobby called me on his cell. What the fuck's going on?"

Bobby peeked out from behind Steve. "Hi, Mom," he said.

* * *

It was all happening too fast, Steve decided.

First, Bobby tangled in a mess that could toss him into the maw of the justice system. Next, Janice showing up, allegedly to help Bobby, the child she'd neglected and abused and abandoned.

"Bobby called me on his cell."

Meaning they'd been in touch, and the kid had never said a word.

Bobby, Bobby, Bobby. How could you?

"If I was you, I'd put that gun down," Janice said to Eva Munoz-Goldberg.

"And if I were you, I'd wash my hair and lose some weight," Eva fired back.

"Gonna ask you nice one more time. Put the fucking gun down before I jam it up your tight ass."

"Now see here—" Myron attempted.

"Janice, let me handle this," Steve said.

"You ain't doing so hot, baby bro." She turned to the Goldbergs. "The way I hear it, little Miss Hot Pants invited my boy to a peep show, so what's the big deal?"

"How dare you!" Myron said.

"Look, dickwad. I'm not throwing stones here. Hell, I was blowing guys behind the school gym when I was twelve. Don't get so self-righteous. Kids will be kids."

"I've heard about you," Eva said. "You don't even know who Bobby's father is."

"Hey, let's call it a night." Steve spoke up, not on his sister's behalf, but for Bobby. The kid had enough problems without these kinds of insults. "C'mon, everybody's nerves are frayed."

"*Chingate*, shyster," Eva hissed. "I heard all about you on the radio. And I know about your father, the dirty judge."

"Let's leave family out of this," Steve cautioned.

"Coke whore. Shyster. Dirty judge. A whole family of degenerates."

"Let the bitch who is without sin cast the first stone," Janice said.

Eva gestured with the gun. "What's that supposed to mean, *puta*?"

"Jesus loves you. Everybody else thinks you're a twat."

Eva took a step forward, but Janice swung first. A combination punch and lunge, astonishingly quick for a woman her size. The punch grazed Eva's cheek, and she probably wouldn't have fallen, except Janice plowed forward, head down. Janice's beefy shoulder caught Eva squarely in the chest. An *oomph*, and both women tumbled to the ground, the Uzi flying into a planter filled with impatiens. The two men were left looking at each other, wondering if they were supposed to throw some punches, too.

"Boob job! Boob job!" Janice screeched as she straddled Eva, the smaller woman's robe thrown open.

"Jesus, Janice, get off her!" Steve said.

"Don't take the Lord's name in vain," Janice scolded.

"Requetegorda!" Eva screamed. "Get off me!"

"Ladies, please," Myron begged.

It was all too surreal, Steve thought. Was he hearing things? Did his sister, who had had her bat mitzvah at Temple Emanu-el all those years ago, just call Jesus "the Lord"?

"How much those hooters set you back?" Janice demanded, holding Eva's robe open. "I was thinking about getting me a pair as soon as I have the liposuction."

"Puta fea," Eva wheezed, Janice sitting on her gut.

"Christ Almighty," Myron Goldberg said.

"Yes, he is," Janice replied.

"Janice, what's all this religious stuff?" Steve asked.

"Jews for Jesus, little brother. In prison, I recognized the true messiah."

"No way."

"Cross my heart."

It just kept getting crazier, Steve thought. A father who'd gone ortho and a sister who'd Jesus-freaked. Just then he caught a flash of movement.

"Look out, Mom!" Bobby shouted.

Myron had picked up the Uzi.

A Jewish periodontist with an Uzi!

Unless the guy was in the Israeli Army, this was a prescription for disaster. Myron seemed to be trying to figure out how to wrap his hand around the pistol grip when Steve took a quick step and uncorked a right-hand punch. His fist caught Myron Goldberg squarely on the chin. Myron fell in a heap, dropping the Uzi.

Steve felt a throbbing pain in his wrist.

On the ground, Myron moaned.

Janice slid off Eva, who was cursing in Spanish. "You did good, little brother," Janice said. "Hey, Bobby. Me and Stevie make a great team, huh?"

"We are not a team." Steve shook his wrist, but the throbbing only increased.

"We're on God's squad," Janice said blissfully.

Myron shakily got to his feet, holding his jaw, saying something that sounded like *"law-shute."*

A police siren drowned him out.

"Gotta split," Janice said, heading for her truck.

"Hey, sis. Stick around for the cops. I might need a friendly witness."

"He that leadeth into captivity shall go into captivity," she said, without emotion, like an evangelical zombie. "He shall have judgment without mercy that hath showed no mercy."

"Nice sermon. What's it mean?"

She dropped her bulk into the driver's seat of the muddy green pickup and started the engine. "You're on your own, little brother."

Twenty-Six

CALL ME IRRESPONSIBLE

Victoria thought she should be both delicate and diplomatic. She could say: *"I question your judgment in striking Myron Goldberg."* Or perhaps: *"For someone still facing assault charges, your conduct might be considered somewhat ill-advised."*

But she settled on: "You're a child! An undisciplined, self-indulgent child."

"C'mon, Vic. I was the peacemaker."

"You're probably guilty of trespassing. And definitely assault and battery."

"I handled it. The cops interviewed me, then headed off to Krispy Kreme."

"So you're not being charged?"

"They're still investigating."

"I should talk to Dr. Goldberg," she said. "Try to talk him out of filing charges."

"I should sue him." Steve held up his swollen right hand. "My wrist is sprained."

They were stuck in traffic on South Bayshore Drive on a muggy autumn morning. Thankfully, Steve had put the top up on the Mustang, or her hair would resemble a floor mop. They were trying to work their way out of Coconut Grove on the morning after the reappearance of Janice, the nabbing of Bobby, and the near-arrest of Steve.

Just another day in the saga of the Solomon family. Do I really belong here?

Steve was like a trapeze artist working without a net. Sooner or later, he would fall. Would she catch him or be squashed by him?

Okay, if Steve's a trapeze artist, what am I?

The gal in tights who rides the prancing elephant?

No, the poor gal following the elephant with the shovel and pail.

She had picked up the circus metaphors from Marvin the Maven, the octogenarian leader of the Courthouse Gang, an unabashed admirer of Steve. Marvin had once told her why he followed Steve from courtroom to courtroom. *"With Steverino, it's like the circus. You never know when a dozen clowns are gonna fall out of a little yellow car."*

But Steve's courtroom antics were usually planned and made some sense, even if they were borderline unethical. These latest actions—clobbering Arnold Freskin and now Myron Goldberg—made Victoria feel that Steve was out of control.

"How's Bobby doing?" she asked.

"Better, I think. He's calmed down."

"Do you want me to talk to him? About girls, I mean."

"Already did. A speech about being a gentleman, respecting girls. I also told him I was disappointed he didn't tell me about Janice the Junkie coming around."

She shot him a look.

"I didn't call her that," he said hastily. " 'Your loving mother' is what I said. 'How could you sneak off with your loving mother like that?' "

"Go easy on him, Steve. He's got a lot going on."

"Yeah, well, so do I."

Steve banged the horn at a Hummer that was trying to nose into traffic from the Grove Isle bridge. "Asshole! Guy thinks he owns the road 'cause he's got the biggest bumper."

Great, Victoria thought. Just what they needed. A road rage incident.

Steve slid down the window on the passenger side, leaned across, and shouted: "Hey, you! Big car, little dick!"

Victoria swatted his hand away and hit the button, closing the window. "What's wrong with you! Don't you know how many drivers in Miami are armed?"

He turned on the radio. "No, but I'm sure you do."

"Your conduct lately simply defies description."

"Oh, c'mon, Vic. Give it a try."

"For starters, you've been both irresponsible and reckless."

A sports talk station came on, the caller and host debating whether Shaquille O'Neal was a better player than Wilt Chamberlain. The consensus seemed to be that Wilt scored more points and more women.

"Could you change that, please?" Victoria asked.

Steve punched a button, and another sports station came on, the host asking callers to choose the sexiest cheerleader from the Dolphin Dolls.

"How can you listen to this garbage?" she asked.

"I like it. Is that being reckless or irresponsible?"

"Juvenile."

"I guess good old Bigby doesn't listen to sports radio."

"Where did that come from? What's Bruce have to do with anything?"

"I don't know. He sort of popped into my head."

Ahead of them, traffic started moving and they inched past Mercy Hospital on the way downtown. Strange, Victoria thought. Just last night, her mother brought up Bruce. Victoria had been complaining about Steve and his penchant for trouble. Weirdly, The Queen had spoken up for Steve. What had she said exactly? Victoria couldn't remember.

Steve gave the Mustang some gas and said, "Good old boring Bruce Bigby."

Omigod.

That was almost exactly what The Queen had said. *"Steve may drive you crazy, but you love him. And frankly, he's a lot more fun than good old boring Bruce."*

"Have you been speaking to my mother?"

"Why would I? She hates me."

Victoria reached over and changed the station. On came Steve's damn Margaritaville music, Jimmy Buffet singing "Growing Older but Not Up." Another of the beach bard's paeans to the good life.

Victoria hit another button, and a deep voice rumbled from the speakers: *"Now in its twenty-third printing,* Looking Out for Numero Uno. *So, log on to Dr. Bill's website and order the book today. With every purchase, get a free Dr. Bill ball cap with the logo 'Me First.' "*

"I'll change that," she said, reaching toward the radio.

"No. Let's see who he's blasting today."

"Now, a special treat. You've heard Dr. Bill pre-

scribe remedies for addiction before. Hard work. Willpower. Self-reliance. Forget groups and steps. Don't waste your time listening to other people's problems. Our guest today helped herself, and you can, too. Remember, folks, 'invincible' starts with 'i.' "

"What's he peddling now?" Steve asked.

"Today's guest is a woman who turned her life around. A woman who was mired in criminality and drug abuse and made the conscious decision to find the power that lies within. Welcome to the program, Janice Solomon."

"Oh, shit!" Steve slammed on the brakes and was nearly rear-ended.

"I couldn't have done it without you, Dr. Bill. You inspired me."

"That's generous of you, Janice. But I give you all the credit. Now, take our listeners through your life, from your upbringing in a dysfunctional family to your descent into drugs, to your rehabilitation . . ."

"What a load of crap," Steve said.

". . . and now your coming home to reclaim the son you love."

The words hit Steve like a one-two combination—jab-hook, jab-hook—and seemed to reverberate inside his brain.

"The son she loves?" Steve nearly spat the words. "She nearly killed Bobby!"

"The son who was illegally taken away from you."

Steve stomped on the gas and pulled through a U-turn, tires screeching.

"What are you doing?" Victoria said.

"We're going to the station. I'm not gonna let him get away with this."

"You can't play on his turf. Remember last time you went on the air?"

"Got no choice. Kreeger's setting the table for a custody fight. I've got to expose him as a fraud."

"He's taunting you. He *wants* you to come after him."

"Fine. He wants a fight, he's gonna get it. Janice, too."

Typical Steve, she thought. Rushing blindly into danger, never considering the consequences.

She sank back in her seat as the Mustang squealed around the turn at Seventeenth Avenue on the way to Dixie Highway. Steve was right about one thing, she thought.

He's not like Bruce at all.

Bruce carried an umbrella, even when the forecast was sunny and clear. Steve windsurfed in thunderstorms, mast pointed toward the sky, daring Zeus to toss lightning bolts his way.

Just now, good old boring Bruce doesn't sound so bad.

On the radio, Janice was going on about how much she missed her son when she was incarcerated and how, alone in her cell, she pledged to clean up her act so she could come home and raise the boy.

"*My brother did the best he could while I was gone. But he's a bachelor, without any children of his own. He's actually quite immature himself.*"

"The Eva Braun of mothers is criticizing my parenting," Steve muttered.

"*No way my brother can do what I can.*"

"Right. No way I'd abandon the boy and nearly let him freeze to death."

"Steve. Don't do anything stupid, okay?"

"*I'm the mother and there's nothing like a mother's love.*"

"I'm not going to do anything stupid," Steve said.

"*I'm so anxious to make up for all the lost time.*"

"But I'll tell you this, Vic. I'll kill her before I let her have Bobby."

Twenty-Seven

LET'S KILL ALL THE LAWYERS

When Steve and Victoria entered the control room, Dr. Bill Kreeger was just finishing his umpteenth commercial for one of his products, a seven-set CD collection entitled: "Stop Kissing Butt and Start Kicking It." Through the window, Steve could see Kreeger and Janice, earphoned and miked, engaged in the mutual stroking of egos.

"Welcome back Janice Solomon, a truly courageous woman who took control of her life," Kreeger said. "Janice, tell my listeners how you did it."

"Sitting in my jail cell, I read all your books," Janice answered. "*Looking Out for Numero Uno* made me realize I needed to love myself. When I finally put myself on a pedestal—that's chapter three—I realized how much my son needed a person as worthy as me."

"Attagirl," Kreeger enthused.

"Attagirl?" Steve said. "A sociopath high-fiving a child abuser."

"Let's get out of here," Victoria said.

"Tell us about your childhood, Janice," Kreeger coaxed.

"When I was a kid, I was in Girl Scouts, and I was a

candy striper at Mount Sinai. Really caught up in the pleasing-others game."

"Chapter four," Kreeger said. " 'The Pleasing Others Fallacy.' Altruism is for suckers. Pleasing others is a waste of time."

"That was me. I baked cookies for shut-ins and babysat for poor families for free. I never got in touch with my inner 'I.' Never learned to say, 'I am *numero uno*.' So naturally, the more I gave, the more I was taken advantage of. Especially by boys."

"Do-gooders do bad all the time," Kreeger agreed. "No good deed goes unpunished."

"Then there's my brother, Stevie."

"Regular listeners will remember Steve Solomon, another family member with a checkered past," Kreeger pointed out, helpfully.

"You got that right, Dr. Bill."

"Well, speak of the shyster." Kreeger gestured toward the window. "Here's your brother now. C'mon in, Solomon. Let's have a family reunion."

"Don't do it, Steve," Victoria said. "Please don't do it."

"I have to, Vic. My inner 'I' says so."

* * *

Twelve minutes later, just after a promo for Kreeger's new video game, "Shaft Thy Neighbor," Steve listened as the shrink prattled on about himself.

"I've been an expert in quite a few custody cases over the years," Kreeger said.

Yeah. The deceased Nancy Lamm's case, for one.

"And correct me if I'm wrong, Counselor, but doesn't the law favor mothers over fathers, much less uncles?"

"Only with very young children," Steve said. "And not when the mother is demonstrably unfit."

" 'Demonstrably unfit.' Now, there's a pettifogger's term for you. So, you don't believe in rehabilitation, Counselor?"

"We talking about Janice or you?"

"Do you really want to go there, Solomon? Because I'd be forced to ask if your shoddy representation of me proved you're a 'demonstrably unfit' lawyer."

"Janice is an unfit mother, and I can prove it."

"You'll have your chance, Counselor."

"Kreeger, why don't you just butt out of my family's personal matters?"

Next to him, Janice laughed. "Too late for that, little brother. Dr. Bill's testifying for me."

"I can't wait to cross-examine him," Steve said.

"More lawyer tricks?" Kreeger said. "Technicalities and obfuscations. No wonder Shakespeare said, 'Let's kill all the lawyers.' "

"Shakespeare had a villain say that," Steve replied, miraculously remembering a long-ago English Lit class at the U. "Dick the Butcher said it in a play, one of the Henrys. His pals were planning to overthrow the government, so the first thing they planned was to kill the lawyers to make the job easier. You're misconstruing the line, just like you're mischaracterizing my sister."

"More legalese?" Kreeger taunted him. "More fine print and sleight of hand. Yes, indeed. Let's kill all the lawyers before they kill all of us."

Janice leaned closer to the microphone. "I think Stevie's capable of murder. When he kidnapped Bobby, he broke Rufus Thigpen's skull."

"I didn't kidnap Bobby. I rescued him from the dog cage you locked him in."

"If I'd been the one in that shed instead of Thigpen, would you have cracked my head open, too?" Janice prodded.

"I'm not gonna answer that."

"Hear that, listeners!" Kreeger said happily. "The shyster invokes the Fifth Amendment."

"This is bullshit!" Steve slammed his hand on the table.

"Please refrain from profanity and violence, Counselor. Janice, should I call security?"

"I'm not worried," she said. "When we were kids, I used to beat the crap out of Stevie."

"Yeah," Steve said. "When you outweighed me by thirty pounds."

"You oughta thank me. How do you think you learned to run so fast?" Janice lowered her voice as if sharing a deep secret. "I used to make him eat mud pies."

"Hold that thought, and don't touch the dial," Kreeger instructed. "We'll be back right after this news break." He pointed toward the control room and took off his earphones. "This is great radio. Solomon, perhaps you can ask Ms. Lord to join us for a while. I'd love to ask her about you."

"Why don't we talk about you?" Steve said as a news announcer droned in the background. "About you and Amanda."

"What's to say? I saved the poor girl, just as you claim to have saved your nephew."

"No, you didn't. You killed her mother to get at her. You're a freaking pedophile."

"Delusions and hysteria. I'd better make a note to add that to your report."

Just then, two uniformed officers entered the studio from the control room. Steve had a disconcerting sense of déjà vu. He'd been arrested here once before, for slugging Arnold Freskin. But these two were City of Miami, not Beach cops. And he recognized them at once. They'd shown up at Goldberg's house last night and taken statements. Rodriguez and Teele. Hispanic cop and black cop, just like on TV. Rodriguez had a thin mustache and Teele sported a mini-Afro, again like a TV cop, circa *The Mod Squad*.

"Hello, Mr. Solomon," Rodriguez said. "Is this your sister?"

"Yes! Take her away, officers. What is it this time: drug possession? Parole violation? Did she rob a bank this morning?"

"Ms. Solomon," Teele said. "Last night, were you present when your brother struck a Dr. Myron Goldberg on or about the face?"

"Yeah. Stevie slugged him right in the kisser."

"Was your brother protecting you from Dr. Goldberg at the time?"

"What do you mean?" Janice asked.

"Was Dr. Goldberg threatening you with a firearm?"

A moment of silence.

"C'mon, Janice," Steve prodded. "Tell them about the Uzi."

"Mr. Solomon, please remain quiet," Teele instructed.

"Dr. Goldberg didn't do anything," Janice said. "Stevie just hauled off and sucker-punched him."

"That's a lie!" Steve was halfway out of his chair when Rodriguez grabbed him by a shoulder and spun him around. Teele had the handcuffs on before Steve could say he wanted to make a phone call.

Kreeger punched a button and yelled at his board operator. "Cut into the news. We're going live. State *versus* Solomon. Chapter two."

SOLOMON'S LAWS

9. Q: What do you call a judge who is old, cantankerous, and flatulent?

A: "Your Honor."

Twenty-Eight

GET THEE TO A SHRINKERY

A week after being booked for slugging Myron Goldberg and released for a second time in a month on his own recognizance, Steve was driving south on Dixie Highway, Bobby riding shotgun, when the pip-squeak said, "I don't want to go to Jewey school."

"To what?" Steve had never heard the expression.

"You know. Beth Am Day School."

"Who said anything about transferring?"

"Grandpop."

"Why, that *alter kocker.*"

Ever since Herbert had gone ortho, he'd been behaving strangely. Not only was he schlepping to temple every Friday night and Saturday morning, he seemed to be celebrating a new holiday every week, either a feast or a fast. Sure, Steve knew about pigging out—without the pig—at Sukkot and starving at Yom Kippur. But there was his old man, celebrating the Fast of Esther, the banquet at Simchat Torah, eating blintzes and cheesecake on Savuot but zilch on the seventeenth of Tammuz. Maybe his old man was acting weird because his blood sugar was riding a roller coaster.

"If your grandfather wants to discover his roots, fine," Steve told Bobby. "But you're staying in public school. It's good to mix with kids of different backgrounds."

"That's what I told Grandpop. I can say 'fuck off' in five languages."

Steve pulled into the left-turn lane and waited for the light to change. Only way to cross traffic during morning rush hour was to wait for a yellow light turning red. To his right was the University of Miami and the baseball stadium where once he won a game by scoring from first on a single. Looking back—the high-fives, the cheers, the late night with a Hurricane Hottie—he wondered if that was the high point of his life.

Just examine the facts.

Victoria, the woman he loved, was stewing over their relationship. All talk of moving in together had ceased. Even staying together seemed problematical. Jeez, they hadn't had sex in an eternity.

Kreeger was pulling his chain like a puppeteer with a marionette. Taunting him with Janice and the threat of a custody fight. Nothing had changed. Every step Steve took, the bastard was one step ahead of him.

Gotta stop playing defense, start playing offense.

And Bobby? If Victoria was Steve's heart, the boy was his soul. Steve would do anything for his nephew, make any sacrifice. Just watching Bobby smile clutched at his heart. There had been damn few smiles and laughs those first months after Steve brought the boy home from the commune. Half-starved, locked up, deprived of social contact, Bobby had withdrawn into a shell. In Steve's house, he would sit cross-legged in a corner, swaying, speaking gibberish, if anything at all. Now, seeing Bobby's growth, watching in awe as his brain sizzled and snapped with electrifying speed, well, it brought tears to Steve's eyes.

So how could you betray me, Bobby? How could you sneak off to see that woman who loved crack more than she loved you?

"Because she's still my mom."

That was Bobby's defense. The night Steve clobbered Myron Goldberg, Steve took Bobby home and made him a smoothie. They talked until dawn, Bobby crying and saying he was sorry he hadn't been honest. A few weeks before, when Janice got out of prison, she had started coming around the neighborhood. At night, she'd sneak into their yard and sometimes look through Bobby's window just to catch a glimpse of him.

Sure, Steve thought. Even with her brain cells burned out by twenty years of narcotics and hallucinogens, Janice had known better than to knock on the door and give her baby brother a big hug. So she'd hung out at the park on Morningside Drive like a regular mom and one day called out to Bobby when he rode by on his bike.

"Why didn't you tell her to fuck off? In five languages."

"Because she's still my mom."

Steve couldn't understand it. And knew he couldn't fight it, either. If he forbade Bobby to see his mother, he'd be the villain. The two of them would sneak around behind his back, make a game of it. He was in a lose-lose situation.

The light blinked yellow, and Steve honked at the Beemer in front of him to *turn the hell left so we don't sit here another fifteen minutes*. The light was red when Steve followed onto Augusto Street, pulling up to the entrance of Ponce de León Middle School. A sea of urchins in shorts, T-shirts, and backpacks was surging toward the front door.

Steve reached over and squeezed Bobby's shoulder. He wouldn't kiss the boy, not when his pals might be watching.

Bobby made no move to open the door. "I don't want to go to school."

"Why not?"

"First period is P.E. Second is Study Hall. Third is Civics, and I've got permission for independent study off-campus."

"Independent study? You getting your master's degree?"

"I can go to court with you today if you want me to."

"You have anything in writing to back up this story?"

"Jeez, Uncle Steve. Don't you trust me?"

"About as far as I can throw Shaquille O'Neal. Now, what's going on?"

"You've got to go in front of some judge, right?"

"Yeah. The Honorable Alvin Elias Schwartz. So what?"

"Grandpop says a defendant should always look as sympathetic as possible. That's why serial killers bring their mothers to court."

"Yeah?"

"I can make you look more sympathetic. I'm Exhibit A in your trial stratagem."

"What kind of word is that for a twelve-year-old? 'Stratagem'?"

"Don't you always say, 'If the law doesn't work, work the law?' "

"Not like this. I won't use you as a prop."

"C'mon, Uncle Steve. If the law doesn't work, work your nephew."

* * *

Victoria paced in the corridor outside Judge Schwartz's courtroom. Morning calendar, the place overflowing with defendants, their wives, girlfriends, and mothers. Bored cops and sleazy bail bondsmen, overworked probation officers and perjurious witnesses—all the jetsam and flotsam of the criminal justice system.

It was a familiar place to Victoria, but still she felt ill at ease. This was the venue of her greatest professional embarrassment. Ray Pincher, the State Attorney, had fired her in Judge Gridley's courtroom, not twenty yards away. She could remember her face reddening, the tears welling, and opposing counsel—Steve-the-Shyster Solomon—hitting on her. An inauspicious beginning to their tumultuous relationship.

Now, hustling down the corridor were two judges— Stanford Blake and Amy Steele Donner—robes flying, chatting away. She nodded to them in the way lawyers do, being polite, but not too familiar. His Honor and Her Honor smiled back.

What were they saying? She could only imagine.

"There's Victoria Lord. She got suckered into a mistrial by Steve Solomon, ended up sleeping with him."

Riding the escalator moments before, Victoria had encountered the head of the state's Major Crimes Division. They exchanged hellos. The man asked what brought her across the bay. Expecting a murder trial, maybe. White-collar crime. Something to ring the cash register at Solomon & Lord, Attorneys-at-Law.

Not . . . *"Defending my partner in his second assault and battery case in a month."*

No wonder she was embarrassed. The humiliation didn't stop with Ray Pincher sacking her. Her partner and lover could be counted on for continuing acts of mortification.

Down the corridor, the elevator door opened and out walked Steve.

With Bobby!

She watched as Steve cruised toward her, slapping pals on the back, howdying prosecutors and defense lawyers alike. Smiling and laughing, a glide to his stride. He could be strolling along a sun-dappled country path on his way to pick strawberries, instead of heading to his own arraignment. He paused a moment to buttonhole Ed Shohat and Bob Josefsberg, two of the top defense lawyers in town. Just Steve's way of letting them know he wasn't in jail, and if they had any cases or clients beneath their dignity, he could use the work.

"Yo, Vic," he called out.

"Yo, yourself. Bobby, why aren't you in school?"

"This is my class project," he replied.

"Bobby's my stratagem," Steve said.

She gave him her *don't bullshit me* look.

"It's true. Bobby's going to stand by my side."

"Just let me do the talking," she said. "All you have to say is—"

"Not guilty. I know, I know."

"Not guilty, *Your Honor.*"

"Okay. You're the boss." He turned to Bobby.

"Look, kiddo, you'll sit next to me and get up when I stand to enter my plea."

"That's your stratagem?" Victoria asked.

"And our theme for the case. I was protecting Bobby that night when I inadvertently struck Myron Goldberg. I stand with Bobby, and he stands with me. We're sending a message."

"With Judge Schwartz's eyesight, I doubt he'll see either one of you."

"He can see okay. It's his hearing that's off." Steve turned to Bobby. "And if His Honor cuts loose a fifty-decibel fart, try not to laugh."

Bobby giggled. "He does that?"

"The old goat passes wind and blames it on the court reporter. So be cool." Steve turned back to Victoria. "Let's go do it. And trust me. 'Not guilty, Your Honor.' Not a word more."

* * *

Judge Schwartz, irascible, aged, and flatulent, was running through his morning calendar of motions, bail hearings, status reports, arraignments, and other procedural gimcracks of the criminal justice system.

Steve, Victoria, and Bobby took seats in the front row of the gallery. Steve spotted Ray Pincher sitting across the aisle. Next to the State Attorney sat Myron Goldberg. The periodontist was sporting a fat lip the color of an eggplant and wearing a soft neck collar for no reason Steve could figure except possible civil litigation.

"Oh, my aching neck."

Goldberg wasn't needed at the arraignment. No testimony would be taken. Why the hell was he even here?

The clerk, a young woman with dreadlocks and no apparent facial expression, called out: "State of Florida versus Stephen Solomon."

The judge peered over the tops of his trifocals as everyone made their way past the bar. "You again?"

"Guilty, Your Honor," Steve called out. "Of being Steve Solomon. *Not* guilty of the charge."

"Didn't ask for your plea."

"I know, Judge, but I promised my lawyer that's all I'd say." Steve and Bobby took their seats, leaving Victoria standing to do the real work.

"What now?" the judge demanded.

"New case, Your Honor," Pincher said. He wore a burgundy three-piece suit. Pincher's trademark miniature handcuffs clinked as he gestured, bowing slightly as if he were a maître d' welcoming diners to his over-priced restaurant. "Mr. Solomon has again committed assault and battery."

"Allegedly," Victoria broke in. "Victoria Lord for the defense, Your Honor."

"Say, aren't you that lady lawyer who got shat on by a bird down in Gridley's courtroom?"

Victoria reddened. "A talking toucan, Your Honor. Mr. Solomon fed it prune Danish."

"Used to eat poppyseed myself, but the damn seeds stick to my dentures."

"Your Honor, Mr. Solomon will enter a plea of not guilty."

"Already did," the judge said.

"In that case," Victoria continued, "the defense waives reading the information and requests trial by jury."

"Fine and dandy. The clerk will set a trial date not

to conflict with the Florida Derby. You like the ponies, missy?"

"Not particularly, Your Honor. We also move to withdraw Mr. Solomon's nolo plea in the earlier case."

"On what grounds?"

"My client was not represented by counsel when he entered the plea."

"Motion denied. Your client's a lawyer. Who'd he hit this time, Pincher?"

"Dr. Myron Goldberg, a neighbor," the State Attorney said. On cue, Goldberg rose stiffly, a pained look on his face. "Dr. Goldberg caught Mr. Solomon's nephew peeping in his daughter's window. In the ensuing confrontation, Mr. Solomon assaulted Dr. Goldberg."

"Not true, Judge." Steve leapt to his feet, and so did Bobby. "I was defending my nephew and my sister."

"Sit down!" Victoria hissed.

"I wasn't peeping!" Bobby insisted.

"First a peeper," the judge said sternly. "Then a flasher. Next thing you know, you're pulling down girls' panties and having your way with them. You know what they did to rapists in ancient Rome?"

"Crushed their balls between two rocks," Bobby said.

"The little perv knows his history, I'll grant him that."

"I'm not a perv!"

"Pipe down, son. You'll have a chance to prove that."

"The boy's not on trial," Pincher reminded the judge.

"Maybe he should be," Judge Schwartz shot back. "He's really starting to torque my tail."

At that, an unmistakable *pop-pop-pop* came from the bench, a Gatling gun of rapid-fire flatulence.

Bobby giggled and said, "Who blew the butt trumpet?"

"That's enough, you little rascal."

"Because it sounded like a bench burner," Bobby continued.

Steve put a hand on Bobby's shoulder, trying to quiet him.

"Are you trifling with me, boy? Do you know who I am?"

"Alvin Elias Schwartz," Bobby replied, scrunching his face in concentration.

"No, Bobby!" Steve ordered. "No anagrams."

"Alvin Elias Schwartz," Bobby repeated. "WAS A SNIVEL ZILCH RAT."

The judge hacked up some phlegm. "I ought to send both of you straight to clink."

"Your Honor," Victoria spoke up. "Mr. Solomon has yet to be tried, and there are no charges against his nephew."

The judge whirled around in his high-backed swivel chair. One revolution. Two revolutions. Three revolutions. The judge disappearing from sight, then reappearing, white fringes of hair above his ears blowing in the breeze. When the chair slowed to a stop, he said: "I question Solomon's mental competence. Where's that shrink's report from the other case?"

Pincher answered, "Not filed yet, Your Honor. Mr. Solomon missed his last appointment."

"If that happens again, he's going straight to jail. Do not pass Go. Do not collect two hundred shekels."

"Judge, don't send me back to that quack," Steve pleaded.

"Get thee to a shrinkery!" Judge Schwartz ordered. "What's the name of that head doctor?"

"William Kreeger," Pincher said.

"That's the one. Go see him. Both Solomon and the kid. I want to know if Solomon's a menace and the little rapscallion's a sicko."

"Your Honor doesn't have jurisdiction over the minor child," Victoria said.

"He's in my courtroom, missy. My fiefdom. It's in the Magna Carta. You can look it up."

"But Your Honor," Victoria pleaded. "Due process precludes—"

The judge rapped his gavel. *Bang!* "That's it, Ms. Lord. Both of your clients go see the shrink." Another *bang*! "Ten-minute recess. My bladder ain't what it used to be."

SOLOMON'S LAWS

10. You won't find it in Darwin, Deuteronomy, or Doonesbury, but it's an essential truth of human nature: We'll all kill to protect those we love.

Twenty-Nine

THE CON ARTIST BLUES

Carl Drake's suite at the Four Seasons was pretty much what Steve expected. Beige sofas with thick pillows in the living room, gray marble in the bath, a curved desk of blond wood in the tidy office. The windows looked across Biscayne Bay, glistening turquoise in the midday sun. Key Biscayne was a green atoll in the distance, a dozen sailboats visible on the far side of the causeway. Just what you would demand for twelve hundred bucks a night.

But who was paying for it? Before he even settled into the sofa, Steve was struck with the notion that The Queen would never get a shilling out of Carl Drake. No matter how much money Drake stole, he seemed to be the kind of guy who enjoyed spending every last cent.

Steve had filed the usual dilatory motions to slow down the mortgage foreclosure, but that could buy The Queen only so much time. Today, he intended to shake some money out of Drake. It was the first of two unpleasant tasks on his calendar, the second being a court-ordered appointment with William Kreeger, M.D.

"What'll it be, Steve?" Drake asked pleasantly, standing at the gleaming marble-topped bar. "Champagne? Cristal."

"No thanks, Carl."

"Wait. I'm good at this. I know from dinner that you drink tequila after dark. Now, as for the daytime . . ." Drake fingered a bottle of single-malt Scotch, then eyed a bottle of Maker's Mark. "I'm betting you're a bourbon man."

"Hemlock, if you have it. Drano on the rocks if you don't."

"Been a rough week, has it?" Laying on a bit of a British accent. Stopping just short of saying "old chap."

"Carl, this is uncomfortable for me," Steve said.

Drake poured himself a Scotch over ice, walked to a facing sofa and perched on the arm. He wore linen slacks the color of melted butter and a shimmering blue shirt, the fabric so soft, it invited petting. "Did Irene ask you to come?"

"She ordered me not to."

"Do you frequently disregard your clients' instructions?"

"All the time. I figure if they were so smart, they wouldn't need my counsel."

Drake gave him a pleasant smile. It seemed to be a well-practiced gesture from a well-mannered, well-accented smoothie.

Steve took a breath and surveyed the room. A portrait of Sir Francis Drake sat on an easel. A map of the seven seas, circa 1550, was pinned to a display board. A polyurethane block embedded with gold coins—Spanish doubloons, Steve supposed—sat on the desk, a seductive tease for any possible heirs of the sixteenth-century privateer. A calfskin briefcase bulged with papers.

Steve turned back to Drake and said: "What do you have in the pockets of those fancy pants you're wearing?"

"I beg your pardon?"

"Wallet? Keys? Take them out."

"Are you robbing me?"

"When I hang you off your balcony by your ankles, I don't want you to lose anything."

Drake laughed, the Scotch jiggling in his glass, a golden whirlpool. "I guess that's called a 'shakedown,' isn't it? But from what I hear, you can't afford any more dates in Criminal Court."

"You're gonna give Irene back her money."

"Oh, would that I could. The money's already gone to pay expenses in the administration of the estate."

"Like room service at the Four Seasons?"

"As a matter of fact, my travel expenses are included. But the payoff to Irene will far exceed—"

"At dinner, you said there were no fees."

"I'm afraid I wasn't totally forthcoming. But I was loath to discuss business on Irene's birthday, and my little deception seemed a good way to short-circuit the conversation."

"You're good, Drake. You're what my father would call 'slick as owl shit.' "

Drake hoisted his glass. "A toast to your father, then."

"Did you know the bank foreclosed on Irene's condo?"

Drake's suntanned face froze momentarily. "The hell you say."

"She's too embarrassed to tell you. Just like you're

too embarrassed to tell her you're a con man. There's
no estate of Sir Francis Drake. You're just pulling a
scam. I'm guessing that ritzy briefcase of yours holds a
first-class ticket to wherever scumbags go when the
Grand Jury starts issuing subpoenas."

Drake stood, walked to the bar, and poured himself
another Scotch. "Foreclosure? I don't understand it.
Irene led me to believe she had millions."

"It's a role she plays."

Drake gave a little rueful laugh. "Seems I'm the one
who's been conned."

"One difference, Drake. Irene didn't steal your
money."

"I never intended to hurt her. She's very special
to me."

"I'll bet you say that to all the widows."

"This is different." He took a long pull on his drink.
His crisp British accent seemed to have been replaced
by flatter tones—Chicago, maybe—and his shoulders
slumped. Losing some of his polish, Drake seemed uncomfortable and out of place, like Vice President
Cheney in a Speedo.

Drake nodded toward the briefcase. "The plane
ticket's there, all right, Solomon. Rio de Janeiro. I'm
usually gone by now. I stayed only because of Irene.
The damn truth is, I'm in love with her."

"Great. Invite me to the wedding. After you pay her
back."

"I wish I could. Truly. But the money's gone."

Steve considered himself a human polygraph machine. Looking at Carl Drake at that moment, the
man's mask slipping away, his brow furrowing, his
voice choked with regret, the machine said the con
artist was telling the truth. For some reason, that only

made Steve angrier. "Dammit, Drake. You say you love her, but you stole the roof from over her head."

"Are you going to hang me off the balcony, then?"

"I would, but I sprained my wrist hitting a guy. I'd probably drop you."

"Then what shall we do?"

"Let's have that drink," Steve said. "Bourbon will be just fine."

* * *

Cabanas—tents of flowing white cotton—blossomed like sails in the breeze. At poolside, Steve and Drake sat in the shade of a sabal palm and sipped their drinks, a soft breeze scented with suntan oil wafting over them.

"You could still go to Rio," Steve said. "There's nothing I could do to stop you."

"Too depressing," Drake said. "That's where Charles Ponzi went."

"The Ponzi pyramid scheme?"

"That's him. Fled to Italy, then Rio. Became a smuggler."

"Must be your hero. Like me following Rickey Henderson. A's to Yankees to Padres to Mets. Stealing bases wherever he went."

"Charles Ponzi died in the charity ward of a Brazilian hospital." There was a touch of sadness in Drake's voice. "I don't want to end like that."

Steve took a second to admire two sun-worshipping young women in bikinis. "Rickey Henderson ended up back in the minors."

"The shame is, I'm quite good at my work," Drake told him. "When I find a mark, I always look for the weakness that lets me pry loose the money."

"Greed, I would think."

"Sure, with the traditional cons. But I was always drawn to people who yearned to be something larger than themselves. You tell people they're descended from Sir Francis Drake, all their defenses evaporate. They dream that their current lives were destined to be greater or more meaningful. Then I turn a seemingly harmless conceit into a way to relieve them of their money."

"You don't sound particularly sorry about being a thief."

Drake shrugged. "We are who we are."

Echoing Irene's words. An incontrovertible fact of human nature.

"So what happened to the money, Drake?"

"I paid off debts. Gambling losses. A real estate investment trust that went belly-up. Even a gold mine that tapped out. I'm broke."

"Why not stay until you rip off enough people to get ahead?"

Drake sniffed at the suggestion. "That's what an amateur would do. A professional knows that it's better to bail out a month early than a day late. I had my usual story ready. Complications with the estate. Must fly to London. That buys a few weeks, and by then, I'm setting up shop in South America."

"And the reason you're not on the beach at Impanema is that you fell in love?"

Drake tipped his glass forward, the ice cubes clinking, the drinker's signal of affirmation. "I wanted to tell Irene everything. Beg for forgiveness. Promise to go straight so she and I could start a life together."

"Where? In the condo that's being foreclosed?"

"As I have no residence of my own, that was a distinct possibility." Drake emitted a laugh that was more of a sigh. "It's turning out rather like an O. Henry story, isn't it?"

"I wouldn't know. Henry Aaron, I might know."

"Oh, I think you understand me quite well. You're a good deal smarter than you let on. And you're an excellent judge of character."

"When I was a kid, I'd go to my father's courtroom and watch trials. For a while, I'd close my eyes and just listen to witnesses. Then I'd cover my ears and just watch. I'd put everything I'd seen and heard together. It was a game I played to figure out who was lying."

"It serves you well to this day. You saw through me in an instant."

"Wasn't that hard. I'm just surprised Irene came to me for help. I'm not on the list of her five hundred favorite people."

"Oh, you're wrong about that. Irene likes you. Worries about you because of that Dr. Bill character. She thinks you're playing with fire there."

That stopped Steve. "What does she know about that?"

"What you say to Victoria she repeats to Irene, who then tells me."

Of course. Mothers and daughters.

"Jeez, next you'll be telling me the last time we had sex."

"Two weeks, Tuesday. Right after *Sports Center*."

"During. The hockey highlights gave us a window."

"I've listened to Dr. Bill on the radio," Drake said. "All that psychobabble to sell worthless books and tapes."

"Do you know about his theory of evolutionary

psychology? We're all hardwired for murder. We're programmed by millions of years of evolution that favors survival of those who slaughter their enemies."

"And all this time, I thought we were just programmed for larceny."

"It's a pretty simple theory. Our genes carry the same murderous impulses as Paleolithic man."

"Interesting," Drake said. "If our DNA instructs us to kill, why fight it? The ideal rationalization for murder."

They each sipped their drinks, mulling it over. "Kreeger says I'm just as much a killer as he is," Steve said, after a moment. "For a while, I thought he was planting that seed in my brain, trying to set me up to kill my sister."

"And now?"

"Some days, he says we're both killers. And some days, we're both heroes. Kreeger claims he rescued a girl the way I rescued my nephew. But what Kreeger really did was sick and twisted."

"It sounds like a game to him. Putting you through the wringer like that."

"Whenever the bastard mentions Bobby's name, a chill goes up my spine."

"He's found your weakness, then."

"My nephew?"

"Your *love* for him. If Kreeger wanted to hurt you, he'd go after the child. Isn't that apparent?"

Too much so, Steve thought.

The way to cripple me, the way to inflict pain without end, would be to hurt Bobby.

What kind of man would do such a thing? Bill Kreeger would. The man who sees himself as the product of millions of years of evolution.

But then, so am I.

Kreeger was wrong about most things, but he was right about something. It's an essential truth of human nature that to protect those we love, every one of us will kill.

OF NYMPHS AND NUDNIKS

With Bobby riding shotgun and Jimmy Buffet singing about "Changes in Latitudes, Changes in Attitudes," Steve drove north on Alhambra in the Gables. The Biltmore golf course peeked out from between the sprawling Mediterranean and Colonial homes. They crossed the bridge over the waterway at Taragona and slowed near at the intersection of Salvatierra Drive.

Kreeger's place was a block away, and Steve was edgy. All his plans had been shot to hell. First, he had tried to simply warn off Kreeger. A tough-guy routine. *"If you come after me, I'll land on you like a ton of concrete."* Yeah, real impressive. Then he'd tried to spook Kreeger with tales of searching for—and finding—De la Fuente. But with the boat captain dead, Kreeger had nothing to fear. Trying to enlist Amanda as an accomplice hadn't worked, either. She'd been lying in wait for Steve. Naked and flirtatious. Clearly put up to it by Kreeger. Maybe to sabotage his relationship with Victoria. Who knew? The bastard was after him on multiple fronts.

And today's plan? A speck of an idea, totally lacking in sophistication.

Illegal, yes. Dangerous, yes. But sophisticated, no.

Judge Schwartz had ordered him to bring Bobby to Kreeger for evaluation. As long as they had to be in Kreeger's house, why not snoop around? Why not burgle the place and see what he could find?

"We're early," Bobby said. "Twenty-one minutes and thirty-four seconds early."

Steve pulled up to the curb and stopped. "I want you to wait in the car. I have something to do."

"What?"

"Can't tell you. And when we see Kreeger, don't mention our showing up early, okay?"

Bobby took off his glasses and cleaned them on the front of his Florida Marlins jersey, his lips pursed. His Solomon & Lord baseball cap was turned around backwards. "Are you gonna get in trouble, Uncle Steve?"

"Why would you say that?"

"Because you're wearing a tool belt and you're not a carpenter."

"It's a jogger's fanny pack, not a tool belt."

"Then why'd you put those lock picks and master keys in it?"

"You ask a lot of questions, squirt."

"Florida Statute eight-ten-point-zero-six," Bobby said. "It's a crime to possess burglary tools with intent to trespass or steal."

That damn echolalia, Steve thought. Bobby had been hanging around the office the day Steve signed up Omar Ortega, a kid charged with possessing a metal ruler suitable for breaking into parking meters. Ortega professed his innocence, even while paying his retainer in quarters and dimes.

"We're invited into Kreeger's house, right, Bobby?"

"Yeah, the judge says we gotta go."

"So I'm not trespassing. I'm just arriving early. If there are any locked doors or cabinets, I might just want to poke around a bit."

"Mom says if you go to jail, I can come live with her."

"Very hospitable of her."

"She said even if you don't go to jail, she's gonna get a judge to give her custody."

"How do you feel about that, kiddo?"

"I know she treated me really bad, but she was so messed up then, I don't think she could help it. I don't hate her or anything, and she kind of needs me because she's all alone. I mean, she doesn't even have any friends."

They sat in silence a moment and Steve felt his stomach knot with fear. In a few moments, he'd be sneaking through Kreeger's house like a cat burglar, but the only thing frightening him was that his nephew seemed ready to desert him. "What are you saying, Bobby? You want to live with your mom because you feel sorry for her?"

Tears formed in the boy's eyes "I know you hate her because of what she did to me."

"I don't hate her. She's still my sister, so somewhere deep inside, I suppose I still have feelings for her."

"And she's still my mom."

That again.

There was a river of sweetness that ran through Bobby that Steve didn't share. Truth be told, those *feelings* he claimed to still have for his sister were mostly homicidal in nature.

"I just want to do what's best for you," Steve said, fighting the urge to yell: *"If I hadn't taken you away from her, you'd be dead by now!"*

"I want the two of you to stop fighting."

"Okay. What else?"

"I want to see my mom, but I want to live with you, Uncle Steve. You and me, we're tight, right?"

Steve felt his muscles unclench. "Okay, I'll see what I can work out with Janice. I'd rather know where you are than have you sneaking out to see her. But I want some proof she's cleaned up her act. Deal?"

"Deal." Bobby reached over and they pounded knuckles.

Steve opened his door and had one foot out of it when Bobby added, "Please be careful, Uncle Steve. If you get in trouble, what will happen to me?"

* * *

A Lexus SUV sat in Kreeger's driveway. Steve figured the owner was a patient, midway through a head-shrinking session. Steve walked along the pink flagstone path that followed the hibiscus hedge toward the backyard. For all he knew, Amanda was sunning herself again, all toasty warm and naked in the midday sun. But before rounding the corner of the house, which would have brought him in line of sight from Kreeger's office window, Steve ducked into the vestibule. The side door to the kitchen was open, and he walked in.

The kitchen could use updating, but it was clean and airy. A pot of coffee sat in its place, still warm.

"Just came in looking for a cup of java, Doc."

Planning his alibi.

An interior door led to a corridor that opened into a living room. Traditional furniture, windows shaded with Bahamas shutters, a seldom-used fireplace. Above the fireplace, a painting. An idealized portrait of Kreeger at the helm of his big boat, *Psycho Therapy*. The shrink appeared a bit taller and thinner. Tanned and fit, one hand on the wheel, one on the throttles. A man in control.

Steve always thought portraits should be reserved for dead ancestors. Wasn't it an act of unbridled ego to commission a painting of yourself? Maybe Kreeger's boat should be renamed *Narcissist*.

Steve took a set of stairs to the second floor, stepping lightly.

Now, just what the hell are you looking for, anyway?

He didn't know. He didn't expect to find a framed document on the wall: *"I killed Jim Beshears, Nancy Lamm, and Oscar De la Fuente. Sincerely, Dr. Bill."*

But you never knew. A diary. An unfinished memoir. Steve once defended a case where his client wrote a to-do list reminding himself to buy a mask and listing the address of the bank he intended to rob.

Steve felt he needed to do something. Find something. Not just wait for Kreeger to make another move.

At the top of the stairs, a corridor. A door was open at the end, and he entered the room.

Master bedroom.

King-size bed. A four-poster. Lightweight duvet, silvery color.

He surveyed the room, trying to pick up vibes from the guy who lived here. In the corner, on a pedestal, a bronze sculpture, the torso of a boy. On the walls, Caribbean art. Brightly colored paintings of partially clothed islanders working on boats and tending fields. Young girls carrying produce.

On a credenza, a man's jewelry box. Steve opened it

without need of master key or pickaxe. Two men's watches, expensive. Several pairs of cuff links. Gold, onyx, jade. Steve ran a finger across the felt lining of the box. Nothing hidden underneath.

Somewhere in the house, pipes rumbled. Steve checked his watch. Another ten minutes before he would get Bobby from the car.

He had been hoping for a computer. Who knew what would be buried in there? Criminals who would never leave fingerprints at a crime scene drop trails of bread crumbs in the "history" window of their laptops. A guy who tried to kill his wife by dropping a roaring hair dryer into her bathtub was found to have electrocution websites plastered all over his hard drive.

But no computer in Kreeger's bedroom. Steve had to look for clues the old-fashioned way. He opened a drawer in the bedside table. A holstered nine-millimeter Glock. Okay, pretty normal for South Florida. In the lower drawer, an old photo album. Yellowing pictures from college and med school. Steve thumbed through the plasticized pages.

A *bang*ing of pipes again from inside the walls.

He stopped at a page of snapshots. A handwritten date on the page, seven years ago. Photos of a woman, late thirties, and a girl who looked to be roughly Bobby's age. On the beach, in swimsuits, smiling at the camera, squinting into the sun. The photographer's shadow crept across the sand toward them. The woman was Nancy Lamm. Steve had seen enough photos during the murder trial to recognize her immediately. The girl was Amanda—Mary Amanda, in those days. Her hips hadn't rounded out, and her bustline was practically invisible, but the features were hers.

Steve sat down on the edge of the bed and turned

the page. Six more photos. No Nancy this time. But
there was Amanda. On Kreeger's pool deck.

Naked.

Just as naked as Steve had seen her two weeks ago.
But these photos were taken when she was perched on
the fence between girlhood and womanhood. A variety of poses, a naked nymph stretching this way and
that, arching her back in one, jutting out a bony hip in
another, throwing her shoulders back, turning sideways to reveal breasts that were barely buds, then facing the camera head-on, legs spread, unashamedly
showing a small tuft of hair, strawberry blond in the
sun. Smiling goofily in one shot, seemingly innocent.
Pouting seductively in another, a child's parody of
pornography. A close-up, just a head shot, showed
something else. A glassy-eyed stare.

Stoned. She was high on something.

Twelve or thirteen. Naked and stoned. There was
something both sad and horrifying about it. As for
Kreeger, could there be any doubt? He was both a
killer and a pedophile. For a moment, Steve imagined
himself as Amanda's father. What would he have
done? Beaten Kreeger with a baseball bat. For starters.
Crushed every bone in his body, starting with the ankles, working his way up to his demented skull.

*Yeah, Kreeger, we're all capable of killing. And
maybe we're all capable of justifying it, too.*

One of the photos jogged something in Steve's
mind, but what was it? He studied the shot. Amanda,
her arms thrown back and shoulders leaning forward,
like a swimmer, on the blocks at the start of a race.

The bronze statue in the corner of the bedroom.

It wasn't a boy at all. It was Amanda, cast in
bronze, her thin torso boylike. Kreeger had chosen to

freeze his memory of her at her prepubescent stage. And those paintings on the walls. The Caribbean islanders. Those young girls carrying the produce. Naked from the waist up.

Getting creepy in here.

He heard a sound, and an interior door opened. The bathroom.

Out walked Amanda, her hair wringing wet, a white towel wrapped around her body. Her startled look melted instantly into a playful smile. "Good morning, sir. You must be the handyman."

He had expected a scream. Not role-playing.

"My mommy and daddy aren't home," she continued in a little-girl voice. "But you can fix anything you want."

Was the childlike tone the way she spoke to Kreeger? Then and now. In this very room, on this very bed. Creepy had just become downright base and vile.

"Nothing here I could fix." Steve dropped the album back in the drawer. "Too big a job."

"Don't you like my pictures?" She giggled. When he didn't answer, she unwrapped the towel and dropped it to the floor. "Which do you like better, the old me or the new me?"

Steve hadn't moved from the corner of the bed. She stepped closer, spreading her legs, pressing her inner thighs against his knees, pinning him in place. Her skin was burnished red from the hot shower, her breasts at eye level, nipples taut. If she moved any closer, he could suffer a detached retina.

"Uncle Bill likes the old me better." Her tone one of mock sadness. "When I was thirteen, I could lock my ankles behind my head."

"You should have tried out for the Olympics."

"Uncle Bill says my boobs are too big now, but I mean, I'm not exactly a cow, right?" She moved her shoulders from side to side, her breasts barely jiggling just inches from his nose.

"Your breasts are fine, Amanda."

"Uncle Bill likes them small. Little tulips, he calls them." She plopped into his lap, her legs spread, facing him, straddling his thighs. "You sure you like mine?"

"What's not to like?" Sounding like his father. Feeling like a schmuck, a real nudnik.

"So why don't you touch them?" A whiny child's voice. "You can, you know. You can kiss my boobies and do anything you want."

He didn't move.

She turned sideways so that one breast slid across his cheek, smooth and warm against his skin. She made a humming sound and said, "You need a shave, but it feels good."

"You're a bad girl."

"So spank me." She slid sideways across his lap and flipped over, arching her back so that her bottom was hoisted just above his knees. He saw the jellyfish tattoo again, tentacles streaming down each buttock.

"If I spank you, will you be good?"

"I'll be so-o-o good." Another girlish giggle. "Unless you want me to be so-o-o bad."

He hesitated, weighing the options.

"What are you waiting for, Uncle Steve?"

Uncle Steve.

The name sounded repulsive on her lips.

He drew back his arm and slapped her butt as hard as he could with an open palm. A one-handed *smack* as loud as a marlin hitting the water.

"Ow! What the fuck!" She leapt off him, yelping,

all traces of jailbait vanished from her voice. "You bastard! That hurt like hell!"

"Sorry, Amanda, but I'm not your Uncle Steve." He got to his feet and started for the door.

"I'm gonna tell Uncle Bill what you did."

"What'd I do?"

"Raped me."

"Right. Gave you a candy bar and had my way with you."

"He'll believe me. And then you know what he'll do?"

"Hit me on the head and dump me into the Jacuzzi? Like he did to your mother."

A laugh came from her mouth, but her eyes were hard, narrow slits. "Is that what you think happened?"

"The jury called it manslaughter. But you and I know better, don't we, Amanda? We both know Bill killed your mother so he could be with you."

"That's crazy." Another laugh, sharp as barbed wire. "You've got everything backwards."

Steve longed to ask the question: *"So what happened, Amanda? What happened the night your mother drowned?"* But sometimes the best cross-examination is silence—the best question, the one unasked. Leave a moment of dead calm, and the witness might just fill in the gap.

"Uncle Bill didn't kill my mom, silly," Amanda Lamm said. "I did!"

* * *

Jogging toward the car, Steve played back what Amanda had told him. She and her mother were spending the weekend at Kreeger's house. Her mother

found her on the pool patio, smoking some weed.
They had a blistering argument, Mom screaming she'd
lose custody if Amanda didn't clean up her act, the girl
screaming back that she gave Bill more pleasure than
Mom did, and the only reason he kept the old lady
around was to be close to Amanda. Her mother
slapped her. Amanda picked up a skimmer pole—the
"pool thingie," she called it—and hit back. Somehow,
her mother ended up in the hot tub and drowned.
Later that night, after the paramedics had carted Mom
away, with the police investigating, good old Uncle Bill
tucked Amanda into bed with warm milk, a handful of
pills, and the promise that he would cover for her.

*But that's not what really happened. Amanda was
lying.*

No. Lying *is the wrong word,* Steve thought.
Amanda could pass a polygraph exam because she believed her own story.

But Steve felt sure she hadn't killed her mother:
Kreeger simply convinced her that she had. How hard
could it have been for him? Amanda was a thirteen-
year-old with a drug problem. Her parents were going
through a horrific divorce. An older man had started
paying attention to her. A devious and manipulative
man who preyed on her insecurities and took her to
his bed.

Steve tried to picture the end of that horrific night,
Kreeger leaning over Amanda's bed. What did he
whisper to her? How did he shape her memories?

"I took care of everything, Amanda. Don't worry."

"What happened, Uncle Bill?"

*"I told them your mother slipped and hit her head.
It'll be all right."*

"What will?"

"You never intended to hit her."

"I hit my mother?"

That was the only version of events that made sense to Steve. Nancy Lamm, who had her own addiction problems, discovered Kreeger was drugging her daughter and having sex with her. Nancy argued with Kreeger, threatening to blow the whistle on him. Kreeger killed Nancy, then convinced Amanda that she'd done it.

But there was no way to prove it.

Now Steve slowed to a walk. The morning air was heavy with humidity. The golf course was quiet. Not even a "fore." Steve approached his Mustang, parked in the shade of a banyan tree. No one inside.

Where's Bobby!

Had he wandered off? He could have sneaked over to the golf course to watch duffers flail away in the scrubby roughs.

Janice! Where the hell's my worthless sister? She could have followed us here. She could have waited, and—

No. No need to do that. All she had to do was call, and the little stinker would sneak out and get ice cream with her.

Kreeger!

Steve whirled and ran back toward the house.

Thirty-One

FIRE OF MY LOINS

Laughter was coming from the ground-floor office. Bobby's laugh. Childlike and innocent, a bird's song on a summer breeze. Steve threw the door open. Kreeger was behind his desk, Bobby sitting cross-legged on a leather chair.

"Hey, Uncle Steve. We started without you."

"Come in, Solomon." Kreeger's smile seemed sincere, as sincere as a wolf smiling at a lamb.

"What the hell's going on?"

"Your nephew is regaling me with his wizardry powers. Shall we try another one, Robert?"

"Go for it, Doc."

"How about my name? 'William Kreeger.' "

"Easy, 'cause it's got so many vowels, and I can make four words." The kid thought a second, then boomed: "WIRE ME RAGE KILL."

"Utterly delightful." Kreeger turned to Steve. "Robert was just telling me about the lovely Maria and the unfortunate incident that led to his coming here."

"She's a fox," Bobby said.

"Indeed, she is." Kreeger picked a wallet-size photo from his desk. "Lovely, isn't she, Solomon?"

"Where'd you get that?" It was a shot of Maria Munoz-Goldberg preening for the camera. Shorts and a sleeveless T-shirt that stopped north of her navel. Her back was arched in a way that showed off her small butt. Except for the clothing, she could have been Amanda, posing for Kreeger seven years earlier.

"I gave it to Dr. Bill," Bobby said. "He's giving me advice on bagging Maria."

"Great. I'll come visit you in Youth Hall."

"Nothing bad or anything. The doc says to just be myself. Don't try to be cool or imitate the guys on the football team, because it won't work. We all have to be ourselves, because if we fake it, smart people see right through it, anyway."

"That's good advice," Steve admitted, leveling his gaze at Kreeger. "Sooner or later, the phonies get caught. And then all their lies, all their deeds come back to haunt them."

"How true," Kreeger said. "Now, Robert, what were we talking about when your uncle walked in?"

"You asked if I thought Maria was a little prosti-tot."

"What!" Steve was halfway out of his chair. "What kind of question is that for a twelve-year-old?"

"Oh, come now, Steve," Kreeger crooned. "You've seen those nubile little cock teasers around the Grove, haven't you?"

"Hey. I don't talk that way in front of Bobby."

"Obviously, you haven't read my essay on verbal honesty. Now, Robert, does Maria have any piercings?"

"A shiny thing in her navel," Bobby answered.

"And I take it she wears clothing that reveals her bare abdomen?"

"Sure.

"As I thought." Kreeger beamed. "A little prostitot."

"That's ridiculous," Steve said.

"We'll see. Robert, have you ever seen Maria's breasts?"

"Not unless you count looking through the window in the dark."

"Well, if you don't try something, she'll think you're gay."

"That's nuts!" Steve thundered. "Bobby, don't listen to him."

"I'm not gay," Bobby said.

Kreeger smiled. "I know that, Robert. But does Maria?"

"Hope so."

"Sounds to me like she really wants you to do her."

Steve leapt to his feet. "That's it. We're out of here."

"In that case, Robert will be detained at Youth Hall, pending mandatory testing."

Steve sank back into his chair.

"Maria never said anything about wanting to do it," Bobby said.

"She won't," Kreeger said confidently. "See, Robert, man is the hunter. For millions of years, man killed the game and took the female of his choice. The female always yields to the strong man. When she says no, she means maybe. When she says maybe, she means yes."

"Wrong!" Steve turned to Bobby. "No means no. Maybe means no. Yes *still* means no because you're too young."

"Bobby, why don't you let your uncle and me talk

for a bit?" Kreeger suggested. "There's a bowl of fruit in the kitchen. And a box of chocolate chip cookies on the counter."

"Awesome. I'll bounce."

Bobby unspooled his legs and headed out.

After the office door closed, Steve got to his feet and leaned over Kreeger's desk. "You can tell the judge anything you want, but I'm not going to let you poison Bobby's mind."

"Relax, Solomon. I'm just testing the boy. I'm worried how Robert might react if Maria rejects him."

"What are you talking about?"

"The way Robert handles stress." Kreeger scribbled a note on a pad. "I'm quite concerned that the boy could become violent with her."

"What the hell are you writing down there?"

"Do you remember that girl who went missing down in the Redlands a few months ago? A boy in the neighborhood had a developmental problem similar to Robert's. The girl's body was never found, and the police lacked evidence, but I feel quite certain the boy was involved."

"Bobby's not violent. In case you forgot, you're the homicidal one, Kreeger."

"So you keep saying." Kreeger rested his hand on the desk, on Maria's photo. "Do you think Robert would mind if I kept this?"

"Yeah." Steve walked toward the window. "And so would I."

Kreeger slipped on a pair of reading glasses and studied the photo. Five seconds. Ten seconds. Way too long. Finally, he said: "Juicy one, isn't she?"

"Sick, Kreeger. Sick and twisted."

Kreeger closed his eyes and murmured: " 'Lolita,

light of my life, fire of my loins. My sin, my soul. Lo-lee-ta.' "

Quoting Nabokov's famous opening lines, admitting his own predilection for pubescent girls. Almost as if he were the patient and Steve the psychiatrist. Did he want help?

"You need to talk about it, is that it?" Steve said, coming back to the desk. "All these years, you've carried this around. Maybe you needed to talk about it when I defended you. Maybe I missed the signs."

Kreeger chanted, as if praying: "Lo-lee-ta. A-man-da. Ma-ri-a." Then he laughed, the cackling laugh of a rooster. "You think Robert's popped Maria's cherry yet?"

Steve didn't even try to hide his disgust. "You don't want help. You just want to wallow in the filth."

"Or have you beat him to it, Solomon? Bird-dogging your nephew's little hoochie?"

"They should send your sick ass to Raiford. You killed Nancy Lamm so you could be with her daughter."

"You know better than that." Kreeger's smile was as sharp as a knife blade. "Or don't you believe a naked woman? Amanda killed her mother, and I took the fall for her. Just as you would have done."

"What does that mean?"

"Let's say that young Robert got rough with Maria and the poor girl died."

"What sick fantasies are you working on now?"

"Just a hypothetical question, Solomon. If Robert killed Maria, wouldn't you do anything to keep him out of prison? Wouldn't you even take the rap for him?"

"That's not what happened with Nancy Lamm. That's just the story you sold a thirteen-year-old girl to keep her in your bed. What drugs did you have her on when you convinced her she killed her mother?"

"Now that I think about it," Kreeger mused, "there is one big difference between the two of us. I admit who I am, and you pretend to be someone completely different than who you are."

* * *

Back in the car, Bobby knew he was in for a goofy lecture. Uncle Steve seemed petrified that any day Bobby would be knocking boots with Maria and she'd get pregnant, which was weird, because so far he had kissed her exactly three times, including once when he missed and ended up with her earlobe in his mouth.

"You know I'd never steer you wrong?" Steve said, before they'd driven a block.

" 'Course I do."

"So you'll listen to me and not that freak Kreeger?"

"Yep."

"You remember what I told you about girls and sex?"

"Have I ever forgotten anything, Uncle Steve?"

"So say it."

"C'mon, it's so dorky."

"Say it, kiddo."

No way around it, Bobby thought, firing out the words. "It shows maturity to keep your purity."

"Attaboy."

"Did you, Uncle Steve? Keep your purity?"

"None of your business."

"That's what I thought."

The "purity" line was so unlike his uncle, Bobby figured he got it from one of those books piled up in the living room.

Raising the Adolescent Boy. Problems with Puberty. Teenagers: An Owner's Manual.

As if I'm a puppy.

Uncle Steve always seemed scared something bad would happen to him.

As if I'm breakable.

Probably because of Mom and the dog shed and a bunch of stuff he didn't even remember.

"Be home before dark."

"Don't put that can of beans in the microwave."

"If your mother calls, I want to know about it."

Sometimes, Bobby wanted to shout: *"I'm not a baby, Uncle Steve."*

Just now, Dr. Bill treated him like a man. Talking about booty like that. Not trying to game him with "purity" and "maturity."

Of course, Uncle Steve hated the guy. Which was weird, because Uncle Steve fessed up that he was the one who cheated back in the murder trial. Driving over here today, he said the doc was dangerous. But he said the same thing about Mom, and Bobby didn't see that at all. Uncle Steve was just so mixed up about all of this. So Bobby decided to keep some secrets. He wouldn't tell Uncle Steve all the things Dr. Bill said. Especially the last thing, right before Uncle Steve came into the room.

"Be a man, Robert. Take what you want. Maria will love it. Trust me. I know."

SOLOMON'S LAWS

11. I won't lie to a lawyer's face or stab him in the back, but if I have the chance, I'll look him in the eye and kick him in the *cojones*.

Thirty-Two

DEFROSTING THE
FROZEN CHOSEN

"You spanked a naked woman?" Victoria couldn't believe this was happening again.

"Not in the way you mean," Steve replied. "It wasn't a *Story of O* deal."

"She rubbed her breasts in your face?"

"Technically, only one breast."

"And you did absolutely nothing to invite the attention?"

"Not a thing, Counselor."

"Your mere presence provokes women to fling off their bath towels and squash their breasts in your face?"

"One woman, one breast," he specified, as if a court reporter were taking it all down.

They were in Steve's Mustang, the radio tuned to the sports talk station. Steve turned up the volume, intending to cut off her questioning, she figured. Victoria listened a moment as a caller complained in grave tones that the University of Miami's touted new wide receiver might, in fact, run the forty-yard dash a tenth of a second too slowly.

She punched a button, turning off the radio. "You were crazy to sneak around in Kreeger's bedroom."

"I was hunting for evidence and I found it."

"You mean the naked pictures? Or the naked woman?"

"I'm gonna nail Kreeger for sexual battery. Amanda was a minor. Extended statute of limitations, relaxed rules of evidence. I can get him, Vic!"

"And how will you persuade her to cooperate? Shower with her next time?"

"All I have to do is convince her that she didn't kill her mother."

"That's all?"

"And that Kreeger's not protecting her. She's protecting him."

"And how exactly will you do this?"

"I'm working on it."

He cut across two lanes and headed up Brickell Avenue, instead of taking I-95 to the Miami Beach flyover.

"Where are we going?" Victoria asked.

"I've got a settlement conference. You can take the car."

"What settlement conference? There's nothing on the calendar."

"Sachs versus Biscayne Supermarkets. The butt-sticking case."

"They're willing to settle, even with an intervening tortfeasor?"

"No one says 'intervening tortfeasor' as sexily as you. In fact, no one else says it at all."

Something wasn't ringing true, she thought as they drove through the canyon of high-rises, home to

Miami's cliff-dwelling lawyers and bankers. "So what's the offer?"

"Nothing yet. But I'll have *mucho dinero* by noon."

So unlike Biscayne Supermarkets, Victoria thought. They fought every slip and fall, no matter how long the banana peel had been rotting on the floor. And this case had even trickier liability problems. Harry Sachs, one of Steve's "repeat customers," as Cece called him, had used the supermarket's rest room and ended up stuck to the toilet seat, which had been coated with Krazy Glue by a prankster. Paramedics used a blow-torch to melt the glue, and the seat peeled off, along with a semicircle of Sachs' butt skin.

"I'm surprised you're getting any offer."

"You know how persuasive I am, Vic. Rolly Ogletree will write me a check before lunch."

Funny, Victoria thought. She'd seen Rolly at motion calendar last week and he'd talked about a fishing trip he had planned for this week. Costa Rica. But she kept quiet. Why would Steve lie about something like that?

He pulled the car to a stop in front of the State Trust Building, a high-rise at Calle Ocho and Brickell. "Wish me luck." He leaned over and kissed her. As he opened the car door, ready to hop out, she said: "Where's your file?"

"You know me, Vic. I don't need no stinking files."

"Uh-huh."

"I keep everything right here," he said, pointing to his head.

He was lying about the Sachs case, she decided. Lying about a conference with Rolly Ogletree. For someone who twisted the truth so often, he wasn't very good at it.

"Good luck, Steve."

Victoria came around to the driver's side, taking her time, watching Steve bound up the steps of the State Trust Building. Sure, that was where Ogletree & Castillo, P.A., maintained its office, defending an array of tight-fisted insurance companies. But something was wrong. She pulled out into traffic heading toward the bridge that would take her downtown, and then across the MacArthur Causeway to Miami Beach. But on impulse, she hung a right onto Brickell Key Drive and parked against the curb.

Okay, Victoria, what are you doing? Surveillance on your boyfriend?

It seemed ridiculous. But with Steve interrogating a naked woman—twice—then his ham-fisted lie just now, what was he up to? Then she saw him in the rear-view mirror. Hurrying across Brickell, crossing to the west side of the street.

Superquick settlement conference, partner.

She watched as he turned north, heading toward the bridge. When he disappeared from sight, she got out of the car and doubled-timed it back to the intersection, a task not so simple in her velvet-toed pumps with the two-inch heels. She stayed on the east side of the street, keeping Steve in sight, staying half a block behind him. It only took a minute. Steve crossed the intersection at Seventh Street, and then ducked into the archway of one of the oldest buildings on Brickell.

The First Presbyterian Church.

Well, at least there wouldn't be a rendevous with a naked woman. But what was he doing there? Steve never even attended synagogue. Why the old church? She jaywalked, dodging traffic, and approached the sturdy building, a four-story Mediterranean Revival structure of stucco and keystone with a copper roof.

She entered through one of the archways, pausing before opening the heavy door to the sanctuary.

What if Steve sees me? How do I explain what I'm doing here? But then, what's he doing here?

She took a breath and walked inside, entering the cool darkness of the vestibule. The place smelled of old wood and wet stones. She took cautious steps, careful to make no sound. The light, a golden hue, filtered into the sanctuary through stained-glass windows. Simple oak pews, walls of bare plaster, a ceiling of acoustical tiles. A spare, clean Protestant look to the place.

Two elderly women sat in a back pew. Then she saw Steve. He sat in a pew at the aisle, one elbow propped on the side rail, his chin in his hand.

Thinking? Praying? Repenting?

At the very least, seeking solitude. Why couldn't he have told her? She had thought Steve lacked the capacity for quiet introspection. But maybe this was where he came for meditation and spiritual guidance. Not making a big deal out of it, just searching for peace in his own way. A flood of warm feelings swept over her. This was, after all, the man she loved. Surely she must have sensed this part of Steve's personality, even though he kept it hidden. She fought the urge to rush down the aisle and throw her arms around him.

No, he deserved this quiet time. She turned and left the sanctuary, wondering if perhaps a house with a yard might be perfectly fine for them after all.

* * *

Steve looked at his watch. He was on time, which meant that opposing counsel was late. It gave him time to think. Had Victoria seemed suspicious? God, how he hated to lie to her. Maybe that was why he'd told a half-truth. This *was* a settlement conference. But it had nothing to do with Harry Sachs and his sticky butt. This was far more personal. Steve had promised Irene Lord that he would get her out of a jam—save her condo from foreclosure—without Victoria ever knowing.

The legal task seemed impossible. Mortgage foreclosures had damn little wiggle room.

"Has the mortgagor paid the mortgagee?"

"No."

"Judgment for mortgagee."

Irene was five months in arrears, and the bank had demanded acceleration of the loan, meaning the entire balance—more than four hundred thousand dollars—was now due. No way Steve could allow the case to go to court.

He heard the *click*ing of leather heels on the tile, turned, and saw Harding Collins moving toward him. Tanned. Tall and trim, with a fine head of gray hair that had been expensively cut. A charcoal suit that shouted Brooks Brothers, and a white shirt with tasteful blue stripes. If Collins weren't a real bank lawyer, he could play one on TV.

"You must be Solomon."

"Sit down, Collins." Steve slid over to give the man room.

"Why on earth did you insist on meeting here?" Collins said.

"I like historic buildings. The wood in here came from the first Presbyterian church in Miami, the one where William Jennings Bryan taught Sunday school."

"I'm very well aware of that."

"Right. Because you're a deacon."

"Not here, of course." A hint of condescension. No, Harding Collins wouldn't attend what amounted to an inner-city church.

"I'm deacon at Riviera Presbyterian. On Sunset Drive."

A Suburban Presbyterian.

Steve considered himself a City Jew, though he had so little faith, he doubted he was entitled to the title. Basically, he'd come up with his own concept of Unintelligent Design, his belief that if a divine entity created humankind, He (or, heaven help us, She) was either dim-witted or a sadist.

Not knowing much about Presbyterians, Steve had enlisted Bobby and Cece for research and investigation. Cece came up with some dirt on Collins, and Bobby announced that "Presbyterian" could be rearranged to spell "Best in Prayer."

"My secretary caught a talk you gave at your church last week," Steve said.

Collins smiled, softened a bit. "Your secretary's a Presbyterian?"

"More like a parolee. But she liked your speech. Something about sympathy and service."

"Gifts of the deacons. Next week, I'm speaking about redemption. Feel free to attend."

"Actually, I play for another team."

"All are welcome," Collins said with a pinched ecumenical smile. "Now, what can I do for you?"

"First Dade Bank has sued to foreclose the condo of my client, Irene Lord. One of your junior associates filed the papers. Unfortunately, Irene's in a bit of financial trouble and could use a break."

"I've heard all the sob stories, Solomon. The family

breadwinner died. The kid's in the hospital. The roof blew off and there's no insurance."

"Yeah, a bunch of whiners out there."

"I represent the bank. My obligation is to the shareholders, not the poor slobs who take on too much debt."

"What about practicing what you preach? Charity, sympathy, gifts of the deacons."

"Religion is one thing, the practice of law is another. You, of all people, must know that."

"Why me of all people?"

"I asked around about you, Solomon. You give sharks a bad name."

"My rules are simple. I don't lie to opposing lawyers or stab them in the back. Head-on, I'll kick you in the *cojones*."

"From where I sit, you're a low-rent lawyer with bargain-basement scruples."

"Actually, I'm a *no*-rent lawyer, but I catch your meaning."

"My answer's the same to you as to anyone else," Collins continued. "No negotiation. Pay up or hit the pavement." His tone had changed. From principled humanitarian to icy defense lawyer in the blink of a time sheet. "So, unless you have a legal defense to the foreclosure . . ."

"Now that you mention it, there's a problem with the papers the bank had Irene sign," Steve said. "The disclosures about the adjustable rates aren't in bold-face. Violates the Banking Act."

"Nice try, Solomon. But every borrower initials the rates clause. That proves actual notice that the rates may go up. And just so you know, we've been hit with lots of consumer lawsuits. I haven't lost one yet, and frankly, I was up against lawyers a helluva lot better than you."

"Different," Steve said.

"I beg your pardon?"

"You were up against lawyers *different* than me. Not better."

Collins laughed as heartily as a poker player who filled an inside straight on the river. "If that's your best shot, I really have to be going—"

"Got one more. I sent my secretary over to the Justice Building the other day. You've had seven parking tickets in the last year."

"I've also jaywalked quite a few times and I might have failed to put out the garbage cans on pickup day." Collins got to his feet.

"Three of the tickets were issued within one block of the Shangri-La Motel on Seventy-ninth Street. You know the neighborhood, Collins? The one the cops call 'Hooker Heaven.' As for the motel, it's what, thirty bucks for thirty minutes?"

Collins sank back into the pew. He shot looks left and right, as if the saints might be eavesdropping.

"Can't blame you for not parking that Mercedes convertible in the motel lot," Steve continued. "But you ought to feed the meters."

"What is it you want, Solomon?" His voice still in even-keeled lawyerly mode.

"The bank gives my client a grace period of eighteen months. Stay all principal and interest during that time. Then she'll resume payments without penalty."

"And if I don't agree?"

Cool and aloof, as if representing someone else. But then, didn't they call Presbyterians the "frozen chosen"?

"Maybe you didn't notice, but the Shangri-La Motel has that camera above the front desk," Steve said. "When you pay for the room, they take excellent digital video. A two-shot of the guy paying and whatever debutante is standing next to him."

Collins' suntan seemed to fade one shade. "You son of a bitch. It's sleazy bastards like you who give the profession a bad name."

"And I suppose foreclosing mortgages is doing God's work?"

"Bastard," Collins repeated.

"Maybe you'd like one of those videos for your talk about redemption."

Collins stayed quiet for a long moment. No more curses. The savvy lawyer seemed to be tallying up the odds. One measly condo mortgage against his life getting sucked down the drain.

I would never, ever follow through on the threat, but you don't know that, do you, Collins?

The bank lawyer barely registered a blip on Steve's personal chart of bad guys. Sure, Collins was a hypocrite. But that ranked pretty far down on Steve's sliding scale of sins. Collins' church work seemed real, and apparently was deeply felt. Maybe his way of repenting for his personal flaws.

So who am I to judge this man?

Florida Bar. Chamber of Commerce. Presbyterian church. Wife and kids and a house in Snapper Creek. In earlier times, Steve thought, Collins would have been called a pillar of the community. Steve wouldn't turn the pillar to salt; the guy simply didn't deserve it.

But I will bluff him till the hookers come home. C'mon, Collins. I'm not robbing the bank. I'm just asking for time.

Collins let out a soft hiss. "It will take a day or so to draw up the papers," he said. Then without a "Good day" or "Screw you," Collins shot one look toward the altar, stood, and walked out.

Steve sat alone, watching dust motes float in the light of the stained-glass windows. He was not particularly pleased with himself. Though it was cool in the sanctuary, he felt his shirt sticking to the pew. He wanted to splash cold water on his face.

Years ago, he had asked his father what the profession was all about.

"Lawyerin's like playing poker with ideas," Herbert Solomon had drawled.

It sounded both romantic and exciting. Like telling a kid that being a cowboy was about riding horses, leaving out all the shit-shoveling. Lawyering, Steve concluded, was more demolition derby than Texas Hold 'Em, and there was at least as much shit-shoveling as at the rodeo.

Thirty-Three

FEELINGS . . . WHOA . . . OH . . . OH . . . FEELINGS

Victoria sipped her Chardonnay and began crumbling blue cheese for the salad. Then she stopped. Steve liked grated Parmesan. She would go with that. But first, she checked the oven. The sweet potatoes—Steve's favorite—were coming along nicely, emitting a syrupy aroma.

This should be his night, she thought. A special night. No arguments, not even a debate over whether figure skating qualifies as a sport. Earlier today, Steve had said he wanted to talk. Not about work. Not about the Dolphins. But about them.

"I want to open up, talk about my feelings."

Yep, he used the dreaded "f" word, the two-syllable one. And this just one day after she spied him sitting in church. A quiet, contemplative Steve. Meditating or praying. Or maybe just thinking about their relationship. So rare in men these days.

She sensed a turning point. And just in time. Everything had become so strained between them.

Maybe it was her fault. Steve had been under so much pressure with Kreeger creeping back into his life. Then there were the two assault-and-battery charges.

And Janice, lurking in the background, threatening to file a custody action.

"You should be more understanding and less demanding, dear."

Amazingly, that's what her mother told her last night. She and The Queen had had dinner at Norman's in the Gables, and over mango-glazed snapper and a bottle of Zinfandel, her mother had expressed warm-and-cuddly sentiments for Steve.

"Stephen has a good heart. Sometimes, I fear you're too harsh with him."

"Me? Harsh?"

"And judgmental. And if I may so, a bit fussy and priggish."

"What!"

"I thought I'd raised you to be a bit more fun."

"And when did you do that, Mother? When you were off in Gstaad or Monaco?"

"Don't get huffy. All I'm saying, a woman has to support her man. Steve's in a real pressure cooker right now. And to throw a hissy fit because he happens to chat with an unclothed girl—well, if you ask me, that's a bit priggish."

Victoria had been too stunned to be angry. The Queen seldom spoke about anyone at great length, other than herself. And it was practically unheard of, a solar eclipse of an event, for her to say anything nice about Steve. But this was the second time in a matter of days that she'd taken his side. So what was going on? Bewilderingly, from the crab cake appetizer to the banana crème brûlée, her mother practically oozed affection for Steve.

"When are you moving in together, dear?"

"What's the hurry?"

"I have my eye on a charming housewarming gift."

"So, suddenly, you think Steve is right for me?"

"Trust me where men are concerned, dear. Despite that thorny exterior, deep inside, Stephen is a loving, caring man who adores you."

Just what were they putting in the sparkling water, anyway?

But the more Victoria thought about Steve, the more she thought her mother was right.

Meaning I've been right, all along. Beginning that night in the avocado grove—Bruce's avocado grove—when I sneaked off with Steve.

He had so many good qualities. His love for Bobby. His quest for justice, even if the road he took was usually off the beaten path. His quirky sense of humor. And, of course, one more thing, something her mother nailed as she sipped her after-dinner cognac.

"May I assume Stephen's good in the sack?"

"You may assume anything you wish, Mother."

"I always liked lanky, wiry men. Stephen looks pretty limber to me."

Right now, Mr. Limber was in the backyard, squirting fluid on the charcoal, lighting a fire for the steaks. T-bones, sweet potatoes, tossed salad, followed by a discussion of feelings, along with Key lime pie. Yes, this was going to be a special night.

Five minutes later, Steve came into the kitchen and headed straight for the refrigerator. What shoes and purses were to women, Victoria thought, the fridge and the TV were to men. He poked around a second and pulled out a cold Sam Adams.

He liked cold beer and rare steak. She liked white wine and grilled salmon. But tonight none of that mattered. Tonight they would get closer than ever. She just knew it.

"How long until you put the steaks on?" she asked.

"A while. You know I like the coals to be glowing. The secret to a great steak—"

"Is the hottest possible fire. Sear the outside, keep the inside juicy. I know, I know. Make mine well done?"

He made a face. "If you say so. Where's the Bobster?"

"In his room, studying."

"Alone?"

She gave him a bittersweet smile. Bobby had been moping around ever since he'd been exiled from the Goldberg house, and Maria had been forbidden from even setting foot on Kumquat Avenue. All by royal decree of the Munoz-Goldbergs.

Complicating the situation was Janice. Steve had begun allowing her to visit Bobby at home, but so far refusing to let her take him anywhere alone. He'd been afraid Janice would snatch him and run.

Now Steve picked up the salad bowl and shook it, shuffling the lettuce, tomatoes, and cucumbers, everything sliced thin, the way he liked it.

"You make a great salad," he said.

"Thanks." She sipped at the wine to let him go on without interruption. When a witness is ready to talk, best to keep quiet.

"You're really terrific in the kitchen," he continued. "A lot of women these days just don't take the time. But the way you balance work and everything else— well, it's pretty impressive."

She picked up the cheese grater and went to work. In truth, her culinary skills were limited to a couple of dishes, but she sensed this was just a warm-up, Steve taking a few practice swings. He looked a little nervous. Apparently, stalking a serial killer was not as scary a task as plumbing his own emotional depths.

"You're good at so many things," Steve went on. "You're amazing with Bobby; the kid adores you."

"It's mutual."

Okay, now we're moving in the right direction, though at the speed of a manatee. C'mon, Steve. Let's go from the nephew's feelings to the uncle's feelings.

"Maybe you and I can talk a bit while Bobby's still in his room," Steve said. "About personal stuff."

She stopped grating the cheese in midstroke. "Sure."

"There are things I've wanted to say to you for a long time, but you know how it is. . . ."

He plucked a tomato slice out of the bowl and let the words dangle in the air. Tongue-tied. Not his usual state. His dark hair was messed, and there was a smudge of charcoal on his cheek. He looked like a kid, she thought, in part perhaps because of his T-shirt: *"I Am Not Infantile, You Stinky Butt Poophead."*

"Go ahead, Steve. It won't hurt."

"So why does it feel like opening a vein?"

"When you're in a relationship, you've got to trust the other person. You can share feelings, expose your fears, your weaknesses." She reached over and wiped the smudge from his face.

He took a breath and sighed, as if to say, *"Here goes."*

She picked up her wineglass and waited. It was a two-sip wait. There was so much she wanted to hear. Words like "love" and "plans" and "future," and even "marriage" and "children." Sure, she knew he was conflicted. Men were like that. They yearn for the love of a woman, and then when they get it, they break into a cold sweat.

"You remember how I always told you about the College World Series?" Steve said.

That puzzled her, but she went with it. "U.M. down by a run in the ninth inning. You got picked off third base to end the game."

"What else? What do I always say?"

This must be some sort of metaphor, she thought, but what could it be? Steve was bringing back the most humiliating day of his life. He'd let his teammates down. So maybe he wanted to say: *I want us to be a team forever, Vic, and I'll never let you down.*

"You always say you got in under the tag," she replied. "The ump blew the call."

"Yeah, maybe the photos make it look that way. But the thing is, I felt the third baseman's glove swipe my hand when I dived for the base. All this time, Vic, I've been lying to myself and everybody else. The damn truth is, I was out."

Okay, Steve, you were picked off. Your team lost. What's it have to do with us?

But she didn't want to appear critical. What was it her mother had said?

"A woman must support her man."

She wrapped both arms around his neck and moved so close, their noses nearly touched. "I understand, sweetheart. You feel your life has been a lie."

"Well, not my whole life. But I feel so much better telling you what really happened."

"So that our relationship can move to a new level?" Prompting him, trying to make it easier.

"What level is that?"

"I thought you wanted to open up, discuss feelings, remember?"

"Yeah. I was feeling bad and now that I told you the truth, I feel better."

"*You* feel better?" She took a step back, astonished. "What about us? What about words like 'love' and 'plans' and 'future'? Where do I fit into your life now that we know you were picked off fair and square?"

Steve seemed startled. He took a gulp of his beer, then moved toward the window. In the yard, white smoke billowed from the hibachi. Either a new pope had been selected, or it was time to put on the steaks.

He turned to face her. "Vic, all these years, I never told anyone else what really happened in that game. I couldn't have told you if I didn't love you."

"Keep going, partner. What else?"

"I'm sorry I've been such a jerk about moving in together. I figured everything was good the way it was. We each had our own space, and I was afraid that if something changed, we'd be headed for the great unknown. So I guess I was scared."

"And now?"

"Life is the great unknown, isn't it? If we shy away from risks, we're running from life."

"So you do have plans? For us, I mean."

"My mind's full of plans, except I call them 'hopes.' When we met, I didn't dare *plan* you'd want to be with me. But sure, I hoped you would. Even when we got together, my hopes all came with fears. The biggest one, you'd wake up one morning and realize you'd made a gigantic mistake. So I couldn't talk about any of this. Even now it's hard for me to believe you want to live with me and help me raise Bobby. As for the future—well, I've got hopes there, too."

She didn't know how far to push him, but she couldn't leave that hanging. "What sort of hopes?"

"You know, permanent stuff."

"Yeah?"

"Marriage. Kids." His voice a whisper.

"Is that what you really want, Steve?" Asking ever so gently, trying not to frighten him.

"Someday," he said quickly. "If all goes well."

Okay, a tiny retreat. But he'd moved a mile forward and only one step backward. Once you say "marriage," the word can't be erased.

Victoria took both Steve's arms and wrapped them around her waist, because the poor guy seemed incapable of movement. Then she cupped his face in her hands and kissed him. As their lips touched, she murmured, "Those are my hopes, too."

She kissed him again and their bodies folded into each other, the contours fitting perfectly, a yin and yang of man and woman. "And by the way, I've studied those photos from the game. You did get in under the tag."

"No, Vic. I remember the glove hitting my hand."

"You remember wrong, lover. You were safe. You've always been safe."

Thirty-Four

A THUMP IN THE NIGHT

Several hours after the words "marriage" and "kids" tumbled from his mouth like skydivers leaping from a plane, Steve Solomon took stock of his life.

I'm a happy man.

Strike that, Madam Court Reporter. "Happy" doesn't quite say it. I'm a living beer commercial. I'm playing volleyball on the beach with the woman I love.

He had shared his feelings with Victoria and it hadn't hurt. They loved each other and had recommitted. They were about to take the giant step of buying a place and moving in together. Steve, Victoria, and Bobby. A ready-made family.

Bobby seemed happier at dinner, too. Steve made him laugh, and the kid worked up his first anagram in a week. Who knew that "President George Bush" could be rearranged to spell "The person is buggered"?

Now Victoria lay alongside Steve in bed. They had eaten their steaks and polished off an entire pie. They had talked some more in the bedroom, had made love, talked some more, made love again, and talked even more.

Steve was just drifting off to sleep, thinking he wouldn't trade places with anyone else in the world, when he heard the *thump*. There was a steady breeze, and sometimes a giant palm frond would break loose from the tree and sideswipe the house on the way to the ground. But that sound was different. He felt too tired and content to get up, but he did, anyway.

The house was dark, and he was naked. He reached under the bed, grabbed an aluminum softball bat, and padded out of the bedroom. In the kitchen, he peered through the sliding glass door. The backyard was an ominous greenish black, the foliage backlit by a neighbor's powerful anticrime spotlights. Something seemed different, but what was it?

It only took a second. The grill cover was on the ground. A metal lid, it should have been leaning against the house, where he'd left it. But it had been moved, maybe two feet, as if someone walking along the house in the dark had stumbled over it.

Steve unlocked the glass door, slid it open, and slipped outside, gripping the bat in his right hand. It was light and whippy. He could crush someone's skull with it, no problem.

He smelled something burning. What the hell?

Cigarette smoke.

Then a woman's voice, out of the darkness. "You've gotten bigger since you were nine."

Heart racing, Steve wheeled around, ready to swing the bat.

"Over here, Stevie."

He wheeled the other way and saw the glow of the cigarette and a heavyset figure reclining on the chaise lounge.

"Jesus, Janice! What are you doing here?"

"Here. Take this." She sat up in the chaise and tossed a towel at him. "You remember how Mom always made me give you a bath when you were little? You hated it."

Steve wrapped the towel—wet and cold—around his waist. "You stoned, Janice? What the hell's going on?"

"Clean and sober. I came to see Bobby."

"In the middle of the night?"

"It's the only time we can talk without you hovering over us like a wicked stepmother. Or stepuncle, or whatever the hell you are."

"I'm his caregiver. I'm his father and his mother, and I'd rather see him raised by wolves than by you."

"You're so great at it, where the hell is he?"

"In bed. Sleeping."

"Yeah, well, I just rapped on his window for ten minutes and he ain't there."

Steve's first thought was that Bobby was sleeping so soundly, he didn't hear Janice at the window. But no, the kid was a nervous sleeper. A car door slamming down the block, a police siren on Douglas Road, a teakettle whistling . . . everything woke him up.

A second later, Steve raced into the house and down the corridor. He threw open the door to Bobby's room and flicked on the lights. The bed was messed. And empty.

"Bobby!" Steve yelled. "Bobby! Where are you? Bobby!"

Thirty-Five

ON BEING A MAN

Steve paced in the living room. Victoria made coffee. Janice smoked.

"Here's what we know," Steve said, straining to be analytical, fighting the fear. "Bobby's bike is gone. That's a good sign. If he'd been snatched, he wouldn't be on his bike."

Steve wanted to believe he was right. When he'd seen the empty bed, his first searing thought was that Kreeger had kidnapped the boy. But no, the bike changed all that.

"That Juban princess," Janice said. "Maybe he went over to her house, and we'll find him up a tree."

"The Goldbergs live a block away," Steve said. "He wouldn't ride his bike. But we gotta check it out anyway. I'll walk over there."

"Not with the restraining order." Victoria came out of the kitchen, carrying a pot of coffee on a tray. "You can't go near their property. I'll do it."

"I'll go along," Janice said.

"No. You'll just start a fight," Steve said.

"Me? You're the one who busted the guy in the mouth."

"Stop it, both of you!" Victoria said it with such authority that they both clammed up. "Time's wasting. I'll go alone. Call me on the cell if anything—"

The doorbell rang. At this time of night, it was a sound as chilling as a scream. Steve's imagination took flight. He pictured a police cruiser, a young officer gnawing his lip, a sorrowful look on his face.

"Are you the next of kin of a boy named Robert Solomon?"

Steve hurried to the door and threw it open.

Myron Goldberg stood there in his bathrobe and sneakers. His wife was half a step behind him.

"Maria's missing!" Eva shoved her spouse aside. *"Desaparecida!"*

Steve's spirits soared. "That's great, Eva!"

"What!"

"Is she here?" Myron asked.

"No. Bobby's missing, too. But that means they're together. It means they're okay."

"But where?" Myron said. "Where could they be?"

Eva pushed through the open door. "If you put them up to this, Solomon—"

"Back off, bitch." Janice walked into the foyer.

"I should have known," Eva said. "Are you behind this?"

"What's the big frigging deal? They'll be back when they're done." Janice gave Eva a double-chinned grin. " 'Course, they ain't gonna be virgins no more."

"Puta," Eva snarled.

"Okay, everybody relax," Steve said. "Let's work together on this. Myron, is Maria's bike gone?"

"I don't know. We didn't look."

"I'm betting it is and they're within a couple miles of home. Where does Maria usually ride?"

"The two of us go down Old Cutler," Eva said. "The path to Matheson Hammock."

"Bobby knows the place, too. That's a start. I'll drive down there, but we'll need people at each of our houses."

"Janice and I will stay here," Victoria said.

Meaning the Goldbergs should head home. Smart, Steve thought. Otherwise, Janice and Eva would surely end up mud wrestling before daybreak.

It only took Steve a minute to step into his running shorts and a T-shirt. He was headed to the door when Janice said: "I need a drink, Stevie. You got any liquor?"

"Bottle of Jack Daniel's above the bar."

"Looked there. Didn't see any Jack."

Steve wasn't about to start searching for whiskey for his sister. But as he got into the Mustang, he wondered about it. What happened to that new bottle of Jack Daniel's, the expensive one, Single Barrel?

* * *

"Ooh, that's strong," Maria said, sipping at the golden liquor. She took another swig, then passed the bottle to Bobby. "Bourbon, right? My dad drinks it."

"Sour-mash whiskey," Bobby corrected, "but people call it bourbon." He raised the bottle to his lips, took a gulp. His eyes watered as the liquid seared his throat.

They were walking at the edge of a mini–rain forest inside Fairchild Tropical Garden, navigating a tangle of woody vines thick as high-transmission wires. It was spooky in the dark, especially if you've seen those movies where killers in hockey masks jump out from behind trees.

Bobby screwed the top back on the bottle and they

continued through the forest. They wound their way past towering ficus trees, giant ferns brushing against their knees, sneakers sinking into the moist earth. Bobby carried a flashlight, but that only made the shadows deeper and scarier. He slipped and nearly fell. Totally uncool, but Maria didn't laugh. Then, hopping over a slippery log, he lost his grip on the flashlight. The beam skittered off to one side, and for a split second Bobby thought he saw the shape of a person, someone looking their way. But when he picked up the flashlight and pointed in that direction, no one was there.

He shook it off. This was maybe the best night of his life, and it was just beginning. An hour earlier, when they had gotten on their bikes, Maria took the ball cap from Bobby's head and put it on, tucking her hair in. The gesture, so feminine, made Bobby's heart ache. Maria was wearing short-shorts and a pink sleeveless T-shirt that had *"Spoiled"* spelled out in rhinestones with a glittery heart dotting the "i." In the light of the street lamps, her complexion was the color of café Cubano, heavy with cream.

They had ridden their bikes along the Old Cutler path, going airborne where the roots of banyan trees poked up through the asphalt. In the moonlight, Bobby watched the gentle curve of Maria's calves as she pedaled, could see a line of smooth caramel skin above her shorts. She was hot, so totally hot. He couldn't believe he was here.

"The next full moon. The rain forest at Fairchild. You'll score, I promise you."

Dr. Bill had told him that. He knew so much that Uncle Steve didn't. Or maybe Uncle Steve knew but wouldn't tell him. Like girls getting hot at the full moon, even girls who weren't hoochies to start with.

They'd ridden down Old Cutler to Matheson, crossing a marshy hammock, inhaling the salty smells, listening to the croaking frogs and the creaking insects. Then, standing alongside a tidal pool, a full moon dangling over the bay, they'd kissed.

The kiss was tentative, Bobby leaning in, waiting for Maria, hoping she'd join the action. She did, smelling of oranges and vanilla, her mother's perfume. The second kiss was softer, slower, wetter, deeper. He'd gotten a raging boner.

Slammin' idea, Dr. Bill.

They'd started hitting the Jack Daniel's then. Rocket fuel, ninety-four proof, according to the label. Bobby's stomach was a little queasy, and his forehead felt sweaty. What they needed was something to eat.

"Bring along something to drink. Vodka or rum or bourbon. The higher the proof, the better. Loosen her up."

But Dr. Bill hadn't said anything about food. Pretzels and chips would have been good. Maybe a blanket, too. And condoms?

But where would he get condoms, anyway? Uncle Steve didn't use them. Bobby had seen Victoria's birth control pills in the bathroom, looking like little candies in a Pez dispenser.

After three swigs of bourbon, two hiccups, and five wet kisses, Bobby and Maria got back on their bikes, rode back through the hammock, then down the path to Fairchild. The gates were locked, so they hid their bikes in a hibiscus hedge and climbed over a fence. Now they were headed through the rain forest toward the tropical fruit pavilion to find something to eat.

The pavilion was a giant greenhouse with a roof shaped like a pyramid to accommodate large trees.

The door was unlocked, and once inside, Bobby set about picking fruit. The lichees and passion fruit he recognized, but he needed to read the little signs stuck in the ground for the rest: jackfruit, langsat, sapodilla, and a bunch of others, scaly and unappetizing.

They sat on a grassy patch, nibbled the fruit, and drank more of the whiskey, kissing between nibbles. The passion fruit was tart, the tiny black seeds crunchy. The jackfruit was spicy hot and the lichees sweet like grapes. None of it went that well with the whiskey. Bobby lay back on the grass, looking at the treetops that seemed to be swaying in the breeze, but there was no wind here.

I'm dizzy. Dizzy from whiskey and kisses that taste like passion fruit.

Maria was talking about a girl at school, a total slut, who after P.E. used a banana to show her posse how to, you know, go down on a guy, but she gagged on it, then spit it up so that it squished out her nose.

"Totally grossed everybody out," Maria said. The story didn't make Bobby's stomach feel any better.

Maria was giggling, going back over details of the banana episode. Bobby was half listening, when he thought he heard the door to the pavilion squeak open, but maybe not. A moment later, Maria leaned over and kissed him again. Then, he wasn't quite sure how it happened, they were lying on the grass, their legs wrapped around each other, kissing and moaning and rubbing their bodies against each other.

Bobby let a hand slip under Maria's T-shirt, but she latched on to his wrist and pushed him away. A second later, he feinted with that hand, then sneaked the other hand under the shirt—*If Pickett had used a similar zigzag, the Battle of Gettysburg would have turned out way differently*—and a second later, he had hold of her bra. The fabric was cottony soft, and he could see the top of it peeking out of her shirt.

Pink brassiere. The letters rearranged themselves in his brain. BARE PENIS RISK.

He tugged at the bra.

"Bobby, don't."

Remembering what Dr. Bill had told him. *"Man is the hunter. Man kills the game and takes the female of his choice."*

"No, Bobby." She pushed his hand away again. Firmly, the way mothers teach them, Bobby figured.

"C'mon, Maria. You want it. I know you do."

Hearing the doc's voice now, as if he were right here watching. *"When she says no, she means maybe. When she says maybe, she means yes."*

"Bobby, I like you. I really do. But let's just kiss for now."

Sweat poured out of him, and his stomach heaved. But his boner was so hard, it had started to hurt. He took her left hand in his right hand and pinned it to her side. Then he slid his left hand around her back and tried to unfasten her pink bra.

"Bobby! No!"

She wriggled left and right, but maybe she just wanted to excite him more.

"The female always yields to the strong man."

He couldn't unsnap the damn thing, so he yanked the bra, and it slipped halfway around her torso.

"Ouch! Bobby, what are you doing?"

"Be a man, Robert. Take what you want. Maria will love it. Trust me. I know."

"You'll love it, Maria," Bobby said, deepening his voice. "Trust me. I know."

Thirty-Six

WHAT GIRLS WANT

The air should not smell so sweet on a night like this, Steve thought.

Top down on the Mustang, the scent of jasmine in the moist air, a full moon ducking in and out of clouds, he drove down Old Cutler Road, more worried than he had let on to the others.

With all the chaos swirling around—Janice and Kreeger, Victoria and Irene, Freskin and Goldberg—Steve wondered if he had been spending enough time with Bobby. Had he let his own problems distract him from the number one priority in his life?

Stop worrying. Bobby's okay.

Steve kept telling himself that. The boy hadn't run away from home; he hadn't been kidnapped. Maria's the first girl who showed him the rhinestone in her navel, so he's experimenting. They're probably necking somewhere under a palm tree, and they'll show up at dawn, sweaty and mosquito-bitten. It's normal.

He's okay, dammit. Stop worrying.

Steve had already checked out Cocoplum, driving down to the bay, then coming back up to the circle at the Gables Waterway. Now he hung a left at Matheson

Hammock. He passed the deserted picnic area and drove parallel to the bicycle path, which wound through a tangle of black-and-red mangrove trees. He stopped at the saltwater pond. No cars in the parking lot. Bicycle rack empty.

No Bobby. And no Maria.

Steve got out of the car and walked around the pond, just yards from the open bay. The tide was out, and a marshy smell hung in the air. A passel of herons tracked across the wet sand, seeking an early breakfast. Across the bay, a few lights twinkled in the condos of Key Biscayne. To the north, the downtown skyscrapers were dark.

The silence was broken by a Boston Whaler chugging out of the channel, an early start for a day of fishing. Over the ocean at the horizon, flashes of lightning brightened a ribbon of clouds. The wind was kicking up, rippling the water. The full moon was obscured by a growing cloud cover but still bright enough to light the sky, like a lamp through a shade. The forecast was for rain, a band of squalls in advance of a cold front.

Steve got back in the car and drove farther south on Old Cutler, pulling into Fairchild Tropical Garden. He'd brought Bobby there a few times, the boy enjoying the peacefulness of the place. Noises still tightened him up. Tranquillity seemed essential to his therapy.

Steve parked at the gate. Everything locked. He got out of the car, leaving the headlights on. Crouched down on a narrow dirt path that ran up to a perimeter fence near the entrance. Next to a hibiscus hedge, bicycle tracks. Two bikes had been here.

Okay, so what?

Well, for starters, the tracks were fresh. It had

rained briefly in late afternoon, and the tracks would have been made after that.

Great. Give yourself a Boy Scout badge, but like I said before, so what?

Well, you couldn't ride past this point. The dirt path dead-ended at the fence. So the bikers must have stopped and parked their bikes here. Maybe they went inside.

Yeah? So . . .

Steve didn't know. Except . . . in the reddish dirt two sets of tire tracks approached the fence, but only one left. So what the hell happened to the other bike?

Just then, Steve's cell phone rang, the sound jarring in the stillness. On the screen, he recognized his home phone number.

"Yeah, Vic?"

"Bobby just rode up."

"Great. Maria at her house?"

"No." He heard the tension in her voice. "Steve—Bobby doesn't know where she is."

* * *

Just before dawn, Steve slid the Mustang to a stop in his driveway and someone screamed.

He hadn't seen Eva Munoz-Goldberg running toward his front door. She nimbly leapt to one side and the front fender just missed her. In great shape from step class or tai chi, Steve figured. Good thing, or he'd be facing vehicular manslaughter charges.

Eva's momentum carried her toward the flagstone path leading to the house. She hopped over a small shrub, then lost her balance on the dew-slick flagstone. The second scream came when she pitched forward, scraping a knee. Steve admired the way Eva scrambled to her feet and headed for his front door without stopping to curse at him.

Bobby's bike was leaning against the pepper tree. Meaning the boy was inside. Steve heard the shouts before he made it to the front door. He found Eva in the living room, her knee bleeding, hair a mess, shrieking at Bobby. "Where is she! Where's my daughter!"

Janice slung a protective arm around Bobby's shoulder and kept her considerable girth between her son and Eva. "Back off, bitch, or you're gonna need some more plastic surgery."

"Thank God you're here, Steve," Victoria said.

Steve wasn't sure which was more disconcerting, Eva screeching or Janice holding on to Bobby. "C'mere, kiddo." He pried the boy away from his mother, hoisted him up by the armpits, and worked both arms under his butt. It's easy to do with a toddler, not a twelve-year-old, even one as gangly as Bobby.

Bobby was trembling and pale and he smelled sour. He looped his legs around Steve's waist and put his head on a shoulder.

"You stink, kiddo."

"Threw up."

He carried Bobby into the kitchen, just to get away from the others. He could hear Victoria telling the two women to give them some space, let Steve handle this.

"I'm sorry, Uncle Steve."

"It's okay. Where's Maria?"

"Dunno. We were at Fairchild. She got mad at me and left."

"What made her mad?"

"I was stupid."

"Yeah?"

"I tried what Dr. Bill said . . ."

Steve felt his jaw clench and a wave a heat flared through his gut. "Dr. Bill?"

"He said I should take Maria there at the full moon because that's when girls get really hot. And then she'd want to do it."

"But when you got there, Maria said no?"

"Yeah."

"And what'd you do?"

"At first, I sort of pushed her. But then I stopped. 'Cause of that dorky stuff you taught me. 'No means no. Maybe means no. It takes maturity to keep your purity.' All that stuff."

"Good boy. But Maria was still mad at you?"

"I guess. I got sick and hurled chunks all over some bromeliads. I went over to the lake to clean up, and when I got back she wasn't there. I got my bike, but hers was gone. I thought she was riding home."

"Did you try to catch up with her?"

"Yeah. How'd you know?"

"Because that's what I would have done. Ride really fast. If she only had a few minutes' head start, you would have caught her."

"That's what I tried. But I never saw her."

Because she was snatched! When she came to pick up her bike, someone was waiting.

It came back to him then. That day in Kreeger's office.

"Just a hypothetical question, Solomon. If Robert killed Maria, wouldn't you do anything to keep him out of prison? Wouldn't you even take the rap for him?"

Steve felt his arms involuntarily tighten around his nephew. Conflicting emotions. Thankful Bobby was safe. But absolute horror at the thought that his girlfriend could be dead by now. Maybe Bobby heard

Steve's breaths quicken or felt his heart thumping. Whatever it was, the boy whimpered.

A second later, Victoria was alongside, running a hand through Bobby's hair. He stretched his neck like a cat that wanted to be petted. A second after that, Janice was there, too.

"Bitch went outside," Janice reported. "How's my boy?"

Bobby shrugged. His arms tightened around Steve's neck.

"Stevie, can I have my son, please?"

"Yes."

"Because you've got no right to keep him away from—" Startled, she stopped. "Did you say yes?"

Steve put the boy down. "We gotta all be on the same team, Jan."

"Why? What's going on?"

"Take Bobby to bed and we'll talk."

Puzzled, Janice draped a meaty arm around the boy and walked him toward his bedroom.

"What's happened, Steve?" Victoria asked.

He could barely get out the words. "Kreeger. He's got Maria. He's going to rape her and kill her. And frame Bobby. All to punish me."

Victoria blinked twice. Then she swiftly recovered. "I'll talk to Eva. You call the police."

Just then, a woman's scream. Steve recognized it immediately. It was the third time he'd heard it that morning.

Steve and Victoria raced outside. Eva was standing next to Bobby's bike. The zipper on the vinyl bag attached to the seat was open. Eva clutched something to her chest. A moment later, when Steve realized what it was, a feeling of dread spread through him like a poisonous tide.

"Where is she!" Eva ran toward Steve, flailing at him. "Goddammit!" Her voice broke between spasms of sobs. "What did he do to her?"

Punches landed on his chest, his shoulder, his arms. One wayward blow glanced off his temple. Steve made no effort to ward off the punches. He was already in such pain, it simply didn't hurt to be hit by a petite woman, her face wet with tears, a small pink brassiere wrapped around her fist.

Thirty-Seven

FROM THE SWAMP TO THE SEA

The cop had a familiar face.

A mini-Afro. A name tag that said *"Teele."* A skeptical look.

Sure, the guy who arrested me at the radio station. The second time.

Bad break, Steve thought. They were standing in Steve's driveway just after seven A.M. Janice was inside, sacked out on the sofa. Bobby was asleep in his bedroom, Victoria sitting watch alongside. Myron and Eva were back in their house on Loquat, giving statements to Teele's partner, Rodriguez.

"Dr. Kreeger is canoeing on the Suwannee," Teele said.

"Canoe-ing on the Su-wan-nee?" Steve used his best derisive tone, dragging out the words. "That is the worst fucking alibi I've ever heard, and my clients have used some doozies."

Teele lowered his voice into serious cop mode. "You're saying Dr. Bill kidnapped this girl and planted evidence to incriminate your nephew, but you've got no proof. Now, I listen to Dr. Bill's radio show . . ."

Oh, great. A fan.

". . . and I think he makes some good points. As for the girl, she could be sleeping in somebody's backyard, and any minute she'll come riding up the street on her bike."

Cops usually assumed the worst because they see the worst. But this guy was an optimist, Steve thought. "So you reached Kreeger on his cell?"

"Couldn't get him. He's up the river past Hatchbend, where there's no service."

Up the river past Hatchbend? Jeez, I'm in Mayberry with Deputy Barney Fife.

"What the hell's he doing up there?" Steve demanded.

"Fishing for largemouth bass, the way we hear it."

"Lemme guess. The woman living at Kreeger's house gave you this cock-and-bass story."

Teele checked his little cop pad. "Mary Amanda Lamm. That's correct."

"Kreeger brainwashed her. She'd say anything he wanted her to."

"Was she lying when she said both you and your nephew are patients of Dr. Kreeger?"

"Not patients, exactly."

The cop made a note on the pad. "So you're not under court order to see Dr. Kreeger?"

"Okay, technically true, but—"

"For sexual deviancy."

"No!"

The cop used his pen to scratch his scalp through the mini-Afro. "I pulled the report, Solomon. The boy's a peeper. And Ms. Lamm claims she came out of the shower one day and found you lurking in her bathroom."

"*Bedroom,*" Steve corrected, a lawyer slicing the

bologna too thin. "I was lurking in her bedroom. But that's got nothing to do with the court ordering me to see Kreeger."

"Right. That would be for your violent streak."

"Look, Teele, Maria's missing. The clock's ticking. By the time you guys get off your butts, she could be dead."

"I hope not, sir. For your sake. Because your nephew was the last person to see the girl. By his own admission, he made unwelcome advances to her while inebriated, and her brassiere was found in his belongings. The way I see it, the only evidence points straight at him."

* * *

Victoria was the first one out of the Mustang when Steve pulled to a stop in front of Kreeger's home. The morning had turned windy and gray and smelled of rain. They'd left Bobby with Janice, but Cece was on the way there to chaperone.

On the drive to the Gables, Victoria had asked Steve if he had a plan.

"Amanda's going to tell us where Kreeger is," he said flatly.

"And betray her lover?"

"There's a glimmer of something good inside her. We just have to tap into that."

Victoria wasn't so sure. "And how do we do that?"

"Good cop, bad cop."

"I assume I'm the good cop."

"Which means you go first. If you don't get any-where, I'll take over."

Victoria remained skeptical but kept quiet. No use in chipping away at Steve's confidence.

Amanda answered the door, for once wearing clothes. Two articles of clothing, to be exact: a red tank top and tight white short-shorts. No bra and clearly no panties, judging from the outline of her taco. No makeup. Hair tied in pigtails. A twenty-year-old trying to look fourteen.

She smiled and said, "Goody, more visitors. Hey, Ms. Lord, did you get that bikini wax yet?"

Victoria shot a look at Steve, who shrugged as if to say sorry.

"Cutie here really admired my landing strip." Amanda gave Steve a flirtatious tilt of the chin.

"Cut the bullshit, Amanda," Steve said. "We've got to talk."

She ignored him, focused on Victoria. "I offered Cutie a closer look, but he said he'd have to think about it."

"How unusual," Victoria replied. "*Cutie* so seldom thinks before acting."

One minute later, they were all inside. A nondescript living room with a sofa and two facing chairs. An old fireplace. A floor of Dade County pine. A coffee table with a bowl of slightly overripe fruit. No personal items, other than the oil painting of Kreeger on a power boat.

"Amanda, we really need your help," Victoria said, her tone pleasant.

"Like I told the cops, Uncle Bill's canoeing upstate."

"We don't think so." Still soft, still pleasant. "We think he kidnapped a twelve-year-old girl. We're afraid what he'll do to her if we don't stop him."

"That's silly," Amanda said, sounding like a preteen herself. She picked up a green apple from the bowl, tucked both legs under herself, and started munching.

Amanda didn't seem overly concerned, Victoria thought. A missing girl. Her lover accused. And here she was, nibbling away on a Granny Smith. Was it possible, Victoria wondered, that Amanda was as much a sociopath as Kreeger?

"Uncle Bill's a lover, not a killer," Amanda added with a sly smile. "And I ought to know."

"Dammit, Amanda!" Steve said, breaking in before he was supposed to. "Kreeger killed a guy named Jim Beshears. He killed a boat captain named Oscar De la Fuente. And he killed your mother."

"Now I know you're lying," Amanda said. "I'm the one who killed the witch."

She said it with a certain amount of glee that Victoria found unsettling. "You were thirteen, Amanda. Kreeger was giving you drugs when he seduced you. Your memory can't be trusted."

Steve picked up the story and they tag-teamed her: "Your mother found out about the two of you and they had a big fight. Kreeger hit her with a skimmer pole and pushed her into the hot tub. Then he convinced you that you'd done it."

"Like I said before, you have everything bass ackwards." Amanda giggled. "I seduced Uncle Bill. I was smoking a little weed, but that's it. Bill gave me some Valium after I killed Mom because I was freaking out. I wanted to call the cops and confess, but Bill said he'd take care of everything."

"He's brainwashed you, goddammit!" Steve said.

Amanda took a dainty bite from the apple. "Where was Mom hit, Cutie?"

"Right side of the skull."

"Uncle Bill's right-handed. If they were having a fight, wouldn't he have hit her on the left side?"

"Pincher covered that. Your mother must have turned and started walking away when Kreeger hit her."

Amanda's *"ha-ha-ha"* seemed contrived, like everything else about her, Victoria thought.

"That's not how it happened," Amanda said. "Me and Mom. We were facing each other. She called me a little whore, said she was gonna send me away to some school for fuckups and I'd never see Bill again. I picked up the pool thingie and hit her as hard as I could. She fell into the hot tub, and I just stood there and watched her drown."

Amanda picked up another apple from the bowl and flung it—*left-handed*—at Steve. He caught the apple and exchanged looks with Victoria.

"Uncle Bill got rid of the pool thingie," Amanda continued. "He came up with the story that Mom slipped and hit her head. The jury didn't believe him. Why should they? It wasn't true."

"I don't believe you," Steve said.

"But I do." Victoria stood, grabbed the apple from Steve, and tossed it from hand to hand as she spoke. "And if I'm right, if you're telling the truth, you owe your life to Kreeger. I'll bet you stayed faithful to him all those years he was in prison."

"I was a good girl. I promised I'd wait for him, and I did."

Victoria nodded in agreement. "After what he did for you—covering up a murder you committed—how could you do anything else?"

"You got it, Ms. Lord."

Victoria took a step toward Amanda. "Which means you'll never betray him, no matter what he's done in the past, no matter what he's doing now."

Amanda winked at Steve. "She's smarter than you are, Cutie."

"I know," Steve admitted. He turned to Victoria, looking defeated. "So if Amanda killed her mother, I lost a case for an innocent man. No wonder Kreeger hates me."

"But you were right about everything else." Still tossing the shiny green apple from hand to hand, Victoria paced in front of the sofa where Amanda sat cross-legged. "Kreeger killed Beshears and De la Fuente, didn't he, Amanda?"

"I'll never tell," she sang in her little-girl voice.

"You know one difference between Steve and me?" Victoria asked.

"I don't know and I don't care."

"Steve would never hurt a woman. It's not in him. But me . . ."

And before Steve saw it coming, Victoria drew back her right arm and threw a punch as hard as she could. Not a jab. And not a hook. A fist that had an apple in it and all her weight behind it.

The Granny Smith smashed squarely into Amanda's nose.

There were three sounds, coming a second apart. The *crack* of cartilage, the *thump* of Amanda's butt hitting the floor, and a *yelp*.

* * *

Steve heard a *yelp*ing sound, realized it had come from him. A stream of blood ran down Amanda's face; a pink bubble emerged from her lips as she exhaled through the torrent.

Did I just see what I think I saw? Did Vic just TKO Amanda with a Granny Smith?

"Fucking bitch!" Amanda bleated, her hands covering her face. "You broke my nose."

"Put your head back till it stops bleeding," Victoria ordered, suddenly the Nurse Ratched of the law business.

"Jesus, Vic. Why'd you do that?"

He was flummoxed. In all their time together, the most violence she'd ever shown was a wicked backhand on the tennis court.

"Don't you get it, Steve? We can plead and beg and try to find that glimmer of humanity you think is inside this sick puppy, but it won't do any good."

"And punching her will?"

"You're a Democrat and I'm a Republican."

"Yeah?"

"You're suspicious of the use of force. But the only way we're gonna get anything from her is to go Abu Ghraib."

"No way."

Victoria had strayed off script. Steve was supposed to be the bad cop, but apparently he hadn't been bad enough.

Still bleeding, Amanda got to her feet. She reached for a cell phone from the coffee table, but Victoria grabbed her wrist and twisted her arm behind her back.

"Ow!" Amanda rasped. "What are you, a dyke or something?"

Victoria snatched the phone with her free hand and threw it hard toward the fireplace. Her aim was high—not enough follow-through—and the phone sailed into the painting of Kreeger aboard his boat. It left a gash in the canvas.

"Bill ain't gonna be happy," Amanda said, no more little girl in her voice. "He loves that picture."

Still hanging on to Amanda's wrist, Victoria used a foot to kick the woman's leg out from under her. Amanda fell to her knees, Victoria tightening the grip and bending Amanda's arm like a chicken wing. Blood flowed from her nose and puddled on the pine floor. Victoria used the woman's arm like a crowbar, pushing higher and higher, until the back of her wrist lay flat against her neck.

"Fuck! That hurts."

"Vic, what are you doing?"

"Trying to save a girl's life. Bobby's, too. Now, make yourself useful and find something to tie her up."

Steve thought it was possible that his lover and law partner had quite suddenly gone insane.

"Where is he, Amanda?" Victoria demanded. "Where'd he take Maria?"

"Fuck you."

Victoria pulled higher on Amanda's wrist until it passed over the shoulder blade. There was a *pop*. And a scream.

"That was your elbow dislocating," Victoria said. "I've done that in tae kwan do. Hurts like the dickens, doesn't it?"

Amanda lay prone on the floor, her wailing interrupted only by her pained breaths.

"Hey, Vic, could you ease up a minute?"

"We don't have a minute. If we don't find Kreeger, that child's going to die. Isn't that right, Amanda?"

No more "fuck you"s. Just some sobbing.

"Let's work on the other arm," Victoria said.

"Wait." Amanda got to her knees. "Bill likes little girls."

"No shit," Victoria said.

Who is this woman?

"He takes them, sometimes. I don't know what happens to them."

"Sure you do," Victoria said flatly. "If they can ID him, he kills them."

"I don't ask him. There was a girl from the Redlands. About twelve or thirteen."

Oh, shit, Steve thought.

"That girl who went missing down in the Redlands . . ."

Kreeger had tried to blame the disappearance on a boy with disabilities. No wonder the bastard knew so much about serial killers. His knowledge fell into the forensics category called "It takes one to know one."

"Where's he go?" Steve now, getting with the program. "Does he have an apartment somewhere? A cabin in the Glades? Where!"

Amanda didn't answer, and Victoria reached for her other arm. This time, it didn't take a snapped tendon. Amanda flinched, then surrendered. She turned her head toward the painting above the fireplace.

Steve focused on the painting, Kreeger and his big-ass sport fisherman, the *Psycho Therapy.* "The boat! He's got her on the boat."

Amanda didn't say a word, but her look told Steve he was right.

"Where's he keep it?" Victoria said.

"Grove Marina," Amanda whispered.

"C'mon, Steve. Let's get going."

"No."

"No?"

"Something's not right. You torture people, they always lie."

He remembered the photos of the boat in Kreeger's office. A dock, a channel, a mangrove island. The island was distinctive, and he remembered seeing it before. It provided a windbreak for the boats anchored away from the dock.

The island. The island. The island.

It wasn't at Grove Marina. Where was it? He tried to focus the way Bobby would. What could he remember? A breakfast. No. A brunch. That restaurant on the Rickenbacker Causeway on the way to Key Biscayne. From the restaurant, you look out over the channel, straight at the mangrove island.

"Crandon Park Marina. On Key Biscayne. That's where Kreeger keeps his boat."

"Then go!" Victoria ordered. "I'll make sure Amanda stays put."

"You're too late," Amanda said. Neither pleasure nor regret in her voice. "They'll be in open water by now."

"Where?"

"Don't know. The ocean, somewhere. Bill does the girls after he gets out to sea. Then he weights their bodies and chucks them overboard. Something about the water's all mystical to him."

Again Kreeger's words came back to haunt Steve. The guy didn't believe in ashes to ashes and dust to dust. He believed in a watery start and a watery finish. What had he called it?

"From the swamp to the sea."

Thirty-Eight

PSYCHO THERAPY

Great sheets of rain pounded the pavement, the winds clocking around to the north. The Mustang sloshed across the causeway, shuddering in the gusts at the top of the bridge.

Steve passed the Seaquarium, the steering wheel in one hand, his cell phone in the other. The 911 operator told him to call the Coast Guard. The duty officer at the Guard base said no, they could not dispatch a flotilla of patrol boats, cutters, and choppers to parts unknown on a citizen's hunch that a crime was being committed somewhere at sea.

He tried the police again. After two transfers and seven minutes listening to recorded crime-stopping tips, Officer Teele came on the line. "Funny you called, Solomon. We've been looking for you."

"Why?"

"Got a bench warrant to pick you up. Seems you didn't show up for anger-management therapy."

"That's bullshit!" Sounding like he needed his anger managed.

"Got Dr. Kreeger's affidavit right here."

"It's Kreeger you should be after. He's got Maria on his boat. He's—"

"You really got to get over this thing about Dr. Bill."

"Goddammit, listen to me! Kreeger killed that girl in the Redlands. He's gonna kill again."

"Okay, Mr. Solomon. Why don't you just come downtown? Then you can tell us all about it."

"Why? So you can arrest me?"

"You're sounding a little paranoid, Mr. Solomon. So tell me, where are you right now?"

Steve clicked off the phone just as he turned into the marina. The car splashed to a stop. Steve jumped out and jogged toward the dockmaster's office, leaping over puddles. A red triangular flag whipped on a pole atop the small building. Small craft advisory, the winds hitting twenty-five knots.

Steve figured Kreeger had a several-hour head start. The *Psycho Therapy* would be in "open water," according to Amanda, but where? He needed to find someone who knew where Kreeger liked to cruise. Maybe someone saw the boat leave the dock. If they could pinpoint the time, it would be possible to calculate the range. Steve needed something—anything—to go on.

Soaking wet in his jeans and T-shirt, he was ten yards from the dockmaster's office when he caught sight of another flag. One pier over. A row of gleaming power boats in the forty to fifty-foot range. Flying from the top of an antenna was a flag imprinted with the image of a bearded man in an old-fashioned suit. The man looked familiar.

Sigmund Freud.

Now, who else would fly a flag with a picture of Freud?

Steve tore across to the pier toward the boat flying the flag. On a concrete piling, a stenciled sign in yellow paint: *"The Freudian Slip."* And on the transom of the white-and-blue sport fisherman tied at the dock: *"Psycho Therapy."*

Bow and stern lines taut, fenders in place. In the cockpit, both fighting chairs encased in their blue weather covers. Same for the console on the fly bridge. No sign that anyone was aboard or had been lately. So, Kreeger hadn't brought the girl here just before dawn. And now, in broad daylight, he surely wouldn't.

Amanda lied! Victoria had twisted her into a pretzel and she still lied.

Steve looked around. Lots of boats, but here not one person on this lousy nor'easter of a day. The rain pounded at the concrete, moving across the dock in seemingly solid walls, then stopping a few moments and starting again. The boats groaned in their moorings. Two seabirds flew overhead, battling the wind. On a nearby piling, a bleary-eyed pelican seemed to be staring his way.

Steve stepped from the dock into the cockpit. A teak deck, weathered and bleached by the sun, channeled the rainwater out the scuppers at the stern. He opened a freezer used for bait. Empty. Moved to a bait prep station, opened drawers. Fish hooks, pliers, knives, some spools of fishing line.

He slid a cushion off a bench and opened the lid to a storage compartment underneath. Fishing gear, deck shoes, life jackets.

No twelve-year-old girls.

Opened the lid on another compartment. Life rings.

An old fishing rod. Three metal buckets, brand-new, the kind you might use to mop the floor. A shovel, not new. It looked like a garden spade, a crust of mud along its curved sharp edge. And a canvas bag, maybe eight feet long, unzipped. Big enough to haul fishing rods or scuba gear ... or a ninety-pound girl. Steve rooted around, running his hands over the canvas, half hoping to find something, half hoping not to.

What would be better? Evidence that she'd been here? Or nothing at all?

But the bag was empty. No little-girl barrettes, no little white socks, no notes saying, *"Help!"*

Then he caught the fragrance. What was it? He stuck his head into the bag and inhaled. Citrus. As if the bag had once held a couple dozen oranges.

Or a girl who borrowed her mother's perfume!

The fragrance Steve remembered from Bobby's room.

He tossed the bag aside and raced to the salon door. Glass in a metal frame. Locked. He grabbed the pliers from the bait station and shattered the glass. The sound startled him. But no alarms sounded. No one shouted. The only reaction was from the pelican, which flapped its giant wings and took off for quieter surroundings.

Steve unlatched the door from inside the jagged glass and let himself into the salon. Dripping water on the polished teak deck. A galley to one side. Stove, stainless-steel refrigerator, microwave, a built-in banquette and table anchored to the deck. On the walls, certificates attesting to the capture of a number of innocent fish in various tournaments. "Hello!" he yelled. "Maria!"

Nothing.

He went down several steps, his waterlogged running shoes squeaking. He checked out the staterooms. Beds made, neat and clean. No one home. He went into the head. A beach towel draped over a shower door. The towel was wet.

She's here! Or she's been here.

He went back into the salon.

"Maria!"

Still nothing. Water sloshed, the fenders squeaked against the hull. In the channel, a fifteen-foot outboard *putt-putt*ed toward open water, a couple of kids ignoring the weather warnings. From somewhere belowdeck, something creaked and something else rattled. Boat sounds. Meaningless.

"Maria!"

He heard a *clunk*. Metal against metal? No, a duller sound. It could be anything or nothing.

"Maria!"

Clunk. Clunk.

Again, belowdeck. He found the hatch in the deck, opened it, took a flashlight from a bracket, and crawled down the ladder into the pitch-black engine compartment. Moved the light over tanks and pipes, stringers and beams, and the two huge diesel engines. Shadows flashed across the bulkhead.

And there, on her knees, tape covering her mouth, ankles and wrists bound with a line attached to an engine mount, was Maria Munoz-Goldberg. Her eyes were closed as she banged her forehead against the deck. *Clunk. Clunk. Clunk.*

Thirty-Nine

RESCUE PARTY

Heart pounding, Steve ripped the tape from Maria's mouth and winced as she cried out in pain. She had red marks above and below her lips, and her forehead bled from where she'd banged it against the deck. Her entire body trembled, starting at her shoulders and running all the way down to her legs and feet. She sobbed, great streaks of tears tracking across her cheeks. Her wrists were bound behind her back with quarter-inch line.

Steve worked at the line, but her chest heaved as she sobbed, and her arms shook, and it took a while to undo the knots. They weren't slipknots. They were knots never intended to come loose.

When the line finally came free, he gave her a moment to rub out the stiffness in each wrist, both raw and bleeding.

"Thank you. Thank you. Thank you." She seemed to be chanting it between sobs. Steve wrapped his arms around her, could feel the tremors shaking her from the inside out.

The air was greasy and stale, and Steve felt the sweat drip down his arms. He tried to untie the line around her ankles, but it was too tight and she was bleeding where it had cut into her. The other end of the line was fixed securely to an engine mount.

"There's a knife in the cockpit. I'll be right back, Maria."

"No. Don't leave! Please."

Steve sat down with her. He'd give her a minute. "Where's Kreeger?"

The name didn't seem to register. Apparently, kidnappers don't introduce themselves. "The man who took you. Where'd he go?"

She shook her head. She didn't know.

Steve wondered if she was in shock. But then the words poured out. She started at the beginning. Bobby was acting up, and she decided to ride home without him. When she got to her bike, a man was waiting. He grabbed her and threw her into his car. A BMW, she noted. He reached up under her shirt and pulled off her bra, touching her. She thought he was going to rape her, but he just crumpled the bra and dropped it in Bobby's bike bag.

"Then he put my bike in his trunk. And I thought this was good. Like, no matter what he was going to do to me, he'd let me go, let me ride my bike home. But after he tied me up and we drove a little bit, he took my cap and put it in my bike bag."

"Your cap?"

"Well, Bobby's cap. That Solomon and Lord one he always wears."

Including the day we went to Kreeger's office.

"Then the man threw my bike in some bushes."

"Near the road?"

"Yeah. A few feet away."

Where the bike would be found. With strands of

Bobby's hair in the cap, his prints and DNA all over it. Another piece of evidence, another nail in the coffin.

"Then he put me in the trunk inside a big bag, and I could barely breathe. I might have passed out, because the next thing I knew, I was down here, all tied up."

She started crying again.

"Did he say anything?"

"Only that we were going for a cruise, but he needed to wait for a store to open. I asked if he was getting sandwiches and drinks, and he just laughed."

A store? It made no sense to Steve, but there was no time to figure it out. Kreeger would be coming back. Steve put a hand on the girl's shoulder. "Maria, we need to get you out of here. I'm going up to get a knife. Is that all right?"

She nodded. "But come right back, okay?"

Steve scrambled up the ladder, climbed through the hatch, and took one step before the lightning bolt hit him. He felt his head snap back. He saw the pain itself inside his brain, an electrical flash behind his eyes. He heard thunderclaps. And then the world went quiet and black.

Forty

THE DEAD WEIGHT OF GUILT

Steve had a sensation of being awakened by being tossed into an icy shower.

But I can't be awake. I can't see anything.

He sensed movement. Side to side and up and down. And a sound. A dull roar.

Okay, the boat is moving, the diesels singing.

He felt the wind rushing by his head, sensed he was in the open cockpit, eyes closed. His face felt raw, like chopped meat, and the salt spray wasn't making it feel any better.

Why can't I move my hands?

A hard, cold rain pelted him, a million freezing needles. A rain so strong, it hissed in the air and *ping*ed as it hit the deck.

He felt the boat ride to the top of a swell, then slide down the trough.

Great. Tied up, semiconscious, and I'm gonna be seasick, too.

A throbbing pain in his skull seemed to beat time with the engines. The boat was moving fast. Open water. Ocean, not the bay. He could tell that from the waves, even though he couldn't see anything.

His mouth felt dry. He licked his lips, tasted blood. He felt the spray hit his neck, the boat splashing down the side of a swell.

So why can't I see anything? Aha, my eyes are closed.

He tried to crank them open. A crowbar would have helped. Eyes swollen shut. He wanted to use a finger to push open an eye, but there was a problem. His hands seemed to be tied behind his back.

He concentrated on his right eye, tried to crank it open. It started to come up slowly, like a Venetian blind pulled by a piece of dental floss. He used his tongue to explore the inside of his mouth. He had bitten though his lip, and he spit out a chunk of tooth.

The rain came even harder, a solid wall of daggers. His teeth chattered. He had never been this cold in his life.

"How you feeling, Solomon?"

Kreeger's voice. The eye opened just enough to see his face, rain soaking his bare chest. The boat on autopilot, Steve figured. With any luck, maybe they'd hit an iceberg. If not, maybe run aground on Bimini.

"Where's Maria?"

"Warm and toasty in the master stateroom. She'll serve her purpose after I dispose of you."

"Bastard."

"That the best you can do, Solomon?"

Steve managed to get both eyes open a crack. "Ugly bastard."

"You don't look so good yourself."

Steve felt like he'd been hit in the face with a base-ball bat. Now he saw it was a shovel. Kreeger was leaning on the garden spade Steve had seen in the storage compartment.

"You'd have two black eyes if you'd live long enough for the bruises to show," Kreeger said. "But as you've no doubt ascertained, this is your last boat trip."

Steve's vision cleared a bit, and he saw that Kreeger was wearing surfer's trunks and was shirtless and barefoot. He looked powerful, with wide shoulders and a deep chest. A dive knife was strapped to a sheath on one ankle.

My feet feel funny. I can't wiggle my toes. What's that all about?

Steve looked down. His feet were in one of the aluminum pails he'd seen earlier, his legs sunk up to his calves in cold mud.

No. Not mud. Wet cement.

"You've got to be kidding, Kreeger."

"We wouldn't want your head popping up on the Fifth Street beach, scaring the tourists, would we, Solomon?"

"You've been watching too much *Sopranos.*"

Steve wriggled his feet, just enough to lift them off the bottom of the pail, but not enough for cracks to show on the surface. The cement was hardening fast.

"Maybe we can work this out, Kreeger."

"The shyster wants to settle the case. What's your offer, Counselor?"

"I get you help. Not guilty by reason of insanity."

Kreeger barked a laugh. "Got a better deal right here. Not guilty by reason of not being caught."

"The cops know I came after you. You'll be the only suspect."

"Suspect in what? There'll be no body, Solomon. They'll figure you either fled to South America to escape your legal problems or committed suicide." He shook his head, almost sadly. "This isn't the way I planned it. You were supposed to be safe and sound. How else to suffer the torment of watching your nephew go through hell?"

Steve focused on keeping his feet moving. A small crack appeared in the wet cement around each calf. The pouring rain was helping, too. If only he could keep the cement from setting around his feet, he would have a chance.

"I blame myself for your predicament," Kreeger continued. "I've never been so late leaving the dock."

"Because you had to go to the store to buy cement, that it? Run out after you killed that girl from the Redlands?"

"Always start with a new bag." Kreeger dabbed at the pail with the blade of the shovel. "Leave no evidence."

"Let Maria go. Like you said, I won't be around to be tormented. Why torture Bobby?"

"I'm afraid that ship has sailed. The girl can identify me. Or do you think that she'll so enjoy our forthcoming encounter that she'd never testify? Maybe start sneaking over to my house instead of yours?"

"Ugly, sick bastard."

Kreeger laughed again. Took the dive knife from its sheath, crouched, and stuck the blade into the pail, testing the cement. Steve kept his feet still a moment.

"Quick-dry," Kreeger said, sounding pleased, "even in this fucking downpour. Be ready in a couple minutes. Now, don't go anywhere, Counselor."

Kreeger scrambled up the ladder to the fly bridge, picked up his binoculars, and scanned the horizon in every direction. Not wanting a passing freighter to see him toss a man overboard, Steve supposed.

He wriggled harder now. The cement was firming up, the tops of his feet encased in a solid block. But he had kept it from hardening along the sides and underneath. If he was stuck to the pail, there would be nothing he could do. But if he could lift his feet out, he had a chance.

Steve tried working on a plan, but his subconscious interfered. The dead weight of guilt bore down on him, heavier than the cement. He'd let Maria down. But not just her.

I screwed up everything.

Foam spritzed over the gunwales and stung his face.

I let you all down.

Bobby would grow up without him. Victoria would move on to another man. Even his father would take it hard. Steve's throat clenched.

Jeez, am I crying?

He couldn't tell. Tears taste the same as the sea.

* * *

Moments later, the sky darkened even more as they rode through a squall. Gusts pushed the big boat sideways. On the bridge, Kreeger pulled back on the throttles. Steve felt them slowing down. In seconds, they were at idle speed. The boat was at the mercy of the waves now, sliding up one face, rocking down the other.

Kreeger slid down the ladder, facing the cockpit, nimble as a sailor hurrying to his battle station.

"There's a thick patch of sargasso weed just ahead," Kreeger told him. "Bet there are some fine sharks looking for lunch down there."

"Let's just get this over with."

"Whatever you say."

Kreeger bent down, dipped the knife into the drying cement. Steve studied the knife. Ridged handle, easy to grip. Titanium blade, maybe five inches long, serrated on one edge, sharp as a razor on the other. You could saw through bone with it.

Kreeger stood, looked down at Steve. "Time to say good-bye, Solomon." There was a tinge of regret in his voice, as if he were going to miss his old buddy.

Steve focused on his own quadriceps. They were the lifters. He didn't know how much weight the cement added to his feet. It didn't matter. He had strong quads and glutes, and an abundance of quick-twitch muscle fibers.

Kreeger looked down, sliding the dive knife into its sheath. As he did, Steve swung his legs up, high and hard. His feet came out of the bucket with astonishing speed. The bucket stayed on the deck. The jagged clump of cement on Steve's ankles caught Kreeger on the forehead. Steve heard the impact, saw Kreeger spin backwards and bounce off the deck. The knife skittered toward the stern.

Steve pushed himself up and tried hopping toward the knife, but he was like a man in a sack race, and with the boat pitching, he fell, then skidded across the slippery deck.

Kreeger got to one knee and wagged his head, as if trying to stir himself awake. Another second and he was on both feet. Shaky but standing. A flap of skin six inches wide hung loose on Kreeger's forehead, and blood poured into his eyes. Rain slashed down. He used both hands to try to clear his vision. *The bastard should have a concussion,* Steve thought, *but look at him. A wounded bull, fixing to charge.* "Kill you, Solomon," the shrink muttered. "Kill all the lawyers."

He staggered toward the stern. Woozy, knees seeming to buckle with each step. Where was he going?

The knife!

Steve saw it, propped on the edge of a scupper at the stern. He couldn't stand. No way to get there.

Spitting blood, Kreeger leaned over, picked up the knife, and wheeled around. He tried using his forearm to wipe the river of blood from his eyes. First one arm, then the other. It wasn't working.

He can't see and I can't stand.

But Kreeger must have seen enough, because he stumbled in Steve's general direction, flailing away with the knife. Wild swings that started above his head and came straight down, like a man using an ice pick. Blood sprayed everywhere from his forehead.

Steve scooted backward on his butt, great white waves sloshing over the gunwales, soaking and chilling him. Kreeger braced himself against the onslaught, then kept coming, swinging the knife sideways now, like a scythe. "Cut your balls off. Your balls off." His voice droning, devoid of emotion.

Steve spotted a graphite tarpon gaff, maybe six feet long, bracketed to the bulkhead. Pushing off with his hands, moving backward on the deck, he slid that way.

Kreeger changed the knife to his other hand. Came at Steve, slashed left, slashed right, edged between him and the gaff, cutting him off. The boat climbed to the top of a wave, seemed to come to rest, then slid back down again.

Steve had run out of room. Inching backward, he'd come to rest against the bulkhead. Nowhere to run, nowhere to crawl. He brought his knees up to his chest, protecting himself from the deadly blows that would come.

Gasping for breath, spouting blood, Kreeger shambled closer.

Steve made one last desperate effort to grab at the gaff, but it was out of reach.

Kreeger stopped three feet away. Wiped the blood off one hand to get a better grip on the knife. The boat slid sideways up a wave, and Kreeger skidded slightly, widened his stance to keep his balance.

Steve felt the boat crest the wave. Would it go over or come back down? After a second it slid down the trough, and Steve straightened both legs, his cemented feet thrust between Kreeger's braced legs. Steve kicked straight up. At the same moment, the boat pitched wildly at the bottom of the wave, the port rail dipping to the waterline. Steve rocked backward hard, felt both knees pop with a searing pain. Kreeger teetered on Steve's ankles like a kid on a seesaw, then sailed over the gunwale headfirst and into the deep blue sea.

Knees flaring as if on fire, Steve hoisted himself up and grabbed the gaff from its bracket. He spotted Kreeger splashing in the water, dangerously close to the props that churned slowly at idle speed.

"Help! Help me!"

A wave washed over him. He vanished, then bobbed up again, kicking and whaling away at the water, trying to close the distance to the dive platform.

Steve hobbled toward the stern, using the gaff as a cane.

Some things you plan, he thought. Some things you do by instinct, by notions of decency and humanity. A man goes overboard, you rescue him. No matter who he is, no matter what he's done. You haul the man aboard, take him in, let the system deal with him.

Steve leaned over the rail, holding the graphite gaff.

Kreeger reached for it, missed, went under again. He came back up, and Steve dangled the gaff in his direction.

But sometimes, all notions of decency and humanity give way to something else. Call it revenge or justice or maybe just certainty. The certainty that Bill Kreeger would never ever again hurt anyone. Or was that overly complicated? Was the explanation simply hardwired into our DNA by millions of years of evolution? Maybe all of us carry the fingerprints of the homicidal animals who came before us.

Threaten me or mine, I will kill you. Yes, I will. Even a normally mild-mannered, semi-law-abiding officer of the court like me will kill you dead.

Kreeger would appreciate that explanation, Steve thought. Proving his thesis right after all these years.

A powerful swell lifted Kreeger, nearly catapulting him out of the water. Down he came, his head slipping underwater. Then, another lift, another slide, this one bringing him closer to the boat. Again, Kreeger grabbed for the gaff. Again, he missed. He shouted something drowned out by the wind's roar. Another wave carried him closer to the stern. Steve held the gaff; Kreeger reached for it; and suddenly, Steve pulled it away. He hadn't planned on doing it. The motion was involuntary, his body not willing to follow his brain's instructions, not willing to save the bastard.

Kreeger swam toward the boat, yelling something. Steve could only make out a single word.

"Just . . ."

The rest was lost in the wind.

Kreeger came closer, reached for the dive platform, shouted again.

"Just like . . ."

What was he saying?

Bracing himself on the slippery deck, Steve drew the gaff back with two hands until it was poised over one shoulder. A batter with his Louisville Slugger.

"Just like me!" Kreeger yelled over the wind. "You're just like me!"

Steve swung the gaff as hard as he could, rotating his hips for power. The flat side of the steel hook hit Kreeger squarely across the temple with a shock Steve felt in both arms. A shuddering impact, like driving the ball up the middle.

Kreeger's head snapped to the side and stayed there, his neck at an unnatural angle. A wave hit, swirling him in white foam, spinning him around, and dragging him beneath the cold, gray sea.

SOLOMON'S LAWS

12. When you cut through all the bullshit of career, status, and money, at the end of the day all that matters is love and family.

Forty-One

THE TEMPLE OF SOLOMON

Steve lay on his back on a rickety raft that rose and fell with the waves. In the distance, lightning illuminated a shroud of fat silvery clouds, and a thunderclap smacked the water. Steve felt the raft pitch and roll, even as he realized he was home in bed. Painkillers will do that.

"God bless codeine."

He had said that to Bobby. Just a few hours ago. Or was it a few years? He didn't know how long he'd been in bed.

"God bless codeine," Bobby had repeated. "BED-SIDE NOSE CLOG."

Steve had laughed, stinging his lip where the stitches pulled at the skin.

"Everyone at school says you're a total mad dawg," Bobby had said.

"If that's a good thing, tell them thanks."

"You're the best, Uncle Steve."

The boy had smiled. They'd pounded knuckles. Bobby doing all the pounding. Steve couldn't lift his arm from the bedsheet. Still, when he saw the boy's grin, he felt he'd won the Nobel Prize for parenting.

A doctor who had once been a client stopped by. Or was he a client who had once been a doctor? Steve's brain was fuzzy. The doc said something about a hairline fracture of the zygomatic bone.

"The zygomatic?" Steve asked. "The machine that chops vegetables?"

"The cheekbone," the doctor explained.

Steve remembered now. He had defended the doctor in a couple of malpractice cases. Lost them both.

There was some sinus damage, too, the sawbones told him. Steve could expect his eyes to tear up unexpectedly. No big deal. That should go away.

"And if it doesn't?" Steve asked.

"Sue me," the doc said.

Crying wasn't so bad, Steve thought. Might be able to use it in closing argument sometime. Then there were the dozen stitches in his fat lip. Plus torn cartilage in both knees. Ice, anti-inflammatories, and rest.

"Don't worry, Steve. You'll be playing eighteen holes in no time."

"Great, Doc, because I've never played one hole my entire life."

Now he was cold. Both knees were wrapped in ice. On the bedside table were a variety of pill bottles, a pitcher of water, and the local section of the *Miami Herald*. A headline blared: "Lawyer Rescues Kidnapped Girl." He would check out the story later. Steve was reasonably certain that it would be more favorable than his last brush with celebrity, an item in Joan Fleischman's column headlined: "Lawyer Jailed Again."

He heard a pounding. Was it in his head? A dull *thud,* then a *crack,* like wood splintering.

Myron Goldberg and Eva Munoz-Goldberg came by. Myron had Steve open his mouth. Complimented his flossing and advised him to get that chipped tooth crowned. Eva gave Steve a deep dish of caramel flan she had baked. He ate it through a straw. Myron said they were dropping the assault-and-battery case, and Steve thanked him as he slurped up the sweet dessert. Eva patted his arm and said he was as brave as Máximo Gómez and Jose Marti.

Apparently, Maria had told her parents how Steve saved her life. How after Dr. Bill went overboard, Steve came to get her, even though he could barely walk and his face was swollen and bleeding. How he climbed the ladder to the bridge, dragging the chunk of concrete on his feet, moaning in pain. How he brought the boat back, banging into the seawall at the Coast Guard station on Miami Beach, then passing out. Steve was glad Maria told her parents all these things, because he couldn't remember any of it.

"Maria says you're a superhero," Eva told him.

"How's she doing?" Steve asked.

"Better than we could have hoped," Myron said.

"*Bien,*" Eva said. "She's with Bobby right now. Studying."

"I'll bet," Steve said.

"He's a fine young man," Myron allowed.

"Of course he is," Eva added. "He's had good training." Then she reached down and stroked Steve's cheek. "*Eres un melocotón en almíbar.*"

Steve wasn't sure, but he thought she'd just called him a peach in syrup. Sweet. Suddenly, he felt a tear tracking down his cheek, then another. Then a torrent.

"You wonderful man," Eva said, her own eyes welling.

Steve decided not to mention his sinus problem.

Cece Santiago came by as the Goldbergs were leaving. The office phones had been ringing all day, she reported, people calling to congratulate him. No new clients yet. There probably wouldn't be. The newspaper story made it sound as if he were on his deathbed. Cece could only stay a minute. She had a meeting with her probation officer. Translation: another wrestling match with Arnold Freskin. And by the way, Arnie already asked Pincher to drop the charges. With both assault-and-battery cases dismissed, Steve wondered if he had any legal work to do.

He dozed for a while and dreamed his raft was sinking. He awoke to find his sister sitting on the edge of his bed, the soft mattress listing to starboard.

"Hey, Stevie. How you feeling?"

"Terrific. I'm starting to understand what you like about narcotics."

"Reminds me, bro. I got a job. Drug counselor over in Tampa."

"Great."

"As for the other stuff, filing for custody of Bobby, my lawyer says I'd be a fool to do it now. You're like a celebrity or something. Plus, I need the job so I can look good in front of the judge when I come back."

"No hurry, Jan."

She studied him a second. "Are you crying, bro?"

"Sinuses," he said.

He dozed off again to the sound of an electrical band saw. Either that, or a million bees were buzzing away in the living room. He awoke and found Irene Lord in the bedroom, running an index finger over the nightstand.

"You need a maid," she said, lifting a fingertip covered with dust.

"How you doing, Irene?"

"Carl left. Just picked up and left."

"I'm sorry. And surprised. I thought he really cared for you."

"I think he does. Yesterday he wired money into my account. From a bank in Moscow."

"Moscow?"

"E-mailed me, too. Said he discovered the lost treasure of the Romanovs. People all over the world are sending him deposits, claiming to be relatives."

"For a con man, he's got a good heart."

"Stephen, have I told you how dear you are to me?"

"Not that I recall, but I've been heavily drugged."

"I think you and Victoria are splendid together. Well, maybe not splendid. But for some reason, you seem to make her happy. And if she's happy, well . . . I'm quite nearly pleased."

She leaned over as if to kiss him, thought better of it, and withdrew. But she did give his shoulder a pat. "Stephen, are you crying?"

"Sinuses," he said.

He fell back into a restless sleep, dreaming of his father. The old goat was building something. Noah's ark, maybe. He felt lips brush his and opened his eyes to find the most beautiful woman in the world kissing him. Victoria was wearing those stretchy workout pants that stop right below the knees and a flimsy sports top with thin straps. The top was cut low and stopped well above her flat tummy.

"You need a shave, slugger," she said. "And your breath smells like a wet donkey."

"What exactly does a wet donkey smell like?"

She kissed him again. "Never mind. I still love you."

"I love you, too, Vic." He licked his swollen lip and said: "I've been thinking about where we should live. If you want a condo, that's fine. You want a townhouse or a real house, that's fine, too. What I'm saying, anywhere is fine as long as we're together."

"You mean that?"

"With all my heart. With all my soul. With my last stinky breath."

She gave him an angelic smile and gently ran a finger across his bruised lip.

The pounding started again. Louder.

"Damn. What is that?" Steve said.

"You don't know? I thought Herbert told you last night."

"Last night, I was running a dogsled in the Iditarod. Although it's quite possible I was hallucinating."

"Come on," she said. "I'll show you."

She eased him out of bed. He threw an arm around her shoulder and she helped him down the corridor.

The living room was far too bright.

What the hell?

There was no back wall. Just a couple of vertical studs, the plasterboard blasted to smithereens. Herbert stood in the middle of the rubble, wearing khaki shorts and a yarmulke, holding a sledgehammer. His bare chest was covered with plaster dust. Steve vaguely remembered something about his old man building the Temple of Solomon, but this still didn't compute.

"The hell you doing, Dad?"

"What's it look like?"

"Vandalism."

"Ah'm extending your house into the backyard."

"Why do I think you're better at knocking down walls than building them?"

"Don't complain till you get mah bill. A new master bedroom with walk-in closets, and a family room."

"What for?"

"For you and Victoria, *schmendrick*."

Of course! His brain was still fuzzy, but it made sense. All the room they would need, even though the roof might sag and the walls would be out of plumb.

"Thanks, Dad. I saw this flat-screen TV the other day. Big as a garage door. Great for the family room."

"I was thinking about a piano for the family room," Victoria said.

"Big TV would be better. High-def for the ball games."

"I looked at this Steinway. The Living Room Grand model. It would be perfect."

"Only if you're living with Rachmaninoff."

"I'd like a grand piano."

"And I'd like a big-ass TV."

Herbert pointed the sledgehammer toward the opening in the wall. "Ah s'pose Ah could add a music room, if we encroach on the property line."

"Good compromise," Victoria said.

"I'm in," Steve said.

He wrapped an arm around both of them and gave a good squeeze. Bobby came into the room from the kitchen, nibbling on half an Oreo cookie. "Hey, Uncle Steve. What's going on?"

"I'm counting my blessings, kiddo. You want a group hug?"

"No way. Hugging's for babies."

Steve let his gaze take them all in. His father, his lover, his nephew. His blessings. He felt his eyes tear up.

"You crying?" Bobby asked.

"Sinuses," Steve lied.

SOLOMON'S LAWS

1. Lying to a judge is preferable to lying to the woman you love.

2. Thou shalt not screw thy own client . . . unless thou hast a damn good reason.

3. When you don't know what to do, seek advice from your father . . . even if he's two candles short of a menorah.

4. If you're going to all the trouble to make a fool of yourself, be sure to have plenty of witnesses.

5. When a woman is quiet and reflective, rather than combative and quarrelsome, watch out. She's likely picturing the bathroom without your boxers hanging on the showerhead.

6. A creative lawyer considers a judge's order a mere suggestion.

7. When you run across a naked woman, act as if you've seen one before.

8. Love is chemistry and mystery, not logic and reason.

9. Q: What do you call a judge who is old, cantankerous, and flatulent?

A: "Your Honor."

10. You won't find it in Darwin, Deuteronomy, or Doonesbury, but it's an essential truth of human nature: we'll all kill to protect those we love.

11. I won't lie to a lawyer's face or stab him in the back, but if I have the chance, I'll look him in the eye and kick him in the *cojones*.

12. When you cut through all the bullshit of career, status, and money, at the end of the day all that matters is love and family.

ABOUT THE AUTHOR

PAUL LEVINE worked as a newspaper reporter and trial lawyer, practicing law for seventeen years, trying cases in state and federal courts and handling appeals at every level, including the Supreme Court, before becoming a full-time novelist and screenwriter. The winner of the John D. MacDonald fiction award, Levine is the author of the Jake Lassiter novels, which have been published in twenty-three countries. *To Speak for the Dead,* the first Lassiter novel, was a national bestseller and honored as one of the best mysteries of the year by the *Los Angeles Times.* He is also the author of *9 Scorpions,* a thriller set in the U.S. Supreme Court. *Kill All the Lawyers* is the third in the series that began with the bestselling *Solomon* vs. *Lord* and *The Deep Blue Alibi.*

He was co-creator and co–executive producer of the CBS television series *First Monday* and has written extensively for *JAG.* He lives in California, where he is at worth on the fourth Solomon *vs.* Lord novel.

It's no Mystery...

Bantam Dell has the finest collection of sleuths around,
from professional P.I.s to unwilling amateurs

SEAN DOOLITTLE

BURN
$6.99/$10.99

RAIN DOGS
$6.99/$9.99

CHRISTOPHER FOWLER

FULL DARK HOUSE
$6.99/$10.99

SEVENTY-SEVEN CLOCKS
$6.99/$10.99

THE WATER ROOM
$6.99/$9.99

RON FAUST

DEAD MEN RISE UP NEVER
$6.99/$10.99

SEA OF BONES
$6.99/$10.99

THE BLOOD RED SEA
$6.99/$10.99

VICKI LANE

SIGNS IN THE BLOOD
$6.99/$10.99

ART'S BLOOD
$6.99/$9.99

PAUL LEVINE

SOLOMON VS. LORD
$5.99/$7.99

THE DEEP BLUE ALIBI
$6.99/$9.99

KILL ALL THE LAWYERS
$6.99/$9.99

Ask for these titles wherever books are sold, or visit us online
at www.bantamdell.com for ordering information.

BD MC2 9/06

THE SUSPENSE WILL KILL YOU....

VICTOR GISCHLER

GUN MONKEYS	$6.99/$10.99
THE PISTOL POETS	$6.99/$10.99
SUICIDE SQUEEZE	$6.99/$9.99
SHOTGUN OPERA	$6.99/$9.99

MORAG JOSS

FUNERAL MUSIC	$6.99/NCR
FEARFUL SYMMETRY	$6.99/NCR
FRUITFUL BODIES	$6.99/NCR
HALF-BROKEN THINGS	$13.00/NCR
PUCCINI'S GHOSTS	$22.00/NCR

ASA LARSSON

SUN STORM
$22.00/$30.00

STEPHEN BOOTH

BLIND TO THE BONES
$7.50/NCR

CODY MCFADYEN

SHADOW MAN
$24.00/$32.00

LISA GARDNER

THE PERFECT HUSBAND	$7.99/$11.99
THE OTHER DAUGHTER	$7.99/$11.99
THE THIRD VICTIM	$7.99/$11.99
THE NEXT ACCIDENT	$7.99/$11.99
THE SURVIVORS CLUB	$7.99/$11.99
THE KILLING HOUR	$7.99/$11.99
ALONE	$7.99/$10.99
GONE	$25.00/$35.00

Ask for these titles wherever books are sold, or visit us online at _www.bantamdell.com_ for ordering information.

BD SUS 9/06